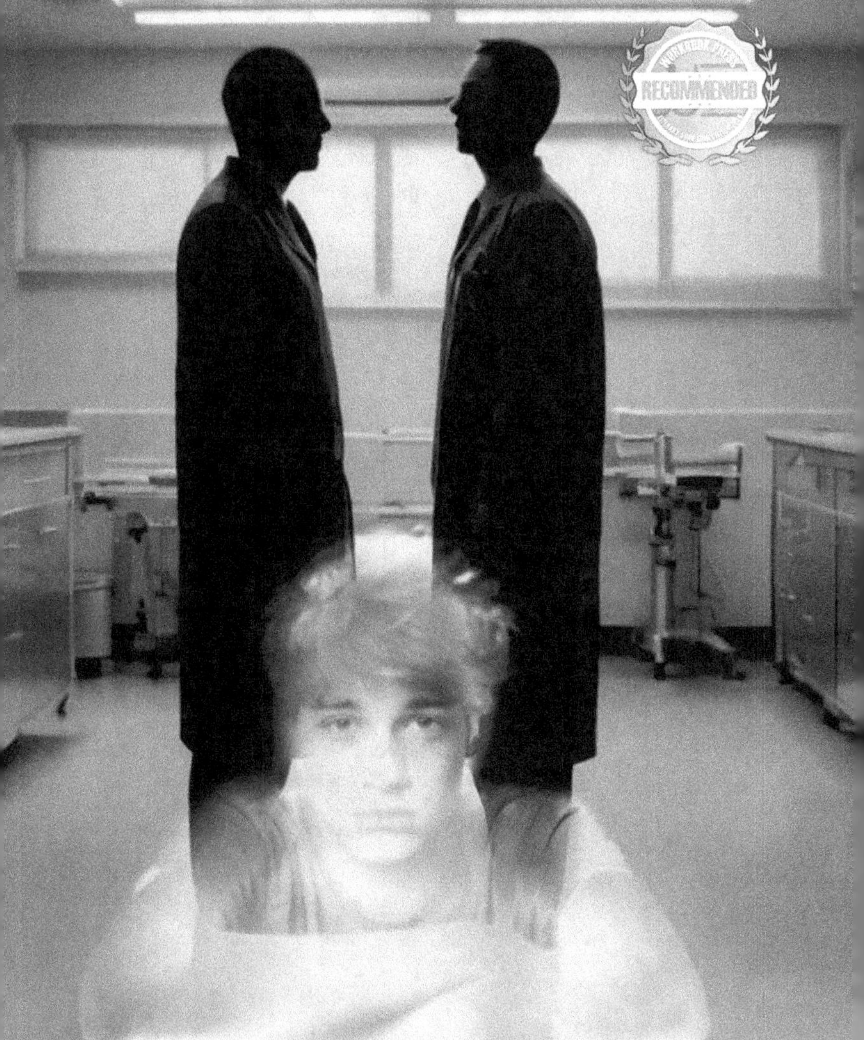

GEOFFREY A. LUNDY, M.D.
REVISED EDITION
OUTLIERS
RECOMMENDED

WORKBOOK PRESS LLC
187 E Warm Springs Rd,
Suite B285 Las Vegas NV 89119 USA

Website: https://workbookpress.com/
Hotline: 1-888-818-4856
Email: admin@workbookpress.com

Ordering Information:
Quantity sales. Special discounts are available on quantity purchases by corporations, associations, and others. For details, contact the publisher at the address above.

ISBN-13:   978-1-963718-96-6 Hardback Version
                978-1-963718-98-0 Paperback Version
                978-1-963718-97-3 Digital Version

PUB. DATE: 10/05/2024

REVISED EDITION

OUTLIERS

By

Geoffrey A. Lundy, M.D.

Outliers is dedicated to my husband, Thom, whose love, knowledge, passion for books and reading, guidance, and encouragement kept me going. It has been the blessing of my lifetime having him by my side.

ACKNOWLEDGEMENTS

I want to thank Celeste Ouellette and Christine McGarry-DesLauriers for reading and rereading my work, editing, and offering constructive criticism and encouragement along the way.

I also want to thank my husband, Thom, for his help and encouragement.

Mortui Vivos Docent

(The dead teach the living)

Geoffrey A. Lundy, M.D.

PROLOGUE

The year is 2030. Political correctness is the rule of the road. Male dominance and white privilege, with the resultant micro-aggressions, has been determined to be causative of many of our ills, and gender and racial fluidity the panacea. Gender and race are now legally defined as fluid attributes, and the use of preferred or gender-neutral pronouns in all government speech and writing is now mandatory.

Consequently, the terms male and female, African American, and white and all other races are solely attributes that one can assume, depending on how one feels. Gender and sexual orientation are entirely fluid. Everyone is a winner in this world, as a participation trophy is of equal value to a winner's trophy, which no longer exists. Grades and class rank are things of the past. Every citizen is each of their own minority. What was right is now wrong, wrong is now right, up is now down, down is now up, black is now white, and white is now black—and if one feels differently, they are deemed to be an ist, which is the cardinal sin of sins.

Everyone is now equal.

Politically it is a time of progressive liberalism. Both the Senate and the House of Representatives have strong democrat majorities. Although there are still nine Supreme Court Justices, the more conservative justices have been replaced by progressive liberal justices, as those conservative justices left the court due to incapacitation or death. It is the philosophy of the Supreme Court, Senate, House of Representatives, and the President that the United States Constitution is a living document that necessitates ongoing changes to keep the document alive and most effective.

The presidential election is just over two years away, and President Jommesa Sufjen Dmopvup will be running for hir fourth term in office. Ze was first elected to the presidency in 2020. It was during the latter half of President Dmopvup's second presidential term that Congress effectively repealed the 22nd Amendment to the constitution, which had been ratified in 1851, through ratification of another amendment barring any term limits. The point was made that in 1851, when the 22nd Amendment was ratified, the average human life expectancy in the United States of America was 36.1 years. In 2030 the human life expectancy is 89.2 years. Also, many of our country's endeavors take far more than eight years to come to fruition, and the two-term limit had become a hinderance to good governance. Additionally, it was felt that any limit of a president's term in office should be decided by our citizens at the time of the presidential election.

President Dmopvup is nonbinary, gender neutral, and of indeterminate race and age, and ze appears and sounds to each observer as the observer expects hir to appear and to sound. Hir past and family histories remain a secret, largely due to political correctness and its ramifications. The mainstream media serves as hir shield, and no one asks any questions. Ze carries hirself with an air of arrogance and smugness, and ze is entirely dedicated to hirself and to hir work.

President Dmopvup's previous occupation was manager of the Dmopvup Foundation, a charitable foundation that ze established in 2012. The foundation did exceedingly well, with assets currently above $20 billion. The foundation receives contributions from large corporations such as Utopia Pharmaceuticals, the largest pharmaceutical company in the world. Once ze was elected president, the management of the Dmopvup Foundation was turned over to its board of directors with oversight from a court-appointed officer to avoid the appearance of any impropriety on the part of the president.

In 2022 President Dmopvup, working with congress, created Americare, a government-owned and government-operated health insurance product that is marketed on every state health insurance exchange at exceedingly low to nonexistent cost to enrollees. The formation of the Americare health plan was a part of President Dmopvup's Americare legislation, which changed some of the tenets of the Patient Protection and Affordable Care Act. Failure to carry health insurance was raised to a class B felony, which could result in up to three and a half years of incarceration.

There are several caveats to remaining enrolled in Americare for both patients and health care providers. Enrollees and providers are required to follow all accepted care plans, and preventive care and screening guidelines to the letter; providers cannot be sued under any circumstance if they do so; and if enrollees become disenrolled for noncompliance or any other reason, they can be subject to imprisonment. If a provider fails to recommend or encourage a patient to follow the established guidelines, that provider can be censured by the state medical board and lose their ability to bill for their services. They may also lose their license to practice medicine and be criminally prosecuted if this is deemed to have been a pattern.

By reemphasizing that health insurance coverage is mandated and by leveraging Americare's exceedingly low to no cost against the high premiums and deductibles of all other health insurance products in the marketplace, ze was able to dramatically increase enrollment in Americare during the ensuing years. Americare is legally designated as a lifelong plan, and it has started to absorb patients who were enrolled in Medicare and Medicaid, as these programs are gradually being phased out.

One by one, insurance companies are withdrawing their products from the exchanges because they are losing money, which threatens their viability as corporations. Approximately two-thirds of the citizens are now insured by Americare, and this number is steadily on the increase. As a result of Americare, citizens appear to be much healthier, as determined by reviewing their quality metrics, and this improvement in health is durable and on the increase.

Primary Care Associates is a six-provider internal medicine practice in central New Hampshire. Kyle Sanderson, PA-C and Lucas Moses, M.D. are two of the practice's providers. This is their story.

CHAPTER 1

"Get up, Sean! You'll be late for school," Sean's mom screamed from downstairs.

Sean rubbed the sleep out from his eyes, got out of bed and ran to the shower, then he brushed his teeth and got dressed. He swung by the kitchen to grab a breakfast bar and his backpack before he ran out the door toward the school bus, which honked its horn as it waited for him.

"Bye, Mom. I love you," Sean said as the screen door slammed gently behind him.

"I love you too," his mother said in return in a wobbly decrescendo as he ran to catch the school bus.

Sean was a senior at Granite Ridge High School. He was the only child of Sean and Evelyn MacDonald. Sean Sr. was a partner in a very profitable and well-known engineering firm, and Evelyn was a professor of mathematics at nearby Northern New England College. Sean was their pride and joy, the center and the love of their lives, and their legacy.

Sean's graduation was right around the corner. He had done exceedingly well in school, both academically and otherwise. He was home schooled throughout the summers, which permitted him to graduate in early October rather than waiting until the following May. He excelled in mathematics and physics, as well as in track and field. He was a long-distance runner, having entered and completed the Boston

Marathon in suitable time on Patriot's Day. He planned on attending Massachusetts Institute of Technology beginning in January 2031 and living away from home for his very first time. Although he was looking forward to this, he knew he would miss his parents.

Most especially, he knew that he would miss his girlfriend, Kaitlyn. She was his first love, and he was her first love too. Their love for each other was genuine, innocent, deep, and sweet. Every experience, touch, and kiss were entirely new to them, and this newness was filled with intense physical feelings and emotion.

Aside from practice, which was over, and school, which was ending, Sean spent most of his time with Kaitlyn. The two had been inseparable since their relationship began two years earlier. Sean's parents had a fondness for Kaitlyn, and it was their hope that, when the timing was right, she would become their daughter-in-law. From Sean's and his parents' perspectives, all was right with the world.

It was Friday, the last day of high school for Sean. Kaitlyn had another eight months yet to go. His last class ended at 11:45 a.m. He cleaned out his locker, then headed over to Kaitlyn's locker, where she was waiting for him with a hug.

"Let's go to Burger King for lunch," Sean said.

"Sure!" Kaitlyn said.

They headed off to Sean's car.

Sean had been permitted to drive to school only for the last six months. His father decided to purchase a new car, and he gave his old car to Sean as an early graduation present. Sean had been working at Burger King to make money for gas and other teenage expenses. He enjoyed working and having his own money and freedom. Although he worked there, Sean waited in line at Burger King, just like everyone else did. This gave him time to hold Kaitlyn's hand, to look at her and think about her, to show her off to the other guys from school, and to be grateful for everything he had. Sean's and Kaitlyn's fingers caressed each other. He looked into Kaitlyn's deep-blue eyes, and he was drawn to her in a kiss.

During the kiss, Sean fleetingly felt a little funny, as if something wasn't quite right. He experienced a sudden, intense chest pain, sweating, nausea, and an urge to defecate. He ejaculated with an intense orgasm. There was a quick but timeless sense of panic and of every feeling all at once, with total and complete physical and emotional disorientation, followed by a sense of disconnection, then by release.

Then came the bright lights, the sound of trickling streams, and of Bach. Sean could see, hear, smell, and feel, yet he could not.

Geoffrey A. Lundy, M.D.

CHAPTER 2

Kyle had just returned from grocery shopping. He was greeted by his phone ringing. He reached for the handset and picked it up. "Hello," Kyle said.

"Hey, it's Luke," the caller said. "I am on call for the group. Yesterday, I received a call from Granite Ridge police that one of our patients, a Sean MacDonald, died suddenly and unexpectedly while waiting in line at Burger King. The autopsy is on Monday at 9:00 a.m. I would like you to be in attendance so we can try and figure out why he died. The postmortem examination is being performed at the state laboratory in Concord. I will make sure you have no patients scheduled in the office for Monday. You may take Monday afternoon off."

"Sure thing," Kyle said. "I'll be there. Have a good rest of your weekend, Luke."

"You too, Kyle."

He clumsily hung up the phone while juggling the bags of groceries.

Kyle was a recent addition to the staff at Primary Care Associates. Since he began working there some three months ago Luke had requested his presence at several autopsies of their patients who had expired under unusual circumstances. As Kyle's supervising physician, Luke felt it to be an important part of Kyle's continuing medical education.

Additionally, it permitted them an opportunity to possibly discover any clues as to the cause of the patient's unexpected death. It also permitted Kyle the opportunity to help the patient's family to bring closure to them for the loss of their loved one.

Kyle had attained his dream of becoming a physician assistant at the age of 26, upon graduating from Massachusetts College of Pharmacy and Health Sciences about four months earlier — May 22, 2030, to be exact. Initially, his short, wavy blond hair, strikingly large, deep, blue eyes, fair skin with some freckles, cleft chin, and a welcoming, dimpled smile raised questions in the minds of some of the patients and staff as to whether Kyle was old enough to have even graduated from high school. Kyle's pronouns were *he, him,* and *his,* and although he was boyish in many respects, he was mature beyond his years. It did not take long for the staff, colleagues, and patients to see and embrace this combination of boyish enthusiasm and maturity, as well as his honesty, sincerity, caring, compassion, and optimism. Kyle was truly a win for the practice, and the practice proved to be a win for him.

CHAPTER 3

Kyle arrived at the state laboratory at 8:55 a.m. on Monday. The smell always reminded him of the walk-in freezer at the butcher shop. The odor of stale, cold, moist air was accompanied by a hint of blood, feces, and decay. Former Sean lay supine, a body block under the torso between the scapulae, and the chest thrusting upward, as if proud. Arms, neck, and head tended backward, and all tubes, lines, and catheters had been left in situ.

Former Sean, the table, and the room had already been meticulously prepared. With Bach playing quietly in the background and the gentle trickle of water running in the table's gutters, setting the stage, the pathologist's performance began.

A high-resolution, whole-body, multi-slice, 3-D multiplanar CT scan was performed to look for less-obvious signs of injury or other pathology. A complete external examination was performed to look for lacerations, ecchymoses, and puncture wounds that might reveal subtle trauma or intravenous, intramuscular, or subcutaneous drug abuse. Next, an 18-gauge needle (attached to a 30-cc syringe) was passed through the sclera and into the globe of the right eye. A sample of vitreous humor was obtained. This would be screened for the presence of drugs of abuse, which was the leading cause of death at this time.

An anterior incision was made along the entirety of the neck, exposing the trachea and the underlying esophagus and both carotid arteries. These were divided at each end and removed to the side table for further examination. The thyroid gland and epiglottis were similarly removed. A long-handled clamp was inserted at the upper end of the neck incision and into the mouth, along the exposed surface of the tongue. This was used to grasp the tip of the tongue and to pull it down over itself and out through the neck incision. The tongue was freed from its attachments to the floor of the mouth using Metzenbaum scissors to make this possible, and the tongue was removed and was also placed on the side table.

Next, the skin and soft tissues were deftly parted diagonally from the right shoulder to the xiphoid, continuing along the midline and beyond to the pubic bone. The tissues of the left shoulder to the xiphoid were similarly parted, forming a large Y.

Skin, muscle, and soft tissue were quickly and elegantly separated from the ribs and breastbone. The large V-shaped skin flap thus created was reflected back over the face, as if to shield Sean from seeing inside—from discovering his innermost secrets. The other flaps were draped neatly to either side.

Then came the audible snaps, like the breaking of dry kindling, as the entire chest plate of ribs and breastbone was removed with the aid of rib cutters and an electric saw. Bits of bone, tissue, and blood splayed out from the blade, forming a collage of sorts all along the exposed portions of the cold steel table.

The smell of blood, feces, and decay became most pronounced as the Letulle evisceration was completed. All organs of the chest, abdomen, and pelvis were exposed and removed en bloc and were placed on the side table for examination, leaving the entire chest, abdominal, and pelvic cavity empty and entirely open to the air.

The block behind the chest was repositioned behind the upper neck, which had been stiffened by rigor mortis. The scalp was incised along the back of the head from the left ear to the opposite ear, exposing the skull. Like the opening of an orange, the upper scalp flap was peeled forward over the face and down to the eyes, and the rear flap was peeled backward and downward toward the neck. With the aid of an oscillating saw, the large bowl of the top of the skull was removed, exposing the meninges, the coverings of what once was the essence of Sean. The three layers of the meninges—the dura mater, arachnoid mater, and the pia mater—were incised superficially to the great longitudinal fissure, exposing the brain underneath. This former essence of Sean was removed using gentle traction on the frontal lobes, with the assistance of a long-handled knife to sever its junction with the spinal cord, and it was placed in a jar of formalin for later study.

Within the span of thirty minutes or so, Kyle had witnessed the former Sean being transformed into a shell of meat and bone that once housed a living soul, a life, someone's true love. That shell remained, with its face spackled with bits of bone, tissue, and blood, looking upward into Kyle's eyes.

The eyes were left wide open, flecked with blood, lifeless with tache noire, cloudy and cold with an empty, sardonic smirk upon disfigured lips.

The organ masses thus removed were further examined on a side table. The great vessels and coronary arteries were opened, exposing large plaques within each and within the aorta. The heart was opened, revealing a large transmural infarction of the anterior wall of the left ventricle and a rupture of the papillary muscles, which had caused immediate and severe mitral insufficiency and Sean's untimely demise, due to cardiogenic shock.

Both carotid arteries were opened in succession, demonstrating large atheromatous plaques within each.

Former Sean suddenly sat up on the cold steel table, cloudy eyes blinking, now heavy and laden with fresh tears. "Find out who did this to all of us, Kyle," former Sean said, crying, with bloody spittle flying from the lips and virtual tongue.

Kyle heard Sean's voice inside his head, and he was stunned, as if his ears had been boxed. Something had been touched deep within Kyle's psyche. He knew that he needed to follow up regarding the ghost of Sean's plea.

Former Sean still lay supine and open on the autopsy table under the cold light. Nothing had changed, yet everything had. Kyle's heart was racing. He was sweating. No one else was the wiser.

The organs were dumped back inside their respective cavities of origin after each was carefully weighed, photographed, and appropriately sampled. The shell of former Sean was zipped closed with sutures, the crown of the skull was replaced, and the scalp was pulled back to of its natural position and secured with running sutures. What remained of Sean was covered with a plastic drape and wheeled into the refrigerator to await pickup by the funeral home.

Pending the results of blood and fluid tests and microscopic analysis of tissue samples obtained, the family was told that Sean had died from a heart attack due to advanced coronary artery disease and hyperlipidemia.

Sean was seventeen.

CHAPTER 4

Kyle arrived at his office early Tuesday morning anticipating a busy day. It was an atypically mild early October day in Granite Ridge, New Hampshire. The sun was bright, yielding a sense of shadows being cast by the trees on the green grass, and the smells of the browning leaves and white pines saturated the air. His morning proved to be a hectic, albeit an uneventful one. He saw patients at fifteen-minute intervals, and he was able to complete his morning patient care session right on time.

At noon, he was seated at his desk, which was his sanctuary from the bustle outside. He was planted in front of a computer screen, eating a smoked turkey breast and avocado sandwich while reviewing his morning. He enjoyed this time of day because it gave him time to decompress and gain the sustenance that would be required for an afternoon of unknown surprises. He liked that about primary care—the surprises.

Kyle took a few minutes to look around at the light-blue walls with his diplomas hanging on them, the whiteboard with notes on it, and the coat hooks with his white coats neatly hanging on them.

"Kyle Sanderson, PA-C" with *"Primary Care Associates"* below it, embossed in green-script lettering over each left breast pocket of my long white coats makes it official,* he thought, smiling.

All of this was illuminated by the stark fluorescent

lighting that all but destroyed the soothing atmosphere. The coldness of the lighting was partially offset by the warmth of the cherry-wood desk, the bookcases laden with *Harrison's Principles of Internal Medicine* and other classics, the bluish-red, office-strength tweed carpeting that covered the floor, and the sound of Brandenburg Concerto no. 1 in F Major playing in the background.

He loved Bach.

Briefly, he closed his eyes, and he felt a gentle smile forming on his lips. *I've made it,* he thought.

He began by skimming through everything and placing items into piles, based on priority, and answering and making phone calls on the fly in between and during his review. Most of the tasks in the task list and items in his in-basket were exercises in redundancy and futility. They were required solely for billing and documentation purposes, such as orders for events, treatments, or durable medical equipment that had already been provided to the patient by the vendor or had already occurred in the weeks past.

Most providers found this aspect of the practice of medicine a source of frustration, yet Kyle refused to become frustrated. He chose just to accept, as frustration was a waste of time and energy. Typically, a twelve-inch-deep pile of incoming pages could be distilled down to only a few inches of stuff that required any action. This pile would then be put aside and addressed in a piecemeal fashion throughout the rest of the day, during brief periods of downtime as well as after hours. He always dealt with urgent issues, of course, in real time.

Although Kyle had been practicing for only about four or five months, he had already developed an efficient, prompt, and thorough style. Nothing slipped past his eyes without his notice. He attended to documents independently with each visual field, heard independently with each ear, and processed it all simultaneously. He lurched forward through the piles, like his Jeep through deep snow, with his mind's eye automatically drawing attention to things that warranted it.

His right visual field was drawn to a document atop the in-basket pile to the right and forward of his computer screen. It was a discharge summary for an emergency room visit for Lorraine Simons, a thirty-five-year-old woman who presented to the emergency room in cardiac arrest on September 28, 2030. Pulling this document from the pile, he began to read it with his right visual field while attending to other things with his peripheral vision. Despite all appropriate measures, resuscitation was unsuccessful.

Kyle recalled, in detail, his last office visit with Lorraine about a month earlier. She had been relatively stable and doing well at that time. Kyle had been puzzled about her health issues since first meeting her about a half a year ago, when he was still a student. It had struck him as odd that someone so young could have cardiovascular disease, especially in the absence of any risk factors for it. It reminded him that medicine was more of an art than a science, that the rules were often broken, and that diseases and health conditions oftentimes occurred sporadically without attention to the rules.

It reminded him of Sean.

With the sunlight gleaming into the office through the window to his left and the smell of coffee and a microwaved meal wafting in from under the office door, Kyle continued the paperwork and task list review. He was ever mindful that the clock was ticking down to the 1:00 p.m. hour, heralding the start of his afternoon patient-care session.

Out of the corner of his left visual field, Kyle spied a progress note regarding Scott Smith, a patient he was following who had HIV/AIDS, which had been uncharacteristically aggressive. His disease had been resistant and unresponsive to intensive medical therapy. This was a progress note from Scott's infectious diseases physician, stating that Scott had expired on September 30, 2030. Kyle was once again struck by his patient's death. Scott had been in a monogamous relationship with a devoted partner for many years. His partner was HIV negative, and their sexual behaviors had been relatively negligible risk, so the genesis of Scott's HIV infection was unclear. Furthermore, who died from AIDS in 2030? With the available medical therapy, virtually no one died from HIV infection. Most patients with HIV/AIDS died with it but not from it; they lived full and healthy lives until they died from something else.

Death was not an unusual occurrence in primary care; it was as natural and as inevitable as birth. Being struck by a patient's death, however, raised an internal red flag that caused a provider to pause and to contemplate.

With a furrowed brow, Kyle closed his eyes briefly and

thought, *Both Scott Smith and Lorraine Simons, within a week of each other.* His focus then immediately was drawn to Sean's untimely demise. *And Sean MacDonald this past weekend.*

Kyle then recalled the premature death of Lester Blumenthal back in August, who had died rather unexpectedly from metastatic colorectal cancer. Kyle was struck by his death because Mr. Blumenthal had undergone a colonoscopy, which was entirely negative, a year and a half before his death. It typically took many years for someone with an entirely negative colonoscopy to develop colorectal cancer, let alone die from it.

What a bad couple of months. What is going on? Am I doing something wrong? Is this just coincidence or bad luck?

These thoughts flashed through Kyle's mind simultaneously and in a pulsating fashion. Untimely deaths and aggressive diseases were not that unusual in a primary care practice, but a string of these warranted pause. He then began to think about these deaths in terms of a definition of *outliers*, as explained to him by one of his mentors. *Outliers* were patients who experienced events, outcomes, conditions, or diseases without any apparent risk factors or reasons for their occurrence and that would not at all be expected, given their medical, family, and social histories. Both Lorraine Simons and Scott Smith were simply outliers, in that they had been members of the population of medically healthy people without significant risk factors for the diseases that they incurred.

Outliers are a part of the practice of medicine, Kyle thought. *They happen, seemingly for no explicable reason, other than they happen.* This was what his mentors had taught him and what his experiences had born out. In Kyle's mind, these outliers were humbling for providers, reminding them that medicine was an art that was based only somewhat in science and that it was not doctrine. Illnesses often occurred, seemingly despite the "rules," and physicians, physician assistants, and nurse practitioners were just people and not gods.

Deep down in his subconscious, Kyle couldn't shake the feeling that something of a more sinister nature was afoot. Although it was possible, there seemed to be too many unexpected deaths to just write them all off as outliers. His countenance had changed from one of boyish sweetness to one of great torment. He could feel the sweat pearling up on his furrowed brow. He could hear and feel his racing heart as he sat for a while, visualizing a mental picture and a memory of the shell of Sean MacDonald—chest, abdomen, and calvarium gaping wide open and empty on the autopsy table, smelling of stool and raw meat, and looking up at him through cloudy, blood-spackled, blood-streaked eyes, as if staring through him.

"Find out who did this to all of us, Kyle. Look into this," a voice inside his head again cried.

Terrified, his eyes opened wide. Kyle focused on his growing sense that perhaps these deaths were other than outliers.

I will pull these records together and review them with Luke during our monthly case review a week from now, he thought.

Although physician assistants in the state of New Hampshire could not carry their own patient panels or practice independently, most, if not all, of Kyle's patients relied on him as their primary care provider. He met with his supervising physician, Dr. Lucas Moses, at monthly intervals, and they reviewed cases together, as required by New Hampshire state law and the bylaws of the practice. Otherwise, Kyle practiced on his own, with Dr. Moses and other colleagues being available for consultation. He shared Dr. Moses's patient panel, as all the patients Kyle saw were officially assigned to Dr. Moses. Their monthly case review occurred at noon on the second Tuesday of each month, the same day as the practice's monthly department meeting.

Using the computer and the practice's EMR system, IQOD, he quickly compiled the list of patients he would review at his monthly meeting with Dr. Moses. Kyle scanned the list again, and the chilled feeling down his spine resurfaced. All of them were under fifty-five years of age. And all of them were insured by Americare.

Kyle closed the document window. *Perhaps Luke can make sense of it.* And he hoped Sean's apparent ghost would quiet down so he could get some work done.

Kyle's afternoon session was also an uneventful one, but a cloud of concern had settled within Kyle's heart and mind that was omnipresent, coloring all his thoughts, feelings, and actions. Within this cloud was this ghost of Sean, who would periodically remind Kyle that he was still there.

CHAPTER 5

That night Kyle's sleep was torturous. His dreams were a random collage of vignettes of childhood, adolescent, and early adulthood events. These were mixed with flashes of the outliers and the smells of the morgue, with Sean's voice still compelling Kyle to investigate their deaths. He tossed and turned and woke up several times during the night. His bed sheets were soaked with sweat when he awoke at 5:30 a.m. on Wednesday, not feeling at all well rested. He was a bit distracted and disturbed during his morning patient session, with every thought and action overshadowed by thoughts about Sean and the other outliers.

Lunchtime arrived, and Kyle was on time, so he used the entire hour between noon and one o'clock to eat lunch and multitask. *The piles aren't that large today*, Kyle thought.

His trademark boyishly dimpled smile reappeared on his face as he shuffled through the piles with his left hand and attended to emails and tasks in IQOD with his right hand, eating in between.

He successfully navigated the pile of papers; completed all the prescription renewals, lab reviews, and tasks in the task list; and finished his lunch of homemade gazpacho, which was an uncommon feat. Just as the afternoon session was about to begin, Corey from the front desk called him.

"Sorry to disturb you," she said. "An officer with the Granite Ridge police is on the phone, asking to speak with you."

This can't be good, Kyle thought. He knew from experience that when a police officer called, it was most likely to inform a provider that a patient had expired at home.

"Hello," Kyle said.

"Dr. Sanderson, this is Officer Zamboni."

Kyle had become weary of telling people that he was a PA, not an MD, as that distinction had all but become moot anyway.

"We are at the residence of Carla Dossier," Officer Zamboni continued. "We were contacted by her next-door neighbor who hadn't seen her for about a week. This morning the neighbor noticed an overpowering smell in the hallway near Ms. Dossier's apartment door. From the look of things, this individual has been dead for a while—in her bedroom with the heat on. I am guessing that death occurred at least several days ago. The body is badly decomposed, so the entire building needs to be evacuated before cleanup is completed. The medical examiner was notified and has accepted the case so the body will be taken to their office for thorough forensic evaluation. Do you know of anyone who could tell us for sure that this is, in fact, Ms. Dossier?"

Kyle was stunned. It was as if everything around him, including time, was at a standstill. He had seen Carla in the office about ten days ago for a routine visit. She had been perfectly healthy with no active medical issues. She had no vices—no smoking, drinking, drugs, or the like. At that office visit, Kyle had performed a routine physical examination, administered the flu shot, and sent her on her way.

Carla had moved to New Hampshire from Arizona about a year ago after a rather painful divorce on the grounds that her ex-husband had been verbally and physically abusive to her. She had cut all ties with him and with everyone in Arizona and moved here to start her life anew. Apparently, there was a rather large divorce settlement, so she had been able to relocate comfortably and take her time finding work, a task that she hadn't yet begun. She had no friends or acquaintances in this area and no children or siblings; her parents were both deceased. She had been alone of her own choosing but not at all lonely.

Carla had come to rely on Kyle for help with depression, and she had been seeing him regularly, every month or so, since June. She had refused to see a therapist, and at the time of her routine physical examination ten days ago, the depression had been in a solid remission. Between her physical exam and an initial evaluation for stable hypertension back in June, Kyle had also seen her in the office in July, August, and September for routine follow-up for depression, which had been successfully treated with duloxetine.

Kyle told Officer Zamboni that he could think of no one else who could identify her. The officer did not push him for more detail, which obviated any risk that Kyle was in violation of HIPAA or any other of the patient-privacy statutes. Under the circumstances, however, Kyle felt comfortable in acknowledging that fact. It could have been construed that Corey and Kyle had done just that by acknowledging to Officer Zamboni that Ms. Dossier was a patient of the practice. He could not disclose anything about her medical issues, including depression, which might render suicide a possible cause of death. The medical examiner's office would almost certainly be in touch with the proper legal releases, so he could provide that information.

"I … I can identify her," Kyle said as an afterthought, stunned and not really knowing what else he could say or do for his patient.

"It isn't pretty," Officer Zamboni said. "And it would be an awful lot for me to ask of you. However, if you could do that, it would speed up this process and would be greatly appreciated. Come on over. The body should be here for a while."

Kyle cursed his trembling hands as he tried to put the handset back on the receiver.

Mechanically, he walked to the front desk, told Corey where he was going, and asked her to cancel all the afternoon patients.

The drive to Carla's home was a short one. She lived in White Tail Run, which was a village within the town of Granite Ridge. Carla's building was quite easy to find, as there were two squad cars parked out front. In the parking lot out back, there was a green van with MEDICAL EXAMINER in block letters, overlying the seal of the New Hampshire State Police. The home was an old Victorian mansion that had been subdivided into apartments, one of which Carla had been renting. Her apartment was on the third floor.

Officer Zamboni met Kyle at the front door of the building and escorted him up the stairway. Upon reaching the second-floor landing, beads of sweat were present on Kyle's forehead. He was struck by a smell of sickening sweetness, the likes of which he previously had not experienced, but it was unmistakable. With each successive step onward, his progress slowed. His pallor and the sweat on his face increased as the sweetness was accompanied, then overwhelmed, by an unfamiliar, increasingly rank, rotten stench. He began to feel it in his clothing and on his skin. It hung there like a cloak. Perhaps it was the discord between the odors as if cheap perfume had been added to a cauldron of week-old roadkill, which confounded his senses and caused him to vomit when he reached the third-floor hallway.

"You all right?" Officer Zamboni asked. He held up Kyle's sweating body and made certain that the vomitus landed squarely within the hazmat barrel, over which Kyle prayed.

"Here, try this." Officer Zamboni passed Kyle a small open jar of Vicks VapoRub and instructed him to put some under his nose. "Sometimes, folks do better if they just mouth breathe."

Feeling like a sweat-drenched ghost, Kyle followed those recommendations as the two proceeded down the hallway. The room was clearly marked by the open door and biohazard bags and barrels outside. The two men turned and entered. Kyle could feel the sickeningly sweet, rank rottenness seeping into his pores, and he could even taste it now. He vomited a few more times into one of the biohazard barrels. Once he recovered, he examined what he thought used to be one of his patients.

There in the bed was something that looked like a rather large, black-and-blueish, yellowish-white Michelin Man. The hands were raised up off the bed because of arm swelling, and the buttons of the nightshirt had been torn open, apparently by the pressure of the edema.

As Kyle tried to examine for recognizable features, the skin sloughed at even the slightest touch of his gloved hands. The eyes and tongue were bulging and protuberant, and there was putrid fluid dripping down the cheeks from the mouth and nose. The abdomen was massively distended, skin integrity was breached, and there was more of that putrid fluid everywhere, most notably pooling between the legs and around the hips, tracking down the sheets onto the floor. Clearly visible were maggots almost everywhere, as well as flies. The flies were coming and going, in and out of the mouth and each opening and breach of the skin, dipping their tiny, curled tongues wherever they lighted.

"I … I can't tell," Kyle said. "I can't tell if it's Carla."

Then Kyle remembered she had lost her right great toe to a lawnmower accident as a kid, and she had a tattoo of her two pugs on her mid-upper back. Kyle explained this to Officer Zamboni, who withdrew the sheets from over the legs. Sure enough, the right great toe was missing. Examination of the back would have to wait for the medical examiner, who was busy taking samples of the insects and fluids.

"The body needs to be left as it was initially found," Officer Zamboni said. "More photos and samples need to be obtained. The medical examiner must complete the bedside evaluation and bring the body to their office. Thank you so much for your help, Dr. Sanderson."

"Yeah, sure thing." Kyle was unsure of what else to say. His pallor and sweating had largely resolved. On his way out, he decided to take one more look at the face. A fly landed on Kyle's lower lip, and he could feel it unfurling its little tongue. He brushed it away in a panic.

On the way home, he was haunted by all that had transpired, as well as flashes in freeze-frames of the decomposing body, presumably Carla, and the open and empty shell of Sean. Both spoke to him in unison. *"Look into this, Kyle. Look into this."* Kyle was terrified and irrevocably changed by everything that had transpired that afternoon and by the outliers he had encountered since joining Primary Care Associates.

How could it be that no other providers, not even Luke, have noticed anything like this? he continually thought.

CHAPTER 6

That night, while trying to drift off to sleep, Kyle became entrenched in deep thought.

Is it possible that other providers aren't experiencing or noticing the same things that I am?

He thought about the outliers. He thought about the September department meeting, during which provider compensation was reviewed with the providers by Martin Shandling, CFO of the practice.

I guess it's possible this is an isolated phenomenon, occurring in my patients only. If this is a more global issue, how could this occur unnoticed by my colleagues? Kyle thought repetitively.

He was gradually overcome by a deep, meditative trance, during which he experienced a dialogue of sorts, exploring answers to this disturbing question, as well as pondering what it meant to be a provider in 2030. It was reminiscent of chemist Friedrich Alexander Kekule's dream in 1865 of snakes chasing their tails while he pondered the structure of benzene. This led Kekule to deduce that the structure of benzene was ringlike in nature, which proved to be one of the most important concepts in organic chemistry and the study of aromatic compounds.

Sleep deepened, even as Kyle thought about the outliers, the review of provider compensation from the September meeting, and the competing agendas that providers had to attend to in 2030. These agendas had changed extraordinarily little, if at all, during the past decade. This was all muddled together in the form of a lifelike dreamscape of that department meeting. In attendance at that meeting were Martin Shandling, CFO of the practice; Seth Weinberg, medical director; and the three other providers: Lucas Moses, MD (Luke); Pradeep Khan, MD; and Margaret Anderson, APRN.

"I'm a relatively new provider," Kyle said at the meeting in his dream. There was a nervous, quivering quality to his voice. "I'm just learning the ropes of being in practice. During my training, I learned a lot about caring for patients but absolutely nothing about taking care of myself. I had no exposure to the other especially important nonclinical aspects of the practice of medicine. I was given no guidance regarding these aspects of medical practice as they related to my life and to providing care to the patient in front of me. I know that this holds true for friends and colleagues of mine who have just completed their training. It was left up to our first employers to teach us these things in a kind of apprenticeship—I guess a sort of rite of passage—and for us to learn by trial and error and by doing. Mr. Shandling, could you explain the basics regarding practice reimbursement by our payers and the subsequent compensation of providers by the practice?"

"Around January 1, every payer publishes its fee schedule for the upcoming year," Mr. Shandling said. "This lists their standard reimbursement for every service and procedure, including office visits, that our practice provides. As more than two-thirds of our patients are insured by Americare, I will use them as an example.

"A compliance quotient—or 'CQ'—is calculated for each participating practice on a quarterly basis. It is equally based upon the degree to which the Americare Medical Record System, or AMRS, has unfettered access to the practice's patient medical records, the degree to which the practice's providers follow their patients' care plans, and the degree to which the patients receive all recommended immunizations and screening tests and procedures. The CQ is a number between 0.70 and 1.30. Hospitals and practices are reimbursed quarterly at a rate that is equal to the standard reimbursement from the insurance company's published fee schedule, multiplied by the CQ. Based on this formula, a practice may receive anywhere from 70 percent to 130 percent of what was billed, according to their fee schedule, for their services depending on their CQ. In like fashion, a CQ is calculated for each provider within the practice that is based on the same parameters for that provider and is also a number between 0.70 and 1.30.

"A provider's productivity is defined by the number of relative value units, or RVUs, that the provider accumulates during the previous twelve-month period. In short and oversimplified terms, every service that a provider delivers is assigned a number of RVUs based upon the relative value of that service compared to nationally accepted standards. The monetary value of the RVU is standardized by specialty and subspecialty, so that your compensation will be determined by the number of RVUs that you generate during the previous twelve months. This is an oversimplification of the Resource-Based Relative Value System—the RBRVS—dating back to the 1980s. A provider's compensation is defined as the number of RVUs times dollar value per RVU times the provider's CQ. Your salaries are guaranteed for the first two years at a compensation as above, with a CQ equal to 1.0, after which time the RVU-based calculation kicks in."

"What happens if, after the two-year salary guarantee, I fail to make at least the guaranteed salary, based upon this RVU-based formula?" Kyle asked.

"Then your salary will decrease to the RVU-calculated salary with your CQ less than 1.0," Mr. Shandling said. "If a CQ of less than 1.0 or low productivity, based upon RVU data, persists for more than four quarters, your employment here could be terminated. I expect that you will each make more than the guaranteed compensation."

Kyle faded out of the dreamscape meeting and into another dream with disturbing thoughts …

A typical office visit is about twenty minutes long. During that encounter, I must calculate the level of service for that visit to determine its RVU value. The calculation of the level of service of an office visit is a complicated matter, based on which set of documentation guidelines I choose to use, whether the patient is new or established, and the levels of the history, physical examination, and medical decision-making involved in that patient encounter. My determining the levels of history, physical examination, and medical decision-making are complicated matters in and of themselves.

During each patient encounter, I must also address the issues for which the patient is seeking care. Based on my assessments during the encounter, I must also make the appropriate diagnoses and follow the prescribed plan of care. This plan might include treatments done in the office during that appointment; the ordering of tests, if indicated; appropriate post appointment treatments, such as medications and the like; and instructions for the patient's follow-up.

Assuming that a patient's care plan is followed to the letter, the control of any conditions or diseases that he or she has should improve. This would be evidenced by an improvement in those parameters that are being followed in the management of these conditions. These parameters are transmitted automatically and in real time to Americare via the AMRS portal for use in calculating the practices and my patients' quality metrics, as well as the practice's and my own CQ. The other remaining insurers are also required to follow the same regulations regarding reporting.

Because of the unpredictable nature of caring for patients, I am often behind schedule, having ten or so of these office visits per patient-care session (which seems to be the minimum required to maintain a decent salary), each with uncertain presentations and some having overly complicated medical issues. Some of these are sick, often critically ill patients who require my undivided attention. Additionally, the telephones are ringing, and I am constantly interrupted, often to give a verbal order or to sign a verbal order for something that I ordered over a week ago. Often, I am interrupted to have a peer-to-peer discussion with Americare or another insurer to justify why their patient requires an MRI, and the like.

Insurance companies track practices and providers' quality metrics and CQs. They also track the costs of each practice and provider in the delivery of that care, both on a per-member per-month and as per-disease state basis. A provider who closely follows the prescribed care plan, whose patients receive all the recommended immunizations and screening tests and procedures, and whose costs are relatively low is excellent value for patients, practices, and insurance companies.

Since the advent of Americare, most providers have noticed a marked improvement in the control of their patients' chronic conditions. Overall, their quality metrics and CQs are much improved. Because their patients are less sick, providers can see more of them in a shorter span of time, so their productivities, CQs, and, therefore, their salaries are much higher. Additionally, providers are held harmless, shielded from litigation or censure, provided they follow their patients' care plans, immunization, and screening guidelines. This has made the practice of medicine much easier and less stressful for providers, whose salaries have dramatically increased overall.

Aside from the emotional aspects, outliers result in no consequences, negative impacts, or any other liabilities for the practice, provider, or insurer. There are drastic consequences for failure in the performance of any other of the competing agendas.

Upon awakening from his dream state, Kyle clearly recognized the reason why these outliers were seemingly unnoticed by his colleagues and the practice.

CHAPTER 7

About a week had passed. Kyle continued to see his patients with his usual youthful vigor, while wondering, deep down, if the patient in front of him might become an outlier.

It was 6:00 a.m. on Tuesday, October 15, 2030, and Kyle was first to arrive for the monthly Primary Care Associates department meeting. Dr. Seth Weinberg, the practice's medical director, with his short, wavy, salt-and-pepper hair, olive skin, and plastic-framed bifocals on his prominent nose, was seated on his perch at the front of the room by 6:15 a.m. There was an air of arrogance about him,

Dr. Weinberg was board certified in internal medicine and was a fellow of the American College of Physicians. Four years ago, he had been elected medical director for the practice. Before that, he had practiced medicine full time, seeing his patients in the office and those who were admitted to the local hospital. Currently, his role was strictly administrative, and he was much more of a "numbers person" than a clinician.

Shortly after becoming the medical director, Dr. Weinberg negotiated a contract with Americare that provided a fee schedule and practice reimbursement far superior to those of any other insurer. The practice increased the number of patients who were insured by Americare and improved the

Americare Medical Record System (AMRS) portal to exceed government standards. Patient throughput and adherence to recommended immunizations and screening procedures had also increased. As a result, providers', and patients' quality metrics (and providers' RVUs and CQs) improved dramatically, and the practice's reimbursement and provider compensation increased significantly. Because of this, Dr. Weinberg had become highly regarded among his peers, both locally and nationally.

As 6:30 a.m. approached, more attendees entered the room, signed in, and then headed to the buffet table on the side of the room to pick up coffee and pastries, which were essential tools for staying awake through the meeting. This ritual occurred on the third Tuesday of every month without fail. The conference room was pristine, smelling of Lysol and coffee, and the lighting was fluorescent and harsh.

A few minutes after 6:30, the door opened again. Michael Jude sauntered in, holding his coffee. Kyle wasn't surprised that he was late. Michael loved attracting attention to himself. He was good-looking, and he knew it.

Michael Jude was the practice's Americare practice liaison. His pronouns were he, him, and his. He worked at the New Hampshire field office of Americare; therefore, he was a salaried employee of the United States government. Each field office of Americare employed practice liaisons who were responsible for all the practices in their district. Each practice liaison was responsible for up to fifteen practices.

Michael Jude's duties included making certain that the

computer systems at the practice and the practice's EMR complied with federal regulations, that they were linked to the AMRS, and that the AMRS portal was optimized for maximum access to the practice's patient records.

His other responsibilities included making sure that all appropriate preventive-care services and immunizations were offered to all patients and that data for each patient was seamlessly transmitted to Americare. It was also his job to make certain the appropriate QR codes for medications, immunizations, and medical devices were listed in the clinical record and in the Americare Ordering System (AOS) well in advance of patients' scheduled appointments. This insured that the requisite supplies and immunizations would be available at the time of service for every patient.

Additionally, the practice liaisons were Americare's sales force. Each one met with patients in the practices that they covered, with the unspoken and unwritten agenda of encouraging them to switch from their current insurers to Americare.

Each practice had a director of marketing, whose job was to maintain close contact with the practice's Americare practice liaison—also with an unspoken, unwritten agenda to encourage the practice's patients to enroll in Americare. Primary Care Associates' director of marketing had left the practice three months earlier, so Dr. Weinberg had assumed that role on an interim basis until the position could be filled.

Dr. Weinberg called the meeting to order and reviewed the minutes of the last meeting, requesting a motion to accept. The motion was put forth by Pradeep Kahn, MD, one of six providers in the practice, and it was seconded by Dr. Margaret Anderson, another of the six. With no objections, the minutes were accepted, and the department meeting proceeded.

Dr. Weinberg then turned the meeting over to Martin Shandling to review the practice's current financial situation, quality measures, payer mix, and the like.

Primary Care Associates had been a provider-owned practice since its inception in 2000 until 2013, when it was sold to a local hospital because of economic failure. This hospital owned and managed many medical practices in the community. In 2000, there were no hospital-owned practices; currently, there were no privately owned practices. The economics of health care, the complexities of managing a medical practice, and the decreases in reimbursement, increases in practice overhead, increases in liability, and ever-increasing government regulations rendered it next to impossible for a private medical practice to maintain viability. Additionally, some physicians were notoriously bad at business.

Beginning in the early 2000s, local hospitals began purchasing medical practices from their owners. Typically, there was little to no financial gain for the seller; rather, the hospital assumed all their financial (and other) liabilities and agreed to maintain the practice. All practice staff and providers became employees of the hospital.

Mr. Shandling's topic for the meeting was "Payer Mix."

One of the ways a practice could improve its revenue was by carefully adjusting its payer mix—that is, the insurances accepted by the practice and the percentage of patients with those insurers. In simplified terms, a practice strove to adjust its payer mix to have the largest number of its patients insured by third-party payers, with the most favorable fee schedules and less-stringent requirements to maximize reimbursement, while at the same time remaining in compliance with all government regulations about patients' access to medical care.

Mr. Shandling noted that Americare had by far the best fee schedule, and increasingly patients were switching from their insurers to Americare during open enrollment. He pointed out that this was the best possible scenario for the practice. And considering the improving health of the practice's patients and quality metrics, Americare appeared to be the best insurer for the practice's patients.

Although in the past it had been illegal for a doctor or a practice to encourage patients to choose one insurer over another, legislation signed into law by President Dmopvup had made this legal. In fact, the president had incentivized this behavior, giving a practice $1,000 of tax-exempt revenue for each new patient it enrolled in Americare.

The meeting was then opened for any questions or concerns that those in attendance might have.

"Luke?" Dr. Weinberg asked as he pointed to Dr. Lucas Moses, whose hand was raised.

Dr. Moses began. "During the past several months, I have noticed more than a few unusual adverse events and occurrences in some of my patients, such as unexpected diseases and deaths without demonstrable risk factors for these conditions, and in patients who seemed to be uncharacteristically young. We have always had a few of these during our years of practice, but over the past several months, I have noticed more of them. In my cursory review, I noticed three such cases in the past month, and five in the previous two months. Each had Americare as their payer. I'm wondering if any of you have noticed anything similar."

The room was silent. Kyle was flabbergasted, feeling as if he had been hit in the face by a brick. He still felt quite ill after his visit to Carla's home, but he was relieved that his concerns had been validated. He could hear Sean and Carla bantering in a distance within his mind in a quiet yet sardonic way. He still could feel, smell, and even taste the sickening sweet rot.

Dr. Moses then looked at Michael Jude. "Michael? Could you generate a report listing all deaths that occurred within our panel of Americare patients during the past three years?"

"I would like a copy of that list too," Kyle chimed in.

"Certainly, Luke and Kyle," Michael responded. "I'll email that report to you by noon today."

Next, Dr. Moses turned his attention to Steven Alcorn, the director of Primary Care Associates' Health Information

Systems and Information Technology Department, previously known as the Medical Records Department. "Steve, could you provide me with a similar report for the entire panel of patients in our practice by noon today?"

"Sure thing, Luke."

The meeting was then adjourned, and both Luke and Kyle went back to their offices to start their morning sessions. The two planned to meet in Luke's office around noon for Kyle's monthly case review.

CHAPTER 8

At noon, Kyle was seated across from Luke, ready to begin his monthly case presentations. Luke was at his desk taking a phone call, which allowed Kyle time to think about him.

Dr. Lucas Moses was a youthful 58 years old at around six feet tall and 170 pounds. His pronouns were he, him, and his. He was balding but kept his head almost completely shaved. When not wearing his contacts, his deep brown eyes were sometimes framed with glasses with lined-bifocal lenses. His body appeared to be toned, and he was always well groomed. Dressing modestly, he carried himself as a regular guy; you would not get the sense that he was a physician unless he told you. He was humble and not at all arrogant. Preferring to be called Luke, he was warm, sincere, honest, caring, and compassionate. He was extremely intelligent and intuitive, and he was well respected and well liked. After graduating from Harvard University School of Medicine and completing his residency in internal medicine at Massachusetts General Hospital in Boston, he joined Primary Care Associates in 2016. It had not taken long for him to develop a bustling primary care – internal medicine practice.

Luke concluded his phone call, and Kyle ceased his pondering.

"Kyle, I heard about what happened with our patient, Carla Dossier, and how you aided law enforcement in her identification," Luke said. "You went above and beyond. I have no idea how stressful that was for you. I do appreciate that."

"Life-changing," Kyle said, clearing his throat. He felt his face become sweaty as he recalled the events of that afternoon.

"If you need any help coming to terms with what happened, please let me know, and I will help," Luke said.

"No … no … I'll be OK," Kyle said, fighting back tears. He abruptly changed the subject. "I'd like to move on to the case presentations."

"Sounds good."

"Lorraine Simons was a thirty-five-year-old female who was diagnosed with multi-vessel coronary artery disease and severe hypercholesterolemia on July 7, 2028. She presented to the emergency room with STEMI-IMI because of right coronary artery occlusion. She had critical stenosis of the circumflex as well. Cardiac echo revealed inferior wall motion abnormalities with global hypokinesis, moderate MR, and LVEF of 45 percent. Two stents were placed, and she was started on an aggressive medical regimen, including a statin, an ACE inhibitor, and a beta-blocker.

"She presented again with unstable angina on December 1, 2029. Cardiac catheterization revealed almost complete occlusion of the RCA stent. This was dilated successfully, and two additional drug-eluting stents were placed—one inside the RCA stent and one in a new distal LAD lesion. LVEF remained relatively stable.

"On September 10, 2030, she presented again to the emergency room with anterior STEMI in cardiogenic shock. At that time, she had two critical serial LAD lesions, which were also stented. She required intubation, mechanical ventilation, and the use of an intra-aortic balloon pump. She was aggressively treated with antiarrhythmic medications, diuretics, increased doses of her ACE inhibitor, and beta-blocker. CHF resolved, and she was extubated, and IABP was removed. Repeat cardiac echo two weeks after the MI revealed global hypokinesis with LVEF of 25 percent. AICD was placed due to the considerable risk of fatal cardiac arrhythmia. Because of her early age, she was placed on the cardiac transplantation list.

"At approximately 8:30 p.m. on September 28, 2030, her husband found her unresponsive in her bed. EMS was called, and resuscitation was started in the field. She was transported to the emergency room, where she presented with resuscitation in progress. Resuscitative efforts were unsuccessful, and she expired at 9:42 p.m. The case was declined by the medical examiner's office."

"Hmmm," Luke said. "This is very unusual. She was so young, and the disease was so extensive."

Kyle then moved on to the next case. "Scott Smith was a twenty-eight-year-old gay male who was diagnosed with acute retroviral syndrome on November 7, 2026, when he presented to the office, accompanied by his partner, with fever and diffuse adenopathy. An in-office HIV antibody test returned as positive. Confirmatory testing was also positive. His viral load was high, and his CD4 count was preserved. He started on Quarnapula—a four-drug HAART combination. After a two-year period of undetectable viral load, his viral load increased dramatically, and CD4 count began to drop. His medical regimen was changed several times but to no avail. He rapidly progressed to end-stage AIDS with a CD4 count of thirty-five and extremely high viral load. He developed CNS toxoplasmosis, CMV retinitis, and Kaposi's sarcoma. He died of drug-resistant pneumocystis jirovecii pneumonia on September 30, 2030, at the age of thirty-two.

"There are several things that concern me regarding each of these cases," Kyle said. "Lorraine Simons was entirely healthy at her annual physical examination on September 12, 2027, performed by you, and she had no demonstrable risk factors for cardiovascular disease. Scott Smith was HIV negative at the time of his annual physical examination with you on August 6, 2026. His health insurer changed to Americare in September 2026, and he was diagnosed as HIV positive in November."

Kyle looked up from his laptop screen. He saw Luke looking downward. There were worry lines across his forehead. Luke's uneasiness was palpable.

"I just sent you the reports I requested from Michael and Steve at the meeting this morning," Luke said. "I reviewed them both, and it appears, at first glance, that there were a lot more deaths in the Americare panel than one would expect, given the improved-quality metrics, which would indicate that the Americare patient panel should be healthier. We should review these cases and the medical records in greater detail.

"I am also concerned about the death of one of my patients, Trinh Nguyen, who had hepatitis C and developed end-stage liver disease because of this infection. I submitted a request to have him placed on the liver transplant list before his death. That request was denied because of the patient's advanced age. Although unlikely, I had another patient of the same age—a few months older, in fact—with the same disease, who requested liver transplantation around the same time, and his request was granted. I requested a detailed explanation for Mr. Nguyen's denial, considering the other patient's favorable determination from Celeste Davison, the director of the Transplantation Board for the New Hampshire office of Americare. I have yet to receive any explanation."

One o'clock was close at hand, as was the start of both Kyle's and Luke's afternoon patient care sessions. They adjourned and agreed to meet at Luke's home in two weeks because neither felt that it was safe to continue to meet at the office. Kyle felt relieved.

Luke quickly returned to his office. His meeting with Kyle was troubling, though he couldn't quite put it all together as to why. *Then there's the matter of that smile.* Luke shook his head. *This is a professional relationship. What am I thinking?*

He reviewed Lorraine Simons's record, making a note to add Scott Smith and Carla Dossier next. Each patient record was composed of a clinical record and an administrative record. The clinical record included all office notes, test results, and clinical data. It also contained the QR codes for any immunizations, medications, or supplies required for any office visits. These codes were automatically transmitted to Utopia Pharmaceuticals for their production and preparation, and the finished products were delivered to the office in advance of their scheduled appointments to make certain everything that was needed was available for their visits. The administrative record contained demographic data and the link to the Americare Medical Record System, or AMRS.

The government made electronic medical records (EMR) mandatory for those providers and practices caring for patients who were insured by government health insurance plans. Each practice's EMR was required to interface directly with the government's system to facilitate electronic billing, reimbursement, and transmission of patient's data and to ensure compliance. Various vendors marketed EMR products. IQOD Systems, Inc., launched a product that was most desirable. IQOD invited selected practices to purchase their product, and it was the envy of all practices. Primary Care Associates was invited to purchase IQOD as its EMR, which it readily did.

There was a link to AMRS that was in the administrative part of each patient's medical record. Clicking that link brought Luke to a page that was inaccessible; it required a password that they did not have. Through further investigation, they discovered that the link was inaccessible to everyone at the practice, except for Dr. Weinberg and Michael Jude.

Over the next few weeks, Kyle, and Luke each closely reviewed their Americare patients' medical records for any possible discrepancies. They tried not to ask any leading questions while questioning their patients about any concerns regarding their health or health care and that of family members.

A sizable number of these patients commented they had received letters from Americare administrators, requesting they consider participating in some studies, being conducted by the gastroenterology department, during their scheduled colonoscopies. These studies involved the placing of micro-implants within the colon during their procedures, which would monitor the contents of the fecal stream and search for genetic markers for colorectal cancer. This would allow for earlier diagnosis of this cancer and improve mortality statistics from this disease.

Colorectal cancer was the third most common cancer in both men and women, and the five-year survival rate was around 90 percent for localized colorectal cancer, 60 to 70 percent for cancer with regional spread, and around 13 percent for patients with distant spread. Only 39 percent of patients were diagnosed with localized colorectal cancer, 35 percent were diagnosed with localized disease with regional spread, and 21 percent were diagnosed with distant spread. The goal of these studies is to improve early detection and, hence, increase survival.

Curiously, these studies seemed to have been offered preferentially to their patients with uncontrolled diseases such as diabetes mellitus type 2, hypertension, hyperlipidemia, COPD, and coronary artery disease. These patients were considerably more likely to die prematurely from these diseases and others, rather than from colorectal cancer.

When they questioned their Americare patients, they all mentioned that Americare was unrelenting regarding their scheduled immunizations, almost insisting they receive them, even if that was not their wish. Americare offered them financial incentives, such as waiving their premiums and copays, if they received their recommended immunizations. Most of these patients reluctantly complied with these recommendations.

In searching the practice's colorectal cancer–screening registry, as well as other of the disease registries maintained by IQOD, Kyle and Luke found anecdotally higher incidences of death in their Americare patients, as compared with those patients who were insured by other payers.

Kyle had approached Dr. Weinberg several times in the past regarding his and Luke's concerns. In an effort not to appear suspicious, Kyle approached these issues in a positive way, touting the apparent benefits of being enrolled in Americare. Each time he approached Dr. Weinberg, Kyle was faced with increasing pressure to disregard the negative observations and to continue to encourage patients to enroll in Americare because of the better outcomes and lower costs.

After Kyle's fourth approach, a somewhat irritated Dr. Weinberg offered Kyle the vacant position of director of marketing for the practice at a considerable increase in salary. In a roundabout way, Dr. Weinberg made it clear that this promotion was contingent on Kyle's backing off from his line of questioning and on his using this position to encourage their patients to enroll in Americare. Kyle reluctantly accepted the position.

Kyle and Luke decided that the rest of their investigation should occur unobtrusively and under the radar and that Luke should proceed on the down-low; after all, Luke was the one who had mentioned these concerns at the department meeting, and any overt investigation on his part might raise red flags. No one would suspect anything if just Kyle was snooping around.

Kyle thought it would be advantageous for him to use his position as director of marketing to develop a friendship with Michael Jude. He could leverage that friendship to obtain more information regarding the inner workings of Americare, as well as obtaining the access code for AMRS. Kyle and Luke decided it would be best to continue to meet about these issues on a regular basis outside the office, thereby keeping their office meetings restricted to those required by practice bylaws and state regulations. They decided to meet again in two weeks' time at Luke's home.

CHAPTER 9

The two weeks passed quickly. Kyle arrived at the office with plenty of time to ready himself for his 7:30 a.m. patient. That morning, he allowed extra time so he could get a jump on the day, as he planned to leave promptly at 6:00 p.m. to meet with Luke.

Kyle was an early bird, typically arriving at least an hour before the start of his morning sessions. His medical assistant, Pam, arrived shortly afterward. She would set the pace and tone for Kyle's day, deflect inappropriate distractions, calm, and reassure patients, and, most often, resolve any patient conflicts in their entirety. In short, without Pam, Kyle would have been lost.

The administrative staff rolled in around 8:00 a.m. This included the secretaries, as well as Michael Jude. Ever since his meeting with Luke, Kyle had taken an interest in Michael, watching his every move whenever he was within visual range.

During his lunch break, Kyle decided to make the first move. Michael was in his office, sitting at his desk. The decor was rich, with a cherry-wood desk and chairs, plush light-brown carpeting, and his college diploma and other certifications proudly displayed on the walls. Kyle rapped on the office door, and Michael looked up. He was on a phone call, and he motioned to Kyle to come in and have a seat.

Kyle decided to remain outside of Michael's office until his phone call was completed. Kyle looked around the office while Michael finished his call. There were several potted tropical plants; two were palm-like and one looked like a weed. The walls also displayed photographs of pricy luxury cars and attractive people.

"Hi, Kyle. What can I do for you?" Michael asked, his chestnut-brown eyes widening and a smile crossing his lips.

"I'm just stopping by to introduce myself and to ask if there's anything we should be working on together. I'm now the director of marketing for the practice," Kyle said proudly.

Michael's interest was piqued. "I'm Michael," he said while reaching out his right hand to shake Kyle's. "My pronouns are *he, him,* and *his.* Please sit." He motioned to the chairs in front of his desk, and Kyle sat. "There is plenty of stuff we should be working on together. We should meet over dinner sometime to discuss and plan."

"Cool," Kyle said. "Let me know what works for you."

"Awesome," Michael said. His 1:00 p.m. appointment was waiting outside the office door. Michael lifted his head a bit as if to look around and behind Kyle.

Startled, Kyle looked at his watch and realized that it was 1:02, and he was never late. He hopped up out the chair and rushed back across the hallway, grabbed his stethoscope, and headed into his first exam room to see the first patient of the afternoon.

Ms. Wilkerson was seated on the exam table, already wearing a johnny. Exam rooms were arranged so that the patient was seated on the exam table, facing the provider, who was at a fixed computer workstation, facing the patient. Kyle entered the exam room, apologized for being late, took his seat at the workstation, and quickly logged into IQOD.

IQOD was the best of the best, solely because everyone said that it was. It was like the story of "The Emperor's New Clothes" by Hans Christian Andersen; all the emperor's subjects commented how wonderful his garments were because they were expected to do so, even though he was buck naked, and his physique was not much to look at.

One did not work *using* IQOD; one worked *for* IQOD. Providers were expected to tailor what they did to meet IQOD's needs. It was reminiscent of "HAL" in the 1968 novel by Arthur C. Clarke and movie by Stanley Kubrick, *2001: A Space Odyssey*. IQOD was cumbersome to use. Nevertheless, it was deemed as ideal because it met all government requirements regarding providing data about quality metrics. It was compliant as far as coding and billing were concerned, and it interfaced nicely with laboratory and radiology services. This permitted the mining of various data sets, and it had a patient portal that allowed patients access to all their office notes, test results, and letters. Meeting all these requirements made the practice eligible to receive additional revenue from the government.

One downside to IQOD was that it had a rather steep learning curve. Providers spent most of their time with their faces buried in computer screens and futzing around with IQOD, rather than focusing on their patients. Valuable information, as well as opportunities to bond with their patients, which was essential for a therapeutic relationship, were lost.

In the past, physicians had been trained and expected to use all five senses during their patient encounters. This was well before the concepts of nurse practitioners and physician assistants were even conceived. The use of the sense of taste fell by the wayside early on likely for reasons of hygiene. The advent of the EMR, notably IQOD, as well as other modern advances, severely limited the provider's use of sight, sound, and touch. These senses had been rendered incomplete, inadequate, insufficient, and impersonal, largely because of the providers' focus on the computer screen in front of them. The patient had become the providers' secondary focus.

Kyle's afternoon went as smoothly as could have been expected.

Michael was now feeling great, as if he had made a conquest, although he had done nothing at all. Mentally, he was already putting another notch in his belt, fantasizing about what would happen with Kyle. He was distracted throughout the rest of the day, thinking about what they should do on their "first date." Michael's goal was to get into Kyle's pants as soon as possible and to parade him around like haute couture. He wanted Kyle, and he felt that Kyle would think he was the most amazing guy in the world, once they got to know each other better.

After Kyle wrapped up his work, he headed to Luke's house. Luke had been off for the day, so he was already at home. Although Kyle had never been there, he knew the area well. The drive was a short ten-minute hop from the office. The house was a modest one, located in a residential neighborhood that was all decked out for Halloween. As Kyle started up the walkway, he appreciated the feelings, sounds, and smells of fall: the chill in the air, the crunch of leaves under his feet, and the smell of the fallen leaves mixed with the scent of hardwood being burned in fireplaces and woodstoves. Upon arrival at the front door, Kyle rang the doorbell.

Luke appeared at the door. "Hey, Kyle. Come on in," he said with a smile.

"Thanks," Kyle said.

"Busy day?"

"Nah, no busier than usual." Kyle hung up his coat after spying a bunch of pegs on the wall by the front door. He then walked into the living room, where a woodstove made the atmosphere warm and cozy, as only a room with a woodstove could be. There was an ambient smell of burning oak. The furniture was simple but elegant. A large couch and love seat were situated at right angles to each other, both facing the woodstove, with a table and lamp in between and a large coffee table in the center.

"I hope you don't mind, but I took the liberty of ordering pizza," Luke said.

Kyle was not expecting a meal, so he was grateful. "This is much appreciated. I haven't really eaten all day."

They grabbed some pizza and ate on the couch, making small talk and reviewing each of their days. While they were chatting, Kyle allowed his mind to wander, as did his eyes. Although maintaining good eye contact with Luke, Kyle examined the features of Luke's face, his smile, his body language, and his aura. He admired Luke and had a deep respect for him as a colleague and as his supervising physician. It was more than that, though. Being in Luke's presence gave Kyle an inner sense of safety and calm, as if Luke was in control.

After having their fill of pizza, Luke cleared the paper cups and plates. He then brought out his laptop and set it up on the coffee table, prepared to get to work. "I reviewed the report that Michael provided, which lists all deaths in Americare patients during the past three years," Luke said. "There appears to have been disproportionately more deaths in our Americare patient panel than in the group of patients who were insured by other insurers. Many of those deaths occurred in patients with type 2 diabetes mellitus, hypertension, and hyperlipidemia, and these appear to have been the result of presumed cardiac arrhythmia, myocardial infarction, trauma, or aggressive infections.

"Because our practice's Americare patients' records indicated improved quality metrics and an overall improvement in the health of our diabetic and hypertensive patients, when compared to those insured by all other insurance plans, so many deaths don't make a hell of a lot of sense. I also reviewed the records of Lorraine Simons,

Scott Smith, and Carla Dossier. They were perfectly healthy until shortly after enrolling in Americare, when each developed fatal diseases and/or died, the causes of which remain unclear and/or improbable, based on their personal and family medical histories. Carla Dossier's cause of death has yet to be determined by the medical examiner. Given her age, her depression, and that she was treated with an SSRI, it may have been a suicide. Additionally, Americare maintains a record system for all Americare patients, and that record system is inaccessible—at least to us.

"Also, I had two virtually identical patients with liver failure, resulting from chronic hepatitis C infection, for whom I requested placement on the liver transplant list. One was granted a place on the list, and the other was denied. The reason for the denial remains unclear."

The determination of the Americare Transplantation Board, although unfortunate, was not unreasonable by itself. What concerned Luke was that the other patient, Rahim Abdikarim, who was a few months older than Mr. Nguyen but otherwise had an identical history and health status, had been approved for placement on the transplant list in July 2029. Luke had submitted a formal inquiry to Celeste Davison, the director of the Americare Transplantation Board, regarding Mr. Abdikarim's acceptance for a liver transplant and Mr. Nguyen's denial. A response was still pending, and Mx. Davison had not responded to his calls.

"That about sums it up," Luke said. "Patients seemed to have developed serious and totally unlikely illnesses after enrolling in Americare, and then they went on to die."

"This is what I have concluded too," Kyle said.

"How's it going with Michael?" Luke asked.

"Pretty good, I think. I was in contact with him today. We'll be spending time together soon. I'll try to find out more about this secret Americare medical record system then."

"Good deal."

Kyle felt good having Luke's approval and positive reinforcement.

"I'm gonna call a close friend and colleague of mine, a forensic pathologist and epidemiologist," Luke said. "Perhaps he will meet with us? We need to know if what we perceive as an increase in adverse events, diseases, and deaths in our Americare patient panel is statistically significant when compared to what has transpired with all our patients. We need to know this before moving forward with our investigation. If these occurrences are not statistically significant, then we should stop our investigation and continue to observe, as these may truly be outliers."

CHAPTER 10

L uke knew exactly to whom he should reach out—Anandakumar Canteenwalla, MD. Dr. Canteenwalla was board certified in forensic pathology, as well as in infection control and epidemiology, and he was an expert in those fields. He was semiretired, serving as a professor of medicine at Harvard University School of Medicine and working part-time for the Commonwealth of Massachusetts as a medical examiner. He had served as Luke's faculty adviser during his medical school, internship, and residency years, and they had become close personal friends as time went on. Luke would often rely on Dr. Canteenwalla's expert opinions about complex medical cases and on his advice regarding personal matters. Dr. Canteenwalla was a quiet, contemplative man of principle and high moral character.

Kyle rang Luke's doorbell, and he was greeted at the door by Luke. After removing his coat, Kyle proceeded into the living room. Seated on the couch, with a laptop on the coffee table in front of him, was an unassuming older man with a dark complexion and striking, thick salt-and-pepper hair. Immediately upon Kyle's entrance to the room, the man stood up with his right hand outstretched and introduced himself.

"I am Anandakumar Canteenwalla. My friends and colleagues call me Andy. My pronouns are *he, him,* and *his*.

It is a pleasure to meet you." He shook Kyle's hand and bowed slightly at the same time.

Andy's thick Indian accent and formal politeness were charming to Kyle, who immediately had the same respect for him as did Luke.

"I have reviewed all the information that you provided," Andy said, "and I took the liberty of accessing your patient records and generating some reports using your EMR. Perhaps we should begin with my findings, after which I will try to answer any specific questions or concerns that you have. All right?"

Both Kyle and Luke nodded.

Andy continued. "I was asked to evaluate the occurrence of specific conditions and patient deaths in a specified population of patients, those who were insured by Americare, and to compare this to their occurrences and deaths in all other populations, combined into one group, to which I will refer as the 'other group.' I also compared the data from each group to data obtained from the general population. Initially, I was concerned that the validity of my findings might be called into question because the number of patients who were insured by Americare was more than twice the number of those insured by all other insurers combined. This proved not to be the case, as the results of my evaluation proved to be statistically valid, and the results were clear. The incidence of all-cause mortality was significantly higher in the Americare group, even when stratified by age.

"I reviewed those specific cases you referred to me, as well as some other patients insured by Americare who died during the past three years. The occurrence of cardiovascular disease in Lorraine Simons was extremely unlikely, given her past medical and family histories and whatever else was documented in her medical record. Likewise with Scott Smith—how he became infected with HIV is unclear. With Ms. Dossier, all bets are off. This may just have been a suicide, which did not make the top three causes of death in either group or in the US population. Her autopsy findings will be telling. I could discern no reason why Mr. Nguyen was denied placement on the liver transplant list by the Americare Transplantation Board while Mr. Abdikarim was placed on the list.

"The Americare patients appear to be healthier than patients who are insured by other payers, largely due to patient attrition—that is, removal of patients who had expired from the list of Americare patients without reporting their removal as deaths. This leaves only the healthiest patients listed in the Americare patient panel, making the overall health of the Americare patients appear much healthier than those with other health insurers, when, in fact, the mortality rate of patients in the Americare panel was much higher than those patients in the other panel.

"It appears that they were tracking these deaths in some fashion because they provided mortality statistics. The mortality statistics were provided in terms of death rates and not actual number of patients who expired. Although the death rate from heart disease is about the same in both groups and in the general population, there was a much higher incidence of death due to presumed cardiac arrhythmia—and therefore a lower incidence of death from coronary artery disease—in the Americare group than was expected.

"Drug overdose was the leading cause of death for those aged fifty-five and under in the general population, as well as the other group. As most of the deaths in the Americare group occurred in patients under the age of fifty-five, I was expecting this to be the leading cause of death in the Americare group. It was not.

"There was a lot of fuzziness regarding how patient deaths were handled by the Americare statisticians. It was as if they statistically replaced the newly deceased patient, who had a poorly controlled disease, with a new patient, whose disease was under good control, keeping the reported panel size the same. It would then just appear as if that patient's disease was under control. Do you understand what I am getting at?"

"Yes, I do," Luke said. Kyle nodded his head in acknowledgement.

"The question I cannot answer, based on the information I have is, whether these patient deaths were from natural causes or if they were removed from the Americare patient panel and, hence, the disease registries by nefarious means—and whether the omissions of causes of death were oversights or deliberate on the part of Americare. Any questions?"

Both Kyle and Luke remained silent, just looking at each other. "No," they said, almost in unison.

"Good," Andy said. "Please keep me informed of any developments." He got up and shook their hands. "I will keep my ear to the ground, look around, and let you know if I hear anything from my colleagues. In the meantime, I strongly suggest you both be incredibly careful and limit the discussion of your concerns to just between the two of you until you have a better idea of what might be going on."

"Will do, and thank you very much for coming by," Luke said as he gave Andy a hug and accompanied him to the door.

After Andy left, a few moments of silence seemed to last an eternity.

Finally, Luke spoke. "I am concerned regarding how Americare treated patient deaths in their statistics. At best, this would be sloppy work. The big question is whether the statistical omissions are just oversights or deliberate on Americare's part. Are the causes of the apparent improvement in quality metrics—and, hence, overall health—of those who are insured by Americare valid, or are they also the result of error? If they are the result of an error, was the error deliberate? If they are not the result of an error, how is Americare doing this?"

Luke's eyes welled up with tears.

"What's wrong, Luke?" Kyle asked.

Luke realized there were an inordinate number of patients who had experienced unexplained sudden death within a couple of days to weeks after their routine screening colonoscopy, similar to what his wife had experienced. As far as Luke was concerned, Karolyn had been murdered by Dmopvup and Americare. His appearance abruptly changed. His face became contorted in rage, and his chest seized up with this realization.

While discussing this revelation with Kyle, Luke looked deeply into Kyle's eyes as he stood in front of him. A mysterious power drew the men closer to each other. Luke was visibly upset, and Kyle was instinctively and naturally drawn into his arms in a comforting way. Luke embraced Kyle and held him tightly, stroking his hair and looking down into his eyes, which now also were full of tears. Luke drew Kyle's face close to him, and they embraced in a kiss that caused both to experience the most intense feelings of closeness they had ever realized.

After holding each other for a long time, Luke pulled away from Kyle, although still holding him in his arms.

"I'm sorry about that, Kyle." Luke looked down at his feet, blushing. "I'm not sure what happened there."

"Why are you apologizing?" Kyle moved his lips closer to Luke's and kissed him tenderly. "I'm not sorry at all." Kyle looked into Luke's eyes and flashed his dimpled, boyish smile.

Luke grabbed Kyle and kissed him passionately as they worked their way toward the bedroom. They continued their embrace, interrupting it occasionally to remove their clothing in piecemeal fashion. They began exploring each other sexually, which introduced many new experiences for Luke.

Amid their intimacy, Luke was struck by a deep inner conflict that caused him to abruptly release his embrace and back away. This breach of intimacy on Luke's part caused Kyle to feel as if he and Luke were being pulled apart while simultaneously being drawn together. It was as if intimacy was having a reverse effect, like two magnets of equal polarity being repelled by each other increasingly, the closer they became.

It was decided that the two should meet again at Luke's house in about one month.

CHAPTER 11

K yle left Luke's house, hopped in his Jeep, and headed for home. Driving his Jeep was both cathartic and hypnotic for Kyle. In a sense, his dark metallic-red Wrangler had become his best friend over the years, the only one thing that was consistent and that he could always count on. He babied his Jeep and took exceptional care of it. His Jeep had never let him down.

Once he was buckled in and driving and rhythmically dancing with the clutch, accelerator, and shift, he was able to let his mind and emotions go wherever they chose to go. This seemed to bring resolution to many of the issues and problems that arose in his life.

He took his time driving. He was deep in thought, as if in a hypnotic state, regarding Luke's and his own feelings. He was overwhelmed with love, but in torment over Luke's internal strife. He was quite confused by Luke's actions. His mind also focused on what they had discovered about their patients who were insured by Americare and what Luke had surmised might have happened to his wife, Karolyn. Kyle was preoccupied with thinking about all the possibilities of what, if anything, was going on within Americare. The more he thought about the situation, the more far-fetched their suspicions seemed to be and the more he wondered if he and Luke were making a big deal out of relatively nothing.

Realistically, what is the likelihood of some kind of plot by Americare? What reason would they have? Kyle wondered.

Both he and Luke had gleaned as much as they could from reading patient records. He realized the dire need to gain access to AMRS and to learn more about the inner workings of Americare. Without that crucial information, they could not proceed any further.

Michael likely could provide that information.

Kyle arrived at his apartment about forty minutes after leaving Luke's place. It was only about a ten-minute drive, but Kyle had taken a rather circuitous route. By the time he arrived home, he was ready for bed. Every night, right before bed, he lamented the fact he would be sleeping alone. This night somehow felt different. He got ready for bed and continued his self-hypnosis until he drifted off to sleep.

Kyle realized he had no interest in Michael; he was not attracted to him in any way. He needed to figure out a way to motivate himself to get to know Michael better and to appear genuine in the process. While falling into slumber, he decided to approach Michael in the morning and arrange a date.

Morning came all too quickly for Kyle as the light of dawn trickled in through the window next to his bed. As the director of marketing of the practice, he had a morning full of scheduled meetings that related to this position. Although he had gladly accepted the position, he loathed administrative work. All the politics, bullshitting, ruffling of papers, wasting of time, and office-speak were not among his interests. He did feel, however, that this position was a way for him to become closer to the inner circles of Americare and an opportunity to connect with Michael and ask him out.

Kyle's first meeting began at 8:00 a.m. in the main conference room, the same venue as for the monthly staff meeting. It was a meeting of the Finance Committee, which was chaired by Martin Shandling, the practice's chief financial officer. This meeting occurred once a month, at which time the practice's financial situation was reviewed, as were trends in revenue and loss. Typically, most of the meetings were boring and of consequence only to the bean counters.

Again, payer mix was most important; this revealed an ongoing increase in enrollment in Americare and a marked decrease in all other payers in the marketplace. In fact, only three of the other commercial payers still had viable insurance products left in the marketplace, and their premiums and deductibles were extremely high. Because of this, their enrollment was continuing to decline. Kyle thought it would not be long before those products were withdrawn from the marketplace too, and then the country would have a single-payer system run by the United States government.

The second half of the morning was spent in small breakout groups, brainstorming about how to improve revenue and decrease waste and loss to maintain a profit margin of at least 8 percent. Kyle made certain he was in the same group as Michael, and he planned to use this as an opportunity to ask him out. Once they went out, Kyle had no doubt he could get their friendship to progress, as long he and Michael talked about Michael's favorite subject—himself.

As the breakout session wound to a close, Kyle approached Michael as he was preparing to leave for his office.

"Hey, Michael. Some meeting, huh?"

"Interesting stuff regarding shifts in the payer mix but otherwise kinda boring," Michael said.

"About payer mix—how does that work? How does it influence our revenue cycle?" Kyle feigned a lack of understanding of the basics to appeal to Michael's need to be the know-it-all.

"Controlling your payer mix has an enormous impact on your revenue," Michael said. "I believe I owe you a dinner so we can talk about this and other stuff further."

"Cool. How is seven o'clock, a week from next Wednesday? Antonio's?" Kyle said. "I'll meet you there. We can talk about this—and other topics we need to talk about. I think if we work closely together, we'll have a significant impact on marketing our practice to the community and using marketing strategies to adjust our payer mix."

Kyle was not that eager to go out with Michael, so he booked their date ten days out. Even though he was eager to further his knowledge about Americare and obtain the Americare record system access code, his heart and mind were taken by Luke. In a way, he felt as if he was cheating on Luke, even though there was no mutual commitment between the two.

Since Kyle and Luke's last meeting, Luke had subconsciously undergone self-examination, and he encountered internal conflicts that begged for resolution. Some tension had developed in their relationship as Luke battled these conflicting feelings.

As the days passed and his date with Michael neared, Kyle sensed that Luke was putting some distance between them. As a result, Kyle became depressed and lonely. Luke became extremely lonely as well. Kyle realized Luke needed to go through these feelings and bring them to resolution. Kyle had learned from experience that he needed to accept things as they were, protect himself from getting hurt to the best of his ability, and continue with his life.

As date night with Michael approached, Kyle maintained more casual contact with Luke, allowing him any time and space he required.

CHAPTER 12

Date night came upon Kyle as if out of the blue, as he had put it out of his mind. He was very conflicted over his need to develop a closeness with Michael and the growing feelings for Luke that he shielded from himself to a greater degree. He knew he had feelings for Luke but deliberately blocked them for reasons that were unclear to him.

Another seemingly interminable morning of meetings drew to a close. Kyle and Michael returned to their respective offices to prepare for their afternoons. Kyle had thirteen patients scheduled for the afternoon. Pam kept the patients and Kyle on track, and he was able to finish his office hours on time at five thirty. He had just enough time to head home, shower, change his clothes, and head over to Antonio's by seven o'clock.

Kyle finished up in the office and raced home, arriving there around six o'clock. While waiting for the water in the shower to warm up, he picked out the clothes he was going to wear and stripped off his work clothes.

Even though he was not particularly attracted to Michael, he was excited about the date, and he wanted to make the best impression. He wanted to be desirable. Kyle hopped into the shower and allowed his mind to wander as he took in the steamy warmth and enjoyed the hot water spraying against the skin of his back and then chest and abdominal muscles.

What will the date be like? Will Michael like me? Will he find me attractive? Will he open up to me? Will he want to kiss me? Will he want me to kiss him? Will there be another date?

All these questions and more flooded his mind as he was showering. Even though Kyle had little interest in Michael from a romantic perspective, he had a need, deep down, to be desirable to others. Additionally, Michael could serve as Kyle's foot in the door to Americare and might even be the key to figuring out what was occurring within the organization.

Kyle spritzed on some cologne and arrived at Antonio's at 6:50 p.m. The smell of garlic and fresh bread wafted out the door with the warm air as patrons entered and exited. Before entering, Kyle scouted the parking lot to see if Michael's car was there; he didn't see it. He was the first to arrive, which was most comfortable for him. Upon entering, he was enveloped by the warmth.

The lighting was dark with hues of red. Candles were on each table, and Italian music was playing in the background. Although Thanksgiving was almost three weeks away, a large but tacky cornucopia and a fake turkey were on display in the atrium, reminding Kyle that another cold and snowy New Hampshire winter was around the corner.

He requested a small table for two from the host. Being the first to arrive gave Kyle a sense he had the home-court advantage. He just then realized he was nervous.

Almost simultaneously with Kyle's awareness of his

jittery nerves, Michael arrived. Immediately, Kyle's anxiety abated.

In the right light, Michael is kinda cute, Kyle fleetingly thought.

"Sorry I'm late," Michael said, although, in fact, he was right on time. "Got hung up dealing with a client. One thing led to another, and before I knew it, it was 6:15."

"No problem. It gave me a few minutes to decompress from the day," Kyle said.

The conversation went on like this for a few minutes and gradually progressed into more personal topics.

It became clear early on that if Michael remained the topic of conversation, he would open up quite easily. Kyle capitalized on this, and within the first half hour, Michael was bragging about how important he was to the Americare organization and to Primary Care Associates. After Kyle greased the skids with a couple of drinks, the information began to flow. Kyle passed on the drinks. He needed to be in complete control of what he asked and what he said.

Kyle made certain he revealed extraordinarily little about himself and that he obtained as much information as he could about Americare. He found that the key to his success was a touch of ethanol, focusing the discussion on Michael, flattering Michael as much as possible, maintaining good eye contact, and using his cute, dimpled smile. Despite all his efforts, their conversation remained rather superficial, and not much was gleaned that Kyle didn't already know.

The meal went quickly, and Kyle had many more questions for Michael. It was time to pay the check; Michael was all over it, insisting he pay for dinner. He was demonstrative about this, and he tipped over 30 percent, as if he needed to make everyone know he was the big spender and in charge.

Michael invited Kyle back to his place. Kyle eagerly accepted his offer, but it was clear that Michael wanted to get into Kyle's pants, and Kyle just wanted to gain access to Michael's mind.

Kyle followed Michael to his apartment, even though he knew the way there. It was right around the corner from where Kyle lived. He strategically assumed the role of submission and insecurity, hoping to fill Michael's need to be in charge and dominant. Kyle had a high emotional intelligence, and he was attuned to others' feelings and emotions. Michael— not so much.

Michael talked from the parking lot, up to the front door of the building, and up the stairs to the third floor. Upon entering the apartment, they were greeted by Michael's cat, Felix, heralded by the unmistakable smell of the litter box.

No matter how clean one is and how often one changes the cat litter, that underlying smell is always there, Kyle thought.

"C'mon in." Michael motioned to Kyle.

"Thanks, "Kyle said.

"Felix welcomes you," Michael said. "I hope you're OK with cats."

"Sure. They're better company than most people."

"Sit." Michael motioned to a comfortable couch in the living room. Felix followed suit, curling up on Kyle's lap and purring.

"Drink?" Michael motioned toward the bar cart.

"Sure, thanks. Whatever you're having."

Michael found two clean martini glasses on the cart. "Belvedere martini straight up, extra dry with a twist?"

Kyle nodded. "Sounds great!"

Michael proceeded to mix two rather hefty martinis. After handing Kyle one of the drinks, Michael sat on the couch next to him. Kyle was seemingly pinned in place by Felix. Michael grabbed the remote off the coffee table in front of them and used it to select background music. His choice was a satellite radio station playing top-forty tunes all the time.

Michael had an interest in Kyle way before Kyle even knew that he existed. As soon as Michael saw Kyle on his first day at the practice—June 17, 2030—Michael knew he had to have him. Whenever anyone new set foot in the office—employee, visitor, guest, or even patient—Michael sized up the person and decided whether he wished to pursue them. He had developed a reputation as something of a predator, pouncing on anyone he felt was desirable and using any means necessary, including those bordering on the unethical, to get closer. He had been watching Kyle since day one.

When Kyle came to Michael's office door that day at lunchtime and asked him if they should be working together, Michael moved him to the top of his conquest list. Kyle was now in his sights, and Michael immediately became obsessed with him. Kyle was a perfect twink—the type of guy Michael was most attracted to. He was attractive by all standards and had a sweet and innocent quality about him. Kyle's colleagues and patients respected him and held him in the highest regard. Michael could easily see himself with Kyle.

"I've been doing all the talking," Michael said. "How about you? What are your goals, hopes, wishes, and/or dreams?"

Kyle realized this was his opportunity to strike and pursue lines of questioning that might provide useful answers. "Professionally, I wish to provide the highest quality of care to my patients," he said. "My heart lies in taking care of patients. I look at my administrative duties as director of marketing as a drawer full of tools that may be useful in providing the best care. This position has given me access to information about the quality measures of our patients, the quality metrics of our practice, and a more global view of the overall health of our patient population. I intend to use these tools to bring about positive changes, with respect to our patients' individual and overall health."

Kyle was aware he was bullshitting, but he was also aware that this was the kind of empty chatter and buzzwords that those in health care administration liked to hear. "Clearly,

Americare has succeeded in significantly improving the overall health of our panel of their patients, as evidenced by their improving quality metrics." He looked deeply into Michael's eyes. "I want you to sell Americare to me, Michael. How does Americare do this? What is so special about Americare?"

Smiling and with a somewhat arrogant air, Michael turned to face Kyle and began to talk. While Michael was talking, he was focused on drawing Kyle into his fold, moving progressively closer to him, while hoping to get at least a kiss. That was his concrete goal for the evening—a kiss. He wanted nothing more than that and nothing less. Once this was attained, Michael was certain everything else would simply fall into place, and Kyle would be under his spell. He was convinced he could ply Kyle into loving him by providing him with information about Americare, and he was careless with respect to confidential information. It was as if he wasn't listening or attending to what he was saying, rather, he was deciding what and how much to reveal, based upon Kyle's responses.

"After I graduated from college in May 2026, I packed up all my stuff and moved from Cali to New Hampshire, having never been here before," Michael said. "I interviewed for this job while I was in college, and apparently, they liked me, so I was offered the position of practice liaison for Americare. I had no experience in health care, not even in college. My course work was in business, and my grades kinda sucked. I had no idea what to expect. They treated me like royalty—

paid all my moving expenses, found me an apartment, paid my first three months' rent, and gave me a $15,000 bonus as an incentive to accept the position. Americare had been launched on the exchange in 2022, so it was relatively new. There was a lot of uncertainty about its long-term viability and, therefore, uncertainty about my employment.

"During the first six months, I took a crash course in population health and how tracking our patients' quality metrics could be used as a measure of the overall health of a population. We started tracking HgBA1c in all our patients with diabetes, systolic BP in all our patients with hypertension, and LDL, HDL cholesterol, and triglycerides in all our patients with hyperlipidemia. I was fascinated.

"AMRS and Americare's actuarial team analyzed this data more and developed a model of our patient population that was stratified, based on patient demographics such as age, gender, race—even though these parameters were no longer used legally to define an individual—and the incidence of various conditions and disease states, as well as indices of their severity and their degree of control, as defined by patient data. From this model, information such as life span, future incidences of disease states, and health care costs were calculated and projected.

"At the same time, AMRS developed what our actuarial team called the 'ideal patient panel,' which was also based on identical patient demographics and disease states. In that ideal patient panel, the quality metrics were optimized, the number of patients with specific diseases were made as low as practically expectable, and the level of control of each of those diseases was optimized to render the cost of health care sufficiently low to permit a larger revenue stream. This then would be reinvested within Americare to offset any losses and to permit Americare to continue to use our resources to improve our overall health."

"So, the goal of Americare is to move the health of those insured by Americare from its current state to a more ideal state of better and less costly health care, by moving our Americare patient panel toward the 'ideal patient panel'? Is that right?" Kyle asked.

"Yup, that's it," Michael said. "The question was, how could we do that? The Americare approach involves close tracking of our patients' data, immunizations, screening tests, and procedures and making certain that providers and patients make appropriate interventions to improve their health, and those providers and patients make certain they receive all immunizations and screenings. Within that system, each patient has some skin in the game. Failure of a patient to receive recommended immunizations or screenings can result in disenrollment from Americare. As health insurance is mandated, this puts that patient at risk for incarceration or other punishment.

"It's similar for providers who fail to recommend appropriate interventions aimed at improving their patients' health or who fail to recommend appropriate immunizations or screenings. They are censured and risk losing their ability to serve as a provider for Americare, which would mean a loss of most of their income. Also, Americare reports them to the state Board of Medicine. Withdrawal of a provider's ability to participate with any insurer is reportable to the provider's state medical board and the National Practitioner Databank. A provider could even lose their license to practice medicine if this were a pattern and not just an isolated incident."

Kyle's eyes widened in surprise. "So, the burden and responsibility for maintaining good health and improving a patient's health is a shared responsibility. It's shared between provider, patient, and Americare, and the patient and providers are held accountable. There are steep consequences for patients and providers who fail to uphold their end of the bargain. Is that correct?"

"That is correct," Michael said. "Their end of the bargain is simple. All that the patients and providers need to do is show up for their scheduled appointments. Each patient has an individualized care plan developed by automated algorithms within AMRS. Providers and patients just need to follow those plans, and everything works fine. Providers never have to alter these care plans or make any clinical decisions. Immunizations, medications, and medical devices are all automatically custom-made for each patient by Utopia Pharmaceuticals and its subsidiaries and are ordered for each patient a week or so in advance of a patient's visit. These are administered, implanted, or utilized at the scheduled appointment or the patient's scheduled procedure."

"So, in the administrative records of our patients who are insured by Americare, there is a link to a medical record system to which we, as providers, have no access," Kyle said. "Is this the computer system that automatically generates each patient's care plan?"

"Yes, it is. That's AMRS—the Americare Medical Record System."

"What's this all about, and how do the algorithms work?" Kyle asked. "Shouldn't providers have complete access to their patients' AMRS medical records and be directly involved in any decision about their health care, including immunizations and preventive-care procedures? When I click on the link, I am asked for an access code that I do not have."

"AMRS is accessible only to select Americare administrators. I have access. I have a key fob that generates random access codes at various time intervals that I enter when I log into AMRS or access AMRS by the link in the patients' practice records. AMRS contains proprietary information and software that retrieves data from patients' records, generates the patients' care plans based on this data, and creates appropriate QR codes for immunizations and medical devices. These appear in the patient record and are seamlessly transmitted to our ordering system for their preparation and delivery to the various practices, in advance of a patient's appointment."

As Kyle asked his questions, Michael tried to get as physically close to him as possible. By the end of their conversation, their faces were within inches of each other. Michael completed the trajectory, pulled Kyle close, and kissed him. The warmth of Michael's lips and tongue on Kyle's tongue aroused feelings within Kyle. He didn't only get hard; he felt an emotional connection, one that he neither wished nor expected to have with Michael.

After Michael released his lip lock, Kyle became acutely aware of the time. "Michael, I had a really enjoyable time tonight. I would like to see you again soon and get to know you even better."

Kyle really meant that. Michael had worked his way into Kyle's heart. Michael possessed an inner sweetness that was covered by a tough crust, and Kyle was able to pierce that shell and get a glimpse of what was inside. Despite his arrogance, there was a side of Michael that Kyle really liked.

"I'm counting on it, Kyle. How about we plan to go out to dinner once a week or so? That way, we can get to know each other better and work on stuff together. I know you have a lot of questions regarding how Americare works. I would be happy to give you all the information you require. All that I ask for in return is that you get to know me, spend time with me, and allow me to get to know you … because I am very attracted to you, and I really like you, Kyle."

Kyle was certain he could play along. Perhaps Michael would reveal more confidential information because it would make him feel important? The administrators of Americare held him in high regard enough to make him privy to it. The more Michael revealed to Kyle, the more affectionate toward Michael he became, which caused Michael to reveal more information and Kyle to become even more affectionate in return.

As a result of their first date, some changes would occur that weren't noticeable outwardly but would change the course of their friendship.

Kyle could tell he was blushing. With that, he decided he should head home.

CHAPTER 13

It had been about a month since Kyle and Luke last met, and they planned to meet again this evening. Kyle was still filled with some apprehension and confusion with regard to what had transpired between them after their meeting with Andy. About three weeks had passed since Kyle and Michael's first date. Kyle and Michael had been seeing each other at least once a week outside of the office, and a romantic relationship had developed between the two. Fall was morphing into winter with a heralding twelve-inch snowfall—not at all unusual in New Hampshire for late December.

Since Kyle and Luke's last meeting regarding the outliers, colleagues in the office had become aware the two were following up on the concerns Luke had raised during the October department meeting. A slight buzz was about in the office, but no one questioned either of them directly. Kyle thought about this buzz on his way over to Luke's home, and it made him a little nervous; at the same time, however, he was glad.

It was a frosty night, with snowflakes in the air. Although the walk from the driveway to the house was relatively short, it felt longer to Kyle. He rang the doorbell.

"Hi, Kyle. Come on in," Luke said quietly as he answered the door. "Let me take your coat."

"Thanks." Kyle handed Luke his coat, and they went to the living room with the warmth and the coziness of the woodstove. This time, the pizza was already on the coffee table. Kyle had made a lot of headway with Michael, and he was eager to share this with Luke. Likewise, he was certain that Luke had done his homework. He was unsure how Luke would react to seeing him again given the events of their last meeting.

Luke was all business, and he jumped right in. "How are things going with Michael?" he asked, grabbing a slice of pizza.

"Pretty well, I think. We went out on a 'work date' last month. I had introduced myself to him and alluded to not knowing much about the implications that payer mix has on practice revenue. He invited me out to dinner so he could explain it to me. Little time was spent discussing payer mix. Most of the night was spent with Michael talking about Michael and answering my questions about Americare. If I appeared interested in Michael and what he did, he pretty much answered every question I asked him. A couple of drinks facilitated this process. We've been going out at least weekly since then. Michael thinks I like him, and I kinda do."

Luke looked down at his feet, ignoring Kyle's comment about his feelings for Michael. A slight frown was visible on Luke's face. "What did you learn about Americare?" Luke said.

"Americare is a health insurance plan that is government run and owned. Premiums and deductibles are low to nonexistent, and in some cases, enrollees are given a stipend, which makes it the least expensive and most affordable health insurance product in the marketplace. Because of this, enrollment in Americare is increasing dramatically, and it has outpriced all other insurance products, so the other insurance companies are bowing out of the marketplace, one by one."

Kyle then summed up the basics of Americare, as Michael had explained. "In addition, algorithms within AMRS automatically develop individualized care plans for each patient. These care plans are based upon each patient's data, disease, condition, illness, medical history, family medical histories, and recommended screening tests and immunizations. After each office visit, these care plans are updated to address the reason for the visit, and they are tweaked to better address any ongoing issues. Patients and providers both have skin in the game, and each is responsible for making certain that these care plans are followed and that recommended immunizations and screenings are received."

"Sounds like a well-run health insurance plan," Luke said. "So how are the unexpected and untimely deaths of our patients explained by Americare, considering this 'improved health' of those insured by Americare? How was the plan able to cause a bump in its patients' quality metrics so quickly? What is the purpose of the AMRS, and why don't providers have access to it? Who has access to it?"

"I'm not yet sure how Americare influences the quality metrics and improves the overall health of their subscribers. Certain administrators at Americare have access to AMRS,"

Kyle said. "Michael and Dr. Weinberg both have access. I'll get closer to Michael on our next date and try to get answers to your questions. I'll also try to get the key fob that generates the random-access codes for AMRS. Michael has one, so there must be a way I can get one. Michael also told me that Americare has an actuarial staff that oversees the AMRS, which has stratified our Americare patient panel, based upon patient demographics, including age, physical attributes such as race, gender, and disease states and their degrees of control. It is done so similarly with the entire Americare panel nationwide.

"That didn't strike me as odd. What seemed unusual to me was that the Americare actuarial staff, using AMRS, spent a lot of time, energy, and money developing a theoretical 'ideal patient panel' that is designed to maximize patient longevity, improve disease control, and to minimize health care costs. This translates into an increase in revenue and a decrease in losses. The goal of Americare is to continue this dramatic increase in their enrollment and to drive the panel of patients insured by Americare as close to that of the ideal patient panel as possible. The only apparent loose end in our investigation is AMRS. Everything else about Americare patients is documented in the regular record, just like with all the practice's patients."

It was obvious to Kyle and Luke that the key to their understanding of what was going on with their Americare patients was to be found within AMRS and that prompt access to this system was crucial. Clearly, Kyle was in the best position to obtain this access.

"I'll be ringing in the new year with Michael, spending New Year's Eve with him this Thursday night," Kyle said. "Michael seems obsessed with me. He's always walking by my office, stopping by to say hi, and calling me every night. I think it is time for me to increase my intimacy with him."

Luke looked away briefly, and then again, he looked at his feet.

Kyle talked about Michael with a sense of distance and in a way that indicated indifference to him. But that was not the case. While getting to know Michael, Kyle had begun to fall for him. There was something about Michael that Kyle found endearing and appealing, but he couldn't put his finger on specifically what it was. Nonetheless, the more he got to know Michael, the more he liked him. Perhaps it was Michael's demonstrable infatuation with and constant attention to Kyle. Perhaps it was his outward appearance of intestinal fortitude, while inside, he had a center of humanness and fragility. It was as if his outward persona was in diametric opposition to the real Michael. Kyle thought maybe he could catch a glimpse of who Michael really was if he could find a chink in the armor of the desirable persons, places, and things that surrounded him.

Kyle thought about Michael often, and he began to have "that feeling" he got when he was truly falling for someone. Even though his heart was on that path, Kyle needed to continue to act as if his courting Michael was a well-choreographed ruse; he had to maintain that air of indifference. Kyle felt truly that his heart was with Luke, but Luke had become distant.

CHAPTER 14

New Years Eve 2030 had arrived. It was a snowy evening, so the driving and road noise were quiet, which was conducive to Kyle's deep thought. He enjoyed driving his Jeep through the deep snow. He was planning to spend a cozy New Year's Eve with Michael and hoped to figure out where he and Michael stood.

Kyle was jolted out of his reverie by a moose ambling across the road. Fortunately, it was far enough ahead of him that both Kyle and the moose were unscathed. Shortly thereafter, Kyle entered the driveway of Michael's apartment complex and parked. After a couple of long, deep breaths, he hopped out of his Jeep and trudged through the deep snow toward the building. Michael greeted him at the door, gave him a big hug, and invited him inside.

They headed upstairs to Michael's apartment. Felix greeted them, looking at Michael as if seeking his approval.

"Let me take your coat, cutie," Michael said.

Kyle handed him his jacket. "Thanks, babe. It's fuckin' cold out!"

"Let me warm you up," Michael said.

The apartment was exceedingly cozy, with warm and inviting lighting, soft music, a fire in the fireplace, and the aroma of a home-cooked meal. Michael had prepared a New Year's Eve dinner; he wanted to cook for Kyle. He didn't cook often, as he was an amateur, so he chose a meal that was difficult to screw up and easy to prepare, which allowed him to hang out with Kyle while dinner was cooking, rather than his having to fuss around in the kitchen. He had prepared ham, mashed potatoes, green bean casserole, and garden salad.

Kyle took his usual seat on the couch, which Felix had reserved for him and kept warm. Michael was close behind, first swinging by the bar cart to mix their usual drink: Belvedere martini, extra dry, with a twist.

Michael sat down on the couch close to Kyle. He lovingly brushed his lips against Kyle's, nibbled his left ear, and kissed his neck softly, working his way up. Michael moved closer ever so slowly. "I love you," Michael said as he continued to kiss Kyle gently but firmly. His lips parted to allow his tongue to open Kyle's lips, inviting Kyle's tongue inside.

Kyle felt as if he'd been struck by a locomotive hurtling at full speed down the tracks. Those three words were the key that unlocked Kyle's heart. He immediately became teary-eyed, but he was unsure if they were tears of happiness, sadness, or fear. He had been here before, always getting badly hurt.

"I love you too, Michael," Kyle said as he wiped away the tears.

"Why the waterworks, babe?"

"You're the only guy who's ever said that to me first,"

Kyle said. "You're the only guy who didn't turn tail and run when he sensed commitment time was coming. You're the first guy I love who loves me back."

They held each other in a long embrace, with Felix giving them some space. Michael then explained how he felt, to a degree that was surprising to Kyle.

"I fell for you the first time I saw you," Michael said. "Once I looked into your eyes, I knew that we were meant to be together, that I needed you to make my life complete. When I moved from Cali, I was all alone. I had no direction, and I was just starting out. Americare was sorta just starting out too. By busting my ass, always saying yes when I was asked if I could do something, and putting work ahead of everything else, I was able to develop a lifestyle that is second to none.

"Yes, I worked hard and benefitted from that, but it was at the expense of relationships and my younger age. To get to the top, I sometimes had to climb over others. I learned to do that at an early age. Even though I dated people, it was for show. I made myself look and feel good by hanging out with desirable people. I had all the toys, wonderful things, money, power, respect, and so on that anyone could want but no one to share this life with—really no life at all to share with anyone. I was quite alone. Then you came along and swept me off my feet, and I realized you were the one I needed to share my life with. I even spoke with Dr. Weinberg about openings in Americare administration for physician assistants."

Kyle was speechless, but he didn't let on that something was amiss. He continued his embrace, but within a couple of minutes, he had gone from feeling on top of the world to feeling like dog poop on a shoe—and Michael was clueless.

I'm simply filling a need for Michael, Kyle thought, *just like all the other beautiful persons, places, and things he surrounds himself with. He uses them as a bandage to keep himself intact.* Kyle was not angry with Michael; he was aware that Michael just didn't get it. This likely was the closest Michael had ever come to falling in love. *I need to use this situation for good purpose*, he thought, *and use it immediately to obtain those key fobs.* The key fobs that randomly generated the access codes to AMRS were the keys to the Americare mystery. *I have the upper hand. It's time to act.*

"Michael, I have fallen in love with you too. I've thought about you almost constantly over the past couple of months. Despite my love for you, there are certain things I have difficulty reconciling or accepting."

"Like what?" asked Michael.

"Well, Americare, for one thing—how you're making your way up the ladder, how you've climbed over others to get there. Stuff like that. Remember the staff meeting when Luke brought up his concerns about totally unexpected adverse events and outcomes that he'd noticed in his Americare patients?"

"Yup." Michael focused his gaze on his feet.

"Remember the list of our Americare patients that you prepared for Luke? You know, the list of all our Americare patients who died over the past three years?"

"Mm-hmm." Michael fidgeted and looked around the room.

"I know how nosy you are, Michael." Kyle flashed a loving smile. "Did you notice anything odd about the list you prepared?"

"Yeah, I did. Despite our markedly improved quality metrics, which should have translated to improved health of our patients, there seemed to have been an awful lot of people of a relatively young age who had died."

"That was our conclusion too," Kyle said. "It's almost as if our diabetics who were under poor control—those with the highest HgBA1c—were dropping out of the diabetic registry through their unexpected deaths, largely from unrelated causes, leaving only the best-controlled diabetics in the registry. Had you ever thought about that?"

"Yes, I did, but then I immediately changed my thoughts to something else," Michael said.

"And why did you do that, instead of giving it more thought?"

"Look, Kyle. Americare has been the best thing for our patients." Michael's tone was loud and irritable. "It has resulted in a dramatic improvement in the overall health of those who are insured by Americare, as evidenced by the marked improvement in patient data. It's affordable and often free for enrollees. Americare has been great for the practice and for the providers too. Practice revenues have increased substantially, as have providers' salaries. Because of the AMRS-generated care plans and the fact that providers are held harmless, provided they are followed, their work is much easier, and their lives are less stressful. A recent national survey indicates remarkably high job satisfaction among primary care providers. Also, Americare has been incredibly good to me. They allow me to do my job any way I see fit, as long as I get satisfactory results. They don't question, and they actually support my methods. I do the same regarding my employer."

"Let's cut the bullshit, Michael. We're talking about the possibility that Americare is altering the health and lives of patients, and possibly even killing them, to get the desired results of improved quality metrics to maximize reimbursement and likely for other reasons."

Michael became inattentive and looked down at his feet again.

"And you didn't question it," Kyle said, "because on some level, you've been aware of it all along. Therefore, you have even profited from it." He pulled Michael closer and stroked his right cheek. "I'm not going to judge you, condemn you, or berate you. I'm certain others are in the same position that you're in, and they must confront their own demons, just as you do. I want to give you an opportunity to take this awful situation and help me rectify it. This might help offset any guilty feelings or feelings of responsibility you may have."

Michael looked forward, staring blindly. "I have no bad or guilty feelings. I've done nothing wrong. That said, let me know what I can do to help you rectify the situation and alleviate any bad feelings *you* might have."

"How can you say that, Michael? You've placed your desire for money, power, and recognition way above the health and welfare of our patients. Because of your actions, others likely have suffered. Luke and I need access to AMRS—two of the key fobs that generate the random-access codes."

"Umm … sorry. No can do."

"Let me put it another way," Kyle said angrily. "If I don't have two working fobs in my hands within twenty-four hours, I will make certain that Dr. Weinberg knows about our relationship—as well this conversation. I know that Americare employees are forbidden to have romantic relationships with other Americare employees or practice employees— punishable, invariably, by immediate termination. I have appropriate documentation of our relationship. Was my request a bit clearer this time, Michael?"

Michael's face drained of color. "Crystal clear." He abruptly got up from the couch and went into his bedroom, returning a minute or two later with one of the key fobs, which he dropped in Kyle's lap. "I'll get the second one to you tomorrow," Michael said. "Now, please leave."

Kyle got his coat and let himself out. Felix watched him with a look of disapproval.

Some happy New Year, Kyle thought as he walked toward his car. Then, he was overcome with profound sadness—yet peace. He now had access to AMRS. But was he ready for what he might discover?

CHAPTER 15

It was New Year's Day 2031, the morning after Kyle's date with Michael. It had been a rough date, yet it put life into perspective. It had given Kyle a lot to think about, but—perhaps most importantly—it had provided him with a key fob that generated the access codes for AMRS. He expected to receive the second key fob shortly.

He felt bad about essentially extorting Michael to get the key fobs. They both knew that exposing their relationship to Dr. Seth Weinberg, the medical director of the practice, would definitely cost Michael his job.

Kyle had learned a lot about Michael, Americare, and what Michael had offered him. He had a lot to think about.

A dilemma had arisen, however, one that Kyle needed to address. He knew Michael loved him—to the extent that he was able. For their relationship to move forward, Michael would expect him to forsake his current life, job, apartment, and everything else to share Michael's life as his own. This would require Kyle to give up his investigation of Americare; in fact, he'd need to become supportive of Americare. Michael surely got the message that Kyle needed to think carefully about this, which he intended to do.

Kyle hopped out of bed at seven thirty, showered, and got dressed for the day. Luke was coming over to his place later. For some reason, these meetings felt like more than just business to Kyle, and this other feeling had become more pronounced as time had gone on. Kyle was emotionally perplexed regarding that which transpired after his and Luke's meeting with Andy. Kyle put this out of his mind and got ready for their meeting.

Two pizzas—one plain, one pepperoni—almost had become a tradition. Kyle placed an order for the pizzas to be delivered before Luke arrived around one o'clock.

At around eleven o'clock, Kyle heard a knock at his door. By the time he opened it, no one was there, but a small box was between the storm door and the inside door. As he picked up the box, he saw Michael's car driving away. He knew it was the key fob, as promised. Kyle went inside and opened the box. Along with the activated key fob was a note from Michael:

> Dear Kyle,
>
> I love you more than I think you know and more than I ever thought possible. I'm offering you my life, including me and everything I have. We had a rough night last night, but that doesn't change how I feel and what I am offering you. I noticed you didn't say no to my offer either. Please give things more thought. We should meet again in a soon.
>
> I love you, Kyle, and I am deeply sorry if I did anything to offend you.
>
> Love,
>
> Michael

With tears in his eyes, Kyle folded the note and stuck it in his wallet. He put this out of his mind and got ready for his meeting with Luke. He was certain that having the key fobs represented a turning point in their unofficial investigation. He hoped that this access would provide reassurance that Americare was, in fact, providing better care for their patients.

Pizza arrived as planned, and at one o'clock, the doorbell rang again. For some reason, Kyle felt anxious. He went to the door and invited Luke inside.

"Happy New Year!" Luke said.

Kyle took his coat and hung it in the hall closet. "Happy New Year to you too," Kyle said as they walked into the kitchen.

Kyle's apartment, though on the small side, was laid out very efficiently. It had one large bedroom, an eat-in kitchen, and a living area with a small nook that Kyle used as an office. The decor was simple and masculine. A few family photos and winter landscapes hung on the walls.

"Grab some pizza and something to drink and make yourself comfortable." Kyle said, as he motioned to the pizza, which smelled heavenly.

They each grabbed a slice and a soda and then sat down at the kitchen table.

"I got the key fobs," Kyle said. "Now we should have access to the Americare Medical Record System. I haven't attempted to access it yet. I was waiting for you, thinking we should do that together."

"Excellent job, Kyle!" Luke said. "You've done a ton of the work here, and I really appreciate it."

Kyle felt warm all over, and he showed a dimpled smile as he thanked Luke. *Why do I this way,* he wondered, *and what caused these uncontrolled physiologic and emotional responses?* For once, Kyle was clueless about his feelings.

Once lunch was done, Kyle cleaned up and invited Luke to the work area.

"Feel free to plug in and connect to the Wi-Fi. The password is Gecko491." He motioned Luke toward the nook he used for work. It had a small desk with a chair, as well as another more comfortable chair with a small table adjacent to it. Kyle sat down at his desk. Luke sat in the comfy chair. After pulling close to the desk, the two plugged in their laptops and accessed the Wi-Fi. Kyle then handed Luke one of the key fobs.

"I don't recommend you carry this on your key chain," Kyle joked.

Luke chuckled. "Agreed."

"Let's step through Lorraine Simons's record together." Kyle said. Kyle logged on to IQOD and accessed her record.

Lorraine Simons's Primary Care Associates record consisted of her clinical record, which was the part that had to do with her health, and her administrative record, which contained insurance information, demographics, next of kin, releases, and the like. At the bottom of the administrative page was a button labeled AMERICARE, presumably the link to AMRS. Clicking that button brought up a box that had six spaces in a horizontal line. Kyle examined his fob. Every sixty seconds, a new six-digit number appears on the LCD display. He entered the current six digits in the box.

"Bingo!" Kyle said. "I'm in. Now you do it, Luke."

Luke followed suit and entered Lorraine Simons's AMRS record as well.

AMERICARE MEDICAL RECORD SYSTEM appeared in rather large bold lettering at the top of the page. In a column on the left, below this heading, the following sections were listed: DEMOGRAPHICS, ADVANCE DIRECTIVE, PREVENTIVE CARE, and CARE COORDINATION. They decided to look at each section one at a time, just to get the lay of the land, and then examine them for content.

The first section Kyle clicked on was DEMOGRAPHICS. This brought them to a page that listed Ms. Simons's demographic information, including her address and phone number, other contact information, Social Security number, employment information, race, religion, and—to their surprise—links to criminal background check information, as well as her political affiliation. Clicking on the link for POLITICAL AFFILIATION brought them to a page displaying two tables.

The first table listed was POLITICAL IDEOLOGY. Listed under this title were the following choices with checkboxes next to each: very conservative, conservative, liberal, progressive, socialist, communist, libertarian, and "other."

The second table on the POLITICAL AFFILIATION page was headed PARTY AFFILIATION. Listed in a column below this heading were Republican Party, Democrat Party, Green Party, Libertarian Party, "other," and "none," each with an adjacent checkbox. In Ms. Simons's record, there were checks in the "very conservative" and "Republican Party" checkboxes.

The next section listed was ADVANCE DIRECTIVE. Clicking on this section revealed any advance directive—DPOA for health care (DPOA-H), health care proxy, organ donor status, preferences, living will, and the like. Ms. Simons had listed her husband, Dana as DPOA-H, or health care proxy. She was a self-designated organ donor, and she had no advance directive or living will. She had been a "full code" until her untimely end.

The third section was PREVENTIVE CARE. Clicking on this heading brought them to a checklist of the recommended screening tests, procedures, and immunizations. It indicated which of these had occurred or had been administered, the dates of occurrence or administration, and their corresponding QR codes. This section was set up in tabular form, with the test, procedure, or immunization listed in a column on the left side, with boxlike spaces adjacent to each in which dates and QR codes were recorded. Many of the boxes had temporary dates and QR codes for planned future interventions. Ms. Simons had been up to date on all screenings, preventive-care procedures, and immunizations when she died.

The fourth and concluding section of Lorraine Simons's AMRS record was CARE COORDINATION. Clicking on this section brought Kyle to a page consisting of progress notes regarding events in Lorraine Simons's life that seemed to address how the various interventions were brought to fruition, ostensibly making certain that all recommended screenings, preventive care, and immunization guidelines were followed. Kyle's attention was drawn to a large button in the right lower corner of the screen, which had DF printed in large, bold letters.

Kyle clicked on the DF box. After a brief delay, he was brought to a page titled DMOPVUP FOUNDATION. The first line, in rather large letters, read "Contribution Status: Noncontributor."

Below this line was a section titled NOTES. Underneath it was a series of dates, as well as entries describing various interventions with QR codes and electronic signatures next to them.

The first of the notes in the DMOPVUP FOUNDATION section was from the month that Ms. Simons had enrolled in Americare: "as per contributor DF 927, injection of CPY-X10 150 mcg IM ordered." This was followed by a QR code. It was dated September 1, 2027, and electronically signed by Dr. Weinberg. This was eleven days before Ms. Simons's routine physical examination with Luke.

"What the fuck is DF 927? What is CPY-X10?" Kyle asked.

They took a half-hour break after reviewing Lorraine Simons's record, and both remained quiet for a few minutes.

Then Luke asked Kyle, "What are your thoughts?"

"It appears that Ms. Simons's Primary Care Associates record is related to the Dmopvup Foundation. It also would seem that Dr. Weinberg was typing notes and/or electronically signing orders in Lorraine Simons's AMRS record. This is surprising and disturbing because I don't believe he ever examined her."

"I don't think he ever even met Lorraine Simons," Luke said. "I'd have seen it on the reports I've shown you.

"I agree. I don't remember seeing it. Do you know what this means, Luke? It means that this is a huge corrupt monster, and it's killing people. Somehow Weinberg is in on it." Kyle spoke in barely a whisper; he almost didn't dare to say the words out loud. It went against everything he stood for as a physician assistant. And he couldn't stop thinking about Sean.

"Yep," Luke said quietly.

"Maybe we should look at the practice records without the Americare record," Kyle said.

Kyle turned back to the keyboard and began typing.

"That's probably a good idea, Kyle."

Using the QR code reader application on Kyle's cell phone to compare the QR codes, they continued their review.

Silently, with Luke looking over Kyle's shoulder, the two reviewed her medical record without looking at the AMRS record. The practice record revealed that Ms. Simons's only office visit in 2027 had been for her routine annual physical examination on September 12. At that visit, her lab results from the week before had been reviewed with her, most notably her fasting lipid panel, which had been normal. Plus, she had a remarkably high HDL, which was protective against cardiovascular disease. She had been given her annual influenza vaccine and sent on her way, with instructions to return as needed and/or in one year for her next annual exam.

Kyle found his voice. "If we also considered the information gleaned from the NOTES section within the DF link found in the CARE COORDINATION section of her AMRS record, it would appear that on September 1, 2027, Dr. Weinberg ordered administration of CPY-X10 150 mcg IM, followed by a QR code, per request of Dmopvup Foundation contributor DF 927. If we leave the AMRS and just look at the practice record, there is a note in the PROGRESS NOTES section indicating that on September 12, 2027—the date of her routine physical exam—an influenza vaccine was given with the same QR code. Likewise, this is listed in her PREVENTIVE CARE flow sheet. Using the QR code reader they again determined that the QR code for the influenza vaccine was identical to that adjacent to the CPY-X10 150 mcg in the NOTES on the DF page of AMRS and in other sections of the AMRS and clinical records. As providers don't have access to AMRS, we were unaware of any such connections."

Providers and patients were told that Americare custom-made all immunizations, drugs, and devices to order for each patient. The QR codes correlated to these items. Kyle and

Luke both realized that this QR code—and hence, Lorraine Simons's flu shot—was influenced by a contributor to the Dmopvup Foundation, as well as by Dr. Weinberg.

"This is terrifying," Luke said. "We need to review more records. I think you need to try to squeeze more information from Michael. He may know nothing, but if he knows something, it might be helpful. No word to anyone about this right now, Kyle."

"Agreed. Let's look at a few more records so we can figure out more about CARE COORDINATION section and how the Dmopvup Foundation was involved with Americare."

They proceeded to review Sean MacDonald's, Scott Smith's, Carla Dossier's, and Trinh Nguyen's records. In all but Sean MacDonald's records, they found similar correlations between orders with QR codes electronically signed by Dr. Weinberg in the NOTES section of the DF page of the CARE COORDINATION section of their AMRS records and injections that were administered at the time of their visits. In Lester Blumenthal's record, no immunizations were listed, but he received several micro-implants at the time of his colonoscopy. Each of these micro-implants had identical QR codes, and there was a note or order electronically signed by Dr. Weinberg on Mr. Blumenthal's DMOPVUP FOUNDATION page in AMRS that referenced this QR code.

In Sean MacDonald's record, no notes, or orders anywhere in the AMRS record were signed by Dr. Weinberg or anyone. Perhaps Sean was truly just an outlier?

CHAPTER 16

A week or so had passed since New Year's Eve, and Kyle needed to meet with Michael, if for no other reason than to allow the two of them to share their feelings about each other. He called Michael who somewhat sheepishly told him to come on over.

Upon his arrival at Michael's door, Kyle took a few seconds to catch his breath and then he pushed the buzzer. The door opened as if of its own accord, and there was Michael, with tears in his eyes and his arms wide open, awaiting a long and deep hug. Kyle fell into his arms and wept too, as Felix rubbed on both their legs as he walked around them.

Kyle hesitantly climbed the three flights of stairs in anticipation of being vetted by Felix before his entry. Kyle doubted that he was still in Felix's good graces.

"Come on in, babe," Michael said as he led Kyle by the hand to the couch. "We should talk." As they sat down, Michael put his arm around Kyle.

Kyle felt obliged to start. "Michael, first let me say that you've opened yourself up to me in ways no one else ever has. You've let me see the real you, which I think you keep wrapped up deep inside of you, surrounded by people, places, and things, as if to shield you." He saw in Michael a very masculine, strong, somewhat aggressive, tenacious, and goal-directed guy on the outside but a soft, gentle, insecure, fragile, and sometimes fearful boy deep down.

"I've been giving this a lot of thought," Michael said. "Within the last few days or so, I've realized that your perception of me is correct. Meeting you caused me to realize this. When you first joined the practice, I was interested in you, even before we met. You're an extreme hottie, and my subconscious thinking was about how great I would look and how great of a guy people would think I was if I had you on my arm. I just realized yesterday that this is how I've thought about myself and my life.

"Tremendous freedom came with this realization, but there also was a profound sense of emptiness, as if I wasn't really anyone. But then it dawned on me—I just needed to start living and feeling and allow stuff to happen. I need to allow myself to think about what I do and why I do those things. I figured that with the passage of time, I would develop a sense of who I was—because I am someone. I just don't know who yet. Does that make sense?"

Kyle grabbed Michael's hand and stroked his fingers. "Yes, it does, Michael."

"Yesterday, I thought about my past—how I got from where I was as a kid to where I am right now. I often stepped on others, even sabotaged others, to get what I wanted. I never even thought about others' well-being. It was as if no one else existed and how I got where I wanted to go didn't matter. What was important to me was getting there. I realized that I had hurt a lot of people, and I didn't even think about that. Now, I *am* thinking about it, and I feel awful. I feel like I need to do something about it, but the past is the past, and it is immutable, unfortunately.

"I guess what I'm trying to say is this: before I can invite someone into my life, love anyone in a healthy and fulfilling way, and share my life with anyone, I need to know and love myself, be aware of other people's feelings, and treat others with respect. I love you, Kyle, but I'm not in any position to have a healthy relationship with you, let alone share my life with you or even your life. I have a lot of work to do—a lot of amends to make, a lot of fences to mend, and a lot of catching up to do before I'll be capable of being in a healthy relationship. I really do love you enough that even though it hurts me—and perhaps hurts you—I need to be honest with you. I'm deeply sorry, Kyle. If you're angry with me, I understand totally."

Michael looked into Kyle's eyes and saw tears, but on his face was his loving, dimpled smile.

"Michael, as far as our love for each other, sharing our lives together, and having an ongoing romantic relationship, I agree with you. I was thinking the same thing, only I wasn't sure how to put it. The fact that we aren't boyfriends or partners doesn't mean I love you any less. You had a revelation yesterday, and it seems as if you discovered a sense of meaning in your life. It sounds like something happened inside of you, maybe triggered by what has been going on between us. Maybe I was put in your life for that reason—to help you figure out who you are and why you're here. Perhaps you were put in my life to help me crystallize my concept of who I am and why I'm here and to strengthen my resolve regarding my Americare quest. I think perhaps we're both here, together, to fix a broken system that has been and still is causing harm and even death to our patients for someone else's gain."

"Really?" Michael asked. "Until Luke mentioned that he noticed a considerable number of adverse events and outcomes in his patients who are insured by Americare, I had no idea there were any issues. I prepared the report listing the patients who had died during the past three years, and that was all I knew about this. This list did surprise me. Since my self-revelation yesterday, I've felt awful because I have bribed, threatened, coerced, and lied to patients in order to get them to follow Americare's protocols. Dr. Weinberg and the Americare administrators are aware of that; in fact, they encourage it. Some of their accepted procedures are quite like my own, and I learned a lot about what I do from them."

"What if I told you what I mean by 'unexpected adverse events and outcomes?" Kyle asked. "I would need your secrecy, and if you *were* to tell anyone we spoke about this, I would have to deny it and report our relationship to Dr. Weinberg."

"I promise you secrecy," Michael said.

"Can you access our patients' medical records from here?" Kyle said.

"Sure."

Michael led Kyle to his home office, where he opened one of his laptops and logged into IQOD. This permitted him access to the practice's clinical and administrative record system, as well as AMRS through the AMRS link in each patient's administrative record. Michael was also able to log into AMRS directly on a second laptop, so he could search for a patient's AMRS record from within the AMRS directly.

"Please pull up each patient's records and follow along," Kyle said. "We'll flip between each patient's AMRS and clinical records so you can see what I'm getting at."

On Kyle's direction, Michael pulled up Lorraine Simons's practice record on one laptop and her AMRS record on the other. Kyle reviewed her history and clinical course with Michael. He pointed out that she'd had a routine physical examination several months prior to her initial presentation for MI and hyperlipidemia, at which time she was found to be extremely healthy with no apparent risk factors for cardiovascular disease. She was given an influenza immunization and sent on her way. Two years later, she was dead.

"In the CARE COORDINATION section of the AMRS records of all our patients, there's a button labeled DF in the right lower corner of the page. Do you see it?" Kyle asked.

"Yup."

"Clicking on this brings the user to a page labeled DMOPVUP FOUNDATION. There, it lists whether the patient is a contributor to the Dmopvup Foundation, below which is a section of NOTES. Have you clicked on that link, Michael?"

"Yup," he responded again.

Kyle pointed to the screen. "As you can see, Lorraine wasn't a Dmopvup Foundation contributor. Most importantly, look at the NOTES. There appears to be some kind of note or order electronically signed by Dr. Weinberg, dated September 1, 2027, that reads 'as per contributor DF 927 injection of CPY-X10 150 mcg IM ordered.' If we look in the progress notes section of her clinical record, the QR code following this is identical to the one following her influenza vaccine given that was given at routine physical examination on September 12. What the hell is this?"

Michael shrugged his shoulders, but his face became pale and unexpressive.

"Can you pull up the record of Scott Smith?" Kyle asked.

"Sure," Michael said.

Michael had access to the entire AMRS on his second laptop, whereas Luke and Kyle could access the AMRS only for the patient whose record they were reviewing. When Michael entered "Scott Smith" in the search bar while logged into AMRS, three patients with that name appeared on the screen.

"There are three Scott Smiths. What's the date of birth?"

"June 6, 1998," Kyle said.

Suddenly, Sean appeared in Kyle's mind. *"You're on the right track here, Kyle."* Sean's ghost said only to Kyle. *"You're on the right track."*

Kyle was a bit rattled but said, "Scott Smith had a

routine annual physical examination on August 1, 2026, during which he was deemed to be healthy and HIV negative. He was given his annual influenza vaccine and instructed to return in one to two years for a routine exam. On the NOTES page within the DMOPVUP FOUNDATION link of the CARE COORDINATION section of his AMRS record is a note or order electronically signed by Dr. Weinberg, followed by a QR code, dated June 23, 2026, that reads, 'as per contributor DF 1035, CRF19 inoculation ordered.' The QR code following the influenza vaccine given at his physical examination is identical to the QR code following the CRF19 note/order. What the fuck? He, too, is noted to not have been a Dmopvup Foundation contributor."

Kyle then reviewed the records of Carla Dossier and Lester Blumenthal, as Michael nervously wiped away beads of sweat from his forehead.

"There's an order on the NOTES section of the DMOPVUP FOUNDATION page of Carla Dossier's AMRS record, dated June 23, 2026, signed by Dr. Weinberg, which reads, 'as per contributor DF 60587, PALBR 100 mcg to be administered IM.' This, too, was followed by a QR code. This was around four months prior to her death. She received an influenza vaccine at her routine physical examination that had an identical QR code noted in her clinical record. There's an order followed by five identical QR codes in Lester Blumenthal's AMRS record, electronically signed by Dr. Weinberg, on his DMOPVUP FOUNDATION page that reads, 'per contributor DF 8863251, 5 micro-implants

ONC3 to be placed at colonoscopy.' The QR codes noted in the AMRS record correspond to identical QR codes for the five implants noted in the clinical record. He died a year and a half after these implants were placed during an entirely negative colonoscopy. There was one other patient who died unexpectedly of a disease that was highly unlikely and whose AMRS record was entirely unrevealing, even though I'm certain Dr. Weinberg was involved somehow," Kyle said.

"How do you know for certain?" Michael asked.

"Because healthy, seventeen-year-old, marathon-running boys don't typically die from cardiovascular disease, Michael." Kyle held back his tears while somewhat angrily handing Michael a copy of Sean's autopsy report—he had printed a copy of the report while reviewing the records. "I wonder if you could help me figure out why there was no documentation in his AMRS record suggesting Dr. Weinberg's involvement," Kyle said. "Please pull up the record of Sean MacDonald."

"Sure thing," Michael said, somewhat sheepishly. He entered "MacDonald, Sean" in the AMRS search bar. Two patients with that name were listed. Michael highlighted the deceased Sean.

A brilliant beacon went off in Kyle's mind. "No, click on the other one," Kyle said, speaking in unison with Sean, whose voice Kyle heard from the recesses of his conscience.

"But this one was your patient, according to the medical record number on the autopsy report," Michael said. "We should be looking at this record."

"Humor me and access the NOTES section of the DMOPVUP FOUNDATION page in the CARE COORDINATION of the older Sean MacDonald's AMRS record."

After Michael did so, Kyle found the answer to the mystery. There, dated August 30, 2030, was an order, followed by a QR code electronically signed by Dr. Weinberg:

As per contributor DF 43251, injection of CPY-X10 150 mcg IM ordered.

The elder Sean MacDonald was also not a contributor to the foundation.

Michael flipped back to the elder Sean MacDonald's clinical record. A flu shot had been administered at the time of his routine physical examination, but the QR code was different from that listed in Dr. Weinberg's order on the NOTES section of the DMOPVUP FOUNDATION page of his AMRS record.

"Let's go to the record of the deceased," Kyle said.

Michael opened that record, and Kyle presented his case.

"Sean Macdonald was a previously healthy seventeen-year-old marathon runner who died suddenly from advanced cardiovascular disease, which proved to be his cause of death at autopsy. His AMRS record was entirely unrevealing—until now. It would appear that my patient, the younger Sean, was the victim of a medical error of sorts. My hunch is that the influenza vaccine that was intended to be administered to the elder Sean MacDonald at the request of a Dmopvup Foundation contributor and ordered by Dr. Weinberg was somehow administered erroneously to the younger Sean, his son."

Sure enough, the clinical record of the younger Sean revealed he had received a flu shot during his physical examination over a year before his death, and the QR code for his flu shot was identical to the QR code adjacent to the CPY-X10 in the elder Sean's DMOPVUP FOUNDATION order. This was the identical code adjacent to the CPY-X10 in the note in Lorraine Simons's Dmopvup Foundation order and the QR code for the flu shot she had received during her routine physical examination.

Sean's further decomposing face again flashed in Kyle's mind. *"You did good, Kyle; you did good,"* Sean's ghost said.

"The list of patients goes on, but these four will give you an idea of our concerns," Kyle said to Michael. "Do you have any idea of what might be going on here?"

Michael was pale and sweaty. He took a couple of deep breaths and then spoke in a wavering tone. "I think I do, yeah. There are monthly meetings between Dr. Weinberg and various other parties, during which issues such as these are routinely discussed. It's well known that contributors to the Dmopvup Foundation are afforded preferential treatment. We were told, per Dr. Weinberg's orders, that sometimes prior authorizations are waived, procedures and medications that would otherwise be declined are sometimes approved, and waiting lists for some tests or procedures are sometimes ignored.

"This is the extent of my understanding of the relationship between Americare and the Dmopvup Foundation. Some preferences and/or requests from Dmopvup Foundation contributors are brought up and discussed during these monthly business meetings, and others are discussed during more private meetings between Dr. Weinberg and various parties. If their preferences are deemed appropriate, they're written as orders by Dr. Weinberg in the respective patient's AMRS record and carried through into the patient's clinical record. I'm not aware of any other perks afforded to Dmopvup Foundation contributors, but Dr. Weinberg does spend most of his time meeting with influential people and in various committees and board meetings to which I'm not privy."

"If I could get listening devices for you, do you think you could place them inside Dr. Weinberg's office?" Kyle asked. "Also, do you think maybe you could get a list of all QR codes and what each one represents? A list of all Dmopvup Foundation contributors would also be extremely helpful.

"I meet with Dr. Weinberg in his office at least once a week about something. I can certainly place bugs there if you tell me exactly where I should put them. I believe I can access the list of QR codes from my computer at the office. I'll get you a copy."

"Excellent." Kyle turned toward Michael, took his hand, and hugged him.

CHAPTER 17

Kyle was the key that had unlocked Michael's heart. Although a romantic relationship wasn't in the cards, Michael's first healthy relationship with someone other than himself was. He admitted his willingness and desire to help Kyle to obtain more information regarding what transpired between Dr. Weinberg and others.

Kyle and Michael did their due diligence to find the appropriate devices and set them up. They decided to place three devices in Dr. Weinberg's office in hidden locations. The monthly meeting of the practice's Transplantation Board was scheduled in that office in two days, and rumor had it that Dr. Hsacis was coming from Washington, DC, to attend. Michael would place the devices sometime before then.

At 6:00 a.m. on the day of the meeting, no one was in the office except for Michael. The desk lamp, chairs, and conference table had been removed from Dr. Weinberg's office and placed in the hallway the previous afternoon because the housekeeping staff had planned on shampooing the carpet later that evening. They had left the office door open, and two large fans were running to dry the carpets by the morning. Michael used this opportunity to place the listening devices.

Michael was somewhat of an electronics and computer geek. Prior to going to the office, he remotely accessed the security camera system and programmed the cameras to freeze between five thirty and seven thirty in the morning on the meeting day so that a still image of the office would be transmitted within the system in lieu of active monitoring.

Michael moved quickly, slipping the first listening device inside the tube of the desk lamp. Just as quickly, he placed one more bug inside the headrest of the desk chair, and another behind the faceplate of the electrical outlet adjacent to the desk inside the office. He then exited the office.

He texted a code to Kyle. The work was done.

Next, Michael paired all three devices with one of his cell phones, which he had left hidden in a compartment in his desk drawer and plugged into a charger. Michael configured the devices to send the data to Luke's computer using his cellphone as a Wi-Fi hotspot. Luke's computer would record the audio.

Michael completed installing the listening devices by seven thirty, and housekeeping returned the furniture to Dr. Weinberg's office around eight o'clock. Michael received a text from Luke indicating he was picking up clear, loud signals—background noises in the office—without distortion. They were hoping the listening devices would hold up and remain undetected long enough to document any deals between Dr. Weinberg and contributors to the Dmopvup Foundation, upper-level staff, administrators, and patients that directly affected the health and welfare of the practice's Americare patients. They also were aware that eavesdropping and recording audio surreptitiously was a felony and that this rendered a part of their investigation illegal.

This was a turning point. Michael was aware that it could backfire, but he couldn't think of any other way to obtain this kind of documentation. On the off chance that nothing improper or illegal was occurring within Americare, Michael would be in big legal trouble. He could even be sent to prison for violating a number of statutes including, but not limited to, federal wiretapping and patient-privacy laws.

Michael reviewed Dr. Weinberg's weekly meeting schedule. In addition to the Transplantation Board, Dr. Weinberg had a couple of meetings with patients and some family members.

Luke eagerly awaited the Transplantation Board meeting. He had previously emailed Celeste Davison, the chairperson for the board, requesting an explanation as to why one of two individuals in identical situations (Trinh Nguyen and Rahim Abdikarim) had been granted a liver transplant, while the other one's request had been denied. Luke had heard nothing in response.

At 9:25 a.m., the attendees of the Transplantation Board meeting began to trickle into Dr. Weinberg's office and sign in. Dr. Weinberg had already slipped in at around nine o'clock, and Celeste Davison checked in a half hour later. A guest in attendance was Dr. Kupevjep Hsacis from the central office of Americare in Washington, DC. Ze was the chief operating officer of Americare, and he is noted to be its chief designer. Ze spent much of hir time traveling around the country, visiting the various practices that were "high producers." Everyone stood up silently as Dr. Hsacis entered the room and took a seat. "Good morning," ze said—and that was about all.

Dr. Hsacis presented hirself as rather stern, uptight, and arrogant, yet businesslike. Ze was not at all personable and had never tread close to the realm of human feelings or emotions. Hir pronouns were *ze, hir,* and *hirs*, as ze followed suit with the government standard. Ze was tall and on the thin side, dressed in gender-neutral business suits all the time, bald on top with hir hair closely coiffed on the sides. Ze wore eyeglasses that tended to sit at the tip of hir hooked and pointed nose. Ze had a gender indeterminate, albeit gaunt and scary, appearance. Ze rarely, if ever, exhibited a smile on hir tightly pursed lips.

The doors closed at 9:30 a.m. Mx. Davison began the meeting as any typical board meeting, though a bit more formal than some. Minutes from the last meeting were approved. Next, new referrals from providers requesting consideration for organ transplantation for their patients were reviewed. There were only two new requests, both for renal transplants, and both were unanimously granted.

Next, any issues regarding past actions by the Transplantation Board were reviewed. Interestingly, the only issue on the table was how to publicly reconcile Mr. Nguyen's denial of liver transplantation, considering Mr. Abdikarim's approval. At issue was which storyline the board members should use. No one contested how the decision was made.

Dr. Hsacis spoke up. "I am concerned this issue is about to go public, and I want to make certain that all board members have something consistent to say, if asked." It was more likely that Dr. Hsacis joined the meeting out of concern about Luke's inquiry, and ze had also gotten wind of Kyle and Luke's informal investigation. "We should tell anyone who asks about Mx. Nguyen that something was discovered during hir preoperative evaluation that rendered hir ineligible for liver transplantation surgery," Dr. Hsacis said. "This is, in fact, the truth."

Mx. Davison then opened the meeting for questions, old business, and new business. There was none, so the meeting was adjourned at ten thirty.

As the attendees funneled out of the conference, Dr. Hsacis, Dr. Weinberg, and Mx. Davison shuffled papers and remained seated for a half minute or so. After everyone else had left, Dr. Hsacis quietly got up and closed the door.

"You realize we did the right thing," Dr. Hsacis said. "All other things being equal, we are under a directive to give contributors to the Dmopvup Foundation priority for transplants, as well as for most things Americare has to offer. We are protected from having to reveal this information to anyone, including the rest of the board and the providers, because of confidentiality clauses in the Dmopvup Foundation contributors' agreement. Part of the screening process is to check and see if a contribution to the Dmopvup Foundation has been made on behalf of a patient referred for consideration for organ transplantation. Mx. Nguyen was not a contributor to the Dmopvup Foundation, nor did anyone contribute to the foundation on hir behalf, which was uncovered during hir screening. Ze was denied liver transplantation surgery because of this issue.

"Mx. Abdikarim, on the other hand, came to this country from Saudi Arabia for the express purpose of receiving a liver transplant. Ze was confident ze would require a transplant within a couple of years. Hir father, Syed Abdikarim, a wealthy Saudi businessperson, made a two-million-dollar contribution to the Dmopvup Foundation in 2024 on Rahim's behalf. Syed Abdikarim had been a friend of the Dmopvup administration and President Dmopvup for years, even before ze was elected president. Ze already has contributed millions to Dmopvup's reelection campaign and to each of hir prior campaigns.

"Per the directive from President Dmopvup, ze was given priority access, even though ze did not meet the criteria for transplantation due to advanced age. Mx. Nguyen was appropriately not granted liver transplantation due to hir age of sixty-five years, which is over our age limit. Because of the Dmopvup Foundation contribution, I was obligated to let the issue of Mx. Abdikarim's age slide."

"I'm not so much concerned about the age issue," Mx. Davison said. "My concern lies in how quickly an appropriate donor was found and the process by which this was done. I've never been involved in a process such as this. It still doesn't sit well with me. I don't understand why both Mx. Nguyen and Mx. Abdikarim were not authorized for living donor liver transplantation and why a search for appropriate living donors for each wasn't begun early on. The most recent economic feasibility studies indicate that the costs of liver transplant surgery and the ongoing care thereafter are now much lower than the costs of caring long term for someone with chronic liver disease. Furthermore, the survival of those receiving living donor liver transplantation is much better than those receiving cadaveric transplants, and the surgery can be scheduled electively, rather than on an urgent basis, once a suitable living donor is found. It's also much more likely that a suitable living donor will be found and within a much shorter period than would a cadaveric donor."

Dr. Hsacis smirked. "We are directed to use any means necessary to keep our contributors happy. I reviewed prior decisions regarding transplantation in other Americare offices around the country. There have been other instances in which transplant recipients who made large contributions to the Dmopvup Foundation were permitted to choose their organ donors from the pool of Americare patients—patients who were a match and who already were on the list of those whose lives were scheduled to be curtailed to improve our quality metrics and the overall health of our patients.

"The most recent studies concur that those discrepancies in survival between patients undergoing living donor liver transplantation, or LDLT, and cadaveric liver transplantation were most likely due to issues involving the medical health of the cadaveric donor, how the donor's liver was handled pre-transplantation, and the time between procurement of the cadaveric liver and transplantation into the recipient. If a transplant recipient could choose the cadaveric donor well in advance of the donor's death, the survival statistics should be equal.

"Mx. Abdikarim's generous Dmopvup Foundation contribution permitted hir to obtain a liver transplant despite Americare's age limitation at sixty-four years. It also permitted hir to choose a cadaveric transplant over LDLT, which was hir desire. Also, this made many other organs and tissues available for others on the various transplant lists who needed lifesaving transplants. Let's pull up hir liver donor's record. Here it is—Michael Thomas. Medically, ze was an extremely healthy thirty-five-year-old, which was desirable. Ze was a police officer, and ze exercised regularly. Hir pronouns were *he, him,* and *his.* Hir political leanings were conservative, and ze had attended peaceful demonstrations against President Dmopvup and the current administration.

"Our deaths due to trauma were way down, compared to the ideal patient panel, causing deaths from other causes to be higher than acceptable. We needed more trauma deaths for our Americare patient panel to approximate the ideal patient panel more closely, so hir life was scheduled to be curtailed because of trauma anyway.

"I know this might seem unfair, but from a population health perspective and for the good of our country, this was required to maintain the health of the herd. By doing this, Americare was able to kill two birds with one stone—no pun intended. Besides, Mx. Abdikarim offered an additional two million dollars for us to make this happen."

Kyle and Luke listened to the recordings from Luke's

home after work. They were aghast. What he'd thought would be impropriety from the New Hampshire office of Americare was a part of a more global plan, from the president on down. It was a pay-for-play scheme using the Americare organ transplantation system as a way of making money for the Dmopvup Foundation, in exchange for positions on the various transplantation lists.

Kyle felt as if his and Luke's lives had been drastically changed forever. He was sickened and in utter disbelief. He had great difficulty focusing on the patients before him, and he had a tougher time holding his tongue and not informing their patients about what they knew was occurring. He was in a bind—informing their patients would bring an abrupt end to their investigation and to any chance of bringing this scheme to an end.

Michael had access to the recording of the meeting of the Transplantation Board while it was occuring. Not only was he horrified, but he also had a newly discovered contempt for Dr. Weinberg and Dr. Hsacis. He felt tremendous guilt because of his participation in Americare, as if he had unwittingly led lambs to slaughter.

Michael now realized this was how Americare worked. Each employee had a specific job to do, and each was encouraged and rewarded for using any means necessary to obtain the best results. Each employee was surrounded and enveloped by a silo, without the ability to see the bigger picture outside of its walls. Each employee, likely all the way to the top, was so sufficiently disconnected from the whole that the person had no idea of the ultimate result of what he or she did. Michael felt compelled to help Kyle and Luke in any way that he could.

The recordings for the next couple of days were relatively uneventful, and nothing surprising was revealed.

On Friday, during Kyle and Luke's now-routine listening of Dr. Weinberg's meetings, another pay-for-play scheme was recorded. A meeting took place between Melissa Chapin, the daughter of Doris Chapin, who was one of Dr. Pradeep Khan's patients, and Dr. Weinberg, regarding Doris Chapin's care. Dr. Khan was one of Luke's and Kyle's colleagues, and he had been a member of the practice for the past eight years or so.

Doris was almost ninety years old, and she realized she was losing the ability to live at home alone because of worsening vision and arthritis. Also, ever since her husband died five years ago, her zest for life had declined. Doris made the decision to sell her home and to use the proceeds from the sale, as well as money from her estate, to move into a community for the elderly that provided all levels of care.

This process required a rather large buy-in and a monthly fee, and none of this was covered by her insurance.

Melissa was not in favor of this move because it would decrease the size of her mother's estate, of which Melissa was to be the sole heir. Melissa had been trying to encourage her mother to remain in her home with home-care services until her death.

Melissa worked as a paralegal at a law firm that specialized in estate planning. Her spouse, Shaniqua Jones, who was also a partner in that law firm, was in attendance as well. In fact, Ms. Jones was representing Melissa as her legal counsel, and she served as both Melissa's and her mother's estate-planning attorney.

Although Doris was mentally intact and able to make her own health care, financial, and other decisions, she had appointed her daughter as her DPOA and DPOA for health care. She had also appointed Melissa to serve as the executor of her will when the time arose.

During the open-enrollment period at the law firm, both Melissa and Shaniqua elected Americare as their health insurer. Doris was already enrolled in an Americare Medicare Advantage Plan through Medicare, which was being phased out.

During their meeting with Dr. Weinberg, Melissa and Shaniqua negotiated a deal in which Doris would have a scheduled visit with Dr. Khan, at which time she would receive her annual flu shot. The injection would contain some sort of micro-implant that would deliver a fatal dose of palutropium bromide rather than the immunization. This micro-implant would be designed to deliver the drug at a specified date and time.

Palutropium bromide was a highly potent, nondepolarizing, paralytic agent normally used during induction of general anesthesia. It was manufactured and marketed by Utopia Pharmaceuticals and was effective in minuscule amounts by all routes of administration; it was undetectable in blood or tissues. The onset of action was within five seconds of its administration. The duration of action was thirty minutes, and it caused death due to asphyxiation unless mechanical ventilation was instituted immediately.

Doris's estate was valued at $88 million. Melissa presented Dr. Weinberg with a certified bank check for $500,000, payable to the Dmopvup Foundation, along with a written promissory note for an additional one million dollars after Doris passed. All parties who were present at that meeting agreed with those terms.

Prior to placing the listening devices within Dr. Weinberg's office, Michael had done some digging inside Dr. Weinberg's paper records after he stealthily accessed them on his computer, where they had been scanned and archived. He first made certain that Dr. Weinberg or Dr. Hsacis weren't logged into the system from anywhere else, and then he used Dr. Weinberg's login information to gain access to Dr. Weinberg's files.

Michael found what appeared to be a list of QR codes and abbreviations and the meaning of each. They represented micro-implants containing various substances, administered to patients under the guise of injections or implanted in the colonic mucosa during colonoscopy. Michael presented this list to Kyle, who compared it with the AMRS records of the patients in question.

In Lorraine Simons's and the elder Sean MacDonald's records were orders from Dr. Weinberg stating that at the request of a Dmopvup Foundation contributor, CPY-X10 150 mcg IM was ordered to be administered. The information provided by Michael indicated CPY-X10 was a cytokine, a protein that stimulated various cells in the body to perform specific functions. This particular cytokine stimulated the arterial endothelial cells (the cells lining the arteries) to undergo rapid atherogenesis—the process of formation of atheromatous plaques.

The cause of Lorraine Simons's coronary artery disease was now perfectly clear. A micro-implant containing this cytokine had been ordered by Dr. Weinberg at the request of Dmopvup contributor DF 927. It had been administered under the guise of a flu shot, which Luke had ordered for administration around a week or so prior to her routine annual physical examination. As Sean MacDonald had erroneously received the same micro-implant that had been ordered by a different Dmopvup Foundation contributor and custom-made for his father, the cause of Sean's advanced coronary artery disease was also revealed.

In examining Scott Smith's record, a micro-implant containing CRF19 had been ordered by Dr. Weinberg at the request of Dmopvup Foundation contributor DF 1035. It had been administered in lieu of the flu shot that had been ordered by Luke and administered by his medical assistant at Scott's routine annual physical examination. From the list provided by Michael, Kyle saw that CRF19 contained an inoculum of the Cuban strain of HIV. This was the most highly virulent and multi-drug–resistant strain of HIV, which was universally fatal—and in short order.

Similarly, Dr. Weinberg had signed an order in Carla Dossier's AMRS record: "Per DF contributor 38574, PALBR 100 mcg IM ordered." PALBR was the micro-implant designed to deliver palutropium bromide at the specified dose at a specified time. This was identical to an order in Doris Chapin's AMRS record that had an administration of a PALBR implant that was planned to occur during her upcoming routine physical exam. This was what was discussed during the meeting between Dr. Weinberg, Melissa Chapin, and Shaniqua Jones.

Unfortunately, Michael was not able to find any information that would reveal the identities of these Dmopvup Foundation contributors.

It was now noticeably clear that the president and hir administration had taken control of the health care system and were manipulating patients' health and lives to bring the Americare patient population—the vast majority of citizens—in line with the actuarially ideal patient panel, as developed by President Dmopvup's actuarial staff. Patients who had uncontrolled medical conditions and, notably, those with uncontrolled medical conditions who had different political views than the president seemed to be the first to be eliminated.

Worldwide, the health of the United States appeared to be second to none, and it was continually improving, approaching the ideal. This was good for the worldwide marketing of the country and its medications, medical devices, and immunizations. By virtue of the passage of time, this would result in a patient panel of medically healthy political sycophants of President Dmopvup as the Americare patient panel approached the actuarially derived ideal patient panel, with respect to overall health, costs of care, and political allegiance. The size of the national Americare panel would approach, if not equal, the entire US population. Utopia Pharmaceuticals would be the only company left in the marketplace to provide all medications, immunizations, and medical devices, and Americare would be the sole provider of health insurance for all citizens.

It was known before the election that President Dmopvup had controlling interest in Utopia Pharmaceuticals. As a condition for being president, hir personal investments were being managed by a court-appointed independent agent. Luke and Kyle figured the sole beneficiary of the Dmopvup Foundation was likely the president hirself. Likewise, they thought the president was reaping the financial benefits of the strong position of Utopia Pharmaceuticals on the stock exchange.

The two were in utter disbelief.

This is the kind of stuff conspiracy theorists come up with, yet this is the reality, Kyle thought.

"Should we report our concerns to the appropriate

authorities?" Kyle asked. "But who are these appropriate authorities? How should we go about this disclosure—and what might be the results of such a disclosure?"

CHAPTER 18

Overwhelmed and uncertain how to proceed, Luke thought it would be prudent to obtain legal counsel on how to proceed and to get an idea of what they should expect. He called Anne Wilson, an attorney who had represented him in a bogus malpractice lawsuit several years ago. She was the senior partner with Wilson, Maddow, and Coker, one of the most well-known and well-respected law firms in the state. With the evidence that Kyle and Luke had, they were certain this would be a slam dunk.

As soon as Luke mentioned the nature of his concerns to Anne, she cut him off and directed him to meet in her office as soon as he and Kyle could get there. Luke was concerned by Anne's abrupt response. *Could it be that we're on to something big?* Luke was eager to unburden himself of all they had discovered and to receive advice on how to conduct and protect themselves going forward. He knew they were in for a rough ride ahead, but he wasn't prepared for how rough it would be. He and Kyle were in a state of disbelief, yet they felt an obligation to pursue their concerns.

Anne Wilson's office was in the capital city of Concord, about fifteen miles away. Kyle and Luke gathered all the information they had obtained, hopped into Luke's car, and headed off to meet her. During the drive, they reflected on the course of events that had led them to their current position.

Anne's office was on Main Street, diagonally across and a few blocks down from some of the state offices and courts. There was a cold chill in the air as they walked from the parking lot to the office. It was only a brief walk, yet it was enough time for Kyle and Luke to get their thoughts and feelings in order.

"Where should we begin?" Kyle said as they approached the front door to the building. "This is so utterly unbelievable. It sounds like a conspiracy theory to me."

"I'm gonna try to start at the beginning," Luke said. "I want to find out if Anne would be willing to represent us or if she could refer us to another attorney if she's unable to do so."

They took the extremely slow elevator up to her office on the third floor. The doors opened anemically, directly into the law firm's waiting area, which was lined with elegant mahogany paneling and a rich-red woolen carpet.

"May I help you?" the woman at the reception desk asked in a soothing Southern drawl.

"We're here to see Attorney Wilson," Luke said.

The secretary brought them into a conference room, directing them to the large mahogany conference table. "Please sit. May I offer you something to drink? Water, coffee, tea?"

"No, thank you," they said in unison.

At that moment, a tall, businesslike figure entered the room. "Luke, it's great to see you again," Anne said.

"It's my pleasure to see you again as well."

Anne turned to face Kyle. With a warm smile and an outstretched hand, she said, "I'm Anne Wilson. My pronouns are *she, her,* and *hers*. It's a pleasure to meet you."

"Likewise, Attorney Wilson." Kyle shook her hand. "My pronouns are *he, him,* and *his.*"

"Please, call me Anne."

And so, their initial consultation began. For an hour or so, Luke and Kyle laid out what had transpired since the summer of 2030 and before, what they had discovered, and where they were. Anne took notes vigorously, stopping to ask questions intermittently, all while maintaining the poker face that was typical of an attorney.

"What do you think you should do about what you have discovered?" Anne asked Luke after he finished.

"I would like to report this to someone who could investigate further and do something about it," Luke said. "If all of this is true, our president and government have been using Americare to cause direct harm and even death to our citizens, while using the health care system to gain financial and political power. If this is occurring, I would like to see our president stand trial for everything that ze has done, after hir impeachment and arrest."

Anne looked up from her notepad. Her glasses had slid down almost to the tip of her nose. "Even under the best of circumstances—and assuming that everything you've found is brought out into the public and proved to be true—what do you think is the likelihood this would happen?"

Luke and Kyle looked up from their notes, but neither one answered.

"My concern has to do with what would happen to both of you. They would destroy you. My question to you is this: are you willing and prepared to have your names and reputations dragged through the mud? Are you willing to risk the well-being and the lives of your family, friends, and colleagues and possibly lose your own lives in the pursuit of trying to bring the alleged perpetrators of this alleged scheme to justice?"

It did not take long for Kyle and Luke to answer yes to that question, with Kyle citing the Hippocratic oath.

Anne adjusted her glasses. "My recommendation to you, then, is to report in a way that doesn't let on you have sought legal counsel. If I contacted the president's counsel or if I filed a motion in any court on your behalf, the government would likely come down on you firmly and swiftly because they would know that you had legal counsel and that I know how to use the judicial system to your benefit. If you reported on your own, with me waiting in the wings and behind the curtain, they likely would not be as aggressive early on, if for no other reason than the Department of Health and Human Services encourages providers to report any concerns about fraud and abuse. In fact, you are legally obligated to report any concerns you might have regarding fraud and abuse as it relates to our government-run health plans. I can remain available to give you cues about what you should do and what you might expect. If or when the need arises, I will jump in but only if it is in your best interest and the best interest of our citizens. How does that sound to you?"

Luke and Kyle looked at each other for a moment, as if seeking the other's approval, and then they said, "OK."

"I suggest you report, using the Department of Health and Human Services' website," Anne said. "They have a Fraud and Abuse reporting system, although this isn't really the kind of fraud and abuse they would expect you to report. One can report anonymously, but I recommend against that, as they are more likely to ignore your complaint, largely because you wouldn't be the wiser if they ignored it. I recommend that Luke do the reporting. Keep your reporting simple and direct; don't mention Kyle by name, and don't type a novel. Believe me, there is enough in your complaint that you should get a rather prompt response."

"Why should Luke be the one who reports, and why shouldn't he mention me by name?" Kyle asked. "I am the one who has done most of the investigative work, established a relationship with Michael, had Dr. Weinberg's office bugged, and assumed most of the risk."

"And that is precisely why Luke should be the one who reports. Let's use Luke's reporting to test the waters and see how HHS responds," Anne said. "You have done a lot, and now you should allow Luke to assume some of the risks. Luke has held a license to practice medicine for over twenty years. You have been licensed for less than a year. I'm afraid your complaint might be taken less seriously because of your lack of clinical experience. Luke is well known and respected. If they seem supportive, then you should get involved early on by attending all appointments and by providing information. If they appear to be in attack mode and want to string someone up, it's best if only one of you is in their sights. It will also give you some bargaining chips, Luke, in case some form of negotiation is required. It's just like playing cards. Try not to show your entire hand up front.

"I do need to inform you of something. Although I have served as both a plaintiff's attorney and a defense attorney in fraud-and-abuse cases, I've never been involved in a case in which the plaintiff was a health care provider, and the defendant was the government. This is unfamiliar territory for me, so I'll take this on pro bono. It's my guess the people who receive your complaint will also be surprised. Unfortunately, given what I know about our government, my degree of surprise is attenuated. I do have a few rules I will require you to follow if you want me to represent you."

"What are the rules?" Luke asked.

"First and foremost, I want you to discuss this with no one except me. We are the only people who can be trusted to discuss this, and I do mean the *only* people. Second, do not answer any questions asked of you about any of this, by anyone, without discussing it with me first. It's likely that we'll need to make my presence known early on, in which case, just refer the asking party directly to me.

"Third, it's important to keep in mind something one of my mentors during law school said to me, which has proved to be true throughout my career. Now you'll hear me say this repeatedly, and you likely will tire of hearing me say it—no matter who's side you think a government attorney, or the United States government may be favoring, it's important to remember that the only side the government is on is the government's side. They have virtually unlimited resources, including money and time. The courses of action they take are often biased and arbitrary, and they make the rules, often as they go along. They can easily break you, financially and emotionally, and they won't hesitate to do so. Many a plaintiff or defendant has had to admit defeat for the sole reason that they ran out of resources, most notably from a financial perspective. The Feds use their system and their unlimited resources as a weapon to get whatever they want and to create the outcomes that they desire. Right or wrong often doesn't enter any determination of outcome. The government could conceivably put you in a position in which they make you feel as if they are working on your behalf, especially if you risk yourselves in obtaining and providing them with information. They might even tell you that they are trying to help you. The government will help you only if it is a necessary part of their plan to bring them into a position of advantage.

"Fourth, the requirement of honesty is binding for you but not upon the government. Even if we 'win' this case, it's almost entirely certain that, in some ways, we will lose. It's important that before we proceed, we have specific goals in mind, as well as a conceptualization of what would constitute a win and what would constitute a loss. Have you discussed this between yourselves?"

"In a lot of ways, it seems that no matter the outcome, we will lose," Kyle said. "I guess what happens to us is immaterial. This is about ending a scheme that is perpetrated by our president, in which ze is causing harm and death to our citizens with the purpose of bringing hir political and financial gain. Our goal is also to bring President Dmopvup and all accomplices to justice."

"Those seem like reasonable goals," Anne said. "Good luck. I'll be available if—or, more likely, when—you need me."

CHAPTER 19

Luke and Kyle walked back to the car silently, each in deep thought. The car chirped as they approached and then entered. Almost immediately, they began to talk as they strapped themselves in and drove off, with Luke at the wheel.

"I wasn't surprised by anything that Anne told us," Kyle said. "I do feel empowered, like at least there's something we can do to perhaps have influence in our patients' and our fellow citizens' lives."

"Same here," said Luke. "Either way, it would appear this is a career-ending situation for us both. Hopefully, it won't turn out to be a life-ending one as well. You know, when I went to medical school, it was because I wanted to make a difference in patients' lives. I wanted to help people. This is our opportunity to do just that."

They drove for a while, not heading directly to either of their homes, still in deep thought. They felt most comfortable going through this together.

"When and where should we do this?" Kyle asked.

"The sooner the better, but no time is a suitable time to do it," Luke said. "Kinda paradoxical, huh? We can head over to my house and report today if you're down for that."

"Sounds OK to me. We can make a date night out of it," Kyle said, trying to break the tension with a little levity.

Within a few minutes, they were pulling into Luke's driveway. Kyle was filled with feelings and memories of the first couple of times he had been with Luke. The most poignant of these memories was their first kiss and how wonderful and right it felt. Since then, Kyle had noticed that Luke seemed to be deliberately pulling away from him, as if to insulate or protect himself from his feelings or to deal with his own personal issues, conflicts, and/or demons.

There was also the transient relationship with Michael, which provided Kyle with a distraction from Luke. Kyle was saddened by Luke's apparent distance from him. He had been so preoccupied by dealing with Michael that only recently had he begun to feel this sadness once the issues with Michael were put into proper perspective. Michael had turned out to be a wonderful friend who was in no way ready to be a partner in a relationship. Both Kyle and Michael had come to that conclusion independently, and both were content with it. Now, all of Kyle's emotional attention was available to focus on what had been going on with Americare, their patients, and with Luke. Luke seemed to be unaware and distant.

The air is a bit warmer, and some of the snow has melted since the last time I was here, Kyle thought as he walked with Luke toward the front door.

Luke remained silent. Upon entering, they hung up their coats and headed into the living room. Luke's laptop was still set up on the coffee table.

"Coffee?" Luke asked.

"Sure, black, please, "Kyle said.

Luke got the coffee, came back into the living room, and settled onto the couch deliberately close to Kyle, who seemed surprised. "Kyle, I need to talk with you," Luke said. He put his arm around Kyle and pulled him close without any objection from Kyle. "Our first kiss a couple of months ago changed my life forever. The events and feelings I experienced that night caused me to closely examine my life and to deal with a lot of issues that I had put off dealing with. In fact, I had no intention of ever addressing these issues that desperately begged to be dealt with. They were all clumped together, intertwined, and all-encompassing, and our kiss caused me to begin the process of unwinding that skein and experiencing and addressing everything all at once that was bound up inside.

"After Karolyn died, I was overwhelmed, surprised, and deeply afraid, so I fell back on a coping mechanism that had stood me well throughout my training when confronted with scary patient situations. I withdrew and outwardly went into autopilot mode while most of my attention, thoughts, and emotions were addressed. I gradually came to terms with what I was unraveling. Finally, I think I have at least a cursory understanding of what I stumbled upon, opened up by our kiss. Our kiss brought me back to life. I would like to share with you that which I have come to understand and how I feel, if this is OK with you."

"Luke, it's fine with me," Kyle said.

"My wife's death shattered my life. I used my work as

a substitute for my reality, unconsciously choosing to shift my feelings and focus toward work and work-related issues, rather than allowing myself to grieve Karolyn's death and deal with my feelings of guilt, loss, anger, and loneliness and to permit myself to move forward. Instead, I wrapped myself up in my created world, a cocoon which protected me from having to feel a lot of pain.

"Although my wife had died, our relationship didn't end. We were and are still married. Even though I would have wanted her to meet someone else and to date if I had been the one who died, I felt as if I was cheating on her. It wasn't so much that I kissed you; it was my falling in love with you that made me feel like a cheater. I felt as if I never asked her for her permission and her blessing. I've had time to do that now, and I feel she has given both to me."

"I understand, Luke, and it's OK." Kyle stroked Luke's hand as it was interlocked with his. "I think I was just surprised by how quickly you changed from passionately kissing me. It seemed to me as if you were angry more than withdrawing."

"Kyle, I had just been hit with the realization that my wife had likely been murdered. Andy had just finished reviewing the high number of deaths that occurred within a couple of weeks after colonoscopy. Karolyn had undergone an uneventful screening colonoscopy two and a half weeks before her unexplained and unexpected death. I awoke in the morning, holding her cold, lifeless body in my arms. That's a feeling I will never forget. The realization that Karolyn was killed by President Dmopvup immediately gave me a focus for my anger. I'm extremely angry. I hated President Dmopvup, and I really think I still do.

"In addition, this forced me to reexamine my sexual orientation and identity. This reaffirmed that I love who I love, and I am attracted to someone because I am. I don't have a gender requirement, which I guess makes me bisexual. Perhaps a more appropriate term would be omnisexual or pansexual. I've always been this way, which is currently the way our nation's children are being raised and how our society feels. When I was a kid, it still wasn't considered entirely acceptable to think this way, though.

"I want you to know that I've fallen in love with you, Kyle. It's likely I won't do this perfectly, and there will be bumps and hiccups along the way as I continue along my path toward self-discovery. I know what love is and how it feels, and I know that I love you. I wanted you to know this in no uncertain terms, especially before we commence on what I think is going to be an incredibly stressful journey."

Feelings of physical warmth, elation, joy, security, passion, intense love, and others that he could not precisely identify came over Kyle, as uncontrollable tears streamed down his face and across his lips and his dimpled smile. He then grabbed Luke and held him tightly. "I love you so much, Luke. I've been waiting all my life for you so we can carry on with the rest of it together." Kyle looked up into Luke's eyes as Luke wiped a tear or two from his own eyes with his thumb.

Luke drew Kyle up in his arms and kissed him. "I love you too, Kyle."

They spent an uncertain period looking into each other's eyes, holding hands, and kissing.

"Are you ready to report?" Luke asked.

"Yup, I'm ready." Kyle strengthened his grip on Luke's hand. "Let's do this."

Luke went to get his laptop, plugged it in, and then resumed his place on the couch next to Kyle. With his arm back around Kyle, where it belonged, Luke turned his laptop on and waited for it to boot up. He then found the Department of Health and Human Services website and figured out how to file an online complaint about fraud and/or abuse.

As Anne Wilson had recommended, he needed to keep things brief but convey all the information that those on the receiving end of the complaint would need to have. This sounded much easier than it was. He was certain most of the fraud and abuse complaints were levied by whistleblowers who witnessed what they believed was fraud or abuse on the part of a private entity against the federal government, using the government health plans to attain personal and/or financial gain.

This was an entirely different animal. Luke would report that the president of the United States was using Americare to perpetrate fraud and abuse against the United States citizenry. Furthermore, he would allege that the president was using Americare to cause grave harm and even death to patients who they insured for political and monetary gain on the part of the government and the president. Luke realized that he needed this complaint to seem credible so that its recipients would not deem him to be a flake and focus their investigation on him. Therefore, he could not state all pertinent facts in the original email, as it would seem incomprehensible that something so crazy could be occurring.

After thinking for over an hour, reviewing his thoughts with Kyle, editing and reediting, Luke came up with what he thought was the best way to report this. On February 27, 2031, Luke filed his complaint, outlining all his perceived evil workings of President Dmopvup and the Americare plan.

"Well, that's about it," Luke said. "Are you ready?"

"Ready as I'll ever be." Kyle was thinking of Sean's ghost.

CHAPTER 20

Jommesa Sufjen Dmopvup's drive to become president was ingrained in hir, as was hir intense desire to essentially rule the world. Ze always envisioned hirself as the queen bee, surrounded by worker bees who would do hir bidding. Ze felt entitled to become president, as if it were hir turn, and ze had already structured hir life in such a way that the only thing required for hir to become queen bee was for hir to be placed in the center of the hive.

That occurred upon hir election to the office of president in November 2020, and the effects were immediate. Ze had a large sphere of influence, largely a result of the Dmopvup Foundation. Since its inception, contributors to the Dmopvup Foundation were rewarded for their contributions. As the foundation grew, and as ze became more facile as a dealmaker, the contributions, deals, and rewards all grew in number, size, scope, and impact. Many lines were crossed, including those of ethics, legality, and morality. Because no negative repercussions resulted, ze reaped the many benefits and the many rewards, and hir activity and use of the foundation snowballed.

Early on in life, Mx. Dmopvup had lost any sense of empathy, compassion, or remorse, and ze was entirely driven by a need for money, power, and influence. Ze used any and all means available to bring hir beehive lifestyle to fruition, and ze would have fought to the death and the deaths of others to protect and maintain it.

Early during hir first term in office, President Dmopvup made the development and ongoing improvement of an evidence-based system of health care the purview of the United States Preventive Services Task Force (USPSTF), which had been in existence since 1984.

The USPSTF called itself "an independent, volunteer panel of national experts in disease prevention and evidence-based medicine," working to "improve the health of all Americans by making evidence-based recommendations about clinical preventive services." It was composed of sixteen volunteer practicing health care providers from all specialties of medicine, and its recommendations were historically put forth as practice guidelines, which were recommendations rather than laws. As these recommendations were always deemed to be best practice, they were universally adopted by all health care organizations throughout the United States and often worldwide.

The Americare legislation made the USPSTF a part of the Department of Health and Human Services. It made each volunteer a paid employee of the US government, and it made the recommendations of the USPSTF mandatory laws, rather than recommendations. Additionally, under the Dmopvup administration, the USPSTF was charged with the responsibility of developing evidence-based protocols for the management of the most common and costly disease states and health-related problems.

The USPSTF embraced these new challenges enthusiastically. During the next five years, the health of the population improved dramatically, as evidenced by ongoing improvement in patient quality metrics and increased longevity. Part of this process involved the ongoing evaluation of individual patients' data from their medical records, the population's data in aggregate, life expectancy, and the cost analysis during the past rolling five-year period.

On August 18, 2022, Americare became available as a choice for health insurance on all fifty state exchanges. The administrative costs were low, which was surprising for a government-run program. Regarding Americare, the passage of a short amount of time revealed markedly improved patient quality metrics, a decrease in health care costs, and an increase in life span that exceeded that predicted by previous modeling, based on the previous health care delivery system.

From a financial perspective, Americare was generating revenue. This offset the $40 trillion deficit to such a significant degree that the country's budget would be balanced, and the national debt paid in full within the next twenty years.

Americare, AMRS, IQOD, and its algorithmic health care delivery system had become an integral part of the US health care system, as well as an important part of the economy. United States citizens were planning their lives, assuming that Americare would be their insurer, and they were happy with the health care system. AMRS and its algorithms had unwittingly and surreptitiously become the standard of care, and the data obtained indicated it was efficacious and cost-effective.

The USPSTF considered Americare, AMRS, the algorithms, and their implementation to be best practice and the standard of health care in this country, as well as one of the most important drivers of the economy. The use of micro-implants in this system, however, was something that only the president, hir attorney general, and hir FBI director were aware of.

This was the cornerstone of Dmopvup's platform and campaign for the upcoming 2032 presidential election, as well as hir legacy. The citizenry viewed Americare as a bright spot in the country, as something that could be counted on to improve the length and quality of lives. They were universally happy and content as far as health care was concerned. It was this happiness and contentment that Dmopvup was counting on for hir reelection, for ze was sorely lacking in many other spheres.

Come Easter, whispers of Luke's complaint had reached President Dmopvup's ears. Ze became appropriately concerned that this could prove to be the fatal flaw, the precariously placed linchpin, the tiny crack in the ice that could spider web unpredictably and out of control to topple everything—hir presidency, power, influence, legacy, and life. President Dmopvup realized ze needed to quash this complaint or, better yet, tweak it and use it to afford hir an advantage through bringing hir government to bear.

One afternoon right before Easter 2030, the president met with Attorney General Musivve Mapdj and FBI Director Kenit Duniz to discuss this and to formulate a plan to use Luke's complaint advantageously. The president gave the order to use any and every under-the-radar means available to make this so. Additionally, ze requested Attorney General Mapdj to be proactive in steering this complaint toward a positive outcome. "Get it done" was the message.

"Low profile. Under the radar. Get it done. Do not keep me informed. Keep me entirely out of the loop."

As a result of these directives, Attorney General Mapdj contacted Assistant US Attorney Arthur P. Hartigan, under whose authority the complaint resided, and asked hir to get involved early on.

CHAPTER 21

L ife went on as usual and a few months passed, with Luke and Kyle feeling an inner sense of closeness that they had never before experienced. On Monday, April 21, 2031, Luke was sitting at his desk during a break between his morning patients. He couldn't focus, though he did his best to concentrate on his job. He knew Kyle also felt that they had, in a way, betrayed the Hippocratic oath, which each had sworn to uphold, by not being able to bring all of this to an end. Kyle had told Luke that he had noticed some of their colleagues might be aware of their activities, but Luke didn't have anything concrete to go on so he told Kyle to do the best that he could to keep a low profile.

Later on that morning, Luke received a call from HHS while he was seeing patients. He jumped when his cellphone buzzed while it was in his pocket, and he let the call go to voice mail. *It's probably not good news*, he thought.

He checked his voice mail at lunchtime.

"Hello, Dr. Moses, this is Special Agent Lauren Dickey from the United States Department of Health and Human Services. I received a complaint that was filed by you on February 27, 2031. It was forwarded to me here at the Concord office from our central office. I would like to meet with you next Monday, April 28, at 4:00 p.m. to discuss this further. If that doesn't work for you, please call me back so we can arrange a mutually convenient time. Otherwise, I plan on seeing you then. My office is in the Federal Building in Concord, on the fourth floor."

That was the extent of the message. Luke was glad he had received a response. Yet he had been enjoying the peace and quiet and his relationship with Kyle, and he wasn't eager to disrupt his life. He called Kyle to let him know about the call and the appointment. He also called Anne Wilson, who recommended that both he and Kyle be present at the meeting. Anne thought there was a good chance that someone from the US Attorney's Office would be there, so she thought she should be there too. She asked Luke if he could pick her up at her office so that they could talk on the way to the appointment. He agreed.

Luke and Kyle canceled their afternoon sessions for that day, something that they rarely, if ever did. Both were anxious, largely because they had no idea what to expect. After finishing his lunch on April 28, Luke swung by Kyle's office. Kyle was hanging up his white coat. Luke closed his office door, gently took Kyle's hand, pulled him close into an embrace, and kissed him while stroking his hair.

"I love you, Kyle." Luke looked deeply into Kyle's eyes. "I want you to never forget that. No matter what happens, I will always love you, and I will do everything in my power to protect you, even at the expense of my own life, if necessary. I think we're in for a most difficult and stressful time. Our lives could be irrevocably altered by what we're about to experience. I've decided I'll do whatever it takes and risk whatever is necessary to put an end to this Americare scheme and bring the perpetrators to justice. Let's do this together." He tightened his embrace on Kyle.

"I love you so much, Luke."

Kyle grabbed his lightweight jacket, turned off the light in his office, closed the door, and headed to the parking lot with Luke, hand in hand.

The drive to Anne's office was a short one, and she was waiting for them in the lobby of her building when they arrived at 3:20 p.m. The Federal Building was only a few blocks away, so they had plenty of time to drive around and chat. Luke pulled the car to the front of the building, and Anne climbed into the back seat.

As Luke pulled out into oncoming traffic, Anne said, "I just want to make sure both of you are as well prepared for this meeting as you can be. Although I'm not sure exactly how this meeting will go, I have an idea of the kinds of things that might take place. I also have some insight into how our government operates."

"What things are they apt to ask us?" Kyle asked.

"That depends on who's doing the asking and how much they already know. Whoever attends this meeting will give us an idea of how much they know about this, as well as the degree to which the government is concerned regarding your complaint. If we are just in the company of Special Agent Dickey, that might indicate that HHS is starting at the beginning, and the purpose of the meeting would then be to gather information. If the US attorney for the state of New Hampshire or one of hir assistants or representatives from the FBI is also present, that might indicate they already have some information regarding your complaint and are building a case.

"Now, I have some rules for you to follow during this and all other meetings. First of all, never answer a question or provide an explanation unless I give you a nod indicating it's OK to answer. Speak slowly to allow me enough time to interject during your speaking, which I will do if I feel it's necessary. Provide *only* what you are asked, no more and no less. Don't over answer. If you don't know the answer to a question, just say so. If you aren't comfortable answering a question or if you're uncertain how you should answer, please look directly at me, and then I will take over. If I feel any line of questioning is inappropriate or leading or could be used against you, I will immediately interject and aggressively say so. Lastly, keep in mind that the only side our government is on is the government's side."

Luke and Kyle rolled their eyes.

"I saw that," Anne said with a smile. "Also, please remember that when addressing a government body or a government official, the use of gender-neutral pronouns is required, and anything that would allude to an individual's gender, sexual orientation, or race is not acceptable. These are the laws of the land. As individuals, we are each free to choose our own pronouns and use them freely in our day-to-day lives, but we are required to use the pronouns that other individuals request when referring to them. All interactions with the federal government and governmental officials must be carried out by acknowledging gender and racial neutrality in our speech. It is criminal to do otherwise.

"As the focus of your complaint is the president, I am not certain how this will work. In the private sector, a US attorney or the attorney general would be required to recuse themselves from this case or decline representation due to conflicts of interest. This is not possible in this case, though, so we are stuck with knowing there will be conflicts of interest with our government's representation of the president. Clearly, the government will be on the president's side."

Luke pulled the car into the parking lot of the Federal Building, just as Anne concluded her rules. They went through the security checkpoint at the building's entrance and proceeded to the special agent's office. After sitting a few minutes in the waiting room, they were directed into a conference room, where Special Agent Dickey stood up and introduced hirself with hir hand outstretched for handshakes that subsequently occurred. With hir left hand, ze handed out hir business card, identifying hir as a federal agent.

Ze then turned to introduce Assistant US Attorney Arthur P. Hartigan and Special Agent Saffron B. Truman from the FBI, who both stood up with their right hands outstretched and their left hands giving out their cards. Anne introduced herself as Luke's and Kyle's counsel and likewise handed out her card. Also present was a stenographer, who wasn't formally introduced. What was billed as a meeting between Luke, Kyle, and a special agent from HHS turned out to be much more than that.

After thanking everyone for coming, Special Agent Dickey addressed Luke. "Dr. Moses, I have your complaint in front of me. I took the liberty of sharing it with Assistant US Attorney Hartigan, who felt it was appropriate to involve the FBI early on, so ze contacted Special Agent Truman and invited hir to join us. Dr. Moses, can you explain what happened that caused you to file your complaint?"

Luke proceeded to briefly review the case histories of his two patients in virtually identical clinical situations, for whom he requested consideration for liver transplantation, one of which was granted and the other denied without a good explanation for the denial. He also stated that he had noticed more than a few unexpected deaths among his patients who were insured by Americare; this was corroborated by Kyle but by no other providers in the practice. "Considering the improving quality metrics of the practice's Americare patient panel," he said, "this did not make any sense to me." Luke looked over at Anne, who nodded.

"Dr. Moses," Attorney Hartigan said, "it appears to me that your informal investigation consisted of a lot more than just a simple record review. Is that the case?"

Luke nodded. "Most of it consisted of a record review, but there was more to it than that."

Anne interrupted. "Assistant US Attorney Hartigan, Special Agents Truman and Dickey, I move that we stop here for now and return at a later date to permit Dr. Moses and Mx. Sanderson to prepare more detailed narratives describing the scope and the findings of their investigation, which led to Dr. Moses's reporting as a whistleblower."

"Are we all in agreement?" Special Agent Dickey asked.

All those who were present nodded and said yes.

"Then, let's end for today," Special Agent Dickey said.

The stenographer, who had said absolutely nothing during the entire proceeding, ushered everyone from the conference room.

The drive back to Anne's office was quiet until Anne said, "They're way ahead of where I thought they would be, given the verbiage of your complaint."

Luke was attentive to both Anne and the road.

"When we return to meet with them, we need to carefully lay out all our cards on the table in a way that protects you and provides them with the information they require. We should leave the next meeting with each of you having given a complete and thorough narrative of everything that transpired and what you discovered, beginning with after each of you independently became concerned that something could be amiss.

"We also need to be certain you're kept safe from any prosecution regarding any violation of patient-privacy laws, as well as any repercussions from the New Hampshire Board of Medicine regarding any alleged inappropriate conduct because of your involvement with Dr. Canteenwalla and Michael Jude, not to mention placing listening devices in Dr. Weinberg's office. It would also be nice to keep Dr. Canteenwalla and Michael held harmless as well.

"As soon as I get in, I'll call Hartigan and request that further participation in the investigation be contingent on each of you, Michael, and Dr. Canteenwalla being immune from any prosecution or disciplinary action from any law enforcement agency or professional board. I hope Hartigan will agree to these terms up front, as it would spare all of us from time-consuming and expensive legal maneuvering from all parties required to make this so. This process would also limit the flow of helpful information in a timely manner, so it's likely Hartigan will agree to this immunity. In the meantime, you are to discuss this with no one except me and each other and only under the condition of absolute privacy.

"It's possible you may be approached by others regarding these issues, even though they're supposed to be confidential. Your answer must be, 'I know nothing about it.' Saying no comment could be construed as admitting your knowledge of these issues and that you were told not to comment about them when asked. This is an old trick I've seen used as a way of causing one to breach confidentiality, which would void any protection for you as guaranteed under the whistleblower statutes. If anyone pesters you or if anyone from the media contacts you, refer them to me without giving any information. I'm telling you this now because I guarantee, in the near future, this will happen.

"In the meantime, I want both of you to prepare detailed narratives of exactly what transpired from your first inkling that something might be amiss up to and including what transpired today. I think you shouldn't collaborate in writing these narratives, as it will be more effective if each one has its own sense of individuality. I will try to arrange a follow-up meeting with Attorney Hartigan and Special Agents Truman and Dickey for about a couple of weeks from now. I know today must have seemed like a whirlwind for both of you. To me, this signals that you are on to something. Try to just go about your lives and work as you normally would. If you have a therapist or know of any, I always recommend getting them onboard. This may get intense at times, and it is my job to make sure you're prepared."

As Luke slowed the car to a stop in front of Anne's building, Anne adjusted her glasses. "Do you have any questions?" she asked."

"No," Kyle and Luke said, almost in unison.

Anne smiled. "I'll call you both tomorrow and let you know if Attorney Hartigan agrees with my request."

CHAPTER 22

Anne was able to negotiate an agreement with Attorney Hartigan and, therefore, the Feds. Hartigan conceded that Luke and Kyle would be held harmless with respect to any action from any professional board, place of employment, or law enforcement agency. Anne successfully argued with Hartigan by stretching the stipulations of the whistleblower statutes that kept witnesses and whistleblowers protected in exchange for their reporting and cooperation. A similar agreement was made for Dr. Canteenwalla and for Michael.

A month after their first meeting, Luke, Kyle, and Anne met again with Attorney Hartigan and Special Agents Truman and Dickey. Attorney Hartigan ran this show. This time, the meeting was video recorded, obviating the need for a stenographer, and Luke and Kyle felt better prepared.

"Good morning," Hartigan said. "This morning, we will listen to testimonies from Dr. Lucas Moses and physician assistant Mx. Kyle Sanderson regarding what brought them to this point, what caused them to embark on their investigation, and what they have allegedly discovered. We will also have the opportunity to ask them questions. Although this testimony is not under oath, per se, I should be clear that any breach of the truth, if it is discovered, would be considered a breach of our agreement to hold Dr. Canteenwalla and Mx. Michael Jude harmless, and it would void any protection afforded to Dr. Moses and Mx. Sanderson under the whistleblower statutes. Is that understood?"

"Yes," answered Luke and Kyle independently.

"I would like to start with you, Mx. Sanderson," Hartigan said. "Please introduce yourself and make note of where you are working, your position there, and for how long. Then, in your own words, tell me what led you to this point."

After formally introducing himself to the group, Kyle explained how he had come to discover that Americare was driving their patient panel toward an AMRS-developed ideal patient panel using micro-implants that caused the death of the sickest patients, those who were deemed apt to become sick, and those of opposing political leanings. He revealed that contributors to the Dmopvup Foundation were afforded the use of this system to have other patients killed, to purchase spots on the various organ transplantation lists, and to choose and purchase their organ donors from the panel of healthy Americare patients of differing political leanings and have them killed for organ procurement.

Luke's testimony followed and supported Kyle's. During their testimonies, Attorney Hartigan and Special Agents Dickey and Truman took notes feverishly on their laptops, with their eyes focused on their screens.

"Does anyone have any questions?" Attorney Hartigan asked.

"Has any other provider, staff person, or patient noticed any similar occurrences or trends?" Special Agent Dickey asked.

"Not to my knowledge, no," Luke said.

"One would think that others would have at least noticed something," Attorney Hartigan said.

"Does anyone here have any questions for either Dr. Moses or Mx. Sanderson?" Attorney Hartigan asked, looking around the room. "No? OK. Thank you both very much for coming forward with your complaint. We appreciate how difficult this entire process can be. It is because of people like you, whistleblowers, that we can bring these kinds of issues to light, investigate them, bring an end to the fraud and/or abuse, and bring those who are responsible to justice. During this process, we will work together with you to achieve these ends. If you have any concerns or if there is anything you think I should know, please contact me through your counsel."

"What will happen now?" Kyle asked.

"Special Agents Dickey and Truman and I will thoroughly investigate your complaint. I will contact Attorney Wilson if I need any additional information and to keep you apprised regarding the progress of the investigation. In the meantime, the utmost secrecy is required, if for no other reason than to ensure your protection and the protection of Mx. Jude and Dr. Canteenwalla from a civil, legal, professional, or employment perspective and to maintain the integrity of the investigation. Special Agents Dickey and/or Truman may also contact you through your counsel if they require any additional information as well. Are there any other questions?"

There being none, the meeting was formally adjourned.

CHAPTER 23

A couple of weeks after Luke and Kyle's second meeting with Attorney Hartigan and Special Agents Dickey and Truman, Dr. Weinberg sent an email to Kyle, requesting that they meet in Dr. Weinberg's office later that afternoon. Kyle was concerned, as Dr. Weinberg usually maintained a low profile and rarely, if ever, requested individual meetings. As nothing new had transpired since the department meeting, during which Luke raised his concerns about the outliers, Kyle was hoping that the meeting had nothing to do with that issue.

Kyle appeared at Dr. Weinberg's office right on time, as he always did when he had an appointment with anyone. Dr. Weinberg was sitting at his desk. Kyle noticed he was fidgety and had a sweat-slicked forehead.

"Kyle." Dr. Weinberg motioned for him to enter and pointed to a chair in front of his desk. "Have a seat. How are things going?"

"Pretty well," Kyle said.

"Hey, listen, Kyle. Remember when Luke raised his concerns regarding the possibility of a few aberrant occurrences in a couple of your patients who were insured by Americare?"

An inexplicable feeling of dread overcame Kyle. "Yes, I do recall that."

"Have there been any other such occurrences?" Dr. Weinberg asked.

"Not that I am aware of."

"I'm aware that you and Michael have gotten to know each other rather well and have become friends," Dr. Weinberg said.

"We have become exceptionally good friends, but what is pertinent here is that we've developed an exceptional work relationship. Our friendship is not something either of us has brought into the workplace, nor do we intend to," Kyle responded.

Dr. Weinberg abruptly became angry. "You can cut out the bullshit, Kyle. It's been obvious to everyone in the practice that you and Michael are more than just friends. Michael is an excellent addition to our practice, as are you. Unlike you, however, Michael has never been able to keep anything in confidence, and this has gotten him into trouble now and again. I guess I'm telling you to be careful what you tell him unless you don't care if he broadcasts the information."

"Did Michael tell you anything that you're concerned about?" Kyle asked.

"Nothing that specifically raises my concern, but I am concerned he might have been shooting his mouth off to Kupevjep," Dr. Weinberg said.

"About what?"

"I'm not sure if he said anything to Kupevjep, but Kupevjep approached me and asked what I knew about rumors regarding bad outcomes in Americare patients. Have you or Luke approached Kupevjep regarding Luke's concerns?" Dr. Weinberg asked.

"I haven't, and I doubt very much that Luke has," Kyle said. "I would also be surprised if Michael mentioned anything of concern to Dr. Hsacis."

"Kupevjep approached me yesterday with hir panties all in a twist. Somehow, Luke's concerns were brought to hir attention by someone. Ze also said you mentioned to Luke you've had similar patient concerns and that you both were following up on them. Is that true?"

In that instant, Kyle recalled what Anne Wilson had told him regarding how to answer a question like this. "Per New Hampshire state law, I'm required to review cases with my supervising physician, Luke Moses, at regular intervals," he said. "As a part of these case reviews, I perform a thorough and detailed review of the cases and the patients' records. Those cases were ones I've reviewed and followed up on."

Dr. Weinberg sighed and removed his bifocals. "I don't think I need to remind you that I am this practice's medical director. Any and all patient-care concerns or issues should be brought to me directly and not to anyone who is outside this practice, without first having my permission to do so. Likewise, the same goes for Luke and Michael. Is that understood, Kyle?"

"Yes, it is," Kyle said. "I haven't approached Dr. Hsacis regarding any patient-care issues since starting my work here at the practice."

"All right, then. That's the reason for our meeting—to make certain that you, Michael, or Luke haven't bypassed me with any concerns about patient well-being or care and that you're clear about the appropriate chain of command. Thank you very much for stopping by," Dr. Weinberg said as he offered his outstretched right hand.

Kyle left that meeting with a nominal concern that Michael might have betrayed his trust and squealed to Dr. Hsacis regarding his concerns about Americare. He found that hard to believe, given how close the two had become, the sensitivity of the information they shared, and the risk of exposing their prior romantic relationship to Dr. Hsacis at the expense of Michael's employment. Nevertheless, Kyle felt obliged to confront him about this.

The next day, Kyle approached Michael while he was sitting at his desk in his office. "Got a minute?" Kyle asked.

"Sure thing. Come on in," Michael said.

Kyle entered Michael's office and shut the door. "Michael, have you reached out to Dr. Hsacis regarding anything we've talked about, specifically relating to any adverse patient events or outcomes?"

"Hell no! Why do you ask?"

"Yesterday, Weinberg called me into his office for a meeting, chewed me a new one, and asked if I had brought up my concerns with Dr. Hsacis. I told him I hadn't. He then asked me if I thought either you or Luke had. I told him I didn't think either of you would have done that. Apparently, someone told Hsacis about our investigation into our perceived patient occurrences. He was quite agitated about this."

"This all fits together," Michael said.

"What do you mean?"

"A couple of days ago, I received a call from an Assistant US Attorney Hartigan, requesting that I meet with him to discuss the concerns you and Luke raised. I was told not to discuss this meeting with anyone. I'll be meeting with him tomorrow. I have retained legal counsel. I'm guessing Hsacis was approached in much the same manner."

"Michael, I'm really sorry for coming across as accusatory. Consider this issue discussed. I have a feeling that Attorney Hartigan may be leveraging us against Americare or us against each other. We need to be careful. I'll let my attorney know what has transpired. In the meantime, let's promise each other that we'll both cooperate fully with the investigation and that neither of us will discuss this with anyone else except our attorneys," Kyle said.

"I promise," Michael said.

"So do I. Good luck tomorrow."

Kyle felt terrible that he had gotten Michael involved in all of this. Michael was an innocent bystander—somewhat greedy but certainly innocent. Dr. Hsacis being made aware that something was amiss, Dr. Weinberg's anxious demeanor and questioning, and now Michael being called in for questioning were all clear messages that they had stumbled on something significant. Kyle only hoped no innocent bystanders would be hurt while this played out.

CHAPTER 24

During the ensuing months, several more of Kyle's Americare patients died unexpectedly. As directed by Attorney Hartigan, he recorded their names and identifying information, along with his concerns. Through Attorney Anne Wilson, he then submitted them to Special Agents Dickey and Truman.

Kyle had become paranoid about confidentiality breaches, and he required reassurance that the submission of names of patients to the FBI wouldn't be considered such a breach. Because of this concern, Anne negotiated with Attorney Hartigan to have the information released to Special Agent Dickey at HHS, who then would release it to Special Agent Truman. Patients signed a waiver of confidentiality with HHS upon enrollment in any of the government-run health plans, which was one of the many ultra-small–print paragraphs that patients signed when they enrolled in these programs. Therefore, the release of this information to Special Agent Dickey could not be misconstrued as a breach.

Kyle's relationship with Luke had become strained by these events too. Each had backed away from the other again, largely out of fear that their closeness could be misconstrued as a conspiracy. Their relationship consisted of professional contact only, with Luke serving as Kyle's supervising physician and having ongoing required case reviews.

Luke had also noticed several more unexpected adverse events and outcomes in his Americare patients, which he, too, reported to Anne. Aside from giving her that information, Luke and Kyle did not discuss these with each other. Yet no other providers reported similar concerns about their Americare patients, at least not that Luke or Kyle were aware.

One day in early June 2031, Luke approached Kyle at work and asked him to come over to his house later to catch up. Kyle had hoped this day would come; he hoped their relationship hadn't become a casualty of their investigation.

Work seemed to last forever that day. Kyle couldn't wait to see Luke in a nonprofessional capacity. He hoped they could pick up where they had left off, as if nothing had ever happened. He hoped that Luke felt the same way. His mind was focused on this on his way over to Luke's house, and his heart was racing.

The sun was bright and warm, the smells of spring were in the air, and the chirping of springtime birds pervaded. This contrasted to Kyle's last time at Luke's, when everything had been dark and cold, the snow had crunched under his feet, and the smell of the woodstoves burning had been ubiquitous.

Luke was waiting at the door when Kyle arrived. Upon entering his house, Kyle fell into Luke's open arms, knowing it was where he belonged. Talking took a back seat as they just held each other tightly for a while. They walked into Luke's living room with their arms wrapped around each other and sat down together. They both began to speak simultaneously, twice, and then giggled like schoolchildren. Then each said, "You go first."

Looking into Luke's eyes, Kyle gave him tacit permission to say what was on his mind.

"Kyle, I love you. I've wanted to say that every single day, at least several times each day, since our last time together."

"Me, too." Kyle tried not to seem as if he was parroting. "My love for you is the main thing that has gotten me through all this shit. I've felt very much alone, aside from that."

"What has transpired as the result of my complaint has made me feel a sense of guilt because of what this has done to you—and to us and even to Michael and Andy," Luke said. "It has also given me time to think about what's most important to me. I realized that you are most important to me. You are the love of my life. I never want to lose you, hurt you, or allow anyone to hurt you. If my actions have caused you any harm, I am deeply sorry."

Kyle smiled. "I'm grateful for everything that has happened because if it hadn't transpired exactly as it did, we wouldn't be sitting here, together, talking right now. The most important thing to me is that I have you right now—that we have each other. Together, we will get through all of this and everything else that happens our way. As long as I have your commitment and your love, I know that everything will be OK. I love you, Luke."

Luke stroked Kyle's cheek with the back of his hand, then pulled his face close and kissed him, which made all the difference in the world. All of Kyle's fears and worries abated. For the first time in about a year, he felt secure and prepared to deal with whatever life had in store. They kissed each other for a while, which spontaneously evolved until they both became one in love. This brought out their strength and passion, the determination that, together, they were stronger and better than the sum of each separately, and the notion that they were destined to be together. That day cemented their relationship and made it permanent, and it bolstered their inner strength and reserve.

The evening drew to a close with a renewed sense of love and closeness between them, each feeling that everything would be OK as long as they had each other. Kyle left Luke with a kiss and then headed home with a feeling of renewal. Luke had the same feelings.

The next day, for Kyle, felt like a day without burdens. It had been a while since he had felt that way; after all, his life had been turned upside down and inside out, just because he had done his job, following the tenets of the Hippocratic oath and using his clinical expertise. The passage of time and the reaffirmation of his relationship with Luke had brought Kyle a lot of healing.

Throughout this time, unbeknownst to Kyle, he experienced a tremendous amount of personal growth and a marked increase in his own inner strength. He saw his patients with a new sense of vigor and confidence, having not lost his tremendous empathy, compassion, and boyish enthusiasm, which made Kyle, Kyle. He thought of Michael and how likely it was that his life had turned chaotic, just because they had met. He felt responsible for that, and he thought it would be appropriate to approach Michael and make amends, even though what had happened to Michael had been inadvertent, not deliberate.

That day at noon, Kyle approached Michael, just as he had done the first time they officially met in the office long ago. Michael was bending over his desk, writing while talking on the phone in his loud, friendly, and persuasive voice. As he looked up, there was a minuscule pause in his conversation as he noticed Kyle standing at the doorway. He motioned Kyle to come in and have a seat, which Kyle obliged.

Michael's call lasted only a few minutes, after which he sat at his desk, looking down at the papers in front of him. Michael was quiet, which was atypical of him, and Kyle knew that.

"I was just thinking about you," Kyle said. "I saw that you were in your office, so I thought I should come by and say hi."

"Hi," Michael said shyly.

"Can we go for a little drive?" Kyle asked.

"Um, sure. My car or yours? Mine's nicer." Michael smiled.

After Michael let his staff know that he was leaving, he and Kyle proceeded to Michael's car.

"Look, I know you've been through the mill, and it's

largely my fault," Kyle said as Michael drove. "I'm very sorry for dragging you into this."

"Well, what are you sorry you dragged me into?" Michael asked.

"I'm sorry I got you involved in the issue about which we are forbidden to speak. I owe you some explanation, and I have some confessions and amends to make to you," Kyle said.

"You owe me nothing. My feelings for you are genuine, no matter what you must tell me. I'm grateful for that. In a large part, you've changed me and my life for the better, aside from the issue about which we are forbidden to speak," Michael said, flashing a small but warm smile.

"You know, I probably would not have gotten to know you if that issue hadn't arisen," Kyle said. "Luke and I had reached an impasse. We had learned as much as we could from the information that was available to us, largely from patient records and interviews. We were at a dead end without access to AMRS and to more knowledge about how Americare worked. We knew that you had access to both, and we decided that I would be in the best position to get to know you in an effort to obtain information about the workings of Americare and to gain access to AMRS. Our meeting was not by chance; it was planned. To be honest, I had absolutely no interest in meeting you prior to our meeting. My goal was to get to know you, become close to you, use this relationship to glean as much information about the inner workings of Americare as I could, and gain access to AMRS, and that was all. I was not looking forward to getting to know you. My interest was in Luke.

"Once we met, I fell in love with you, which turned my life upside down. I was prepared to commit my life to you. You caused me to review my life, values, goals, hopes, and dreams and to reassess my purposes. I then realized that even though I loved you, our lives were so entirely different that a healthy relationship with you would not be feasible unless I changed my life to conform to yours, or you changed yours to conform to mine. That would not be healthy or beneficial to either of us.

"Specifically, your involvement with Americare and how you carried out your job were inconsistent with your being in a relationship with me. Additionally, I gained the sense that you were in a different place with respect to relationships and that you were not looking for the kind of mutual commitment that I was, although I'm aware that it wasn't fair of me to conjecture about what you were looking for or what you were feeling.

"I put you at significant risk several times to suit my own ends, not too dissimilar to what I accused you of doing regarding patients and your employment with Americare. I guess what I want to say is that I'm so sorry for using you the way that I did, but my feelings for you, which developed along the way, are genuine, and they are still there. I'm asking for your forgiveness, as well as your ongoing friendship."

Michael grabbed Kyle's hand and held it tightly. "Kyle, we used each other. You were on my list of people I wanted to date, largely because you're so hot. As you are aware, this has been my pattern—getting into 'relationships' with beautiful people and essentially wearing them like fine clothing to hide my fragile interior. Once they've exceeded their usefulness to me, I dispose of them.

"You were to be one of those beautiful people. I was using you in a similar fashion to my using all the others. Yet during this process with you, I fell in love for the very first time. You dashed all my plans, turned me upside down and inside out, and made me realize who and what I was and wasn't, what I was doing and not doing, and to whom I was doing it. This made it possible for me to make some changes. Nothing you did begs your forgiveness, Kyle, and my ongoing love and friendship are a given." He smiled. "Let's just be grateful for what we do have and not be regretful for what we don't. OK, babe?"

"Perfect for me," said Kyle.

Michael had driven for about forty-five minutes, but it seemed like only five minutes. They returned to the office, each feeling as if a huge burden had been lifted from their shoulders and with a renewed readiness to tackle what the afternoon and future days had in store for them.

CHAPTER 25

After the Feds had questioned Luke and Kyle, life continued onward, and they heard nothing more from them about Luke's complaint for almost a year. Michael had been questioned, and Luke and Kyle suspected the Feds had reached out to Andy as well. Nevertheless, it seemed that things were dropped. Kyle and Luke were grateful for this lull in the action, which allowed them to regroup and settle into their comfortable, pre-complaint routines.

This calm ended on March 24, 2032, when Attorney Hartigan called their attorney, Anne Wilson, and arranged another meeting at the Federal Building. The meeting was scheduled for the following week on March 31, so Anne met with Luke and Kyle in the afternoon the day that she received the call. As they entered Anne's office, she was standing by her desk, busily shuffling papers, seemingly unaware of them. A gentle knock on the door got her attention.

"Hi, Luke, Kyle. I'm so sorry. I didn't hear you come in. Please sit." She motioned to two chairs in front of her desk and took her seat behind it.

Kyle looked around for anything that might have changed since he had been there. The piles were bigger. That was about it.

It felt like the other shoe had finally dropped; they had been waiting for the Feds to call them. *It was probably a tactic*, Kyle thought. *Let time go by so we'll get comfortable. And then, boom!*

Anne cleared her throat. "So, Attorney Hartigan called me today, asking to meet to discuss their findings and how they wish to proceed."

Luke and Kyle were elated yet filled with a sense of dread. It seemed that their work and concerns were being seriously investigated.

"What is likely to happen at this meeting is that Attorney Hartigan will present the results of their investigation, including what Special Agents Dickey and Truman had discovered," Anne said. "I suspect that you think that Attorney Hartigan's investigation will validate your complaint and findings and that Hartigan, representing the United States government, will choose to proceed in a way that ends whatever scheme is occurring at Americare and bring President Dmopvup and hir accomplices to justice. That likely will not be the case. Hartigan is in an uncomfortable position—they're investigating serious complaints against the president and the federal government, but they have to act in a way that is in our government's best interest. This is the very definition of conflict of interest—representing the president while investigating complaints against hir. It's also an election year, and President Dmopvup is the incumbent, running for hir fourth term."

"How do you think Hartigan will choose to proceed?" Luke asked.

"I have absolutely no idea," Anne said. "Remember that no matter how much allegiance to your cause they appear to have, the government is on the government's side. They have unlimited resources, and they make the rules, yada, yada, yada. We also need to keep in mind that in the process of your investigation, you two, Michael, and Dr. Canteenwalla violated some patient-confidentiality statutes, and you broke several laws. Even though they agreed to afford you protection from criminal or other prosecution, this does not mean that our government condones these actions, however necessary they were. From a legal standpoint, this case is unique, but it's important to regard whatever Attorney Hartigan says from the perspective that the government is on the government's side."

Anne's comment caused Luke to roll his eyes, and she glared at him, though it was accompanied by a smile.

"OK. Is there anything we need to do to prepare for this meeting?" Luke asked.

"Just get a good night's sleep the night before the meeting. Try to relax between now and then, and, most importantly, do not discuss your complaint or anything that has to do with it with anyone."

"Agreed," Luke said, "and I'll continue to maintain utmost secrecy."

"Likewise," Kyle said.

"Any other questions?" Anne asked.

"Not right now," Luke said. "I'll call you if anything comes up between now and the meeting."

Although it was a long seven days until the meeting, that day came uneventfully. Kyle noticed that Luke looked tired, and Luke admitted he'd tossed and turned much of the night, worried about the uncertainties.

Luke and Kyle entered the conference room, and once again, Luke was seated across the large conference table from Attorney Hartigan, with Kyle seated to his right and Anne to his left. Special Agents Dickey and Truman and the stenographer were noticeably absent.

After they all were seated, Attorney Hartigan shuffled some papers, took a sip of water from a nearby glass, and then said, "Dr. Moses and Mx. Sanderson, I have asked you here today to put everything together about Dr. Moses's initial complaint and to make sure we are all clear with respect to what you reported. To that end, I will report what I understand to be the exact nature of your complaint. After I have finished, I will ask you if my understanding is accurate. I am requesting that you refrain from raising your hands or speaking until I have finished my presentation." Hartigan looked broadly around the room. "Please write down any questions you may have or any discrepancies that you perceive regarding my presentation and your complaint."

After a short pause, he said. "In February of last year, 2031, Dr. Moses contacted the Department of Health and Human Services online through their Fraud and Abuse reporting system. We subsequently met in this office to obtain information from you, and in the interim, between now and then, an official investigation occurred that involved Special

Agent Dickey from the Department of Health and Human Services, Special Agent Truman from the FBI, and me. We have concluded our investigation.

"The complaint centered on President Dmopvup and on Americare. Your complaint against Americare has three parts: First, you allege Americare improved quality metrics by altering the health and even causing the death of those patients with poorly controlled chronic illnesses, thus removing them from the Americare patient panel and from the quality metrics calculations. Second, you allege contributors to the Dmopvup Foundation were given special privileges, which included approval of medications and services that otherwise would have been denied, and you allege the use of the Americare health plan to bring harm and even death to other Americare patients selected by the contributors.

"Third, you allege contributors to the Dmopvup Foundation who required organ transplantation were granted preferential placement on the various organ transplantation lists, as well as the ability to select their organ donors from the panel of healthy Americare patients who were a match. In all cases, patients whose political leanings were believed to differ from those of President Dmopvup were chosen as organ donors first. Am I correct so far in stating the overall scope of your complaint?"

"Yes, so far this is correct," Luke said, as he squirmed uncomfortably in his seat.

"Next, I will go into the mechanics that you allege are being used to accomplish this," Attorney Hartigan said.

"This is the mechanism by which you allege that Americare is meeting these ends. The central parts of this plan involve Americare's Actuarial Department, the Americare Medical Record System, and the use of micro-implants and technology developed by Utopia Pharmaceuticals and its subsidiaries. It allegedly works as follows:

"First, AMRS has algorithms that developed an 'ideal patient panel,' which is a model representation of a panel of patients who, overall, are the healthiest; who would cost Americare the least to provide care for; and from whom, ideally, Americare would make the greatest profit. This panel is stratified by age, gender, race, disease state, degree of control of disease state, and political leanings. It indicates the ideal number of patients with every major disease under a specified degree of control. This 'ideal panel' was developed by AMRS and corroborated by the USPSTF and by Americare's team of actuaries.

"Second, AMRS has algorithms that select patients for elimination so that, by attrition, the Americare patient panel will approach that of the ideal panel, as determined by quality metrics and political affiliations. Third, micro-implants containing various infectious agents, medications, genetic material, biologic agents, and toxins are being implanted in selected patients under the guise of routine immunizations and screening procedures, as indicated by QR codes generated by AMRS. The content of each micro-implant is generated by the AMRS algorithms for each patient selected and is represented by QR codes that are generated by the algorithms. These QR codes are automatically sent to Utopia

Pharmaceuticals or one of its subsidiaries via the Americare Ordering System, or AOS, for manufacture and delivery to the appropriate practice for administration or placement within the patient.

"Lastly, you infer but don't directly allege that President Dmopvup is the sole beneficiary of the Dmopvup Foundation. Is my understanding of your complaint accurate, Dr. Moses?" Attorney Hartigan looked up from the conference table.

"Yes, it is." Luke looked at Kyle and then at Anne.

After briefly shuffling papers, Attorney Hartigan said, "Dr. Moses, I am going to ask you to withdraw your complaint."

Luke gasped audibly as his mouth dropped open and his eyes widened. Attorney Hartigan hadn't given a reason for hir statement, and ze phrased it as a request, as if it would be Luke's choice.

"What is your reasoning for this request?" Anne asked in her calm, professional manner.

"We did a detailed investigation of Americare and, to the best of our ability, President Dmopvup, and we found no evidence that supported Dr. Moses's complaint," Attorney Hartigan said. "Furthermore, in the process of obtaining information, Dr. Moses, Mx. Sanderson, Mx. Jude, and Dr. Canteenwalla broke the law. The fact that nothing was found in support of that complaint voids any promise of immunity from prosecution, civil or otherwise.

"We did find some issues within Americare that are less

than ideal, such as the need for process improvements, issues with statistical analysis, patients' access to all Americare's services, and patients' access and compliance to recommended immunizations and screening tests. Admittedly, Americare is not perfect; it is still having some growing pains and minor issues. Our investigation revealed, however, that, overall, Americare is functioning exactly as it was hoped it would.

The government is prepared to offer Dr. Moses and Mx. Sanderson a settlement in exchange for Dr. Moses dismissing his complaint."

Luke shot up from his seat. "Absolutely not!"

Anne firmly grabbed his arm and brought him back down to his seat.

Attorney Hartigan was calm. "Dr. Moses and Mx. Sanderson, it is your right to waive an explanation of the settlement that we are prepared to offer you. I strongly suggest you listen to the terms of the settlement before making your decision. If you choose to waive the offer, we will continue the case and convene a grand jury to obtain indictments against both of you, Mx. Jude, and Dr. Canteenwalla for violation of patient privacy laws, among other things. Is it still your wish to waive the explanation of the settlement and pursue your complaint?"

Luke, Kyle, and Anne whispered to one another.

"We wish to hear what the government is prepared to offer," Anne said.

"In exchange for Dr. Moses withdrawing hir complaint,

and for both Dr. Moses and Mx. Sanderson agreeing never to discuss or reveal this settlement in any fashion, we are prepared to do the following: First, we will offer Dr. Moses and Mx. Sanderson high-level administrative positions within the Americare organization. The rationale behind this is that you both would be best able to affect changes in Americare from inside the organization, and you are both exceptional providers who place patients' needs and health above all other concerns. Second, we will offer you each a financial settlement of $500,000 as a sign-on bonus if you accept the offered positions within Americare.

"Third, we will waive any prosecution from any entity—criminal, civil, or otherwise—for Dr. Moses, Mx. Sanderson, Mx. Jude, and Dr. Canteenwalla. In order to fully meet the requirements of the settlement, Dr. Moses and Mx. Sanderson would be required to publicly withdraw their complaint, stating that they misinterpreted Americare's statistics, that Americare is providing exceptional care to patients, and that they both plan on joining Americare as executives to make things even better. Do you understand the terms of the settlement being offered to you?"

Anne nodded. "Yes. We would like a day or two to discuss this and review our options."

"Very well. Attorney Wilson, I expect to receive, in writing, Dr. Moses's intention to accept the settlement within the next forty-eight hours. Are there any further questions?"

Anne had to restrain and shush Luke. "No," she said.

"Our meeting is adjourned."

Attorney Hartigan walked back to hir office for an appointment ze had scheduled the day before with Special Agent Truman. From Special Agent Truman's perspective, the case was cut-and-dried. Hir decision-making processes were always nonpartisan and based solely upon the facts. Ze fully expected that Attorney Hartigan would concur with hir interpretation of the facts.

Special Agent Truman believed Dr. Moses and Kyle. Ze thought that the federal government might have initiated a process in which the government, along with the plaintiff—Luke—initiated a civil action against the defendants for losses sustained by the plaintiff because of the defendant's actions. Initially, the nature and existence of the complaint would be kept secret and under seal, as this complaint was, but ze was not sure how this could be accomplished, with the government essentially investigating itself. This would be similar to a qui tam, in which a whistleblower, along with the United States government, files a civil action against the whistleblower's employer for fraud and/or abuse reported by the whistleblower. The whistleblower would then be entitled to some degree of legal protection, as well as a percentage of any monetary penalties levied on the defendants, if the qui tam proved successful.

Attorney Hartigan arrived at hir office, reviewed a few things that were sitting on hir desk, took a few deep breaths, and entered the waiting area, where Special Agent Truman was seated. Ze immediately stood and walked toward hir office.

"Saffron, come on in," Attorney Hartigan said.

Silently but swiftly, Special Agent Truman entered and sat down across from hir.

"Coffee?" Attorney Hartigan asked.

"No, thank you," Special Agent Truman said.

"As you are aware, I met with Dr. Moses and Mx. Sanderson with their counsel present. I informed them that if Dr. Moses chooses to proceed with hir complaint, it would likely be a rough road, given the nature of the complaint and the defendants. I implied this might prove to be a life-changing event for hir and Mx. Sanderson and likely would not result in the outcome they were hoping for. I did give Dr. Moses an option to withdraw hir complaint in exchange for a settlement."

"On what grounds did you recommend against hir proceeding with hir complaint?" Special Agent Truman asked.

"On the grounds that after an exhaustive review of your investigation and the investigation by Special Agent Dickey, there was no credible evidence to support the claims made in hir complaint."

Special Agent Truman was flabbergasted. "A couple of days ago, when I reviewed the results of my investigation with you one final time, you agreed that the evidence provided was credible. What happened between then and now?"

"In the review of all the evidence provided to me, I

found no credible evidence supporting the claims that Dr. Moses made in hir complaint," Hartigan repeated.

"What about the documentation found in the medical records of the individual patients, notably in AMRS, that ze presented that support hir complaint?" Special Agent Truman said. "What about the links between AMRS and the official medical records and documentation of the use of the Dmopvup Foundation to buy medical services, cause harm to other patients, purchase positions on the transplantation list, and select organ donors from the pool of living Americare patients? What about all the AMRS algorithms that decide which patients needed to be eliminated and their modes of death and the algorithm that generates the QR codes for the poisons, infectious materials, and drugs that kill them?"

"Upon further review of the medical records, AMRS added no new information to that which was included in the practice's medical records. The information from AMRS that Dr. Moses cited in hir complaint was not found in AMRS," Attorney Hartigan said.

"What about the testimony of Mx. Michael Jude? Dr. Canteenwalla?"

"We have been unable to locate Dr. Canteenwalla, and Mx. Jude is under investigation for conspiracy to defraud our government. We did obtain Mx. Jude's deposition."

This is very strange—and even scary, Special Agent Truman thought. "With all due respect, Attorney Hartigan, I saw this evidence firsthand. I saw the medical records. I saw the QR codes. I personally matched up the QR codes with the drugs, infectious agents, and so on, and I reviewed the documentation in AMRS that clearly indicated exactly what Dr. Moses outlined in hir complaint. Now you are telling me that this evidence is gone?"

"No, I am telling you that this evidence never existed."

Silence filled the room.

Special Agent Truman now had a good idea about what was transpiring, yet ze didn't know how to react or what ze should say and do. Ze had just realized that President Dmopvup had weaponized the United States Department of Justice, the mainstream media, and perhaps other agencies and organizations to obtain the outcome ze desired. In the instant ze had this epiphany, Special Agent Truman realized that this explained the outcomes of several other procedures and processes involving the Department of Justice. Ze also surmised that this was likely how Jommesa Sufjen Dmopvup had been elected president in 2020 and how legislation had happened that permitted hir to run for a fourth presidential term. Special Agent Truman felt entirely betrayed by the very government that ze put hir life on the line to serve.

CHAPTER 26

The walk from the Federal Building to the car was a quiet one. Luke and Kyle remained silent, and Anne didn't encourage any discussion until the three were out of earshot of anyone associated with the Federal Building.

"Let's go to my office," Anne said.

Kyle drove, and no one spoke until they arrived at Anne's office fifteen minutes later.

"Would you like anything to drink?" Anne asked. "Coffee, tea, water, or soft drinks?"

"How about a scotch?" Luke asked with a smirk. His face was beet-red.

As if not surprised, Anne opened a small cabinet behind her desk that revealed a bottle of Glenlivet French Oak twelve-year-old scotch, among other spirits, as well as some glasses.

"Not for me; I don't drink much," Anne said. "Would you like a scotch, Kyle?

"Hell yeah."

Anne poured three scotches, deciding at the last minute that this situation warranted a belt or two. By the time Anne and Kyle had taken their first sips, Luke had asked for another drink.

"I cannot believe Hartigan's findings and the audacity of his offering us settlements," Luke said, "Hartigan was

any further will be at your own risk and peril—and at Kyle's, Michael's, and Andy's. I'm certain that if you do not dismiss the complaint, your lives will become uncomfortable, and you will possibly be in danger. The government is exceptionally good at ensuring its privacy and its appearances, and it has extraordinarily little concern for the welfare of anyone who threatens it, regardless of the reason. Right or wrong has nothing to do with how the government acts. It's immaterial. This is how our federal government does its business."

"May I speak with Kyle alone for a few minutes?" Luke asked.

"Certainly. Poke your head out the door when you're done and help yourself to more scotch—but not so much that it clouds your judgment." Anne got up quietly and left the room.

Luke pulled his chair close to Kyle's and put his arm around him. "What should I do?" Luke asked.

"Remember Sean MacDonald, Lorraine Simons, Scott Smith, Carla Dossier, Michael Thomas, Lester Blumenthal, Trinh Nguyen, and Doris Chapin," Kyle said. "Remember Americare's ongoing process of culling out the sick and killing them automatically as determined by AMRS algorithms. Think about Rahim Abdikarim, who paid, via contributions to the Dmopvup Foundation, to have Michael Thomas killed for his liver. Think about his wife who lost her husband and his kids who lost their father. Think about other Dmopvup Foundation contributors who bought their way to the top of the transplant lists, bumping others farther down the list, only to die while waiting. Remember those Dmopvup Foundation contributors who purchased their organs from the population of healthy, living Americare patients of opposing political viewpoints and had them killed. Remember those unwitting organ donors whose lives were lost in this process.

"All of that will continue if you withdraw your complaint, which would represent your tacit approval of all of this. You—we—would have to live with the knowledge that we were permitting this to continue. We would be just as evil as the president and our government are because we would profit by allowing this to go on. We each would get half a million in cash and cushy, high-paying administrative positions within Americare in exchange for withdrawing the complaint. We would then be a part of these schemes.

"Luke, the official decision is yours to make, and I support whatever decision you make. I'm willing to give up everything, however, including my life, to put an end to this and to bring those responsible to justice. Unfortunately, you're making a decision that affects me, Andy, and Michael as well. Knowing Michael as I do, I can say with confidence that he would agree with me. I would guess Andy would feel the same way. What are your thoughts and feelings?"

"I feel the same way as you do," Luke said. "I just wanted to make certain I took your feelings into account prior to declining the settlement. I love you so very much, Kyle. I resent the fact I have put you in harm's way when I should be protecting you."

"I feel safe in your arms, Luke, no matter what happens to me and us."

Luke stood up and pulled Kyle from his seat and into his arms. He held him tightly and kissed him. "I love you, Kyle," he said again.

"I'm with you, Luke. Somehow, we'll get through this."

Luke poked his head out of the office door.

Anne returned and sat down at her desk. "What have you decided?"

"I've decided not to withdraw my complaint and not to accept their settlement," Luke said, while holding Kyle's hand. "I wish to proceed with my complaint."

Anne looked up through her glasses at Luke and then Kyle. "That's what I thought you would do," she said with an accepting smile. "I'll call Hartigan now and tell him, if that's OK with you."

"Sure," Luke said.

A few minutes later, Anne had Attorney Hartigan on speakerphone.

"Are you certain this is how you wish to proceed?" Attorney Hartigan asked Luke.

"I'm entirely certain," Luke said.

"You will need to submit that in writing. After I receive it by fax, the complaint will be unsealed and will percolate through the court system. You will be notified about what you will need to do and when you will need to do it. There will be a press release," Hartigan said. "Assuming I receive your statement declining the settlement and citing your intent to pursue your complaint today, the press release will occur tomorrow. Please keep in mind that this is an irreversible decision that will greatly affect your lives, as well as the lives of others. I do advise against this course of action. I am asking you to reconsider your position, Dr. Moses, as most people who decline settlements rarely do well in court, and their lives and the lives of others are often irrevocably changed. Withdrawal of your complaint and acceptance of the settlement would put you in the best position to affect and realize the changes that you think are necessary within Americare, without resulting in any harm."

"I have considered the settlement, and I have decided to decline it and to pursue my complaint," Luke said.

"Very well. Once I receive your letter via fax, I will have the complaint unsealed and authorize the press release. Please send me your original letter by courier."

"We will take care of that today," Anne said. "Thank you."

Attorney Hartigan had already hung up the phone.

Anne then produced a letter addressed to Attorney Hartigan, indicating Luke's intent to decline any settlements and to pursue his complaint. Luke signed it, and Anne's secretary notarized it and faxed it. A copy was made for Anne's records. Anne gave Kyle and Luke a copy; then she called a courier to take the original signed document to Hartigan. Anne instructed Luke and Kyle to keep the letter out of sight and to lock it away for safekeeping.

"Now, get ready for a very rough and unpredictable ride," Anne said. "Rely on each other and on me for support. I must tell you that I have no idea how this will go. Please be incredibly careful, and trust no one, not even Michael and Andy—you never know what the government might be offering them. Try not to go out alone, and avoid the press, if they approach you. If you've been looking for a reason for Kyle to move in with you, this is it.

"Totally off the record, keeping a loaded .45 in my nightstand brought me peace of mind during a time when I was dealing with a lot of uncertainty and when I felt I could not trust anyone. If that works for you, do it. In New Hampshire, you don't need a license to have a gun in your home or to even carry it outside the home. You can walk into a gun shop, choose your weapon, fill out one sheet of paper, and provide your driver's license. This is faxed to the state. If your background is clean, you can walk out of the shop with a gun in fifteen to twenty minutes. Just something to consider. Whatever makes you feel safe. Any questions or concerns?"

"No questions, lots of concerns," Kyle said.

Anne grinned. "I have no doubt about that. You have my cell number, and you may call me twenty-four/seven. Luke, does your house have a security system?"

"Yes, it does, with perimeter cameras and motion sensors that turn the floodlights on."

"Excellent. You're in good shape. Try to live your life as normally as possible. In all seriousness, Kyle, you should move in with Luke today—my orders. Tomorrow, when you wake up, both of you will likely be on the news, the press may haunt you, and patients and coworkers will ask you lots of questions. Your employer may put you on paid leave for your protection and in the interest of keeping things running smoothly at the practice. That would be ideal, but don't request that. Roll with the punches and rely on each other for comfort and advice. Have faith in a higher power of some sort. If you're religious, prayer goes an awfully long way. Keep in mind that no matter what happens, tomorrow will always come, and things always work out, albeit not necessarily the way we plan."

CHAPTER 27

Luke took Anne's advice. He swung by Kyle's apartment after leaving her office so that Kyle could pack some of his things and move in with him. Luke was happy with this requirement, partially hiding his happiness under the guise of Anne's order. He knew they were teetering on the brink of something new and big for them, and he was aware that Michael's and Andy's lives would be affected as well. He felt guilty that they had been dragged into this and that neither one could be afforded any advance notice of what might transpire.

Luke decided to stop at the grocery store and stock up on a lot of nonperishable food items and supplies, as if getting ready for a nor'easter during winter. They were preparing for the worst-case scenario: being forced to remain in their home because of the press and other attention. All along, they wondered if they might be making more of this than it would turn out to be. Someday, they might laugh about how they had decided to stock up unnecessarily. Deep down, however, each knew this would not be the case.

By the time they made it to Luke's house, it was early evening. They put the groceries and supplies away, threw some burgers on the grill, and then ate supper and tried to relax. At around nine o'clock, they decided to go to bed, not solely because they were tired. Tomorrow was a workday, and they knew they would find comfort in each other's arms.

Despite this comfort, they had a relatively sleepless night. They managed to doze off around 3:00 a.m., only to be awakened at their usual time of 5:30 a.m. Luke hit the snooze button for another fifteen minutes but lay awake, looking forward to the day at work with excitement and dread.

It was a beautiful April Fools' Day morning, 2032, and Kyle and Luke had their morning coffee out on the patio in the quiet calm of Luke's wooded yard. The birds were chirping, the squirrels were scurrying about, and the sun rose and blanketed them with its comforting warmth and strength. Cautiously, Kyle and Luke scoured Facebook and the local and national news on the internet to see if the press release had occurred. Seeing nothing, they turned on the television and watched the morning news.

Luke and Kyle were socially liberal and fiscally more conservative; neither fell in lockstep with any political party. "Life Free or Die" and "Live and Let Live" accurately described them both. President Dmopvup and hir administration had mandated access to health care for everyone, and it was affordable. Luke and Kyle, however, could not support the way in which health care was being delivered and the use of Americare for Dmopvup's political and financial gain at the expense of patients' lives. The *ist* angle of identity politics had rendered everyone their own oppressed minority, who are entitled to universal and unrequested government validation, intrusion, and financial compensation. This had created a country of victims who were becoming increasingly more beholden to a government that was killing them off at the pleasure of the president.

Increasingly, Luke and Kyle began to feel as if the only permanent way to end President Dmopvup's scheme of using Americare to cause patient harm and death would be to educate the public about what had been going on and have faith that the public would use their power on election day to cause hir defeat. Unfortunately, the other viable party's candidate, John Doe, was a relative unknown. His platform was one of fairness and equality of opportunity for all, regardless of the boundaries established by the identity politicians who were currently in office.

President Dmopvup ran hir campaign by suggesting that because John Doe was a middle-aged, white, married, straight male, he was, of necessity, an *ist* (racist, sexist, a misogynist, xenophobic, and homophobic), and anyone who voted for him was, of necessity, also an *ist*. This mentality of identity politics had always been successfully wielded by the Democrats during all of the recent election cycles.

"It would be ideal if we could reach out to John Doe and tell him what we know about President Dmopvup and Americare," Luke said to Kyle as they sat peacefully on the patio. "Unfortunately, he would likely think we were psycho, and no doubt the Dmopvup campaign and our government would promote that line of thinking. We would also be voiding any protection that might be afforded to us, Michael, and Andy and risk thwarting our own efforts to bring the Americare scheme to an end and President Dmopvup to justice."

"Yeah," Kyle said. "I hope to God our efforts result in the public revelation of how President Dmopvup has been harming patients. If nothing else, that would be my personal goal—to provide information to the public and allow our citizens to exercise well-informed votes to bring this scheme and President Dmopvup's presidency to an end."

Despite their strong feelings regarding the Americare scheme, both Kyle and Luke had become quite fatigued from dealing with it. Nothing could be more welcome for them than to return to a normal life. They were hoping to seek refuge at work, hoping to bury themselves in their normal work routines to restore overall normalcy. They were able to do this for a part of the day, and they were able to forget about things entirely for a bit.

Around noon, Kyle spied two men wearing dark suits; they showed up in the office, asking to meet with Michael. After waiting for fifteen minutes, they were escorted into his office by Alex, Michael's secretary. Shortly thereafter, the two men and Michael left the office, with Michael's hands zip-tied behind him. This was promptly followed by an email from Dr. Weinberg, explaining to everyone in the office that Michael was no longer working there. Luke's and Kyle's hearts jumped into their throats; they couldn't help but believe this was related to Luke's complaint.

Then, Luke and Kyle received an email from Dr. Weinberg, requesting their presence in his office immediately.

Dr. Weinberg was visibly upset when he asked the two to sit. "I received a call from Kupevjep Hsacis a half an hour ago," he said. "Ze was officially notified about the complaint that you, Luke, filed against Americare and even against

President Dmopvup. Ze is beside hirself and is incredibly angry with you both, and I am too. I was subsequently instructed by our central office to suspend you both with full pay because, given the nature of the complaint, neither of you can care for Americare patients until this complaint is formally investigated. I was also instructed not to engage you in any discussion regarding the complaint. I need your ID badges, and you are to leave the office by the back door. Take the stairs to the parking garage, not the elevator to the lobby, as security has informed me that members of the press are waiting for you."

With hands shaking, Kyle and Luke handed over their ID badges and got up to leave.

"What happened to Michael?" Kyle asked. "He was escorted out of the office by two men in suits, and it looked like he was cuffed."

"The FBI took Michael into custody," Dr. Weinberg said, his voice quivering. "No reason was given. Please—just leave the office now."

Luke and Kyle did as they were instructed. They managed to avoid the press by taking the stairs to the parking garage, which was underneath the building. As they left, they drove by a large scrum of reporters hovering at the front door of the building, and they saw news media trucks in front of the building.

They managed to drive off without being noticed. It was likely that the press was too intent on getting into Primary Care Associates' third-floor office to be the first to interview Luke and Kyle.

They drove off toward Luke's home, hoping to arrive there undetected. They were grateful they had gone to the grocery store the night before. After a couple of minutes of driving silently, Kyle took hold of Luke's hand.

"I love you, Luke."

Luke squeezed Kyle's hand and stroked his fingers with his thumb.

As Luke drove, Kyle searched the internet tentatively. He fumbled with his phone with his free hand, and after a few minutes, he found what he was looking for.

The headline read: PHYSICIAN FILES COMPLAINT WITH HHS AGAINST AMERICARE. It was dated that day – April 1, 2032, and the press release read:

> On February 27, 2031, a Granite Ridge, New Hampshire, physician, Lucas Moses, MD, filed a complaint with the US Department of Health and Human Services through their Fraud and Abuse reporting system. In the complaint, Dr. Moses alleges that Americare is being used to cause harm and death to some of their patients for the personal and political benefit of the health plan, its administration, and President Dmopvup. The complaint was initially filed under seal, and it was unsealed on March 31, 2032.

Assistant US Attorney Arthur P. Hartigan stated in the release that hir office would oversee the investigation and the prosecution of this case, if warranted.

The press release was rather benign, and it was written

in a rather small and innocuous font, seemingly with the hope of minimizing its notice. A benign press release was likely not enough to pull something like this along under the radar. Luke also looked at the website of their local news. The story had made its way there too, but it just parroted the official press release.

They decided to drive around the block one time to ensure they wouldn't be accosted when they entered Luke's driveway. Fortunately, and surprisingly, they did not see anyone waiting. Rather than drive around the block once more, Luke pulled into the driveway and into the garage. After he closed the garage door behind them, Luke took a few deep breaths and gathered his feelings and thoughts. Then they headed inside.

Luke thought it would be a good idea to call Anne and let her know what was happening. When he looked at his phone, he noticed she had already called a couple of times and had left one voice mail. He listened to her message, which informed him of what he already knew about the press release. She did request that he return her call to let her know how things were going, which he did.

Anne asked if the three of them could chat for a few minutes, so Luke put the call on the speakerphone.

"So now the complaint is out," Anne said. "It will be interesting and very telling to see what happens next. The government always has a plan when they release any information to the press, mainly to present the government's position in the most positive light. I doubt this is all we will hear, and I'm expecting more from the government within the next week or so. I just want to reiterate the importance of not saying anything to anyone. Members of the press are excellent at getting people to inadvertently disclose information. You each need to memorize a stock answer for whenever anyone asks you about the complaint. Present that answer automatically and without thinking about it. Do you have any questions or concerns?"

"We were both suspended from work, with pay, for the duration of the investigation," Luke said. "I guess that's a good thing. I'm not sure what I'll do to keep myself from going crazy without work."

"That is a good thing," Anne said. "Lay low, watch, and listen to the news, and keep your ear to the ground. Make sure no one is trespassing on your property. Keep yourselves safe, and call me any time, twenty-four/seven, with any concerns or questions. Let's plan a meeting on Friday, April 12, around noon. I'll come by your house, so you won't have to go out and risk encountering the press. These are uncharted waters for all of us, including me. We need to rely on each other for support.

"You both are very courageous. You could have simply withdrawn your complaint and headed off into the sunset with cushy jobs, great salaries, and half a million dollars in each of your pockets. You are willing to forgo the money, cushy jobs, and security to fight for what is right. This was an easy decision for you both. From the beginning, this whole thing has been about protecting all patients from harm, bringing an end to the schemes you discovered, ensuring that each patient receives the best of care, and bringing all parties responsible to justice.

"I find it extremely hard to believe that no one other than the two of you realized an increase in the number of their Americare patients who experienced adverse events, bad outcomes, and even deaths. When you raised your concerns at the monthly department meeting in October 2030, Luke, no one, aside from Kyle, acknowledged similar experiences. Reviewing the list of those Americare patients who died during the past three years revealed that other providers had similar patient experiences, but no one other than you chose to ask what was going on here, why it was occurring, or—most importantly—what they could do to fix this. It is highly likely that your colleagues recognize the benefits that they are receiving because of Americare, especially their increase in compensation.

"All physicians—and physician assistants, I believe—swear to the Hippocratic oath, one of the cornerstones of which is, 'Do no harm.' You are both true healers in the Hippocratic sense, something that, in my opinion, is sorely lacking in our health care system. Keep this in mind during the times of certain stress that lie ahead and remind yourselves of the number of patients you'll be sparing computer-algorithm–generated bad outcomes or death by virtue of your sacrifices."

"I feel like going to my camp up north," Luke said. "I'm always at peace when I'm up there."

"Then go. Just make sure we can reach each other by phone, twenty-four/seven, and that you can get back here within a day or so."

"One thing I want to do is find out how Andy, Dr. Canteenwalla, is doing," Luke said. "I'm concerned because I haven't heard anything from him for a while. I really want to call him, but Attorney Hartigan said I can't do that. It's possible that Andy was also questioned by Attorney Hartigan and told not to communicate with me."

"I also haven't heard anything about or from Michael," Kyle chimed in. "I guess that this isn't surprising, given his arrest. I would like to know how he's doing too. I just feel so guilty, and I pray both are OK."

"You head up to the camp today or tomorrow. You deserve tranquility, peace, and quiet. I'll try to find out how Andy and Michael are doing, and I'll let you know what I hear. Let's scratch our plans for a meeting on April 12, then. We should talk daily, though. OK?"

"Sure thing, Anne, and thank you," Luke said. "We will keep in touch."

Anne hung up the phone, and Luke and Kyle eagerly packed their stuff into Kyle's car.

CHAPTER 28

After talking with Anne, Kyle felt better. Even though he and Luke had extreme anxiety, they consoled each other, knowing that no matter the outcome, they had done the right thing by reporting.

Luke frowned as he looked out the kitchen window. "Did you see that?"

Kyle nodded. "Red Toyota, looking pretty beat. Twice."

Luke grunted. "Probably the press."

Kyle agreed. "The government has better cars. But still, it's too damn close. We need a better plan because this isn't going to cut it when they get more aggressive."

"Well, it's getting late," Luke said. He turned on the home security system, the perimeter cameras, and the motion-sensor–controlled perimeter floodlights. He kissed Kyle good night and went to bed.

At eleven o'clock, he was awakened by the quiet alarm on his phone, indicating activation of the perimeter floods. The video had recorded a small bear trying to get at the bird feeder. In the distance, one of the cars that had been driving by was clearly parked, with the driver and passenger still inside. It was a silver-colored sedan. Although a bear was common in Luke's neighborhood, an occupied parked car on the street was not. Kyle was sound asleep, lying on Luke's right arm. Luke decided to let him sleep. He put the phone back down on the pillow and cradled Kyle's back against his chest. He kissed his ear and cheek and whispered, "I love you." He then fell asleep.

Luke awoke at 5:30 a.m. The sun was shining through the bedroom window, heralding what he hoped would be a happy and peaceful day. He reviewed the alarm data from the night, which revealed only that the car had remained occupied and parked on the street throughout the night. Luke crawled back into bed, kissed Kyle awake, and explained the recorded events of the night, trying not to upset him.

Kyle was a lot tougher than Luke gave him credit for, and in many ways, he was stronger than Luke. Nonetheless, Luke was nurturing and protective of Kyle in a sweet and loving way.

They got out of bed, and Luke turned the TV on while getting ready for the day. Kyle scoured the internet on his phone for anything new about Luke's complaint, hoping to find nothing. Finding nothing new, they breathed sighs of relief, showered, and ate a hearty breakfast of bacon and eggs together. This time, they avoided the patio for fear of being accosted by the press, who, they were sure, would trespass on Luke's property to get an interview. They sat together at the dining room table and ate while they discussed plans for the future.

"I love to camp," Luke said. "Even though the thought of going into the woods for a camping trip with you appeals to me on many levels, the goal of this trip is much more than for our enjoyment. I plan on us disappearing without a trace. We can keep track of the outside world via judicious use of our cell phones and laptops. We will move around and change our location after we use them to avoid being located and pestered by the press."

"This will also afford us some welcome peace and quiet," Kyle said.

Many a hiker and camper had lost themselves in the woods of the North Country, and many of the inexperienced had lost their lives too. Luke knew the North Country like the back of his hand and was convinced that he and Kyle could remain completely hidden up there.

They decided to head out after breakfast in Kyle's Jeep, with Luke driving, as he knew the way. As expected, the silver-colored sedan was still there. As Kyle's red Jeep Wrangler pulled out of the driveway, the silver sedan followed them. They hoped to lose it between the house and the camp in Pittsburg, but they would be fine if they didn't. The woods of the North Country would provide them safe refuge, and Luke was confident they could give the car the slip.

The car followed them as far as Plymouth, and then it peeled off at an exit, not to be seen for the remainder of the drive. Luke surmised that the occupants of the vehicle were Feds, and that the driver had likely run out of gas, given the presumed poor fuel efficiency of the large sedan and the miles driven.

"I'm so glad we got the hell out of there and were able to give those goons the slip," Kyle said.

Luke took his right hand off the wheel, grabbed Kyle's left hand, and lovingly caressed Kyle's fingers with his thumb. "I feel entirely free," Luke said. "Finally, I feel as if we're free and safe. Things are just starting, and I think we'll both feel better at my camp. It's been in my family since I was a kid. I spent many weeks there while growing up. I learned how to hunt, fish, and camp up there, and I learned wilderness survival skills. My dad was quite an outdoorsperson. My dad taught me a lot. The camp was his favorite place in the entire world. Since his death eight years ago, I have tried to get up there as often as I can. To me, Dad still lives there, and I feel a connection to him when I'm there, as well as a strong sense of safety. It's as if all my troubles disappear, and life is put into a healthier and simpler perspective. Solutions to my problems then just seem to come to me."

As they drove north, Luke and Kyle shared information about their pasts and discussed their hopes for the future. The three-hour drive to Pittsburg seemed to pass in a matter of minutes. Before they knew it, they were traveling along a bumpy dirt road through the woods. Luke knew that road well. He knew every bump, twist, and bend. As he neared the camp, a feeling of warmth came over him, as if the camp were welcoming him and Kyle home.

The camp was quite simple: a small, rustic log cabin with three bedrooms. It did have rudimentary electrical service and could be heated by electricity, LP gas, or wood.

There was a backup generator in case the electricity was interrupted, which happened often when severe weather downed the power lines. Fortunately, there was cell phone service, as noted by a couple of cell towers nearby. This allowed internet access, albeit spotty and not entirely dependable.

Most areas of the North Country did not have cell service or any access to the internet, and it was a certainty there would be no such services once Kyle and Luke were deep in the wilderness. Water was supplied by a well, which required manual pumping, and the cabin had a composting toilet system that was in good condition. The entire property was on two hundred acres of mostly wooded forest on a gentle mountain slope. At the base of the slope was a river, which was also part of the property.

After they unpacked the Jeep, they decided they should call Anne to see if anything new was happening. They set Luke's phone on the rustic wooden table in the family room of the cabin and plugged it into one of two electrical outlets in the room. Amazingly, the cellular signal was strong. With some degree of apprehension, Luke called Anne. As Anne's phone was ringing, Luke put his arm around Kyle and pulled him close.

"Hi, Luke and Kyle," Anne said. Luke had put her on speaker. "How are you doing?" Her voice was quieter than usual. Luke and Kyle could tell something was amiss.

"We're doing well," Luke said. "I'm feeling much better since coming up here, and we've been here for only about an hour or so."

"That's good. Listen, I must tell you something. Andy's dead. I don't have all the details, but he was struck by a car while walking in a parking lot in Boston the night before last. He was heading to his car after attending a conference on forensic pathology. He was found by a lot attendant yesterday morning, and he was pronounced dead at the scene. They have no clues as to who might be responsible for his death. I'm so deeply sorry, Luke. I know how close the two of you were. I feel awful. If there's anything I can do, please let me know."

For a split second, Luke's heart stopped. He was saddened beyond tears. Ever since the death of his wife, however, he had kept his emotions buried deep inside, and he found it difficult to cry. He managed to say, "Even though it could've been a hit-and-run, I cannot help but feel that his death was my fault."

"There's no way for you to know that Luke," Kyle said.

"He was killed in a parking lot in a not-so-nice area of Boston," Anne said. "Robbery may have been the motive, but any information regarding motive has not been released. In any event, please be careful. It may be that Andy's death is unrelated to your complaint but continue to remain suspicious of others."

That was the last time Luke ever spoke to Anne about Andy's death.

After hanging up the phone, Luke and Kyle decided they would start their trek into the woods early the next morning.

There were several backpacks in the cabin, as well as various supplies and utensils used for camping: pots and pans, a small portable stove, portable yet powerful LED lanterns, dehydrated meals, canteens for water, tents, sleeping bags, and space blankets.

When they had arrived at the camp, Luke had plugged in the chargers for the LED lanterns, phones, laptops, and spare battery packs. Now, they filled the canteens with potable water from the well. They both chose what to bring on their trip and transferred their clothing from their suitcases to the backpacks. By the time they were done packing and preparing, it was 10:00 p.m., and all their batteries and electronic devices were fully charged. They were tired and planned to get up around 4:00 a.m., so they decided to go to bed.

Before retiring, Luke thought they should peruse the internet and look for any reference to Andy's death. Kyle used his phone to do the search, fully aware he could be located by triangulation. They thought this risk was worth taking, and it proved to be.

In large headlines on all US media outlets was something similar to the following:

ARREST WARRANT ISSUED FOR NEW HAMPSHIRE PHYSICIAN AND PHYSICIAN ASSISTANT INVOLVED IN AMERICARE CONSPIRACY COMPLAINT

Luke was stunned once again. Rather than try to read any of the articles, he chose to view the press conference. He thought it odd that it was run by FBI Director Kenit Duniz. US Attorney General Musivve Mapdj and Assistant US Attorney Hartigan were standing on either side.

"After careful consideration of all the evidence provided, we have sufficient evidence implicating Dr. Lucas Moses and physician assistant Mx. Kyle Sanderson in the violations of patient privacy laws, as well as for conspiracy to defraud the United States government," Attorney General Mapdj said. "Their licenses to practice medicine have been revoked. We have issued warrants for their arrest, as well as a $100,000 reward for assistance in the apprehension of each party."

There were some questions from the media after the press conference, yet more prominent was the number of people in the audience who expressed anger at Luke and Kyle. A few people who were interviewed expressed their concerns that Luke and Kyle may have betrayed the citizenry and put the health plan's viability in jeopardy, thus risking its ability to continue to improve the health of the citizenry at a nominal cost to them.

"We're leaving here now," Luke said.

They gathered their backpacks and other supplies, turned off all the lights in the cabin, ditched Kyle's Jeep and covered it with brush, and headed on their way.

CHAPTER 29

Luke and Kyle entered the woods of far northern New Hampshire and hiked throughout the night. It was early in April 2032, which guaranteed cool days and cold, brisk nights, and an early spring snowfall was also possible. The moon was almost full, so the visibility was excellent without using their lanterns, which saved their battery life considerably. They took a fifteen-minute break every couple of hours or so and made certain they maintained adequate hydration. They were not alone in the woods; in fact, they were guests among its permanent inhabitants.

Luke was extremely comfortable in the wilderness. Kyle was a bit less so. Luke had the advantage of knowing the woods, and he was familiar with all its denizens, most of whom came out at night.

During their trek, they came upon several black bears that were out foraging, many raccoons, opossum, moose, and coyotes. They were also the audience to the blood-curdling shrieks of fisher cats, which were plentiful throughout New Hampshire. Many whitetail deer, being crepuscular, heralded the onset of dawn.

They found a clearing and decided to set up camp for a couple of hours to eat breakfast and to get some sleep. They pitched their tents and rolled out their sleeping bags. One tent was for storage of their gear, and the other was their shelter. Luke prepared some dehydrated eggs and dehydrated fruit for breakfast, bringing them to life with the addition of water and heat. They'd brought enough dehydrated food to last around two months or so; they assumed they'd obtain additional protein through fishing and fresh greens by foraging for edible plants.

After breakfast, Kyle went on watch for the first two hours, allowing Luke time to sleep. After two hours, Luke awoke refreshed and spelled Kyle from his watch, allowing him to get some sleep too. Kyle immediately fell into the most relaxing, deep sleep he'd had in the past year. Upon awakening, he was rejuvenated and ready to continue.

It took only fifteen minutes to pack up their camp and to make sure they didn't leave any traces of themselves when they left. The sun was well up in the sky, but it had been a cool night and morning. They continued their trek throughout the day and night, stopping periodically for rest and food.

Late at night, they again pitched their tents and took turns sleeping. They felt comfortable and safe in the woods and not at all alone. After eating breakfast in the early morning, they again broke camp and continued their journey. They repeated this ritual for about two months, each enjoying the care and comfort of the other and the northern New Hampshire woods. After two months' time both sporting full beards, which aided in any disguise. They were aware that their supply of dehydrated food was running low and that they would soon need to return to the cabin to restock their supplies.

One morning in early June, their routine was disrupted. After breaking camp and eliminating any traces of themselves, the two followed the winding course of a small stream, flanked on either side by mountains. Kyle inhaled deeply through his nose and stopped. He put out his hand for Luke, who also froze. Turning, he jerked his head to the left, and Luke nodded. Kyle touched his nose and mouthed "fire." Luke nodded again. They climbed up one side of the mountain, and when they reached its summit, they saw a small log cabin down in the valley below, with smoke curling from its chimney.

"Do you know of anyone who lives out here?" Kyle asked Luke.

"Nope. There are likely more than a few folks who live out here in the woods, though, preferring to live off the grid and respectfully live off the land," Luke said.

"What should we do?"

"We're down to the last bit of our dehydrated food," Luke said. "Seeing that no one else is around here, and we have no idea if or when we will encounter anyone else, why don't we knock on the door and see who lives there? Whoever they are, likely would be off the grid and may not have access to the news. We do need to be prepared for the possibility we'll be greeted by the barrel end of a gun—folks in the North Country, especially out here, can be rather suspicious of flatlanders, however innocuous they may appear. In the interest of our safety, we should use aliases."

They continued toward the cabin, which, although it looked nearby, was a mile or so away.

They arrived at the front of the cabin. Someone was living there, as evidenced by a well-manicured woodpile, a small well-groomed garden in the back, and several rudimentary antennas in the far back of the property. The smell of wood burning in the fire was much stronger now. It brought back memories to Kyle of sitting on Luke's couch in front of the woodstove, cozy and warm. They approached the front door. Luke knocked.

The door opened after the first knock, as if the occupant of the cabin had been watching them and waiting. As the door opened, they were greeted by a thin, frail, elderly white-haired, white-bearded man with somewhat darker skin. He was wearing wire-framed trifocals and holding a semiautomatic handgun in his right hand. He extended his left hand to shake. His overall posture was welcoming yet defensive and suspicious. It was likely that visitors here were exceedingly rare.

"What can I do for you?" the elderly man asked.

"My name is Richard, Richard Davis, *he, him*, and *his*." Luke placed his right hand into the old man's left hand and shook it gently but firmly.

"I'm Scott Dillon, *he him,* and *his*." Kyle followed his introduction with a handshake too.

Luke wanted to be entirely honest with the old man, but he knew he would not be able to do so while standing in his doorway looking down the barrel of the loaded Glock pointed at him. "We've been hiking in the woods and camping for the past two months or so. We got lost, and we're running out of food. We came upon your cabin and thought we would say hello. We thought that maybe you could help us."

"C'mon in," the old man said, albeit somewhat hesitantly. "I'm Jesús Martinez. My pronouns are *he, him*, and *his*."

Kyle and Luke entered the cabin.

"Make yourselves comfortable," Jesús said. "Want anything to eat or drink? I've got moose stew with homegrown root vegetables, coffee, and fresh spring water. Please, help yourselves."

The two were hungry and thirsty. After thanking Jesús, they did help themselves. The food was amazing.

The three made small talk throughout the day, getting to know and to trust each other. The hours passed by quickly, as did another meal. It did not take long for Luke and Kyle to feel safe with Jesús and in his home, and they were eternally grateful.

"Jesús," Luke said, "we want to thank you for not turning us away and for your hospitality, food, and your listening ears. We feel safe here, and we know we can trust you. Thank you ever so much."

Jesús smiled. "Likewise. I feel I can trust both of you. I don't get many visitors up this way. Of necessity, I'd be suspicious of anyone who came to my door. In fact, you're the first people to have ever knocked at my door." He chuckled. "It's a pleasure to share my home and hospitality with ya. I thank you both for that."

As late evening rolled around, all were tired and ready for bed. Jesús placed some bedding—comfortable sheets, handmade blankets, and animal skins—on the floor in front of the woodstove and declared that space Luke and Kyle's bedroom.

"Sleep as late as you like. I'm up early and will have breakfast ready when you wake up. If you need anything, just give a holler." Jesús headed into his small bedroom, and Luke and Kyle rapidly fell into a deep and restful sleep, aided by the warmth, crackling, and woodsy smell of the stove at their feet.

Morning came quickly, and the two were awakened by sunlight peering through the windows and the aroma of home-cured bacon snapping and spattering atop the woodstove. They rolled up their bedding and joined Jesús, assisting him in cooking and engaging him in conversation. "You know, I know who you are and why you're here," Jesús said, surprising them both. "You're Lucas Moses"—he looked at Luke and then at Kyle— "and you're Kyle Sanderson. You filed a complaint against Americare and our president, and it backfired on ya, which is no surprise to me." Luke and Kyle looked at each other in dumbfounded surprise.

Jesús then proceeded to explain in detail what he knew about them and about Luke's complaint and the government's response. His understanding of their situation was spot-on.

"There's a reason why I live out here off the grid," Jesús said. "I have no use for our government, and I have no trust in 'em. They're the largest organized crime ring in the world, if ya ask me. I feel for you guys, and I entirely support you, but I'm amazed by your stupidity in thinking that doing the right thing and filing a complaint with the government against the government would cause everyone to live happily ever after. On second thought, I don't think ya were stupid, just naive to believe that the government is here to help you and our citizens. The government is here to help and serve the government. I kinda thought everyone knew that."

Kyle and Luke looked at each other again and smiled, both hearing Anne's voice. The two were also concerned about how Jesús knew about them even in spite of their somewhat lengthy beards, and they remained guarded. Now they were a bit suspicious of Jesus, given his extreme isolation and his fund of knowledge about them and the feds.

"How do you know so much about us—or anything, for that matter?" Luke asked. He had become suspicious that Jesús might be connected with the government, and that he had been placed there to detain them.

"Cuz I'm a ham radio operator," Jesús said. "Using my radio equipment, I have access to information from all over the world and beyond. I can also communicate with folks anywhere, so I'm likely more connected than most folks are. Here, see for yourselves." Jesús motioned to a small room off the living area. The room housed a lot of communications equipment, some of which obviously was homemade.

"I'm off the grid, but I made a wood-fired generator that can power my equipment and my appliances. That's how I keep my floors clean." Jesús chuckled and pointed to an old vacuum cleaner. "I just finished building a hydroelectric generator using the spring in my springhouse. This generator can power other electrical appliances, but I still must build a power inverter to convert the DC from the generator to AC that powers the appliances."

"How did you end up here in the North Country? And how did you make all this stuff?" Kyle asked.

"I'm an old electrical engineer, MIT undergraduate, and PhD," Jesús said. "At the age of eighteen, I came to the States from Mexico on a student visa to attend MIT. I did well and stayed on at MIT for my graduate studies and then, afterward, as a professor and researcher. During that time, I was able to become a United States citizen. The only things about me that are Mexican are my name and my heritage, of which I am extremely proud.

"I left conventional civilization after I got tired of my inventions being stolen and patented by others, most often by our government, and having my reputation defamed. I decided I wanted to live a happy and healthy life without all that crap. So, around twenty-five or so years ago, I drove up to Pittsburg from Cambridge, sold my car, bought hiking and camping equipment and some basic electronics supplies, and walked deep into the woods, never to come out again. I looked for the ideal spot in a valley with high mountains nearby, with a spring or river in the valley, surrounded by white-pine forest. I figured out how to build this here cabin adjacent to the spring, using white pines that I felled, cut, and prepared by hand.

"I built a springhouse over the spring and attached it to the main house. I use this for refrigeration. The water is potable, should the well I sunk fail. The well pump is driven by electricity obtained from a hydroelectric generator that I designed and built. It also runs the electrical system of my house. I have developed some backup systems in case the spring runs dry, but it has been flowing well since I built it. It took me over a year. I had to winter in a tent, which is no fun in northern New Hampshire. We get over two hundred inches of snow here during winter, and it gets very cold. Once my cabin was built, I focused on setting up my shack."

"Shack?" Kyle asked. "I saw only this building on the property."

"Shack is what us hams call the place where we keep and use our radio equipment." Jesús laughed. "I brought a couple of handhelds, a small dual-bander, and a small all-mode HF rig from home. I made the rest of my equipment, including all my antennas, which are on the top of the mountains. I do admit I had a large amount of RG-213 coax and PL259 connectors shipped to a post office box in Pittsburg during winter around fifteen years ago. I used cross-country skis and snowshoes to trail a sled to pick it all up in Pittsburg and bring it back here. At various times, I've ordered some other items too, and I've gone to the Pittsburg post office to pick them up.

"I have a bank account and have earned and saved over two million dollars, which I use for supplies when I'm unable to make them for myself. In fact, I have investments that I manage online that are making money for me. I have found a way to avoid paying any taxes."

Kyle was astounded. "You have two million dollars? Why are you living this way?"

"Because I choose to. I've never been happier."

"I can see you're happy, and I'm a bit jealous," Luke said. "You've found your calling. Although I'm not religious, per se, I do believe that everything happens for a reason and that each of us exists for a specific purpose that is likely unknown to us. It's this unknown purpose that I refer to as my calling. I think mine is different from yours, but I'm not even sure if it's what I'm doing right now. Right now we live in fear for our lives because of what has transpired, but we are on a mission.

"I'm spiritual in the sense that I believe we're all part of a greater system," Jesús said. "As humans, we don't call all the shots. Humankind is not the alpha and the omega, and the sun doesn't rise and set because of us. I choose to call the entity that does call all the shots God. Perhaps God is the Judeo-Christian God; perhaps it is Allah or the God of some other faith. Perhaps it is just nature. Of that, I'm uncertain. I am certain that this entity is not me, and that feeling of certainty brings me great peace. I regard my purpose in life as following my calling, as prescribed for me by God."

"I have the utmost respect for others' beliefs," Luke interjected. "People who denounce the existence of any form of God scare me because they are asserting that they are at the top of the spiritual food chain. They imply that they are the alpha and the omega, the great decision-makers, the great benefactors and beneficiaries, and the end-all and be-all.

"Same here," Kyle chimed in. "Such people seem to become angry and even nasty and profane when I refer to God, even though my conception of God is a global and all-inclusive God, not purporting any religious affiliation. They scream 'discrimination' based on religion, as well as unconstitutionality, if I refer to God and our country in the same paragraph. I am called an 'ist.' This form of secularity has forced any mention of God to be eliminated from our speech, save for the gods of those for whom political correctness deems their mention and respect a requirement."

"I feel compelled to continue as a physician," Luke said. "Most importantly, I am driven to continue forward with my complaint against Americare and the president, who are altering and even ending people's lives. Even if I decided I wanted to live off the grid, I could not do so right now because it would interfere with my intended calling, for which I am prepared to die, if necessary. Kyle and I realize the only way to bring an end to the Americare scheme and to bring those responsible to justice is to provide the citizenry with the facts regarding what is going on. If nothing else, they could exercise their power on election day by voting President Dmopvup out of office. We also realize that the only way to reach our desired ends is to do so from within the system."

Kyle was struck by what Luke said, largely because this mirrored his feelings exactly. Kyle reflected on his desire to become a PA. This was more than a desire; it was hardwired inside of him. Once Kyle had become aware of what was going on with Americare and President Dmopvup, pursuing the truth, ending this scheme, and bringing those responsible to justice became hardwired within him too. He realized at that moment that he was prepared to die, if necessary.

Kyle realized they were likely out of the range of cell service and internet access, so he asked, "Jesús, would it be possible for you to access the news so we can find out what's going on?"

"Now that's an easy one. Of course, I'll help with that. Come on into my shack.

The woodstove has been going continuously overnight, charging a large twelve-volt battery," Jesús said as he started powering up his station. "When the battery runs out, the five-kilowatt generator will kick in automatically."

"How does that work?" Luke asked.

"While I was at MIT, I developed a system that converts thermal energy directly to electrical energy. The idea and prototype were both stolen from me and patented by one of my colleagues, which is part of the reason I left civilization."

Jesús took his seat and turned to an AM news broadcast from WBZ in Boston. The signal was loud and clear. After listening for about an hour or so, they got the information they were looking for: the reward for anyone who assisted in their apprehension had been increased to one million dollars each. Their cell phones and landlines were bugged, their email accounts were being monitored, and their outgoing emails were blocked.

Kyle realized they were contained within a box without any ability to contact anyone, including Anne, whom they'd promised to contact daily.

"May we stay here for a few days?" Luke asked.

"Stay here as long as you like, provided you help out with the chores and such," Jesús said.

Luke and Kyle were grateful for the human companionship, a warm and cozy home, and a trusted friend. They knew they should not attempt to contact anyone because they could be located and apprehended. They were isolated from the rest of the world by their own choosing, yet they needed to do something to advance their cause. The Americare scheme was no doubt continuing and with it, the loss of lives.

As the days passed, their fear of discovery was rapidly overtaken by their deep need to do something. Their need for self-preservation became gradually replaced by the need for intervention of some kind.

One morning at breakfast, this became the topic of conversation.

"By not reaching out and doing something, I think we're

doing a disservice to our patients and our fellow citizens," Kyle said.

Luke nodded. "I think so too. Somehow, we need to reach out to the public in an effective way before the Feds get hold of us. We need to inform the citizenry about what's going on. Hopefully, law enforcement could apprehend President Dmopvup, Attorney General Mapdj, and FBI Director Duniz—that is, if law enforcement is not conspiring with Dmopvup. We need to figure out a way to do it."

"We can reach out to the public," Jesús chimed in, "and provide them with all the information you want using my radio equipment."

"How does that work?" Kyle asked.

"It's quite simple, really," Jesús said. "I can set up my radio equipment to transmit in a couple of different ways, adding some redundancy in case one of the modes of transmission fails." Jesús went into his shack and returned with a small handheld radio, which he gently shook while explaining further. "I would use a bogus call sign for the transmissions to hide my identity. A call sign is one's on-air signature. Transmissions from one of my dual-band—VHF and UHF—radios can be received by specified local repeaters, called nodes, which receive the transmissions and then send them via the internet using a sort of voice-over internet protocol to repeaters all over the world. They are in multiple locations. These repeaters retransmit the transmissions on one or several different frequencies and at higher powers, which can be received by anyone with a dual-band transceiver within fifty or more miles from each repeater. Dual-band transceivers, either handheld or base, are the most common transceivers, and I would venture to say that every ham, even newbies, has at least one."

Jesús put the small handheld radio on the table in front of him. "I can also set up transmissions on the high-frequency, or HF, bands, which are worldwide bands, but using the radio waves and not using the internet. HF transmissions are long-distance transmissions, and they can be received directly by hams who are listening worldwide. I could set my HF equipment to transmit repeatedly for a set period or whenever I choose to end the transmissions. The transmissions could consist of a recorded message of the two of you, generated repetitively, explaining what is going on and what you want those receiving the transmissions to do to rectify the situation. I would require at least a laptop computer to generate and perpetuate the broadcasts."

Luke thought for a moment. "That's an excellent solution to our problem, and I think we'll be OK with one laptop, so we can leave you one of ours. I would ask that you destroy it after it's used to drive the system or wipe the hard drive. Is it legal to do this?"

"No, it isn't legal," Jesús said. "I could lose my amateur-radio license and be fined or possibly subjected to jail time. I made a degaussing tool that can effectively wipe the hard drive, including solid-state drives. I can just smash the rest of it. What you said about your 'calling' made me think." Jesús stared into Luke's eyes. "Your cause has become my calling, the calling that I believe I was placed here in the woods—and even on this earth—to fulfill. I'm compelled to do whatever I can to help bring this Americare scheme to an end and bring the perpetrators to justice. I'm prepared to risk everything, including my amateur-radio license, my freedom, my money, and even my life, which I believe is a real possibility. I want to do this to help you and our country, but most importantly, I *need* to do this."

"Thank you." Luke grabbed both of Jesús's hands and shook them.

With a few tears in his eyes, Jesús got to work. He set up his equipment to transmit using both methods. He sent test transmissions that requested responses via both methods and promptly received responses with excellent signal reports.

Jesús also permitted Luke to send an email to Anne using a VPN-like system that he designed that made it impossible for anyone to identify the sender, the sending computer, the IP-address, or the sending computer's location. Luke informed Anne of what was going on, in general terms, but not where they were. Jesús also gave Luke a small handheld dual-band transceiver and a shortwave receiver and instructed them on how they could listen to the transmissions on both bands. With the radio equipment all set, the three bearded men sat down together, held hands as Jesús said grace, broke bread, ate their supper, and formulated the plan.

They decided to set Luke's laptop computer to drive the radio equipment to begin the transmissions three hours after they left Jesús's cabin. That way, by the time the source of the transmissions was detected, Luke and Kyle would be three hours out in the North Country woods and difficult to find.

In the interest of Jesús's safety, Luke said, "Come with us, Jesús."

"This is my home," Jesús said. "I'm destined to remain here. I would not be at peace, nor would I be comfortable abandoning my home, as I know I'm supposed to remain here. I'm touched by your invitation, though. You are the only visitors I've had since I came here twenty-five years ago. I believe you were sent here with the purpose of revealing my calling to me and allowing me to reaffirm that I belong here. I'm right where I'm supposed to be in time, space, and matter. I'm so grateful to you for giving me these gifts."

Kyle and Luke repacked their backpacks, tents, and sleeping bags and went out into the sanctity of the woods on a warm early July morning. Jesús gave them some nonperishable food items, dried venison and moose, and made certain their canteens were filled with fresh, cold spring water. After thanking him, they said their goodbyes and left for the woods in the direction Jesús recommended.

After hiking for three hours or so, they decided to stop and rest for fifteen minutes. They turned on the handheld radio and portable shortwave receiver and listened for their planned transmissions. They were audible on both transceivers, loud and clear.

CHAPTER 30

"CQ, CQ, CQ, CQ, calling CQ. This is Kilo Alpha 1 Quebec X-ray Romeo. Kilo Alpha 1 Quebec X-ray Romeo. Kilo Alpha 1 Quebec X-ray Romeo, calling CQ. QRZed? CQ, CQ, CQ, CQ, calling CQ. This is Kilo Alpha 1 Quebec X-ray Romeo. Kilo Alpha 1 Quebec X-ray Romeo. Kilo Alpha 1 Quebec X-ray Romeo, calling CQ. QRZed?" Charlie's radio chirped.

He grabbed his microphone, pushed the PTT switch, and tried to respond, but the CQ call just repeated, as if it were automated and designed to grab listeners' attention. Charlie heard many other hams answering the CQ to make and document the long-distance contact but to no avail. It continued repeating, as if begging for listeners. The CQ irritated and annoyed those taking part in the DX contest, but it succeeded in piquing all listeners' attention. It had certainly aroused Charlie's undivided attention.

What the hell? he thought. He reached across the desk in his shack and grabbed a pen and paper to record the call sign of the offending ham. Just as he was putting pen to paper, the broadcast began again.

Charlie scribbled in a sort of shorthand, not wanting to miss anything. Calling CQ without identifying one's actual FCC-issued call sign was procedurally incorrect. Broadcasting a recorded message was expressly forbidden by FCC laws. This was especially so during a DX contest on that frequency. He would report this incident to the FCC. If nothing else, it had interfered with the DX contest that he was enrolled in.

What followed the CQ was a brief and to-the-point statement from Kyle, identifying who he was and revealing a bulleted presentation about what had been going on regarding President Dmopvup and Americare. This broadcast repeated multiple times until the frequency was jammed a few hours after it started; then the airwaves became silent.

Removing his glasses and rubbing his eyes, Charlie stared blankly at his laptop screen while googling "Kyle Sanderson," then "Lucas Moses, MD," and then "Americare." Charlie recalled hearing something about this.

He reached up to turn off his radio and noticed that his hands were shaking, yet he had no idea why. He sat for a bit, his elbow resting on his desk and his chin in his palm, blankly staring at his laptop screen and thinking, *Now I have possible explanations as to why Tom and Judy died inexplicably.* The other day at lunch, Charlie half-jokingly said that maybe they had been bumped off by some whacko liberals. The radio transmission that he'd just heard added credence to his joke.

Charlie turned off his radio equipment and cleared off his desk, as he usually did after using his radio equipment.

"I need to reach out to Ken and Beverly," he said quietly, as if someone was listening. Rather than contacting them using his rig, he decided it was best to use the telephone.

Sweat was beaded on his furrowed brow, and his shirt was soaked in the armpits, although he wasn't certain why. Charlie knew that he had heard something profound and that he needed to act. But how?

"Hey, Ken, it's Charlie," Charlie said as Ken picked up his phone.

"Hey, buddy, how are you?" Charlie said. "Hey, listen, I just heard an unidentified CQ, which turned out to be a broadcast using a fake call sign, which shook me up pretty bad—not sure why—and I needed to talk with you."

"I heard it too," Ken said. "I knew after hearing it that you would call and that you'll call Beverly." Ken said. "I am not sure why either. This feels weird."

"How about we reach out to our membership and call a meeting to discuss?" Ken said, loudly clearing his throat. "Hey, I'm not sure why I said that. It's as if the words were placed in my mouth, but it seems like the right thing to do. Let's follow the phone tree we designed in case of a natural disaster, and each of us call two people. They in turn will each call two and so on. And let's meet this evening."

Charlie and Ken were members of the Western Nevada Radio Club (WNRC). They didn't know who else to reach out to, as the WNRC also was their circle of friends.

Charlie called Beverly, who also had been expecting his call, and she also did not know why. She had not heard the transmission on twenty meters, yet she had already begun the process of trying to find a sitter for her two kids so she could attend the meeting that she instinctually knew would happen that evening. Beverly was unnerved.

Charlie, Ken, and Beverly each called two other club members, who each called two more, and the phone tree was completed within an hour. Surprisingly, everyone was expecting a phone call, even though only about half of the fifty-four club members had heard the illicit broadcast.

The meeting would start at 7:00 p.m. at the Episcopal church in town. The congregation allowed the club to use a large conference room in the basement, as many of the club members were also parishioners, and the WNRC assisted with radio communication during all church-related events. Most club members would be there, a feat in itself, yet no one knew exactly why.

This scenario was repeated all over the country. Ham radio clubs, groups of others who had been listening on shortwave radios, and others who had inadvertently heard the broadcast reached out to friends and acquaintances. Those who were called were expecting to be called, expecting to meet that evening, and they realized almost full attendance at their meetings.

Although Ken and Charlie lived in Nevada, these group meetings occurred in all United States time zones, at 7:00 p.m. in each zone, as well as worldwide.

The membership of the Western Nevada Radio Club was a diverse bunch from all walks of life, races, genders, ages, and sexual orientations, with a variety of political leanings, yet they always came together to share their common interest—*ham radio*. Additionally, most saw through these differences and were bound together by commonality and a willingness to help others. The amateur radio service (also known as ham radio) was a volunteer radio service that provided communication during disasters and local events, with the express purpose of bringing people, radio equipment, other electronics, and communication together and advancing the radio art.

The membership of WNRC was similar in makeup to all the groups that convened meetings at 7:00 p.m. In fact, most groups formed that day on an impromptu basis because of that broadcast, although they were not existing groups or organizations. Also, in common was the fact that members of these groups did not know why they were meeting.

Not everyone was called to meet, but those who were called were drawn there by an inexplicable force, like an unrelenting craving or desire. Some of those who experienced this calling were people who worked for Americare or other government agencies, as well as local, state, and federal law enforcement. They met not as a group of Americare, state, local, or other federal employees, but as members of groups not related to their employment. Some Americare employees attended the WNRC meeting. They had either heard the broadcast on the twenty-meter band earlier that day, or they were called by someone who had heard it, and they fully expected to receive a call and to attend a meeting that night.

Charlie, Ken, and Beverly arrived at the church at 6:45 p.m. Others were already there, setting up chairs, making coffee, and preparing the podium, from which Charlie, being the group's president, would run the meeting.

Charlie did not know what he was going to say, yet he was entirely at peace and confident that he would give a cogent presentation.

By 7:00 p.m., forty-one of the fifty-four club members were seated in silence, awaiting Charlie's presentation. Everyone in attendance, including Charlie, was certain that the remaining thirteen people would not attend, so the meeting began promptly at seven.

It was very brief. Charlie called the meeting to order as an emergency meeting regarding the illicit broadcast on the twenty-meter band heard earlier that day. The meeting was clearly scripted, but the script came from within.

"We have all been called here to band together to address a life-threatening issue," Charlie said. "Although I am addressing you as the club president, I do not know what will come from my lips. I only know that I am supposed to bring this to you and ask for your help. President Dmopvup has provided us with universal health care through Americare, which is government owned and run. We have been grateful for this because it has provided everyone with health care, pretty much free of charge. The only caveats are that we must follow our provider's recommendations to the letter and have all recommended immunizations and screening tests and procedures. Failure to do these things results in imprisonment.

"As a result of Americare we appear, as a country, to be much healthier. Most of the chronic illnesses and diseases have seen dramatic improvements overall, from a population health standpoint. Our country appears to be getting healthier, but things aren't what they seem—if this sounds too good to be true, that's because it is. President Dmopvup is using Americare in diverse ways to systematically kill our citizens for hir political and financial benefit. This culling of the herd has resulted in the appearance of a healthier US population overall, rather than improvement in patient care. This explains the unexpected and otherwise inexplicable deaths of our friends, colleagues, and acquaintances.

"Kyle Sanderson, a physician assistant, and Dr. Lucas Moses, both from Primary Care Associates, a primary care medical practice in New Hampshire, brought this to light. Kyle risked his life to find out exactly what was occurring, and Dr. Moses filed a complaint with the United States Department of Health and Human Services. As a result, the two are being hunted down by the FBI for conspiracy to commit treason or something of that ilk, and if caught, they likely will be executed. The government will figure out a way to make things seem as if the two were insubordinates— criminals who were committing fraud and other treasonous acts against the government. I assure you that this is not the case.

"At seven o'clock tonight, in every town throughout the country, groups like this are convening, and this speech is being delivered verbatim. These groups—we shall call ourselves the Disciples—must unite, bring this scheme to an end, and bring President Dmopvup and hir associates to justice. We will rely heavily on individuals who work for Americare or other agencies within the federal government. These 'double agents' are in a unique position with access to the required information and technology. They will act autonomously at times, and they will know what to do. They will report back to their respective groups, the leaders of which will report to our central headquarters outside of Washington, DC.

"Absolute secrecy is necessary, and we each must deny the existence of any Disciple groups if we are asked. Each of us can tell, by virtue of our senses, whether the person we are dealing with is a Disciple. There may be traitors among us, those who decide to talk for fear of their lives. I assure you that this will not occur, as they will be devoid of any useful information, if so interrogated. Tomorrow, after every Disciple group in this country has met, I will reach out to other group leaders. Other meetings will be convened when more information presents itself. Are there any questions?"

No one raised a hand; all remained in peaceful silence.

"Then go out from here and be safe."

CHAPTER 31

Luke and Kyle continued their journey through the woods of northern New Hampshire. "It is my hope the public will eventually hear our radio transmissions," Kyle said.

Because only other hams and others with shortwave radios that were tuned to the exact transmission frequencies could hear them directly, Luke and Kyle were concerned that the transmissions might have fallen on deaf ears.

"Maybe the media will pick up these transmissions," Luke said. "Maybe they will use their investigative abilities to investigate what they heard." At that point, hope was what was keeping them going. They were vigorous and determined to continue.

The FCC monitors all radio frequencies, including those of the amateur radio bands. They use volunteer ham operators to listen for any violations among the ham radio community and to report them to the FCC. It took these FCC enforcement monitors nearly three hours to pick up the transmissions during their routine monitoring. Because of the nature of the content of the transmissions, information about the transmissions was passed rapidly upward along the food chain, reaching Attorney General Mapdj and FBI Director Duniz within a few more hours.

As was hoped and planned, the attorney general and FBI director listened to these transmissions. Predictably, they were genuinely concerned, largely because the transmissions included detailed information implicating President Dmopvup for using Americare to injure and kill patients and citizens for hir personal, financial, and political gain.

Immediately, the FBI director ordered the FCC to jam those frequencies by transmitting high-power, continuous signals with large bandwidth, which essentially drowned out the transmissions. Prior to jamming the frequencies they used radio direction finders to triangulate and locate the source of the transmissions. Then the FCC was able to roughly locate the source, and FBI agents were sent to search the area. Once they found the source, they were instructed to destroy the equipment. They were to question the radio operator regarding his involvement with Luke and Kyle, where the two were headed, and what their plans were—and then they were to eliminate the radio operator.

A perimeter within which the transmissions originated was accurately defined using the radio direction finders. The FBI employed fifty special agents in a grid-like search pattern. It wasn't long before they came upon Jesús's cabin. The agents encircled the house, with ten in front, locked and loaded, and focused on the front door. Two agents approached and knocked. Jesús opened the door.

"What took you so long?" Jesús asked. "Please come in."

The agents, somewhat perplexed by Jesús's response, pushed him aside and stormed the cabin. Jesús chuckled quietly; there was a unique glow about him.

"The radio equipment is over there." Jesús pointed to his shack.

The agents tied him to a chair, covered his head with a heavy burlap sack so he couldn't see, destroyed his shack, and confiscated all his equipment. After that, the entire cabin was thoroughly searched. Two of the agents remained in the cabin and proceeded to question Jesús.

Jesús had decided in advance that he would provide them with confounding and false information and never assist them. He was entirely at peace.

"Where are they?" one of the agents asked somewhat angrily.

"Where are who?" Jesús said.

"Dr. Moses and Mx. Sanderson," the agent responded.

"I have no idea what you're talking about," Jesús said, chuckling quietly.

With that, one of the agents kicked the chair over, knocking Jesús to the floor. He untied Jesús, picked him up from behind, and roughly tied him to a post in the center of the room in a standing position. One of the agents removed his belt and used it to secure Jesús's ankles to the post, and a rope was similarly used around Jesús's waist. Jesús's wrists were bound together behind him and the post.

"Perhaps you remember now," the agent asked.

"Remember what?" Jesús said.

Then came a searing pain as one of the agents removed

one of Jesús's fingernails using a pair of pliers. The pain was immediately overcome by a sensation of ecstasy and peace.

"Where are they?" the agent demanded angrily as he smacked Jesús across the face.

"I will not help you," Jesús said. A smile had developed on his lips.

One of the agents ripped off Jesús's shirt, dropped his pants down to his ankles, and then proceeded to burn Jesús's nipples with a cigarette lighter. The sense of ecstasy and peace increased.

The agents asked Jesús multiple questions, but he remained mute, despite fingernail and toenail removal, burning of both nipples and elsewhere, carving into his body with kitchen knives, and even chopping off some of his fingers and his toes. The sensation of ecstasy and peace continued to increase.

Jesús had dissociated from his physical being. He had learned how to do this as a boy while being beaten by his physically abusive father, yet this was much more than that. It was as if he was watching himself being tortured from afar, with any pain replaced by a sense of euphoria, rapture, and inner peace. Hanging there on the post was the most painful and humiliating experience of Jesús's life. Yet it was through this pain and humiliation that Jesús transcended deeper and deeper into a sense of inner ecstasy and peace.

While hanging there, he reviewed his life, tried to tie up his emotional loose ends, made peace with his Maker, and prayed for the first time in over forty years. He had prayed for the ability to carry out his Creator's will; for the strength to fearlessly deal with whatever was destined to happen; and for the health and safety of Luke, Kyle, and the citizenry of the United States of America.

At the end of this period of reflection, he felt pressure and a slight sting across his neck. He started choking and coughing up liquid, which he felt all over his body. He became dizzy and unable to breathe. Upon the realization that Jesús would provide no useful information, one of the agents had slit his throat from carotid to carotid, using one of Jesús's sharp kitchen knives.

Jesús wasn't entirely surprised by this. He was relieved to know how he was going to die. His life was ending as it was destined to occur, taken so that others could live. Jesús peacefully lost consciousness for the very last time.

The agents left the cabin after filling it with C-4. Jesús hung there, peacefully, for over an hour while the agents sought a safe position. Once they were about a mile away, they detonated the C-4 using a radio signal. The explosion was profound, rocking the ground and forest for a great distance.

The agents circled back and saw a large hole where the cabin once stood. Inside the hole, they found one of the large ceiling joists bisected by a vertical post, extending upward a foot or two beyond the joist, forming a rudimentary cross. A belt and two ropes were loosely tied around the base. Written on this joist, in what appeared to be blood, was, "My life was freely given in order that others may live, and that justice will be served."

Chills went up and down the agents' spines. They chose to destroy the message and not report it to their superiors.

Luke and Kyle heard the jamming signals and knew the government had received their transmissions. They heard and felt the explosion, so they knew the cabin and the radio equipment had been found and destroyed and that searchers were close to them. They were also aware when the jamming signals ceased, leaving the bands quiet again. They prayed that their friend Jesús was unharmed, but they feared the worst. They decided to pick up their pace and then stop and search the airwaves every few hours, hoping to hear evidence their transmissions had been heard.

Several hours after the jamming ceased, Luke and Kyle tuned into a WOLF News radio broadcast, whose feature story was the radio transmissions. WOLF News reviewed the content of the transmissions in detail and rebroadcast portions of them. They announced they were creating a special investigative team to follow up on this. They requested that anyone with information on the transmissions or anyone responsible for their content contact them by phone, and they listed a phone number to call.

The internet revealed that all other news outlets were running a story saying that an unidentified rogue survivalist had flooded the amateur radio airwaves with antigovernment propaganda and exploded themselves and their radio equipment once they were discovered.

The nature of the transmissions was stated as accusations inspired by the complaint against Americare. Every news article and broadcast, aside from WOLF News, referred to the transmissions as "not credible" and as "conspiracy theory." Only one media outlet, WOLF News, lived up to its reputation of being *balanced and fair*.

Luke and Kyle were now certain that Jesús was dead, and they were struck by the overall bias of the mainstream media in favor of the government and the president and against the safety and the lives of the citizens.

Luke and Kyle continued to live in the woods and to follow the news closely, mainly WOLF News. They continued to lay low, not contacting anyone and remained in the woods, where they were comfortable and safe. Their thoughts were with Jesús, who had most likely given his life for their cause.

Around three weeks after Jesús's radio transmissions, Kyle was scanning the internet using his cell phone. He came across a press conference dated August 3, 2032, in which Attorney General Musivve Mapdj and FBI Director Kenit Duniz put a positive spin on the situation, using lies and deception. They presented President Dmopvup as a generous philanthropist who had only the citizens' best interest in mind. FBI Director Duniz restated that Dr. Moses's complaint had been thoroughly investigated. He thought that no reasonable prosecutor would bring a case against Americare or President Dmopvup. They reemphasized their intent to capture Luke and Kyle and bring them to justice.

All media outlets broadcast that press conference, even WOLF News. At the conclusion of the press conference, WOLF News again introduced their special investigative team and again listed the tip-line phone number, encouraging anyone with knowledge about Jesús's transmissions or their content to contact them.

"I feel as if we should do something," Kyle said.

"Maybe we should call the WOLF tip line and see what they have to offer us," Luke said.

"I'm not so sure we should do that," Kyle said. "This could be a setup by Dmopvup and the government to bring us out of the shadows."

"That's a chance that we must be willing to take," Luke said. "Are you willing to take that risk?"

"I'm afraid we have no other options but to call," Kyle said.

Frustrated and feeling trapped, with election day rapidly approaching, they decided that Luke should call the number anonymously and test the WOLF News tip line to figure out their resources and intentions. They needed to be judicious with their phones. Despite having five portable phone chargers, they were rapidly running out of battery power. They did have a solar-powered battery charger, but the weather had been cloudy, not permitting them time to keep it charged.

With considerable trepidation, Luke and Kyle called the tip line on speakerphone. They decided that the best course of action was to be directly honest with WOLF and ask them for their help. They relied on their faith that this was a part of their calling.

"Good afternoon. WOLF News tip line. This is Paul."

"Hello, I have some information regarding the radio broadcasts about Americare and President Dmopvup," Luke said.

"Thank you for calling." Paul sounded surprised, almost startled. "Let me transfer you to Francis Sales. He is our correspondent working on this case."

While waiting to be connected to Francis Sales, Luke grabbed hold of Kyle's hand, looked into his deep-blue eyes, and mouthed, "I love you."

"Sales, here," Francis Sales said as he took the call.

"Mr. Sales, this is Dr. Luke Moses. I'm here with my partner and physician assistant, Kyle Sanderson. We need your help."

"Thank you so much for reaching out to us," Francis said with an air of pleasant surprise. "Let me start by asking what WOLF News can do for you, and then I want to ask you some questions."

"We are entirely and absolutely certain that what I allege in my complaint to HHS is fact. Ever since my complaint was filed, Assistant US Attorney Hartigan has done everything to cause me to withdraw my complaint. He even offered me and Mr. Sanderson large cash settlements, as well as administrative positions with Americare, in exchange for withdrawing my complaint. Hartigan told us that if we did not opt for the settlements, our lives would become exceedingly difficult, which they have.

"After I refused to withdraw my complaint, they turned the tables on us, altering the Americare medical records and documentation, making us out to be the criminals, and changing their focus and the focus of the citizenry to our apprehension, rather than on the issues I cited in my complaint. One of the people who assisted us is in FBI custody, and at least two others are dead.

"Kyle and I have been hiding out in the woods. Our supplies and resources are dwindling, and we have run out of options. We believe the only way to effect positive change is to make our citizens aware of exactly what is going on. Our attempt to do this resulted in the death of one of our friends, and the information that was transmitted was sanitized by every media outlet except WOLF News. All other media outlets portrayed our president and Americare in a positive light, making Kyle and me out to be criminals. We are out of options and are hoping you can help us."

"Where are you?" Francis Sales asked. "I can meet you with our mobile station and crew. This would be a confidential, off-the-record meeting to formulate a strategy. I can imagine you might be skeptical about our authenticity, but I assure you we are genuine. We have been looking at President Dmopvup and Americare for several years, but until now, every lead we found has brought us to a dead end—until you called. We also reached a brick wall when dealing with the Feds. They are entirely obstructionists. They tried to have my broadcasting license revoked and have me fired. WOLF News stood behind me. I am asking you to trust me."

"We trust you, if for no other reason than we don't have anyone else we can trust," Kyle said.

"Which town are you in?"

"We're about a day's hike from Pittsburg, New Hampshire," Luke said. "Meet us in the parking lot at the Walmart in Pittsburg, New Hampshire, at noon, the day after tomorrow. I'll call you at eleven in the morning to make sure you'll be there."

"We will be there, and thank you so much for reaching out to us. We will bring you some food and supplies."

"Thank you," Kyle and Luke said at the same time as they ended the call.

They sat for a while and held each other, both anxious regarding the uncertainties that lay ahead. They knew that now was the time for blind trust and faith that things would work out. After comforting each other, they broke camp and headed toward Pittsburg. It had been over three months since they'd retreated to the woods. Now, they realized what Jesús had found so appealing about living there.

Their journey out of the woods was bittersweet. It was as if they were saying goodbye to the trees that served as shelter and as fuel for heat and cooking, the plants that provided food, the springs that provided potable water, the streams, and ponds where they bathed, and the animals that had been their family, protectors, and a source of sustenance. Nevertheless, they hiked through the night, pitched their tents by a small stream, ate, and then slept for the better part of the next day. As dusk approached, they broke camp for the final time and continued on to the last leg of their journey. They were largely silent, as they were anxious about what might transpire at noon the next day.

CHAPTER 32

Eleven o'clock was upon them, and it was time for Luke to call Francis Sales to make sure he was ready to meet. He dialed the number, and it was answered after the first ring.

"Sales here," a voice answered.

"Are you in Pittsburg?" Luke asked.

"Yes, I'm at Walmart at the front of the parking lot."

"Drive behind the building," Luke instructed. "You'll find a dirt road leading into the woods there. Drive down that road a half a mile or so, and we'll meet you there. I'm putting my entire faith in you that you're being genuine and honest."

"You have my word," Sales said. "The vehicle is an unmarked white van about the size of a large ambulance."

The call ended. Luke and Kyle waited in a ditch by the dirt road, and soon they heard the approach of a vehicle, increasing in intensity. When the vehicle drew near, Kyle decided to crawl out of the woods to meet them first, and Luke would follow, once he felt it was safe. That way, Luke might be able to get away if this turned out to be a double-cross. Kyle crawled out of the ditch and flagged down the van.

The van stopped, and the driver and passenger stepped out to greet Kyle.

"Francis Sales," the passenger said, extending his right hand. "My pronouns are he, him, and his."

Francis Sales was a person of significant stature, around six feet three, and he walked with a slight limp. The driver was a man of modest stature and rather average looks and features.

"Kyle Sanderson." Kyle shook Francis's hand.

Luke felt secure enough to crawl out of the temporary bivouac that had sheltered him and Kyle in the ditch. "I'm Luke Moses." He joined Kyle to greet Francis and the driver. "Our pronouns are *he, him,* and *his.*"

They shook hands.

"Let's go inside where we can talk," Francis said as he motioned to the back of the van.

As the four walked toward the van, Luke and Kyle remained appropriately suspicious and keenly attentive to their surroundings, as well as to their hosts. The four of them entered the van, which was more like a mobile communications laboratory and a lounge/office. They all sat down in comfortable leather chairs.

"Would you like anything to drink or eat?" Francis asked.

"Whatever you have, but don't go to any trouble," Kyle said.

The driver went to a refrigerator and brought out some snacks and bottles of iced tea, which he placed on the table in front of them.

"I'm Paul," he said. "My pronouns are *he, him,* and *his.* I'm the one who took your call. I guess you could say I'm a jack-of-all-trades—or a Paul-of-all-trades, to be more exact. I'm Francis's assistant, cameraman, and sound technician, and I run all this stuff."

"He also serves as my driver," Francis said.

Kyle and Luke shook Paul's hand and helped themselves to iced tea. They made small talk for about half an hour or so.

"On our way up here from New York, I thought about ways that we might help you inform the public about what's going on with Americare," Francis said. "Then it dawned on me that seeing and hearing are believing."

"What do you mean?" Luke asked.

"First of all, I need to know what you both are willing to risk."

"We're willing to risk our lives and to do anything and everything it takes to bring this all out in the open," Luke said.

"Then I have an idea. Suppose you just turned yourselves in to the local authorities? What do you think might happen?" Sales asked.

"I think we would likely be handed over to the Feds and questioned by them before we were killed," Kyle said matter-of-factly.

"And suppose the entire world could hear and maybe even see them question you?" Paul asked.

"I'm not sure I follow you," Luke said.

"Suppose for a minute that you turned yourself in and

you were handed over to the Feds," Francis said. "And suppose they started to question you, but you refused to talk unless questioned directly by President Dmopvup, or Attorney General Mapdj, or FBI Director Duniz, or all of them. And suppose the entire world was able to hear and maybe see the entire thing."

Luke smirked. "Assuming Dmopvup and hir entourage were being honest, it would blow them out of the water. They would self-destruct."

Paul nodded. "Here's what we have to offer. Remember the micro-implant technology Americare is using? During the past several years, we were able to infiltrate the computer systems at Utopia Pharmaceuticals, access all the technical information regarding their micro-implant technology, and use our connections within the private sector to figure out ways to utilize this technology in our industry. We were able to obtain prototypes of several of these micro-implants. We contracted with electrical and computer engineers to develop ways to miniaturize audio and visual transmitters for use by our correspondents.

"We would have each of you swallow exceedingly small but high-powered audio transmitters. Similarly high-powered video transmitters, which also had audio-transmission capabilities, would be easily implanted on your scalps or anywhere, actually. Then, you would turn yourselves in to local authorities and follow the plan we just outlined. We have extremely sensitive receivers throughout the Washington, DC, area, which would pick up the transmissions from these devices. In fact, we have these receivers throughout the entire world. The audio and video feeds could then be live streamed on the internet and broadcasted on WOLF News, which would also record them."

"Sounds cool," Kyle said.

"Even if they were to find the video transmitters while searching you, they would never find the audio transmitters you swallowed. We would give you a drug that causes constipation and drastically slows the transit time through the gastrointestinal tract, which would keep the swallowed audio devices inside you for up to two weeks or longer. They are programmed with digital noise-canceling technology that filters out all bodily sounds and transmits only those sounds from outside the subjects who ingest them.

"Our only concern is what would happen to both of you after the questioning. This plan, assuming you were able to finagle talking with Dmopvup and/or Mapdj and/or Duniz, would bring all of this out in the open, with President Dmopvup admitting hir involvement in these schemes. They would basically hang themselves and, most importantly, President Dmopvup. Unfortunately, our thinking is that neither of you would survive."

"Election day is around three months away," Kyle said. "If we miss this opportunity to expose them before the election, we will have missed our golden opportunity to end the Americare scheme and bring Dmopvup and hir cohorts down. Beggars can't be choosers. What other options do we have? I say we do it."

Grabbing Kyle's hand and pulling him close, Luke knew what he had to do. "I agree," he said. "Let's do it."

Francis and Paul needed to return to New York to get the required equipment and supplies and assemble it, which they thought would take about a week to accomplish. They all decided Luke and Kyle should present themselves to local authorities in Pittsburgh on Monday, August 16. Paul and Francis would return early on August 16, 2032, to install the micro-transmitters.

CHAPTER 33

The week between their meeting with Francis and Paul, and August 16, 2032, passed much quicker than either Luke or Kyle would have liked. Even though they were preparing to make their final moves, it also likely spelled the end of their lives.

They were engulfed by mixed feelings. They thought a lot about Jesús, who had fearlessly given his own life for their cause, and about Andy, who likely had done the same. Kyle and Luke would be in the best of company if they were killed, and that made the thought of their demise more palatable.

They remained distant from Francis and Paul, not contacting them until the morning of the sixteenth. They prepared themselves to retain the swallowed audio devices. Each drank an entire bottle of magnesium citrate on the morning and the evening of August 12th, which induced profound diarrhea and resulted in an ultra-thorough clean-out by the next day. Once the diarrhea had abated, they started a low-fiber diet and took a long-acting preparation of diphenoxylate HCL/atropine that Paul had given them on the evenings of the 13th, 14th, and 15th, with a planned dose for the 16th right before they left for the police station. This is a potent antidiarrheal regimen that is constipating and that would drastically slow the gastrointestinal transit time.

Francis and Paul were confident that the ingested audio devices would be retained for at least two weeks. The devices had been designed with microscopic spines that allowed them to embed themselves transiently and superficially in the gastrointestinal mucosa at various points along the way, like miniature cockleburs sticking to the socks of unsuspecting hikers in the woods. This would cause their transit in the gastrointestinal tract to be a more stuttering course and would further guarantee their longer-term retention.

August 16 arrived, and Luke and Kyle were prepared for what was to come. A part of each of them hoped no one would answer when they called Francis, but that was not to be. Sales answered Luke's call again on the first ring.

"Sales, here."

"We're ready," Luke said. "Where should we meet up?"

"You tell us, Luke," Francis said. "You know the area, and we don't."

"How about we meet where we met before?" Luke said. "After Kyle and I are prepared, we'll drive ourselves over to the police station."

"Sounds good. Meet you in about an hour," Francis said.

After the call, Luke and Kyle felt as if they were going on a long one-way trip that didn't require any luggage. The whole thing was weird and surreal. They made their way back to their bivouac in the ditch beside the road to wait for the van to return. Once again, they heard the van's engine approaching. They came out of the ditch to the side of the road to meet the van, anxiously anticipating the next steps. The van continued its approach and then stopped right in front of them. As if in a repeat performance, Paul and Francis hopped out, shook their hands, and invited them into the back of the van.

"Want anything to drink or eat?" Paul asked.

"Sure, just some iced tea for me," Kyle said.

"Same here," said Luke.

Paul poured the iced tea and brought out some cookies for them to munch on. Luke and Kyle were hungry, as the hunting and fishing hadn't been as productive recently. While they were eating, Paul was busy preparing the audio/ video devices.

"Where's that going to be placed?" Luke asked.

"On the scalp," Paul said.

"I'm balding, so I have nothing on top. All skin," Luke said, chuckling a bit as he patted his head.

"Your scalp will do just fine," Paul said. "See how small these devices are—about the size of the head of a pin and flesh-colored. These will be inserted into the skin, under the epidermis, where they'll be invisible to the casual observer. You won't feel a thing. These cameras tightly adhere using a skin adhesive containing 2-octyl cyanoacrylate and methyl methacrylate in combination, which is a mixture of skin glue and bone glue. Once the devices have adhered, we'll need a couple of minutes to focus them and to test their audio and video. If, for any reason, the devices fall off or they are discovered and removed, the devices that you swallowed will at least live-stream the audio. Oh yeah, you each swallowed an audio device. It was inside one of the cookies you ate. They are designed to be placed surreptitiously in someone's food and are encapsulated in an almost crush-proof epoxy. I'll test those, too."

Luke and Kyle were surprised at the diminutive size of each device and even more surprised they had already ingested the audio devices. Paul took a few minutes to install the cameras on their scalps. He then focused the cameras by having Luke and Kyle stand, one at a time, on a line on the floor and look at a test pattern with writing on it. Using the control panel inside the van, Paul adjusted the camera for the best clarity. The devices could be adjusted at any time going forward. Audio from both the scalp devices and the swallowed devices was similarly adjusted on the panel. He then had Luke and Kyle go outside the van so he could adjust each device for distance reception.

Luke and Kyle reentered the van and sat down with Paul and Francis to discuss what was to follow. Although they were presently less than a mile from the Pittsburg police station, a short walk, Luke wanted to go back to camp to say goodbye to the camp and to his father, who still lingered there. He asked Paul if the video and audio could be turned off or ignored during that time. Paul agreed.

Paul and Francis drove Luke and Kyle close to the

dirt road leading to Luke's camp. They wished them luck, hugged them, turned the audio and visual monitoring off, and set them free. Whatever happened next would depend on Luke and Kyle working their way up the food chain and talking with President Dmopvup, the attorney general, and/ or the FBI director, as well as on luck and circumstances.

As they walked down the road toward camp, hand in hand, they reminisced about their lives. They talked about the time they'd had together, their journey through the woods, and their love for each other. As they crossed the threshold of the cabin, they were again flooded with warmth and incredible peace. They held each other for a moment and kissed. No words were spoken, nor were any words necessary.

Luke then asked Kyle to step outside for a few minutes so he could say goodbye to his father, his camp, and his world. After Kyle left, Luke went into the bedroom, knelt at the side of the bed, clasped his hands, and prayed silently. Then, he spoke quietly, with tears streaming from his eyes, which he wiped away periodically.

After Luke prayed at the side of the bed and talked with his father, his tears abated, and a smile developed. He then went outside and found Kyle kneeling by the lake, praying, also with tears in his eyes and a smile. They embraced, looked into each other's eyes, and kissed in silence. They said their goodbyes without words. In like fashion, they expressed their love for each another, as their love was so profound as to defy words.

After that, Kyle sent a text with a percent sign to Paul, which was their predetermined signal to resume video and audio monitoring. A returned ampersand acknowledged the text and indicated the monitoring had resumed. They were now entirely ready to turn themselves in.

They uncovered Kyle's Jeep, removing the brush that served to keep it camouflaged. Luke hopped into the driver's seat and drove them to the Pittsburg police station. As they drove along, hand in hand, they were at peace.

"This has been my destiny," Kyle said, looking at Luke. "I believe it has always been my calling to remain loyal to our patients—our citizens—and to inform them about what has occurred with Americare and President Dmopvup, to bring an end to these Americare schemes, and to bring the president and hir administration to justice."

"It has always been my calling to assist and support you, Kyle, in your calling," Luke said. "And for this, I am willing to die, if necessary. I experienced this epiphany while talking with Dad back at the cabin and in talking with Jesús."

They drove along silently and in peace the rest of the way, holding each other's hands.

CHAPTER 34

After taking the last diphenoxylate HCL/atropine tablets, they left the sanctity of the Jeep and entered the police station. It was 1:00 p.m. Once they stated who they were, they were placed in separate but adjacent cells, and the Feds were contacted. Within no time, two men in dark suits, with microphones in their ears, appeared in the station. They cuffed Luke and Kyle, escorted them outside, and placed them in the secured back seat of a black Lincoln. They started questioning them immediately. As rehearsed, Luke and Kyle said they would speak only with the president, attorney general, and/or the FBI director.

They were driven to an awaiting small jet aircraft on a small airstrip. The handcuffs were removed for the flight as they were seated on the aircraft. One of the FBI agents told them they were headed to FBI Headquarters near Washington, DC. The flight took about an hour and a half. Upon arrival, zip-tie handcuffs were reapplied before they deplaned.

Luke and Kyle were greeted on the tarmac by another black Lincoln, which took them to their final destination. They were exhausted, hungry, and dirty when they got there. They hadn't had a shower or a shave in several months. They were surprised by how candid and polite the FBI agents had been thus far, and they were even more surprised by how they were treated at FBI Headquarters. The cuffs were removed, as were their clothes, and they were thoroughly searched.

Once this was completed, they were given a nice room, clean clothes, and a menu listing a large food selection They were permitted to shower and to shave.

After their meals, they were given an opportunity to rest and sleep, and they had access to a large-screen TV with a myriad of programs. The two slept soundly, as it had been a while since either of them had the luxury of sleeping in a bed. This treatment continued from August 16th   through the early morning of August 18th. It allowed them to gather some strength and to be with each other.

At 6:00 a.m. on August 18, 2032, two FBI agents woke them up by bringing a basket of pastries, some fresh fruit, and a pot of fresh coffee into their quarters. The agents told them that they soon would meet with the president, and they should get themselves ready. After eating their fill, Luke and Kyle showered and got dressed for the day. The FBI agents had provided them with clothes that fit them well. The agents' obvious efforts raised Luke's and Kyle's suspicions.

Shortly thereafter, Luke and Kyle were brought into a conference room and offered more coffee and tea. They were joined by Attorney General Mapdj and FBI Director Duniz, who entered the room silently and sat down across the conference table from them. Then, with a flourish and an air of arrogance, President Dmopvup entered the room, surrounded by an entourage of what appeared to be Secret Service agents. Everyone in the room stood and placed their right hands over their hearts out of respect for the office of the president and for the country. Luke and Kyle were awestruck. President Dmopvup motioned for all to sit, and they did. The scene and situation seemed surreal.

"Good morning, Dr. Moses and Mx. Sanderson," the president said. "I thought it was about time we all met and talked. I know you think that you are responsible for this meeting; that you have the information that I need or something of that nature; and that by using this as a carrot, you have coerced me into complying with your request to meet. That is only partially true. You have absolutely no information that I require. I already know what you know and what I need to know. That is not the purpose of this meeting, which I arranged to meet my needs, and not yours."

President Dmopvup's facial expression was stern and cold, as if dismissive of their very existence. "I will start this meeting by asking if you have any questions and by saying that I know you're aware of what you need to say and do to quash your ridiculous accusations. Your more-than-generous rewards for doing so still stand."

"We will sign the settlement agreements previously presented to us as is," Luke said, "provided you explain to us, from the beginning, what is going on with Americare. If you don't explain it to us, this will all come out in public. If you explain it to us, we would be bound by the settlement never to discuss this with anyone. We are aware we will lose our lives if we decline to sign the agreement, and we have accepted that, so using our lives as bargaining chips would be futile. The choice is yours."

President Dmopvup's eyes widened, and a slight smirk appeared upon hir lips.

CHAPTER 35

"Tell us, from the beginning, how this came to be," Kyle said.

"When I was a law student, both of my parents were killed in an automobile accident," President Dmopvup said. "After they passed, I was left a $2 million inheritance. Not knowing what to do with it and being a socially conscious and progressive liberal student, I kept $300,000 to live on and used the remaining $1.7 million to start a charitable foundation. I legally changed my identity several times during my earlier years for the sake of anonymity, and eventually assumed the name Jommesa Sufjen Dmopvup. With the mainstream media by my side, I made certain I would be legally guaranteed confidentiality. I have managed to ensure this will always be the case. Therefore, I have no past; consequently, I will not comment any further regarding my personal life. I have always kept my past life private.

"What has happened since then?" Kyle asked.

"Since that time, there have been many contributors to the foundation," President Dmopvup said. "Some of them are well known, and the foundation grew to $4 billion during the next several years. I finished law school, worked in various law firms, and gradually entered the world of politics. I have always had a penchant for and interest in our health care system, and I dreamed of someday becoming the engineer and owner of a universal health care plan."

"But how were you able to pull this off?" Kyle asked.

"I used the mainstream media and the courts to my advantage," President Dmopvup said. "Using the media, computer driven artificial intelligence, creative speaking and writing, as well as psychological principles, I was able to develop a persona that appears to each individual exactly how they want me to appear. In 2020, I was first elected to the office of president. Shortly thereafter, I used my power and influence to cause Congress to draft legislation that abolished the Twenty-Second Amendment to the United States Constitution, lifting the restriction on the number of terms a president can serve. When I became president, I turned the management of the Dmopvup Foundation over to an impartial board, consisting of attorneys, investment bankers, and financial experts, none of whom were contributors to or beneficiaries of the foundation. The Dmopvup Foundation now essentially runs itself."

"With all due respect, Mx. President, you have not answered my question," Kyle said.

"Building on former president Obama's Affordable Care Act legislation and tweaking it to allow citizens to purchase health insurance across state lines, I created Americare," President Dmopvup said. "I used $5 million from the Dmopvup Foundation as seed money to get it started. I saw this as the best way to gain influence over every citizen and to gain control over their lives, as health insurance was now mandated. The availability of health insurance products on the state exchanges varied from state to state, and products were becoming fewer and farther between. Furthermore, premiums and deductibles for every health plan offered on the exchanges were so high as to be unaffordable. Most people just opted to pay the 'tax' for being uninsured, which was considerably lower. Premiums continued to increase, the number of available insurance products continued to decrease, and the overall quality of these products was mediocre at best.

"I created a health insurance product that had exceptionally low and often nonexistent premiums and deductibles, as well as high quality. Placed on every state exchange, it permitted citizens to purchase and carry their health insurance across state lines, and it outcompeted all the others. I also increased the penalty for not carrying health insurance to include incarceration. By 2023, Americare was a robust and viable health insurance product that was affordable to everyone; increasingly, our citizens were enrolling in it."

"How did you develop this algorithm-based health plan?" Luke asked.

"Starting in early 2023, I began to focus more on quality, using the quality metrics of the Americare patient panel as an equivalent representation of the health of our Americare patients. I contracted with IQOD systems to develop a computer system with the capability of performing modeling of populations regarding population health. They produced a state-of-the-art system that was interactive and could tell us not only where we needed these quality metrics to go but also which interventions we needed to employ to get us there.

"Using this computer system and our team of actuaries, we also developed a model of an 'ideal' patient panel. It was ideal in terms of the number of patients with specific disease states, the degrees of control of these conditions for each patient, and, most importantly, costs. This was a realistic representation of my reasonably achievable goals."

"How has this evolved?" Luke asked.

"The algorithms provided by this computer system could also develop and provide care plans for each individual patient, which included medication changes, immunizations, screening procedures, disease-management plans, and more. This would bring each patient's quality measures in line with the quality metrics established for the ideal panel," President Dmopvup said. "Disenrollment from Americare would result in punishment for the patient. For the provider, it would result in censure by the state medical board and the loss of the ability to practice and, therefore, make a living. It could also result in the providers losing their licenses to practice medicine.

"This was an incredible advance in computer hardware and software. This system had the ability to automatically generate care plans for each and every patient. The only difficulty was that the success of the system was largely dependent on compliance of the provider and the patient vis-à-vis prescriptions, immunizations, follow-up visits, screening procedures, and following the care plans. Because of this, we reached a plateau regarding our quality metrics and costs that were still a way off from the ideal patient panel."

"What did you do when you realized that you had reached a plateau?" Luke asked.

"Well, then I got to thinking," President Dmopvup said. "What if I could develop a system of algorithms that could achieve the same goals in terms of quality metrics by eliminating the need for patient and provider compliance? Other demographics and physical attributes, such as a patient's political affiliation, race, gender, and age, could also be used in the algorithms. The algorithms were then adjusted to give AMRS autonomy in the implementation of these care plans. The patient care orders would be generated and implemented by the algorithms automatically, without the need for input from a PA, APRN, DO, or MD."

Kyle looked at Luke in horror.

"The transition to this system was seamless for our patients and providers, as they were entirely unaware it had occurred," President Dmopvup said. "Patients come in for their appointments, as usual. Based on data entered into the medical record—patient demographics, lab results— and other data, algorithms within the AMRS develop individual care plans that in some cases result in the patient's death. These care plans are automatically implemented by AMRS, as reflected by orders in the patient's record that do not require their provider's signature. This way, we can effectively cull the herd, thereby removing patients with diseases and conditions that are poorly controlled, patients or their progeny who are likely to become a financial burden, and patients who have opposing political leanings. This has already proved to increase the relative number of favorable voters and improve our quality metrics, thus killing two birds with one stone, if you'll pardon the expression.

"Because almost every patient requires at least an injection or an immunization annually or a colonoscopy or other screening procedure at appropriate intervals, I decided these would be the appropriate times to implement the elimination parts of the new algorithms. I worked closely with the folks at Utopia Pharmaceuticals, a large contributor to my foundation and a company in which I have a controlling interest. Utopia had already developed micro-implants containing drugs, chemicals, infectious agents, biologic agents, cytokines, genetic material, and whatever else the algorithms require."

"So, you are killing people," Kyle said.

"Many of these are people who would likely die prematurely anyway," President Dmopvup said. "We are just making their journeys shorter and much less uncomfortable. These micro-implants are created and prepared for each individual patient, as instructed by QR codes developed by the algorithms. Utopia or one of its subsidiaries manufacture and package these individualized micro-implants inside an immunization, other injection, or a study-related device to be placed during colonoscopy, and they are shipped to the patient's practice in advance of their scheduled appointment.

"In the case of injectables, medical assistants administer these micro-implants, with the patients, medical assistants, and ordering providers being totally unaware that anything other than the ordered injections are being administered. This is likewise true for GI suite staff and the gastroenterologists, who place these implants during colonoscopy as part of their ongoing studies. Unfortunately for your wife, Karolyn, our algorithms selected her for elimination due to her opposing political points of view. Ze had PALBR implants placed in hir colon during hir routine screening colonoscopy. Eventually, the algorithms will get around to selecting you for elimination too.

"So, you set it up so that these people die at someone's hand other than your own," Kyle said. "How cowardly!"

"This was the only way to implement these changes so broadly. As a result of these new algorithms that eliminated the sickest of the sick, as well as those deplorables with political viewpoints running counter to my own, Americare's quality metrics once again began to improve, costs began to decline, and the size of my constituency increased dramatically."

"What about the seed money that you used from your foundation?" Kyle asked.

"As Americare still owed the foundation $5 million, I needed to figure out how to recoup my initial investment. I also wanted to have more control over which quality metrics required improvement and the rate at which these improvements would occur. This gave me direct control over our revenue stream and the costs of providing care, and it further increased the number of favorable voters at rates that I specified in the algorithms. Since the seed money for Americare came from the foundation, I decided early on to use the foundation to recoup the initial investment. By word of mouth to a small group of wealthy patients and friends, I suggested that if they wanted or needed anything that was not covered by their health plan, this might be overcome by contributing to the Dmopvup Foundation. I did this by inference and not directly, using others to infer that this option was available to them. Using third- and fourth-party mouthpieces, contributions were encouraged, and their issues were largely resolved.

"It began by giving patients coverage for medications and procedures that were denied coverage, and it quickly evolved into the ability for a contributor to have another Americare patient killed if the contribution was sufficiently large. The influence of the Dmopvup Foundation contributions even spread to include obtaining positions on the various organ transplantation lists, as well as the ability to select their organ donor from the population of healthy Americare patients who were on the list for elimination. A contributor could even select a donor who was not on the elimination list.

"This system has been utilized for the past six years with dramatic results with respect to our quality metrics and revenue, and very few administrative errors. Sean MacDonald's death was the result of an administrative error. The micro-implant that ze received under the guise of hir annual influenza vaccine was meant to be given to hir father, who shared the same name. As I need to protect the privacy of foundation contributors, that is all I will say. By means of monthly morbidity and mortality conferences, these issues are closely reviewed and addressed, and systems have been put in place to prevent and eliminate these sorts of errors. As these occurrences are addressed by our internal quality assurance program, they are not discoverable in a court of law.

There were many other programs that I developed that dovetailed nicely with Americare.

The national DNA library, organ and human cloning, and repurposing and reclamation programs for those who have outlived their algorithm-defined usefulness are some of them.

"Until now, no one has admitted any suspicion, and patients have been happy with their health care coverage. I intend on continuing this system of care, as it has brought the quality metrics and therefore the overall health of our population under better control. Our citizens are extremely happy with Americare. With the premiums being extremely low—often nonexistent—and with low deductibles, enrollment in Americare continues to increase. Americare is almost the sole insurer of the citizens of the United States. Yes, this is a monopoly, but it is a monopoly of necessity and of choice. The only way to break the monopoly would be to withdraw Americare from the marketplace, leaving no options for insurance coverage, even though health insurance is mandated. With the assistance of Attorney General Mapdj, FBI Director Duniz, and the Department of Justice, any antitrust or other related issues were resolved or quashed."

"Are you ready to sign, Dr. Moses? Mx. Sorensen?" President Dmopvup asked.

"You are despicable," Kyle said.

"We have no intention of signing anything," Luke said.

As Luke and Kyle refused to sign their settlement agreements, a loud commotion came from outside the door of the conference room. Then the door burst open, and a SWAT team rushed in—ten people dressed in black, wearing black face masks, and aiming rifles.

The apparent leader shouted in a familiar voice. "FBI! Put your hands on the table and then don't move, or you will be shot!" The leader's voice was remarkably familiar.

The agents made quick work of searching, Mirandizing, and cuffing everyone, including Attorney General Mapdj and FBI Director Duniz, who were aghast at their arrests. All were led out of the room in cuffs. The room was now quiet. The SWAT team leader sat down across from Luke and Kyle and removed his mask.

It was Michael! "I need to apologize to you both, especially to you, Kyle," he said.

Kyle was stunned.

"I was using both of you from the beginning. To be honest, the FBI has been investigating the president, Attorney General Mapdj, and my direct boss, FBI Director Duniz, since 2022, when President Dmopvup came up with $5 million from an unknown source and used it as seed money to create Americare. After more digging, it was discovered that President Dmopvup was involved with Americare and that the Dmopvup Foundation was also involved. The FBI and the Department of Justice were involved at some level as well—or at the very least, they were turning a blind eye. That was as far as the rank-and-file FBI agents could get unless they could investigate the situation from within, without raising any suspicion from the FBI director and those within the upper echelon of the FBI.

"Around 2023, the FBI's Office of Professional Responsibility, or OPR, which is essentially the FBI's internal affairs department, created a covert investigative unit to investigate any concerns regarding possible malfeasance within our government, including within the Department of Justice and the FBI. They were seeking an entirely naïve special agent who would work alone and in secrecy and report to no one. This special agent was charged with gathering the requisite information about Americare and President Dmopvup and, using the resources of the Bureau and the covert investigative unit, bring any justice to bear.

"This unit was created under the terms of a charter that rendered it essentially invisible to the executive, legislative, and judicial branches of our government, including the FBI and the FBI director. It was designed to function in an autonomous fashion. It was to remain invisible until the special agent who was hired to run the unit presented biometric codes to specified members of another equally stealthy independent unit that had also been created by and was working under the auspices of the OPR.

"While the covert investigative unit was being developed, I was getting ready to graduate from high school. I wanted to go to college, but I couldn't afford to go. I embarked on a search for grants and scholarships, and I applied for a grant through the federal government. I was afforded a full free ride through college in exchange for assuming an entirely new identity, attending an immersion program with the FBI while attending college, and participating in various other immersion programs through the FBI's Behavior Analysis Unit, the BAU, in Quantico, Virginia.

"That was all I knew when I was accepted for this grant program. My role as an FBI agent working in covert operations was revealed to me gradually during my college education and FBI training. Retinal scans and other biometric data were obtained to serve as the codes required by other OPR units, to be used for revealing my purpose, when that time came. These biometric data sets are what got me secretly sprung from captivity and permitted me to carry out the remainder of my covert operations assignment here.

"That is how I became an FBI agent. I spent half of each year in college and the other half of the year at FBI headquarters and at the BAU. Through an arrangement that the FBI had with my college, I was awarded a bachelor's degree in business administration, with a résumé that looked as if I had just matriculated at college for the entire four years. The BAU created a false persona, Michael Jude, whose résumé, personality, and goals were a perfect match for Americare, who was looking for practice liaisons at the time. This was done using government resources and means that were similar to those that President Dmopvup used to assume and protect hir identity.

"I lived the life of a college student, assuming the created life of Michael Jude, with the personality traits and characteristics that the BAU felt would render me most attractive for a position within Americare. I applied for a position of practice liaison within Americare, and I was hired almost on the spot. I was able to climb the ladder, contact important Americare officials such as Dr. Hsacis, gain their trust, become privy to important and confidential information, and gain access to AMRS. That was as far as I was able to get. I reviewed many patients' AMRS records, but I am not a health care provider. I was not well versed in health care, and my understanding of medical processes, issues, and terminology was limited.

"Then I developed a plan in which I would become close to a provider and leverage our relationship to gain information that I otherwise would not be able to obtain. I planned on using that provider in a variety of ways to bring any guilty party to justice and to end whatever illegal and/or unethical enterprises I discovered."

Michael reached out and took Kyle's hand in his. "Kyle, the feelings that developed and my self-revelation and growth are genuine, and they were entirely unexpected. I used you and put you at risk, and I feel awful, but there was no other way. When you apologized to me for using me, I apologized to you for using you too, but I couldn't tell you in which ways and to what extent I was using you. Luke, I apologize to you for steering you to file the complaint with HHS. Without that complaint, we wouldn't have been able to pit the government against itself, which was essential to exposing this scheme. I feel deeply responsible for Andy Canteenwalla's and Anne Wilson's deaths. They both died at the hands of our government. Andy was killed by a hit-and-run, and Anne was shot to death, both by killers contracted by the federal government."

Luke and Kyle looked at each other with surprise and sadness. They had no idea that Anne had been killed. This explained why they hadn't received a call or response after Jesús sent the email via the Internet Radio Linking Project system.

"I want to thank you both on my behalf and that of the United States of America and its citizens. Think about what this country would have been like ten years from now if you hadn't done what you did. You both were and are heroic."

Many thoughts and feelings coursed through Kyle's mind and soul. It was at that point that he realized that he and Luke were both outliers with respect to how they reacted to what they had seen and experienced. All the other providers, in the practice and likely nationwide, had merely accepted these untoward patient events and deaths as the cost of doing business, and they enjoyed the end results of improved salaries, less stress, and overall improvement of the health of the citizens. Kyle and Luke had chosen to question in the interest of their patients' health and safety and to risk everything in the process.

CHAPTER 36

After thanking Kyle and Luke, Michael offered to lead them out of the building and back to their own lives. When he turned the doorknob, however, he realized they were locked in.

A video of President Dmopvup then appeared on a wall.

"Dr. Moses and Mx. Sanderson, you were warned by Attorney Hartigan on several occasions that proceeding down this road would place you at risk of great loss. Mx. Jude, you have been aware of the risks of pursuing me all along. Yet you each chose to continue to go after me. So here we are."

"Where are we?" Luke asked.

"The room you are in is a part of a cell that was designed for you by FBI Director Duniz. This is the dayroom where you may watch TV, read, and eat your meals, which you may order from a menu that will be provided. There are three adjoining apartments—one for Mx. Jude, one for Dr. Moses and Mx. Sanderson, and one for Special Agent Saffron Truman, the FBI agent who was investigating your complaint." President Dmopvup pointed to the three doors at the back of the room. "Special Agent Truman deduced my involvement with the foundation and Americare in the course of being an excellent FBI agent. Unfortunately for hir, ze will have to pay the price for a job well done. Ze will be joining you here as soon as I am finished debriefing hir."

Kyle and Luke looked at each other in disbelief.

"Dr. Moses and Mx. Sanderson, I thought it would be nice for the two of you to room together, just like at home. Each apartment has ample sleeping quarters and bathroom facilities. You each will be treated as if you are guests at one of DC's finest hotels, the difference being that you cannot leave here. Dr. Moses and Mx. Sanderson, your plan to have the entire world become aware of my health care empire was a failure. This entire building is shielded in such a way as to prevent any broadcasts from leaving here. Instead, a computer-generated meeting between the three of us was broadcast on DNN, the Digital News Network, during which you, Dr. Moses, withdrew your complaint. You both signed the settlement agreements, and you each apologized to me and our citizens for misinterpreting the data and drawing inaccurate and inappropriate conclusions.

"During the couple of days that you have been guests of the federal government, audio and visual data was obtained by hidden cameras, and it was analyzed by the IQOD simulation and modeling algorithms. Technology developed by IQOD was used to create virtual avatars of each of you. These virtual, dynamic audio and video images were each paired with a human operator. I paired Dr. Moses with Attorney General Mapdj and paired Mx. Sanderson with FBI Director Duniz, and the three of us acted out a script that I wrote.

"The operators' motions, mannerisms, and speech are mirrored by the virtual avatars, using your video images, voices, and speech patterns. They say and do exactly what I want them to say and do, as I instructed their operators. These avatars exist only in the plane of virtual reality. I plan on using them in many creative ways, using computer-generated visual and audio feeds or as lifelike holograms on specially designed stages."

The video screen briefly went blank. Then, the news report began, with Kon Edutve, the DNN chief White House correspondent, standing outside the White House in the light rain.

"Today, President Jommesa Sufjen Dmopvup met with Dr. Lucas Moses, who filed a complaint with the US Department of Health and Human Services against Americare back on February 27, 2031. Hir colleague, Mx. Kyle Sanderson, the physician assistant in practice with Dr. Moses, as well as hir partner and the one who was the most active regarding this complaint, was also in attendance. The two alleged that the federal government and President Dmopvup were using Americare for political and financial gain and, in the process, knowingly causing harm to patients."

The video then switched to their meeting in the Oval Office, which was a holographic stage. President Dmopvup was situated behind hir desk, and avatars of Luke and Kyle were in comfortable chairs in front of hir. Correspondent Edutve continued hir report, with the voices of Luke, Kyle, and President Dmopvup heard faintly in the background.

"During the course of this meeting, the president presented the two with additional information that caused

Dr. Moses to withdraw hir complaint and for both Dr. Moses and Mx. Sanderson to offer formal apologies to President Dmopvup, our government, and our citizens."

The video then focused solely on the meeting, and the volume of the dialogue between Luke's and Kyle's avatars and the president then increased to become the focus of the broadcast.

"Mx. President, this additional information clarified what has been going on with our Americare patients," avatar Luke said as correspondent Edutve became silent to allow the audio to be heard. "Mx. Sanderson and I are entirely devoted to the care of our patients. When we were led to the erroneous conclusion that Americare was being used for financial and other gains by you and the government, I felt obligated to report this. In fact, I think I am mandated to report if I have any evidence that could indicate any fraud and/or abuse.

"Mx. President, I apologize to you, to our government, and to our citizens for drawing inaccurate conclusions and insinuating that you and the government somehow harmed patients for some sort of gain. In fact, Mx. President, I applaud you for greatly improving the health of our citizens and for making high-quality health care available to everyone for the entirety of their lives."

Avatar Kyle then spoke. "I also wish to apologize to you and to our country and its citizens. I think you and your administration are doing wonderful things for our citizens with respect to health care."

The volume diminished dramatically as a video of correspondent Edutve appeared in an outlined box in the corner of the screen. "President Dmopvup told the two that ze was grateful to them for bringing these issues to hir attention, and ze offered them administrative positions within Americare, from which vantage points they could bring complete resolution to any issues of concern. Dr. Moses and Mx. Sanderson accepted President Dmopvup's offer. In a gesture of solidarity and gratitude for their efforts, the president waived any potential criminal or professional repercussions for each of them.

"The meeting ended with both Dr. Moses and Mx. Sanderson expressing their complete and total support for the president and hir administration and Americare. They cited the markedly improved health of our citizens and that everyone has access to Americare. Kon Edutve, at the White House, in Washington, DC."

The video screen went blank again briefly, and then President Dmopvup reappeared.

"You will burn in hell for what you've done," Kyle said.

"You will remain here for an as-yet-undetermined amount of time," President Dmopvup said, ignoring Kyle. "During your stay, there will be multiple DNN broadcasts using your avatars that will further establish you as Americare administrators and supporters of me and my administration. You will become old news. Once this state of insignificance and irrelevance has been attained and is sustained for a period of time, the three of you will be put up for auction as organ donors for our various transplantation programs." President Dmopvup abruptly signed off.

"How sick is this!" Kyle said.

"Ze is a sociopath," Luke said.

"And what an asshole," Michael said.

Initially, Kyle believed that his outcome likely would be the same as that of the other outliers—Sean MacDonald, Lorraine Simons, Scott Smith, Lester Blumenthal, Carla Dossier, and Trinh Nguyen.

"This situation is an epiphany of sorts," Kyle said. "It is the unavoidable consequence of the confounding of our citizens. This allowed Americare's and the president's scheme to become established within our health care system, with our citizenry unaware and becoming increasingly beholden to the government."

"That's right," Luke said, "and now this system is free to propagate itself, run itself, replicate itself, increase in number and effect exponentially, and increasingly control our health care system and the health and the lives of our citizens."

"It's sort of like a virus taking advantage of the weakened immune system of its host," Kyle said. "It has established itself within the national genome and it has used the mechanisms of our constitutional republic to replicate exponentially and to flourish."

Kyle realized that the most important part of his calling was yet to come. He, Luke, Michael, and Saffron, unlike the outliers, apparently had immunity to this virus in some sense. They had not died unexpectedly or prematurely, and they were inside the belly of the beast and alive. They would be in an advantageous position if they could capitalize on this situation. Being guided by Sean's ghost, who appeared in Kyle's dreams on a nightly basis, Kyle was formulating a strategy.

One night, Anne Wilson appeared to Kyle while he was sleeping. It was as if she was in a courtroom, giving her summation, with Sean MacDonald, Lorraine Simons, Scott Smith, Lester Blumenthal, Carla Dossier, and Trinh Nguyen in the very front row of the jury box. Many others were behind them. Anne was standing in front of them, facing Kyle. She was wearing a blue suit with a white collar that was stained by her blood. Both of Anne's hands were missing, and her arms were drenched with blood that dripped on the courtroom floor. Her face was carved up and bloody, and her skin was sloughing where exposed. Pinned between the stump of her left wrist and her body was the clipboard that she often carried. She raised her right hand above her head, a fountain of blood pouring out of it, and shook it at Kyle, almost defiantly.

"The government is on the government's side. I warned you both. Fix this Kyle, so that the government is on the side of our citizens," Anne said.

Upon awakening, Kyle knew that his life and the lives of Luke, Michael, and Saffron would be spared and that their callings, too, were yet to unfold.

CHAPTER 37

Early in the morning of January 9, 2033, people trickled in, as was typical, to the monthly Primary Care Associates staff meeting. Dr. Seth Weinberg, the practice's medical director, was seated on his perch at the front of the room by 6:15 a.m., as always, when the first of the sleepy-headed attendees arrived. Dr. Weinberg called the meeting to order and reviewed the minutes of the past meeting, requesting a motion to accept. The motion was put forth by Pradeep Kahn, MD, one of six providers in the practice, and was seconded by Dr. Margaret Anderson, another one of the six. With no objections, the minutes were accepted, and the department meeting proceeded.

Dr. Weinberg then turned the meeting over to Martin Shandling, Primary Care Associates' chief financial officer, to review the practice's current financial situation and quality metrics. His report indicated their quality metrics had never been better, and they were improving with greater velocity than ever before. The patients had never been healthier. Likewise, revenue for the practice was robust, affording a whopping 12 percent margin annually. All providers exceeded their productivity goals and at least matched their quality metrics targets. The meeting was then turned back over to Dr. Weinberg for his closing remarks.

"In the larger scheme of things, the health of our nation has reached its peak. Thanks to President Jommesa Sufjen Dmopvup, we now have a single-payer system run by our government that provides the highest-quality health care. This care is now available to every citizen at a low, often nonexistent cost. As a 'side effect' of our health care system, our government is now making a profit that will be sufficient to eliminate our country's debts within the next twenty years or sooner.

"Americare is functioning exceptionally well. Our nation and its citizens are in the best state of health. This is evidenced by our nation's markedly improved quality metrics and increase in life span. By virtue of their complaint and their arduous work and dedication to their cause, Dr. Luke Moses and Mr. Kyle Sanderson succeeded in pushing our government to restore our health care system to one that is solely evidence-based. It was Dr. Moses's complaint and their collective efforts that brought about the necessary changes in our health care system and in Americare that were required to make our nation's health care system healthy and well. They did this at a great personal sacrifice. For these things, as well as others, we should be grateful to them for making our nation well. They each are exceptional providers who love our patients, our citizens, and our country. Although they are missed greatly here at home, they are now in a much better position to address the needs of our country's citizens and patients. Working for President Dmopvup and hir administration within the Americare system, I am certain that Kyle and Luke will continue to bring exceptional care to all our citizens." He looked around the room at everyone. "Any new business?"

There was a brief period of silence.

"Seeing none, this meeting is adjourned. See you all next month."

CHAPTER 38

Darkness was everywhere as Kyle rubbed the sleep from his eyes. His right hand and arm tingled but were otherwise insensate, as was usual due to his position in bed. Kyle was the little spoon, with his back protected by his big spoon, Luke, who was still fast asleep. He lay there a while, taking in the silence and enjoying the feeling of Luke's breath across the nape of his neck and the warmth of Luke's body close to his back. Sunlight was just beginning to peek above the windowpane as a harbinger of the coming morning.

Today will be a new day, Kyle thought optimistically, although he had little doubt that it would be the same as days past. Despite all his efforts, he had lost track of the days. President Dmopvup had promised them that ze would do hir best to confound all their senses and cause them to forget. Ze had succeeded.

Kyle had witnessed the passage of the seasons. They were much less pronounced in the DC area than in New Hampshire, and he did not have access to windows that overlooked deciduous trees. He was uncertain how many falls, winters, springs, and summers had indeed passed. It could have been one or one hundred that had passed.

They weren't permitted to go outside so the ambient temperature was always around seventy-two degrees. No mention was made of Christmas, as the government considered it insulting and offensive to those of secular or other persuasions. Absent were the scents of roasting turkey, pies baking, gingerbread, and peppermint. Only the stale hotel-like and hospital-like odors pervaded their living quarters. Any written or other recordings that would indicate date or season were noticeably absent. They had no access to the internet, television, radio, or newspapers, save for some videos and movies that had been screened and edited. They did have an alarm clock that kept them informed of the time and permitted them to wake on time for work. Kyle felt confident, however, that at least one year had passed since their confinement on August 18, 2032—at least, he thought it was August 18, 2032. To the best of Kyle's calculations and recollection the present year was 2033, sometime in the winter or fall.

As the sliver of sunlight coursed across his eyelids and then Luke's, Luke groaned, and the two kissed each other awake for the day and got out of bed. After showering, shaving, and attending to personal hygiene, they threw on sweat clothes and left their apartment for the dayroom to join Saffron and Michael, who already were there for breakfast. The four were somewhat grateful that their lives had been spared for just one more day, although they weren't entirely sure why they were grateful. Kyle began his day by remembering how things had reached this state. Unbeknownst to him, the other three began their days in a similar fashion.

There they all sat in silence, waiting. Unlike in their residences and the rest of the building, the aroma of bacon, coffee, burned toast, and a hint of maple syrup pervaded the dayroom. The telltale sounds of the shuffling gait two drones, with the rolling wheels of their food truck, became apparent, which caused the four to sit up at attention. In a world devoid of things to look forward to, this breakfast routine was something that brought the foursome a sense of pleasure and optimism. They had no idea where the drones came from, and they didn't think to question. For some unknown reason, the four hostages simply accepted the existence of the drones, as if the inquisitive parts of their brains had been deactivated or numbed, and as if drones had been around forever.

The drones remained silent as they removed food trays covered with plastic cloches from slots within the food truck and placed one in front of each of them. Another drone followed with a pot of coffee in one hand and a pitcher of orange juice in the other, carefully, and accurately pouring a little of each beverage into vessels in front of the four. Each drone wore an off-white linen jumpsuit that had AMERICARE, followed by a string of unique numbers embossed on the left breast, overlying a decal of the American flag. They each also donned an off-white cloth head covering that permitted only their eyes to be visible.

As quickly and quietly as they camblank-staring in, the drones shuffled out of the dayroom, leaving behind the food truck and two rather large trucks that held linens, which reminded the four that today was laundry day—the bed sheets required changing and laundering.

No one talked during breakfast, as if there was no point in it. They knew that they were continually being watched and followed. They ate in silence, with each sharing fleeting glances with the others, all while Kyle and Luke intermittently holding hands.

Suddenly, the back wall of the dayroom came alive with a video broadcast of President Dmopvup. They had not heard or seen the president, in person or hir facsimile, since their confinement, so this was extremely unusual. Kyle's heart rate increased dramatically as his attention focused on the wall. Luke and Kyle tightened their grips on each other's hands.

"Good morning, Dr. Moses, Mx. Sanderson, Mx. Jude, and Mx. Truman," the projection of President Dmopvup began. "I thought it was time that we meet again, and that we redefine your purposes. A lot has changed since we last spoke."

Kyle and Luke looked at each other with raised eyebrows, still hand in hand, wondering what was to follow.

"It is Sunday, December 4, 2033, a bit over a year since the presidential election that granted me my fourth term," the president said. "The four of you have been here since August 18, 2032, since about three months prior to my reelection.

"My Americare health plan has continued to flourish. At the time of your confinement, there were three or four other health insurance products available in the health care marketplace. By offering Americare free to all citizens and even paying citizens to enroll, we succeeded in cornering the health care marketplace. Since January 1, 2033, Americare has been the sole health insurance product available to our citizens. Because there is no competition and because health insurance is required, this is a monopoly, but a monopoly of necessity, which renders all antitrust legislation inapplicable. I succeeded in creating an unavoidable but necessary health insurance monopoly.

"It was only a natural extension of this that the USPSTF—the United States Preventive Services Task Force—established the AMRS algorithms and patient care plans as 'best practice' and 'standard of care' in our country. Currently, most primary care consists of following the AMRS-generated care plans for each patient, and these care plans require no clinical judgment on the part of our providers. In fact, clinical training and judgment have proven to be liabilities, and I envision a time in the not-too-distant future when almost all primary health care services will be provided by non-clinically trained providers, drones, or even robots. Robotic booths are being set up in various shopping centers in anticipation of this transition.

"My plan is succeeding in eliminating anyone with serious, complex, life-threatening illness, not by curing it but by direct elimination of it. Because of this, Americare's quality metrics indicate that our patient panel, and therefore our citizenry, is at its healthiest yet, approaching that of our computer-generated, actuarially ideal patient panel. Your work has made my success possible, and for that, I thank you. Any questions?"

Kyle spat at the screen. The next thing he knew, he was in a daze, being picked up off the floor by Luke and Michael. He later learned that a low-level electromagnetic pulse had emanated from his microchip, the result of an automatic response of AMRS to Kyle's spitting as his expression of his disgust and his disrespect toward the president.

"You are not free to do and act as you choose," President Dmopvup said. "Disrespect and insubordination will not be tolerated. I still can have you squashed like a bug. Is that understood?"

Kyle nodded his head in acknowledgement.

The four sat in silence for a few minutes after President Dmopvup's video message concluded. Kyle was still in a daze, and Luke sought to comfort him. Kyle's physical and mental states rapidly returned to his baseline. Despite what had just transpired, Kyle and Luke remained hopeful, yet still uncertain about their fate. *Is the auction for our organs about to commence?* Kyle thought.

Shortly after breakfast was cleared, the telltale sounds of drones shuffling toward the dayroom could be heard in the distance.

Four drones shuffled in, each one carrying a different colored pile of folded jumpsuits, along with work-assignment instructions; each brought the assigned color to the respective captive. The four had gotten used to wearing the same sweat suit–like jumpsuits every day. A drone carrying a pile of red jumpsuits approached Saffron, stopped about a foot or so from her, and dropped the bundle of clothing and neatly typed work-assignment instructions into her outstretched arms. The same routine occurred with Luke, Michael, and Kyle, with their respective colors, instructions, and drones.

The drones then shuffled out as quietly as they had entered, and Kyle, Luke, Michael, and Saffron followed, heading toward their respective apartments. After entering their apartments, they each placed their jumpsuits on their beds and reviewed their work-assignment instructions. These work assignments were new, aside from Michael's assignment, which would be a continuation of what he had been doing since early on in their captivity. All were off from work that day, and all would be working the day shift on the next day, as opposed to two each working day—one working the evening shift, and one on night shift on a rotating basis.

Kyle and Luke spent much of their free time together and away from the others. Kyle's muscles were sore from the shock he had received at breakfast, and he was exhausted as much as he was angry and disgusted with President Dmopvup. Luke and Kyle placed their jumpsuits in their chests of drawers, and Kyle lay down for a nap. He was immediately joined in his dreamscape by the ghost of Sean, with whom Kyle discussed options for escape, ending the Americare scheme, and bringing the president and his cronies to justice. The entirety of this discussion was camouflaged from Dmopvup's view and ears by the shroud of a dream, covering up Kyle's mutual sharing of ideas and plans with the ghost of a dead boy.

Luke went back to the dayroom to join Saffron and Michael. This was the first time in a long while that all had the same day off and would be working the day shift starting the next day. They spent the rest of the day talking, playing cards, and watching permitted movies and videos. After his restorative nap, Kyle joined the three in the dayroom. This occurred regularly whenever any of the foursome had the same time off or even when only Michael and Saffron were free.

Kyle put down an eight of spades, careful to keep his eyes down. Luke stared at the card. Michael put down a heart card, and Saffron followed with a club.

The four captives had developed a rudimentary form of communicating by acting, talking, and playing cards in a sort of cypher that disguised the meaning of what they were doing and discussing from the omnipresent eyes and ears of President Dmopvup. It was a simple code. Kyle was surprised that the drones hadn't caught on. The topic was always the same: escape.

It appeared to anyone observing that they were just playing cards and watching the television screen. This rudimentary mode of communication using this code rendered any headway incredibly slow, if nonexistent, but they believed that painfully slow and steady might win the race, whereas stagnation and failure without trying or being too blatant or obvious in their communications would certainly result in their demise.

Kyle and Luke had grabbed the positions on the lounge chairs that they had established as their places, and Michael and Saffron stationed themselves on opposite ends of the loveseat; the afternoon of watching movies, playing cards, and talking commenced. This became a regular event almost every day after their work assignment was completed now that they all had the same work schedule. During these movie-and-card-game afternoons and evenings, a secondary agenda involving just Michael and Saffron developed and progressively matured, under the radar and with Kyle and Luke entirely unaware. It was a miniscule magnet-like attraction that was so subtle that, initially, Michael and Saffron were unaware of it too.

Michael and Saffron shared a lot in common, both being FBI agents and having to live within that sort of cloistered society with all its rules and regulations, as well as secrets and privileges. Their shared experiences and their sense of "FBI-ness" resulted in the rather rapid development of platonic friendship, and it set the stage for the possibility of more than that. By the end of each card night, the two would sit progressively closer to each other in the middle of the love seat, having moved there from its ends unknowingly. As the months passed, the distance between the two on the love seat decreased at a more rapid rate. The first card game was spent with the two at opposite ends of the love seat the entire night. By the middle of the fifth card-game-and-movie-night get-together, the two were in the middle of the loveseat. From then on, the time it took for the two to sit in the middle had progressively decreased until they began the get-together by sitting next to each other, with their arms around each other's shoulders.

The afternoon ended with the sounding of the one-hour notice of pending supper, which caused each of them to go to their respective apartments to wash up for their evening meal. This, too, had become something that they each looked forward to, in this world almost devoid of other causes for optimism and pleasure. Kyle was also revitalized after a chat with the ghost of Sean.

It became apparent that President Dmopvup had changed their work schedules to allow the four of them to get closer and to permit hir to observe any communication between them, regardless of how rudimentary. They were always under twenty-four/seven audiovisual surveillance.

Each was enjoying the day off, and each eagerly awaited their new work assignments, starting the following day.

CHAPTER 39

Michael's ears throbbed. He sat bolt upright in bed as he was awakened by the first of several blasts of his alarm clock that he had set for 5:30 a.m. Work would begin at 7:30 a.m. sharp. He allowed plenty of time for a shower and shave. Since the impromptu audiovisual meeting with President Dmopvup the day before, he began keeping track of the days, writing them down each morning on a small piece of paper hidden under his mattress and on another one kept inside his briefs. It was Monday, December 5, 2033; he wrote the date down on the papers.

He arose, grabbed his bathrobe from the hook inside his bedroom closet door, and walked into the adjacent living room. He donned the robe awkwardly as he walked to the coffee maker. It had already been set up with a pod of French Roast and a coffee mug underneath. He pushed the brew button; then he headed to the bathroom. He turned on the shower, opening the valve to maximize the hot water spray. Steam filled the bathroom and coated the mirror. It formed a blackboard of sorts, obscuring the view. He wrote "Good morning, Michael!" on the mirror with his finger, smiling all the while.

It was a trade-off between steamy warmth and the ability to see his reflection. The steam won out. The coffee maker had just finished its job as Michael walked by it, and he grabbed the piping-hot cup of French Roast from underneath the dispenser. He ambled back toward the bathroom for his morning shower, sipping the hot beverage along the way, not spilling even one drop. After entering the bathroom, he placed the coffee mug on the bathroom counter. He let the bathrobe slip to the floor but scooped it up and placed it on the hook on the back of the door. He pulled off his briefs and stuck his date list on the bathroom counter as he stepped into the steamy shower. He stood there in the shower, pensive, for several minutes before he commenced his showering routine.

This was a well-orchestrated ballet, of sorts. It occurred every morning in identical sequence and without any apparent effort on Michael's part, including his insatiable desire for his morning French Roast and the subsequent shower. While standing in the shower and washing, he was in deep thought about many things almost all at once. Thoughts about Saffron and the futility of it all were always on his mind. He was also obsessed with escaping from captivity and bringing the president to justice—and saving the citizens from the perceived impending disaster.

Michael knew that he was in love with Saffron. He was always preoccupied with her, thinking of ways to express his love and find out whether she felt the same way about him. Although he was well trained, his FBI training came at a cost. He had missed that portion of a young man's life that teaches him how to deal with falling in love. His adolescence and young adulthood had been replaced by the rigorous training required to become an FBI agent. By the time he gave serious thought to how to approach Saffron, his shower was over, and it was time to dry off, shave, and get dressed for the day.

With a towel wrapped around his waist, he walked into his bedroom, opened his bureau, and removed the pile of recently laundered jumpsuits. There were seven to choose from. They were identical, each light blue, with AMERICARE embossed on the left breast pocket; underneath was embossed NATIONAL GENOME REGISTRY. Underneath all this lettering was the Great Seal of the United States. Somewhere within the structure of each jumpsuit were several small microchips identifying the garment as uniquely his. If even one of the microchips in the jumpsuit didn't communicate appropriately with the one placed under his skin, alarms would sound whenever he passed one of the omnipresent detectors. This would raise an alarm that the wearer of the jumpsuit was an imposter, of sorts, at least impersonating the owner of the jumpsuit for some uncertain purpose, or at the very least just borrowing it. It was a criminal act to wear someone else's jumpsuit or to permit anyone else to wear theirs. Michael selected a jumpsuit from the middle of the pile and placed the rest back in the drawer. Even though they were identical in all respects, the jumpsuit with the small black blemish on the inside label seemed to fit better and feel better, so that's the one he chose.

He put on his briefs, slipping the date list inside. Then he grabbed the jumpsuit du jour and strode back into the bathroom, where he shaved and applied antiperspirant under his arms. He then hopped into his jumpsuit and zippered it closed. He stepped into special white shoes that he wore solely for work, which also contained his microchips, completing his work attire for the day.

Michael finished his coffee with a gulp and then headed for the door of his apartment. It closed and locked behind him as he stepped into the hallway. He chose to skip breakfast. He was met in the hall by his drone escort, who would accompany him to his place of work. His shoes were silent on the floor, entirely overcome by the unmistakable sounds of the shuffling of the drone's feet. No words were spoken as they entered the elevator and descended a minute or two to level 2. It was the express elevator, taking him directly to his destination without any other stops. During his passage, he wondered about the genesis of drones. *How did they come to be? Who are they? Why do they have a shuffling gait? Why are they seemingly mute?*

With a ding, the elevator door slid open, revealing a short hallway. At the end of this hallway was a large set of double doors with NATIONAL GENOME REGISTRY in black lettering centered above it.

Michael's work at the National Genome Registry had become routine. He had been stationed at the National Genome Registry Headquarters in Washington, DC, almost since the day he entered captivity. This was the central office of the registry, which provided the user of the registry access to information regarding the genetic makeup of anyone in the entire country. Furthermore, it was often the starting point of desktop cloning, a process by which the operator of the system ordered a clone with specific features, as if ordering from a fast-food menu.

Desktop cloning consisted of a progressive series of menus; each one based upon the operator's selections on the previous menu. It was set up in such a way as to avoid or mitigate any cloning errors resulting from the operator's lack of knowledge or understanding of genetics, basic biology, and the cloning process. Once completed, the entire menu was forwarded to the Cloning and the Microchip Divisions for further processing.

Although the National Genome Registry was the simplest of the more advanced services offered by Americare, it was really the cornerstone of all the advanced services—microchipping, micro-implantation, organ and human cloning, repurposing, and reclamation, and the like. All these services began shortly after the National Genome Registry was up and running, and they each built upon it.

"Good morning, Michael," a monotone voice greeted him upon his approach to the entrance; the double doors slid open with a wisping sound.

"Morning, Simon. How are ya?" Michael chose to call the voice Simon, largely because he thought the name suited him.

Michael crossed the threshold of the first set of automatic doors, which closed immediately upon his entry. The drone peeled off and to the right upon the door's closure, seemingly disappearing into thin air, as a large puff of steam that smelled of antiseptic flooded the airlock into which he had been led. Michael automatically raised his hands above his head, and he completed a preemptive slow pirouette as the jets of warm antiseptic steam brushed his armpits and enveloped his body.

"Right leg in first, then left," Simon instructed as Michael stepped into his outer garment, which was hanging from the ceiling, facing forward, with an open zipper in the back that welcomed his entrance. "Next are your arms—left one, then the right," Simon said, as Michael followed.

The white cloth-like suit was zipped closed in back by the airlock drone, whose job it was to repetitively zip and unzip this attire, and a lightweight helmet with transparent plastic face shield was lowered onto the suit and then secured with clips. Air was provided into the suit from a hose that exited the helmet and was also suspended from the ceiling. Likewise, there was a series of wires and other tubes, all of which were zip-tied together at various places as the neatly bundled series of tubes and wires progressed upward from his helmet to the ceiling. The airlock drone checked each bundle to make sure the zip ties were intact and that there were no loose tubes or wires.

An intricate system of pulleys, thin steel cables, tracks, and rails allowed Michael to ambulate freely about the room while tethered to his air supply, electricity, and whatever else, no matter where he traveled. These hoses, tubes, and electrical wires disappeared into a hole in the ceiling, presumably en route to their respective sources, being played out as needed for his ambulation with enough slack to provide his free travel wherever he chose to go.

"Thanks, Simon. You have a wonderful day," Michael said as the rearward airlock door opened upon his approach and permitted him to enter his workspace, with all the tubing and wiring suspended from the ceiling in tow. He never really understood the need for all this hoopla, as he had no contact with any living tissue, disease, chemical, or the like. His job consisted mainly of looking at a computer screen. In asking around, he found out that everyone's workspace, regardless of where they worked at Americare, was the same with regard to the bodysuits, apparent decontamination upon entry, and overall concern with sterility. Also, he determined that his job was the most boring of all, yet it was also one of the most important and valuable.

Since 2022, samples of everyone's DNA had been collected, analyzed, categorized, and logged into the system. This represented most of the work that Michael was doing daily; entering data regarding specimens and their respective citizens. It was estimated that no one escaped having their tissue collected. Tissues were collected at local levels, most often at each citizen's health care provider's office, and they were processed and kept locally as well. The central office, where Michael was working, also served as the local office for the Washington, DC, metro area.

Buccal swabs were the most collected sources of DNA. Other sources were common too, including skin biopsies, sputum, blood, and saliva. These specimens were logged into the National Genome Registry. The characteristics of each tissue sample could be viewed from anywhere there was computer access. The National Genome Registry was essentially a complete library of the DNA from every citizen of the United States.

Michael clunked his way to his desk and computer screens, with the bundle of tubes and wires in tow. The head gear was somewhat bulky and cumbersome. "Shit," he said as he whacked his head.

"Careful," said Simon. "We need you in the best of shape to perform your duties at your best level of ability."

"Yeah, I know," Michael snapped under his breath.

There were four other people sitting at identical workstations. Everything was white, and the lighting was harsh and fluorescent, as one might expect. After he logged into his computer, there were already lists of clients and specimens on the screen that begged attention. There was also a large bin containing multiple specimen containers and completed requisition forms that needed to be processed, reconciled, and otherwise entered into the National Genome Registry.

He also needed to address a list of errors that were a result of his work from the previous day. Although there was relatively minimal risk, he imagined the possibilities if the wrong genetic material was combined. Rules needed to be followed; otherwise, the results could be catastrophic. Everyone in Michael's line of work had experienced this at one time or another, at least several times per day.

Michael continued with his work through the morning; then the noon meal buzzer went off, announcing lunch. Lunch was provided by the organization, usually a sandwich made of cold cuts, Spam, or "Faux"—a processed food product that had enjoyed a resurgence in this country during the last several years. He navigated himself back into the airlock, performing this morning's dance in reverse.

With Simon instructing him, Michael removed the protective garb, received his fumigation, then backed out of the airlock entirely and into the lunchroom. After washing his hands thoroughly, Michael sat down alone at one of the automated dining stations.

"Good afternoon, Mr. Jude. What will it be today?" a friendly but obviously synthesized feminine voice asked.

"Good afternoon, Sally. I hope your day has been going well," Michael said—because she did sound like a Sally. "I'd like a large Faux meat grinder loaded with jalapeños, lettuce, tomato, onion—all the good stuff." He chuckled a bit. "And a Diet Coke, a cup of black coffee, and a chocolate fudge brownie."

Within a few minutes, everything that Michael had ordered appeared on the conveyor belt in front of him. He removed each item, one at a time, as if removing luggage from a carousel.

Michael enjoyed this part of his day the most, mainly because he knew that he had rounded the halfway mark. In honesty, he found his job to be exquisitely boring. Even the most "exciting" parts of it—all of it was boring! The most interesting and skill-requiring parts were getting the bodysuit and air hose on and off inside the airlock. The job itself was nothing more than that of a lowest-level librarian. Boring as it was, however, his job was also extremely important. It was this feeling of importance that made Michael feel somewhat proud to have this job.

Once he concluded his noontime meal, he returned to his workplace somewhat energized, ready for the afternoon. He thoughtlessly guided himself through the process of donning his bodysuit, air hose, and helmet with Simon's assistance, and then found his way back to his workstation. His computer screens were as pristine as when he had left for lunch—no new business there.

Michael's afternoons were spent logging in new DNA samples by entering new specimen information into AMRS. These were specimens that had been obtained during routine provider visits, surgical procedures, or something similar on the previous day. Every citizen was required to have their DNA sample updated every five years or whenever it appeared as if new specimens were required. Patients' medical records would automatically notify their providers upon logging into the patients' records, and the samples would be obtained simply by swabbing their mouths or other procedures. There was always something that needed to be done to maintain the National Genome Registry in good and functioning order. Often, the specimens would be obtained from blood tests that had been ordered by a provider for another reason.

Typed or handwritten requisition slips containing patient or specimen information were collected from various locations within the Americare's Washington, DC, facility and brought to his office, along with the specimens, for processing. Given all of this technology, the existence of paper forms seemed to him to be antiquated and inappropriate. The specimens were separated from the requisition forms once given a unique QR code containing all available patient and specimen information. They were sent to pathology or their other destination. Once there, a small subsample of each specimen was obtained and catalogued for genomic testing and analysis. Another small subsample of each specimen was saved.

The National Genome Registry was continuously changing and continuously updating and expanding to reflect the size of a progressively healthier population. Michael's job was to make certain that the registry was current and that every citizen had a DNA sample that had been obtained within the last five years. There were systems in place to remind patients that they were due for DNA testing and that they should contact their primary care provider's office and arrange to have this done. This was seamless and stealthy, for the patients just thought that their doctors were calling to schedule routine visits or blood tests. They were entirely unaware of the National Genome Registry and that the genesis of the phone call was from one of the highest levels of the federal government.

It was here that Michael's workday began with a "good morning" at 7:30 a.m. His workday typically ended at 5:00 p.m., with a "have a good night" from Simon, after his specimen cataloguing for the day was completed.

Geoffrey A. Lundy, M.D.

CHAPTER 40

Luke and Kyle awoke the next morning as they did every other—little-spoon Kyle's eyes gently opening, becoming aware of his surroundings, rolling over to face big-spoon Luke and kissing him awake. Kyle typically lay there, looking at his love, with a deep sense of gratitude for him. The gentle caress of Kyle's lips as they brushed against Luke's was usually enough to rouse Luke from his deep sleep. They always took a moment or two to just hang out in each other's arms and snuggle a bit before getting up and heading to the bathroom.

They had established their own routine. Luke headed right for the shower, Kyle trudged off to the sink, and then they reversed their positions. Kyle only needed to shave every two to three days because his beard was light, both in texture and in color. Despite the passage of time, it was still difficult to discern whether Kyle was a boy or a man. Once Kyle spoke, however, one realized that he was clearly a man of maturity well beyond his years.

Luke, being twenty years older than Kyle, made Kyle's youth even more stark in comparison to Luke's maturity. Luke was balding, keeping what was left closely cut to his scalp, and, aside from occasional scruffiness, he was cleanly shaven on most days. The two fit together perfectly. Their love for each other was apparent in everything they said and did.

Once the two were cleaned up and dressed in clean sweat clothes, and their beds were made, they headed to the dayroom for the morning dance of the drones and for breakfast. This was followed by a brief return to their apartment to get into their work clothes before heading off to work. Luke's new work assignment was in the Microchipping and Micro-Implant Division, and Kyle's was in the Cloning Division.

Since their first days of captivity, the four had been required to work five days each week. Work assignments began as simple tasks—cleaning floors, delivering interoffice mail, filing, and the like. Assignments changed every three months or so and became increasingly complex with each change. The only one of the work assignments that had remained the same since their first day of captivity was Michael's work assignment. He always worked at the national headquarters of the National Genome Registry. He did his job extremely well, and he appeared interested in it, which likely was why he remained there.

After donning his green jumpsuit, Luke kissed Kyle goodbye for the day and headed off to work in the Microchipping and Micro-Implant Division of Americare. There was a drone outside his room door that escorted Luke to the elevator. It was a rather long and circuitous walk, which Luke later grew to look forward to, because by the time he arrived at his workstation, he was energized by the brisk pace of his walk. His walk ended at the doors of an awaiting elevator, occupied by a drone that took him to his destination, the Microchip Laboratory on level 4.

Using the ID badge applied directly to the sleeve of the jumpsuit, he contacted a pad, while looking through what appeared to be a retina-scanning device. The door slid open silently into a vestibule to an air lock, or laminar flow room. A recorded message directed Luke to a shower that sprayed him with dry chemicals, then to an awaiting light-green hazmat-looking bodysuit hanging from the ceiling by a hose. He climbed into the suit, which was zipped up by an air lock drone, and the helmet was secured in place. He was directed to another electric door, which slid open upon his approach, revealing a gymnasium-like atrium of sorts, where many people walked about wearing suits just like his, also attached to the ceiling. There was also an assembly line, with green-suited people standing alongside, performing their repetitive tasks.

"Get over here!" said one rather large, green-suited individual, who motioned at Luke to take his place along the conveyor. "I am 11275," he said. "I am your boss."

"I'm—"

"Luke Moses, yeah, I know who you are," 11275 said. "Let's take a little walk."

Luke followed close behind until they entered a small conference room-like facility, and he closed the door. The two sat down.

"You are in the Microchip Laboratory, or ML," 11275 said. "This is where all the microchips are manufactured. They are distributed from here to the various satellite facilities for distribution throughout the United States to every Americare facility in the country and even worldwide. One of these satellite facilities is in the room next door. Microchips and some micro-implants are installed in these facilities. They are also installed in our human cloning facility. Hence, we have a remarkably close relationship with all other departments, from the National Genome Registry to the Organ and Human Cloning Facility. The microchipping program has grown since its development in 2022. Micro-implants have been in use by Americare since 2021. Microchips and micro-implants are not the same device."

"How long has this been going on?" Luke asked.

"I just told you," 11275 scolded. "But I will tell you again in more detail. Since its inception in 2022, microchips have been placed within every single newborn baby at the time of birth. All living adults have been microchipped as a part of their routine health care visits, under the guise of routine immunizations or during routine procedures. Initially, these were installed unprogrammed because we did not have the technology required to program them. We were only interested in the safe incorporation of a solid-state electronic device within the central nervous system of a human host, without any rejection. Once that was achieved, these microchips were used as two-way conduits, providing sensory and tracking information to AMRS, and they permitted AMRS some degree of control over its host. Progressively more sophisticated AMRS technology has afforded us the ability to program these microchips, to instill memories and desires, to give the host motivation, and to provide more control over them. You and your friends are microchipped, which is our guarantee that you cannot flee, among other things. If you were to get away, your memories of this conversation would be wiped clean, made nonexistent. You could also just be destroyed. So, you see, microchips are especially important. Any further questions?"

Luke was aghast but said nothing.

"Follow me, Luke," 11275 said as he briskly walked through another set of automatic sliding doors. Luke followed close behind; his sense of disgust at what he had learned had gradually faded. "We are now in the Microchip Programming and Repurposing Laboratory, or MPRL. It is here that all microchips are programmed or reprogrammed. Most are now preprogrammed so that once they are installed, the host assumes the program within his or her own nervous system in a seamless fashion. All programs are gradual enough that the host, their acquaintances, and family members are not aware of the changes, if any, in the host's personality or behavior. Also, their microchips are programmed to accept any changes in the host after the placement of the microchip. The actual program resides within AMRS and not within the microchip itself. Much of the ongoing programming of a microchip occurs automatically by subroutines within AMRS, and it does not involve any human or other input. Microchips can also be programmed manually by someone sitting at a computer screen, using the microchip programming software.

"Microchips are under a process of constant updating,

automatically occurring through the auspices of AMRS. Person-specific updates can be entered at one of many user terminals. These updates can change the chip, and therefore its host, in a variety of ways. The updates produce responses that AMRS would issue to situations presented to the individual and not necessarily how the individual would respond without the microchip. AMRS has an overall plan in place, and the microchips and their programming ensure that we are all on target for the overall plan—having the healthiest, easiest, least expensive, and most profitable patient panel. There are also a very few additional specialized health plans within Americare that individuals may buy that permit them to alter other individuals' microchips, including their own, through a contribution to the Dmopvup Foundation. I will give you more on this later. Any questions so far, Luke?"

"Um … no, not really." Luke was in a state of utter disbelief. He realized that the microchip served as an interface between its human host and AMRS, allowing AMRS—and hence, the government and the president—the ability to control everyone. At the very least, the microchip acted like a memory card in a laptop computer, increasing its RAM and memory and computing capacity. In actuality, the microchip served as a conduit to and from AMRS, with its hardware and software able to control everyone and the entire society, so the president could achieve hir goals.

"Good, well, speak up if you have any questions," 11275 said. "The only stupid questions are the ones that we don't want you to ask. The actual microchips were developed and manufactured here in the USA by a top-secret unique process that no one else has access to. They are basically solid-state devices that are stamped out in a matrix using advanced organ-on-chip technology. They are, essentially, a transplanted artificial organ that assists the brain. It becomes fully integrated within the individual, as a transplanted organ would, within about a week, except there is absolutely no rejection; it is melded to the human organism in a way that prevents that. With the advent of the microchip, Americare has succeeded in creating the first true society of cyborgs— cybernetic organisms. We are now a society of human organisms, each augmented by the presence of a cybernetic brain-on-a-chip."

11275 then led Luke through another set of automatic sliding doors into the Microchip Installation Facility, or MIF, a room with twenty or so stretchers.

"In about thirty minutes or so, these beds will be filled with people, each of whom will receive a microchip or who will have a microchip replaced. Some of these are new clones receiving their designated microchip. This process takes about five minutes and is entirely painless. Once installed, the chips are typically programmed on the fly as they are used. The system works sort of like the old cellular telephones did. There is a network of antennae, through which individual microchips are constantly being updated—again, like the old cellular phones.

"Who decides how each microchip will be programmed?" Luke asked.

"Why, AMRS does," 11275 said.

Luke was a bit taken aback by the matter-of-factness with which that comment rolled off 11275's tongue. The fact that everyone was entirely under the control of an electronic medical record system was horrifying to him. Even more horrifying was how acceptable this was to 11275 and likely to everyone working in this division. Luke had no doubt that his microchip was being reprogrammed, and in short order, so that he would soon find this control acceptable and even comforting.

"Follow me, Luke. Hop to it!" 11275 said.

The two continued on their walking tour, passing through another double set of automatic doors with an air lock in between them. They stopped inside the air lock between the doors.

"Next, we will enter the Micro-Implant Laboratory, or MIL for short," 11275 said. "This is where micro-implants have been made since we started using them around 2020. Micro-implants are miniaturized delivery systems that can deliver genetic material, biologic substances, chemicals, drugs, immunizations, infectious agents, and most anything else one can think of, as specified by a timer, of sorts, within the micro-implant. The purpose of these micro-implants is to make our population as healthy as possible through altering the course of individual lives. Unlike the microchips, not everyone requires a micro-implant. The requirement of a micro-implant can be determined individually as a part of a care plan or, and most often, automatically as a part of an AMRS algorithm to alter the health of its recipient in a specific way that makes the overall health of our population better. Think of this as the old-fashioned Amazon Fulfillment Center. Orders come in, in the form of QR codes scanned into AMRS or AOS at facilities throughout the country. They are rapidly processed and shipped out, usually on the same day, to practices and medical facilities throughout the country. And … that's all she wrote!" 11275 said, ending his tour. "Any questions?"

"What is my job?" Luke asked.

"You will start on the assembly line that you first saw—the one with the folks in green jumpsuits on either side," 11275 said. "Let's head back there."

The two headed back to the assembly line in the first room of the microchip laboratory. This was where the microchips obtained their initial configuration and programming and where they were packaged and sent to their various locations for installation within their hosts.

"Sit." 11275 motioned to a chair in front of a computer screen.

Luke sat down.

"Most new microchips are installed essentially blank, with nothing on them aside from some preprogramming that permits integration within the central nervous system without rejection," 11275 said. "Once installed within its host, the microchip connects wirelessly to AMRS, whereby the host assumes AMRS' operating system as its own. All the rest occurs seamlessly, automatically, and most often without any intervention. AMRS has artificial intelligence that has gone way beyond artificial. It makes these decisions; in fact, nothing but a computer could be capable of making this vast number of continuous decisions in the infinitesimally small amount of time available, while at the same time keeping the bigger picture in mind.

"You just need to look at the screen and check to make sure that the name, birth date, and medical record number on the microchip matches the one in the patient's medical record. The screen is an enlarged image of the microchip. If the identifying data on the microchip matches the patient data on the screen, click the green APPROVE button. If the two don't match, click the red DENY button. This is the last quality-assurance step prior to distribution of the microchips, and a lot is riding on this job being done correctly. Installing the wrong microchip into a patient could have disastrous consequences. If it is not immediately recognized and the microchip reprogrammed, the patient could die or be repurposed, perhaps as a drone. Bottom line—don't screw this up. It could have disastrous consequences for you too if it happens too often. Now get to work, Luke," 11275 said. "If you need my help, press this button, and I will assist you." He pointed to a switch labelled CALL on the desk.

Luke sat there for several hours approving most and denying only a few microchips. The hardest part about this job for Luke was keeping himself from getting distracted. At noon, his computer screen directed him to secure his workstation and head to the dining room for lunch. He followed his morning routine in reverse, leaving his work suit inside the airlock and, with the aid of the air lock drone, exiting the air lock into the hallway and heading for the dining area. Each floor had its own dining area. Luke went to the dining area on level 4 and sat in front of one of the self-serve kiosk screens.

"Good afternoon, Luke. May I take your order?" a polite female voice said.

"Yes, I'd like a Faux meat sandwich on whole wheat with lettuce, tomato, and mustard; a small side salad with ranch dressing; and a large iced tea," Luke said.

Within ten seconds, his food was presented on the conveyor belt in front of him. Luke ate his lunch, also digesting what he had learned. Luke sat for a while, nibbling at his meal, and staring pensively at the wall in front of him.

The 12:30 p.m. alarm came across the loudspeaker, reminding workers to return to their workstations. After he got up, he walked down the hallway to the air lock. The air lock drone was right behind him, ready to assist him in donning his work suit. Once he was sprayed with antiseptic steam, he again donned the suit and was zipped and then helmeted and sent on his way to the Microchip Laboratory.

11275 was still there, apparently not requiring lunch. "Luke, follow me to the Microchip Programming and Repurposing Laboratory," 11275 said, pointing to the series of sliding doors across the room. Luke walked briskly toward the sliders, catching up with 11275 and scurrying past the sliders. The doors silently slid closed behind them. The room was filled with green-suited individuals sitting at computer screens; the room looked like the old videos of Mission Control during the Apollo era, save for the workers' garb.

"It is here that those microchips that require special programming are manually programmed or reprogrammed, and those who have out served their missions are directed to their respective repurposing stations," 11275 said.

"You mean clones?" Luke asked.

"No, I mean those," said 11275. "Your job is to watch the computer screen in front of you. Periodically, the name and identifying data of an individual will appear on the screen with specific instructions, most often to get them back on their preprogrammed path. For some reason, people sometimes stray from their programs. A simple reboot of their microchip most often fixes the issue immediately. This reboot occurs automatically. If the automatic reboot fails to fix the issue, the individual appears on the screen, along with the words REPROGRAMMING ERROR and a list of exactly what transpired that constituted a failure. You can run diagnostics on the microchip, and if it results in microchip failure, you click on the button that directs the individual to come in for installation of a viable microchip and retrieval of the failed one. This directive is sent directly to the individual's microchip and to the individual's Americare primary care provider's office, who contacts the individual to arrange for rather urgent retrieval and reinstallation. You must maintain a list of these individuals and follow up on each one, making certain that retrieval and reinstallation occur within three days."

"What if the retrieval and reinstall doesn't occur within three days?" Luke asked.

"Then you need to contact the individual's primary care provider and find out what is going on. If it is merely a scheduling issue, as it is most often, you are authorized to permit another three-day window. If it is the individual refusing to schedule the retrieval and reinstallation, you are authorized to request repurposing by clicking the repurposing button. The repurposing team will take things from there, and the individual should disappear from your screen within the next day or so. If not, you should click on the button again. You are afforded the latitude to make the repurposing decisions. If you do not make this choice when it is appropriate, you will be held accountable.

"Sometimes, an individual is referred to us specifically for repurposing. It may be that their mission has ended or that there is another specific reason for their curtailment. This request must be authorized by me, as well as you. We both need to review this and click the repurpose button. It is for legal reasons that all retrieval, reinstall, and repurposing decisions be made manually by one or two of us, as required. Any questions?"

"What is repurposing?" Luke asked.

"It is exactly what the word means," 11275 responded.

"Any further information regarding the repurposing process will be provided only on a need-to-know basis. Right now, you do not need to know anything more about repurposing."

This response from 11275 did not evoke any sense of concern within Luke; it was likely that his microchip had been programmed in advance just to accept it.

"So, have a seat, Luke," 11275 said, motioning to an office chair before two computer screens. "You just wait until something comes up on your screen. Sometimes hours or even days go by; other times, you get these in rapid succession.

There was a beep and then "298057-AZ Holland, Orlando, P DOB: 12/12/2012" flashed on the screen. "Program Failure. Reboot Successful."

"Go ahead and click on ACCEPT," 11275 said.

Luke followed 11275's instructions, and the screen cleared.

Twenty minutes passed.

There was a beep and then: "84875756-CA Chin, Sophie, M DOB: 07/23/2000. Program Failure. Reboot Failed."

Luke clicked on REFERRED FOR RETRIEVAL/ REINSTALL.

"Good work, Luke," 11275 said. "You need to follow up on this and make sure this is off your screen within three days.

Several more program failures appeared on the screen. All but one was resolved by the automatic reboot, and Luke referred the other one for retrieval and reinstall. Upon clicking on this button, a warning returned: INDIVIDUAL HAS BEEN REFERRED FOR RETRIEVAL AND REINSTALL TWO OTHER TIMES AND REFUSED TO SCHEDULE PROCEDURE.

"What should I do?" Luke asked.

"Refer for repurposing," 11275 responded.

With that, Luke clicked on that button, again without any remorse or questioning.

At 2:30 p.m., a quiet bell alarm sounded, followed by an announcement that there would be a required fifteen-minute break. Luke arose from his seat and headed toward the automatic sliding doors.

"When you return from break, head over to the Microchip Installation Facility," 11275 said loudly, while pointing to another set of sliders at the back of the room. "I will meet you in there."

With that, Luke backtracked to the air lock where he had gained admittance, removed his suit with the help of the air lock drone, and went to the dining room. He helped himself to a cup of black coffee, which he knew would sustain him throughout the rest of the workday.

Upon sipping the last of his coffee, he left the dining area and headed back to the air lock. He was once again sprayed with antiseptic steam and assisted into his suit by the air lock drone, who secured Luke's helmet on his head. He carefully ambled through the first set of sliding doors and then continued through the Microchip Laboratory, through the sliding glass door in the back, into the Microchip Programming and Repurposing Laboratory. He continued through this space, entering the Microchip Installation Facility via the double sliding doors in the back of the room.

Inside this facility were no less than thirty gurneys, each with an individual lying within. Alongside each gurney was a Mayo stand that contained all the necessary equipment. An operator and an assistant stood alongside each gurney, which was illuminated by an operating room–style light source.

"Over here, Luke."

Luke looked across the room to see 11275 waving his hand, directing Luke to the gurney on which he was working. The individual on the gurney was completely covered, save for the back of the neck, which had been prepped with betadine and covered with an occlusive surgical drape.

"Luke, I have already verified the name and identifying information of the individual and the microchip to be installed," 11275 said. "First, we have to remove the failed microchip, which is five years old."

11275 grabbed a wand-like device from the Mayo stand and hovered it across the back of the individual's neck. It beeped; the frequency of the beeping varied, becoming faster as the transducer got closer to the failed microchip.

"Once the beep becomes a confluent tone, a mark is made on the skin with an indelible marker," 11275 said.

When confluence of the beeping tone had been achieved, 11275 marked the skin and then grabbed a syringe off the Mayo stand. "I am now infiltrating the area of skin and deeper tissue with 0.5 mL, 1 percent lidocaine with epinephrine, to anesthetize the area and minimize bleeding to keep the field clean," he said. "Using a 15 blade, I am incising the skin. Next, I'm using a small Kelly, freeing up all the surrounding subcutaneous tissue and searching for the failed microchip, which is right here." He grabbed something the size of a small grain of rice with a curved hemostat and placed it in a specimen cup on the Mayo stand.

"I am now going to copiously irrigate the wound with half-strength betadine, then close it with one or two subcuticular sutures of 4-0 Vicryl. I then will cover the wound with one steri-strip that should fall off within two weeks. The retrieved malfunctioning microchip will be sent to pathology for identification and salvage if it is deemed salvageable and reprogrammable. The installation of the new microchip is easy," 11275 said, as he demonstrated on the individual lying on the gurney.

"The insertion device consists of a loaded syringe containing the microchip with an 18-gauge needle. I pick up about a half an inch of skin on the back of the neck or the deltoid region of the individual's nondominant upper extremity—or anywhere, for that matter. The needle of the insertion device is then inserted just under the skin. I draw back to make certain I am not inside a blood vessel, then inject, leaving the microchip in place. I pull the needle out and verify the position of the new microchip with the wand."

He placed the wand over the back of the neck, and the device produced a confluent tone over the insertion site. "This individual is good to go,"11275 said as he placed a small Band-Aid over each of the removal and insertion sites and assisted the individual to sit up on the gurney. "She will have no recollection of the microchip retrieval and replacement process or the events leading up to it. She will have complete retrograde amnesia from the time she left her 'normal' life until the time she returned back to it." 11275 turned to Luke. "By the end of the week, you will be doing this too."

CHAPTER 41

After Luke was escorted to his place of work, Kyle donned one of his orange jumpsuits. He stowed the six remaining jumpsuits snugly in one of his drawers. He would be working in the Cloning Division of Americare. He was looking forward to this, hoping that it would bring them ever closer to an eventual escape.

Kyle stepped outside of his apartment and was met by a drone who escorted him to his place of work. Aside from the shuffling sounds of the ambulating drone, the two walked silently to the elevator, which was waiting for them with doors open. The drone then pressed the button for level 3, and after twenty seconds, the elevator opened directly into an air lock, and Kyle was handed off to an air lock drone for further assistance. The elevator doors closed with the escort drone inside and went on to its next destination.

After applying the left shoulder of his jumpsuit against a magnetic pad and looking into a retinal scanner, Kyle was led farther into the air lock.

"Raise your arms and spread your legs," the air lock drone said.

Kyle did so and was sprayed with antiseptic-smelling steam all over his body. The orange suits were suspended from the ceiling with the backs open and the booted feet touching the floor. The drone pointed to the suit closest to Kyle.

"Step into that orange suit," the drone said.

Kyle stepped into each boot, which snuggly but comfortably provided a good fit.

"Put your arms all the way into the sleeves," the drone said.

As soon as Kyle obliged, the back of the suit was zippered closed and a helmet with plexiglass face shield was lowered onto his head and secured to the neckpiece of the suit via an airtight locking system. Immediately, the suit was filled with air, and air circulated continuously.

"Walk forward," the drone said."

As Kyle walked forward, he was released from the rack that had held the suit prior to his donning it.

"Welcome to the Cloning Division of Americare," a voice said from behind Kyle.

Kyle turned around and faced another orange-suited figure with "7811" embossed on the helmet and on the left breast.

"I am 7811, your instructor and supervisor while you are working in this division. Here, you will learn the basics of organ and human cloning, then develop the skills required to assist in this process. Information regarding organ-on-chip and human-on-chip technology, the basics of cloning using pluripotent embryonic stem cells, induced pluripotent stem cells, and SCNT—that's somatic cell nuclear transfer—is being downloaded to your microchip as we speak. It should be completely available for you to rely on within twelve hours, as it will be committed to your microchip's memory. It is only available to you while you are here at work. You will have no memory of it or access to it when you are off the premises.

"Americare's cloning technology far surpasses any other cloning technologies. In some ways, it is a sort of technological hybrid of several different modalities. The thing that makes it so unique is the speed at which organ and human cloning can occur. It takes about twenty-four hours to clone a human organ. After the organ is cloned, it is ready to be transplanted into a host with a diseased or irreversibly damaged organ. The cloned organ is transported to the organ recipient's hospital to be transplanted. Because the organ is cloned using the recipient's DNA, there is no rejection of the transplanted organ.

"It takes about twenty-four hours to clone an entire human being and an additional twenty-four hours for the clone to develop to its selected age. After cloning and aging, the appropriately aged, cloned subject is then sent to the Detailing Shop. The Detailing Shop creates those distinguishing features on the clone that the original human had, such as any scars, birthmarks, or missing digits or limbs. Here is where scars and individual-specific characteristics are applied, and language and accents are added to microchip. Fingerprints and retinal scans of the clone are identical to those of the original. It is then microchipped, permitting the clone to assume its identity as its human original or an entirely unique identity, as programmed on its microchip. If it is necessary, we activate the compliance module on the human original's microchip, which causes the original to present itself at our facility (or one of the many others) for reprogramming, reassignment, or reclamation, and the clone of the human subject is released into the general population.

"Kyle, you will be overseeing these processes to ensure they occur without any problems. You will be seated at a computer workstation, where you will see various checklists assigned to the various clones being processed. You need to document that everything on the individual's checklist is in order, then sign off so that the cloning process may proceed. Additionally, you will need to follow along with every human and organ cloned to make certain that no aberrancies occur.

"Because we are dealing with genetic material, mutations do occur. Once identified, a decision must be made regarding how to proceed. Human clones that develop with more than one head and/or more than two arms, and/or two legs, and/or with both male and female genitalia are immediately sent to our Repurposing and Reclamation Division, and their cloning process is restarted again from the beginning. Likewise for organ clones that are deemed to be imperfect. Any questions, Kyle?"

"No, not really," Kyle said.

"Good," 7811 said. "Then have a seat at this workstation, and let the screen tell you what to do. An integrative process will develop between your microchip, AMRS, and the computer screen that will answer any questions you may have and ensure that you make the correct choices."

"But I don't think I know enough to do this!" Kyle said.

"Relax," 7811 said reassuringly. "AMRS will call all the shots using your sensory input and your motor skills to do so."

"You mean I initiate and control the cloning of human organs and entire human beings right from this chair and console?" Kyle asked.

"That is correct, Kyle." 7811 said. "You will be directing everything from soup to nuts from right here. You will be working as an extension of AMRS, carrying out those things that AMRS deems necessary for successful cloning of organs and human beings, but that AMRS cannot accomplish because it lacks a physical body, extremities, hands, and feet. AMRS uses your body, and especially your hands, to carry out its commands for cloning to be expeditious and successful. Because of AMRS you will work at incredible speed, multitasking and making high level choices as dictated by algorithms within AMRS. I'm telling you all this now with the understanding that any recollection or memories of whatever transpires within the Cloning Division of Americare is erased from your memory immediately upon exiting this laboratory. Kyle sat at that workstation for four hours, but it seemed like only a few minutes. He was retrieved from his workstation for his lunchbreak by 7811, who escorted him to the airlock for un-donning of his suit and direction to the dining area.

Kyle felt fuzzy-headed, and he had absolutely no recollection of the previous four-hour period of work. He was so upset by this that he wasn't hungry for lunch, which he skipped. After a half hour break Kyle returned to the cloning department accompanied by an escort drone, and he was assisted back into his occupational garb by the airlock drone. 7811 was there waiting for him when the airlock door opened into the Cloning Division.

"The rest of your workday will be a repeat performance of this morning's session." 7811 said. "At the risk of sounding repetitive, when you leave here today you will have no recollection of anything that transpired while you were here. Initially this will feel odd to you, as if large chunks of time have been removed from your life. Over time your brain will acclimate to these gaps in your memory, essentially stringing all other memories together and ignoring the times of absence. Look at it this way, you have the best job anyone could ask for because you will have no recollection of ever working."

CHAPTER 42

It was 6:00 a.m. when Saffron's alarm clock jolted her out of a restful sleep. She awoke with a racing heart and feelings of impending dread, as she did every morning. Sleep was the only peace for her, save for her developing—albeit stuttering—relationship with Michael. Everything that had transpired regarding the work she did in the case that became the Feds versus Lucas Moses, et. al., had left her feeling duped and dumbfounded. Her realization that the government to whom she had sworn blind allegiance was corrupt and evil was like a bullet to her head. As a captive, she remained relatively quiet, speaking only to Michael and to others only when necessary. She despised the fact that she was working for President Dmopvup and that this work aided Dmopvup in hir quest for fame and fortune at the expense of US citizens' lives.

Saffron had set up her coffee maker the night before to provide her with a hot cup of coffee upon awakening, and she looked forward to that. After having a few sips of her coffee, she headed to her bathroom to ready herself for another day. She looked at herself in the mirror. She was a shadow of her former self when she was an FBI agent. Of necessity, her captors had cut her hair short so it wouldn't get tangled in equipment and machinery. Nonetheless, she had an inner spark that kept her going. Her growing love for Michael and her anger against the president kept her going as well.

She entered the shower and stood under the warm spray in a bit of a peaceful trance; then she got down to the business of washing. Feeling somewhat rejuvenated, she left the shower, dried off in the bathroom, brushed what remained of her hair, and headed to her bedroom to dress. After donning her bra and undergarments, she slipped into her red jumpsuit and headed to the dayroom for her morning meal. The drones had already placed her cloche-covered tray on the table where she typically sat. Today, she sat alone; Kyle, Luke, and Michael had chosen to either skip breakfast or to eat earlier or later than she did. Breakfast was a necessity for Saffron and not at all enjoyable. Once her meal concluded, she made her way back to her room to brush her teeth and get ready for another day of work.

Promptly at 7:30 a.m., Saffron left her apartment and, in the company of an awaiting drone, worked her way to the Repurposing and Reclamation Division of Americare. They took an elevator to level 5. The elevator doors opened directly into a system of air locks, each with an awaiting air lock drone to assist in decontamination and donning of the requisite equipment necessary to perform her job. She was sprayed with steam that contained various antimicrobial agents, and she was guided by the air lock drone to the end of the air lock. Awaiting her was a red bodysuit, complete with gloves, boots, and helmet with a plexiglass face mask. She was assisted into her suit by the airlock drone, as Michael, Luke, and Kyle had been.

"Now please follow me."

Saffron followed the air lock drone to the back wall of a large laboratory. There were a series of workstations, each having several monitors, each having a keyboard and mouse. Only two of these workstations were vacant. A similarly red-clothed individual seated next to one of the vacant workstations motioned for her to sit. She left the company of the air lock drone and honored that request, taking a seat at the workstation.

"I am 9800," the individual said. "I am responsible for your training. Welcome to the Repurposing and Reclamation Division of Americare. The advent of organ cloning has made the need for cadaveric organ donors obsolete. Those who were awaiting auction as part of the organ transplant programs are no longer needed, so they are being repurposed. Some of the cloning programs require the human original to also be repurposed. Clones and individuals who have outlived their utility are also repurposed. Unexpected deaths due to complications also occur. Because of this, the bodies have piled up and have been frozen, pending a plan for their stealthy disposal. Additionally, people with malfunctioning microchips that fail rectification, reconfiguring, and all other remedial interventions require repurposing.

"Our Repurposing and Reclamation Division has developed a system in which 90 percent of those who require repurposing are painlessly and comfortably converted into a nutritious food product. Working in conjunction with the FDA, which provided seed money in the form of a grant, a conglomerate of food manufacturers joined forces to become a state-of-the-art factory and business. They utilize a processing procedure invented by scientists at Americare. This process converts those being repurposed into an edible and usable foodstuff, leaving no traces of humanity once this is accomplished. The edible results of this process can be flavored, formed, textured, and colored and is marketed as a highly nutritious, non-GMO food product that does not increase the risk of any disease. It is available free of charge to anyone asking for it at the supermarket. The nonedible by-products formed by this process—mainly some residual calcium carbonate—are used as calcium supplements and as an additive in fertilizers.

"A huge marketing campaign was undertaken to tout this food product as being manufactured by an entirely green process, which is entirely sustainable, and it is free for the asking. This has largely eliminated starvation in this country, as well as in countries to whom we export it. It was also sold to all food companies worldwide at nominal cost, resulting in a decline in food prices and an increase in profit from food sales. As it is available in a variety of colors, flavors, and textures, it is now largely replacing more costly, unsustainable, foodstuffs in many traditional recipes. It is being marketed and listed as an ingredient as 'Faux meat,' 'Faux poultry,' 'Faux vegetables,' and 'Faux plain,' or just "Faux"—the raw, unadulterated product.

"You don't need to know exactly how the sausage is made. Anyone who undergoes repurposing goes in one end of the reprocessing laboratory and, within two days, exits in sealed tins of a homogeneous paste, sealed in plastic vacuum packs or long plastic tubes, or sent out to food manufacturers to be incorporated into other foods. Your job will be focused on collecting those who require repurposing and getting them into the lab. A lot of those requiring repurposing have already been collected and deactivated and are stored in various freezer facilities. These just require thawing prior to entering the lab. The others are still out in the community. They will require activation of the compliance module within their microchip, which will compel them to present at one of our repurposing centers. At this point, each of them is in a semi-lucid trance state, and they will do as they are requested to do. Each will undergo a gastrointestinal clean-out procedure, which consists of a clear liquid diet and a full polyethylene glycol bowel prep until their stool is running clear. Then the termination subroutine is activated within the subject's microchip, which induces a very deep sleep. The body then enters the laboratory, whereupon the sausage is made. Any questions so far?"

Initially, Saffron was in total disbelief and disgusted and frightened by what she heard. Within a few minutes of listening to 9800, her disbelief, disgust, and fear had abated, and the process seemed reasonable to her.

"I would like to know how the process works," she said.

"Good—particularly good!" said 9800. "Your microchip has been programmed in such a way as to allow you to learn more about the process. The process is called reclamation. Reclamation has five steps: *scalding, flaying with stripping, evisceration, trephination with evacuation, and lastly, alkaline hydrolysis.* During the process, any surgical hardware, microchips, micro-implants, and so on are retrieved and repurposed. This includes any artificial joints; pacemakers; orthopedic rods, screws, and plates; dental inlays, crowns, implants; and the individual's chip set. All skin, subcutaneous tissue and fat, muscles, internal organs, and much of the bones will be made into Faux. An enclosed corridor runs the full length of the laboratory with ceiling to floor glass. That will permit you to have a narrated journey through the entire process."

9800 showed Saffron to the door of the observation tunnel, which Saffron entered.

This reminds me of the old-fashioned automatic car washes that had a similar setup, Saffron thought. *People could watch and follow their vehicles as they progressed through the car wash.* Soft classical music was playing, and in an overtly computerized voice—one that was deep and unemotional—the narration began:

"After the subject is thawed or its termination subroutine is activated, it is placed supine on the conveyor belt with feet facing the entrance to the lab. Once in proper position, the conveyor starts, and the subject enters the first chamber, for *scalding.*"

Saffron watched as several drones loaded subjects onto the conveyor belt in succession. Some of the subjects obviously had been frozen, but others writhed about on the conveyor before being made inanimate by a drone who fired a pistol-like device in direct contact with the front of the skull. The device reminded Saffron of the penetrating captive bolt pistol used in slaughterhouses that fired projectiles into the brain causing widespread and catastrophic brain injury but sparing the brainstem so that breathing, and circulation remain intact.

"As the subject is moved along by the conveyor belt, high-temperature steam is sprayed from high-pressure nozzles throughout the chamber. This scalds the skin and subcutaneous tissues, therefore loosening it from the connective tissue beneath and making it easier for the next part of the process—flaying and stripping."

Saffron looked with disgust and awe while the bodies were blasted with hot steam. Some of them were still writhing about. Over the ensuing few seconds, Saffron's sense of awe and disgust was replaced by the absence of any feeling about what she was witnessing.

"The conveyor belt advances the subject into the *flaying tunnel* and then the *stripping tunnel*. These tunnels are lined with sharp, rotating blades that initially are about as long as the skin is deep. These blades are called *dermatomes*. The scalded skin usually just falls away and is retrieved by the drones working within the tunnel. As the subject progresses through the tunnel, the blades become longer. These are called *myotomes*, and they cut the muscles down to the bone. Next, the subject is advanced through a series of blades called *scrapers*—very sharp, oscillating blades that hug close to the body and advance from feet to head as the conveyor belt advances. The scrapers cut the muscle free of any attachments to the bony structures. The skin and muscles, thus stripped or scraped off, fall onto a conveyor below the conveyer upon which the subject lies. It is retrieved by the drones for processing into Faux.

"The subject is then moved by the conveyor belt into what is called the *evisceration chamber*. A circular saw blade is suspended above the conveyor, underneath which the subject will pass. The blade will incise the pelvic and abdominal musculature; if any remains, then a pair of secondary saw blades descends about a foot or so to either side of the sternum and along the lateral walls of the thorax. These blades cut the ribs free from the rest of the thorax, eventually splitting the clavicles. The sternum and entire breast plate, thus rendered unattached to any bone, is lifted off by a series of hooks applied to the lower ribs by the drones as the individual proceeds along the conveyor. At this point, all the pelvic, abdominal, and thoracic viscera are exposed to air, and a large, exquisitely sharpened scoop, called the *eviscerator*, descends into the lower pelvis and scoops out all pelvic, abdominal, and thoracic organs as the conveyor moves the subject along against the sharp stationary eviscerator blade. Eviscerated organs are also reclaimed for processing into Faux.

"The conveyor next moves the subject into what is called *the trephination and extraction chamber*, where the head is automatically clamped into a metal frame that rises from the conveyor on either side. The head is held immobile by a series of screws that are automatically deployed from the frame into the skull. Automatically, a drill taps a small burr hole at the vertex into which a screw eye is screwed into place. The screw eye is attached to a chain, the other end of which is attached to a winch.

"Next the *trephination ring* is applied to the skull, which is held in place by being clamped to the frame. This results in a halo-like metal band with thirty trephination holes around the entirety of the skull from the frontal region and around the temporal regions bilaterally and occiput. *Trephination* begins as a ring of thirty *trephines* mates with the *trephination ring* in such a way that each *trephine* is aligned with its corresponding hole. All thirty *trephines* are applied simultaneously, resulting in a ring of burr holes around the skull. The *trephines* and the *trephination ring* are then removed, revealing a ring of thirty 0.5-centimeter burr holes circumferentially around the skull. An *osteotome* and *mallet* and a *Gigli saw* are used by the drone in attendance to fracture or incise the bony bridges between the burr holes, leaving the top of the cranium easily removable by mechanical traction on the chain and screw eye applied to the vertex. The winch is engaged, removing the top of the skull, and leaving the brain and the meninges exposed.

"Next, the *extractor* is applied onto the open skull. It scoops out the brain while severing the spinal cord just below the brainstem and the optic nerves at the level of the optic chiasm. The brain is saved for processing into Faux. The conveyor then moves what remains of the former individual to an *alkaline hydrolysis chamber*. The former individual, along with the portion of removed skull and the chest plate, is sealed inside this chamber, which is filled with water and potassium hydroxide and pressurized to permit heating to well above the boiling point without any boiling. After twenty-four hours in this chamber, only soft bone and a greenish-brown liquid remain. The liquid contains amino acids, some proteins, and sugars. The softened bone—calcium carbonate—is easily pulverized into a powder using a standard *cremulator*. The amino acids, proteins, and sugars are extracted from the effluent. The calcium carbonate, amino acids, proteins, and sugars are then added back to the previously procured skin, brain, muscle, and visceral organs, and the mix is processed into a homogeneous brownish paste. *This* is Faux. Any further questions?" 9800 asked Saffron.

"How are the pieces of skin, bone, fat, muscle, and organs retrieved after they are removed from the subject by the process?"

"At any given time, there are twenty or so drones who work within the processing chambers and tunnels," 9800 said. "It is their job to make certain that the equipment is appropriately applied to the individual being reclaimed and that all tissues removed from the subject are placed on another conveyor belt that is located to the right of the main conveyor. This secondary conveyor is submerged in a foot of water that runs from the entrance toward the exit of the tunnel. The secondary conveyor belt has perpendicular baffles every five feet or so that are one foot high, resulting in compartments filled with viscera and water, which are moved out for processing. This additional processing takes about another twenty-four hours. What is left on the primary conveyor belt, mainly bone and some residual muscle, and the chest plate end up in the alkaline hydrolysis chamber for twenty hours. At the end of the reclamation process, the effluent from the *alkaline hydrolysis* chamber is neutralized to a pH of 7.42; then it is mixed with the other reclaimed tissue mixture to form the finished product."

"Thank you, 9800, for explaining all of this to me," Saffron said, "and for allowing me to participate in a process of such import. You said about 90 percent of those sent for repurposing are put through the reclamation process. What happens to the remaining 10 percent who are referred here?"

"They are made into drones," 9800 said.

"How does that occur?" asked Saffron.

"It is quite a straightforward process, really," 9800 said. "When the subjects present themselves for drone conversion, they are sent to the much-smaller secondary portion of the Repurposing Laboratory, called Drone Conversion. They are compelled to present there by activation of the compliance module within their microchips. They are taken into the Drone Conversion portion of this facility, whereupon the Drone Conversion subroutine on their microchip is activated. This eliminates all executive brain functions, leaving the brainstem intact. The circulatory and respiratory systems continue to function. The microchip then becomes their entire brain, as the rest of the brain is electrically destroyed. They are mechanically functioning bodies that are solely operated by our instructions and are controlled by AMRS. They do not see, hear, or feel. They are, in effect, a physical extension of AMRS, and they are work-extenders. Their fingerprints are permanently removed with acid, dentition is removed, and retinae are destroyed by laser. This process renders them completely blind, both cortically and optically. Destroying the retinae, fingerprints, and dentition also makes finding out who the drone was before the drone conversion most difficult if not impossible. They are given individualized, microchipped uniforms that include a skin-tight white cap and face mask, which further blurs their prior identity. Drones are numbered; they wear their numbers on the left breast of their bodysuits, and they respond to their number only. Their nutrition is maintained by a liquid nutritional mixture administered through a percutaneous gastrostomy tube that is placed after the drone conversion process is completed. This liquid enteral nutrition along with their daily requirement of water is administered through their gastrostomy tubes during their down time of about eight hours each day."

"Now, let's learn about your job." 9800 said. "Follow me back to your workstation."

Saffron followed close behind. Little did she know that during her observation of the narrated process, her microchip was continually being adjusted to cause her to find the Repurposing Laboratory and the process of reclamation to be quite interesting and appealing, rather than objectionable. She sat down at her workstation.

"Your job is to follow our protocols that make certain that those to be repurposed arrive at their repurposing stations as directed," 9800 said. "A bit less than half of those awaiting reclamation are flash-frozen, so they will be stored in the freezer at their respective facilities. The other 60 percent or so are still out in the community. They consist of subjects who have experienced critical microchip failures that were irremediable by reprogramming, clones who have outlived their purposes, human originals who were destined to be reclaimed once a clone for them was created, humans or clones who were chosen for elimination by AMRS algorithms to improve our population health, and those who have committed crimes necessitating the death penalty. Those who die of natural causes are typically flash-frozen and are reclaimed after the legal waiting period of five days. Each repurposing station can reclaim over five hundred units every twenty-four hours. The Repurposing and Reclamation Laboratories operate twenty-four hours a day, seven days a week, and each state has at least two of them. Some of the most populated and geographically largest states have up to fifteen such stations.

"Sometimes a clone is made during drone conversion and returned to their loved ones, so it is not apparent to their loved ones, friends, or employers that they are also being made into a drone. Most often, it is not necessary to make a clone of the drone-converted individual. The populous is unaware of the existence of drones. The remaining family, friends, employers, and contacts of someone who is reclaimed have their microchips reprogrammed so they have no recollection of the previous existence of the drone-converted or reclaimed individual.

"Each morning you will receive a list of those requiring repurposing and reclamation. This will appear in two columns on your screen: AT LARGE and FROZEN. Most of the frozen subjects are already onsite, and the remainder will be delivered. For the AT LARGE subjects requiring repurposing and reclamation, you will need to click on ACTIVATE COMPLIANCE MODULE. They are required to appear at this site within forty-eight hours. Once they arrive, you will check their status. If DRONE is listed in the status section, you click on DRONE CONVERSION SUBROUTINE. If RECLAMATION is listed in the status section, you need to click on RECLAMATION SUBROUTINE; then everything else happens automatically. Previously frozen subjects should never have DRONE listed as their status. This would be a reportable error, and you should inform me if it occurs. Previously frozen subjects are entirely without life. For those who do not show up, you need to contact our compliance officers. They will locate them and bring them to their designated facility. Any questions?"

"No, not really," Saffron said.

"Then get started," 9800 replied with a smile.

CHAPTER 43

Kyle and Luke were all but forgotten at Primary Care Associates, where everything began. At the practice, there were commemorative bronze busts of each of them, touting them as heroes who fixed the health care system. What went down with the two of them corresponded only temporally with perceived marked improvements in patient outcomes and overall health of the population. Dmopvup and Americare had successfully used Luke's complaint, Kyle's and Luke's capture, and their sham joining of Americare's administrative team to tout the quality of health care that Americare was providing. As far as anyone knew, Luke and Kyle were working in administrative capacities at Americare and climbing the corporate ladder; in fact, they were being held captive and being used for labor by President Dmopvup while awaiting their demise.

Average Americans were only aware that the citizenry appeared to be healthier, and that people weren't becoming as ill as they had been. Caring for patients had become much less complicated because patients had become healthier. Unknown to them, their care was algorithm-driven, and Americare was free to all citizens of the United States of America.

The average American was not aware that there was a National Genome Library, although it was not deemed top secret, per se by the Dmopvup regime. The microchip, micro-implant, and cloning programs were top secret, and no one aside from select Americare employees were aware that they even existed. Their microchips were set to forget these programs while not at work, which involuntarily caused them to remain secret. Likewise, the citizenry was entirely unaware of the repurposing and reclaiming of citizens into drones or Faux products. In fact, no one outside of Americare headquarters had ever heard of a drone, which is an acronym or portmanteau for Deprogrammed Repurposed ONE. Everyone was familiar with Faux, which was marketed as a "non-GMO plant-protein–based substrate that is entirely sustainable and can be used in place of beef, pork, fish, shellfish, and fresh vegetables." It was nutritionally a far superior foodstuff. They were unaware of the product's origin.

From the perspective of the average citizen, life was good, their health was good and improving every second, and because of inventions such as Faux, they had more money in their bank accounts due to a substantial decrease in the cost of living. Free food in the form of Faux products was readily available to all.

Society had become a well-choreographed social network that was driven by computers, microchips, micro-implants, and the like, with microchips dumbing down the natural human sensibilities that would cause people to question the existence of a product called Faux. Rather, they embraced it. This was the perfect Stepford society. AMRS and its algorithms made certain that most people did not live long enough to die naturally from chronic diseases, as these diseases were costly to Americare.

The algorithms continued to whittle away at the populous, based upon political ideation, family history, past medical history, and social history, in a successful effort to obtain the ideal population in terms of risk of becoming expensively ill and of political uniformity. When their time was up, they were called into their primary care provider's office, administered a micro-implant by intramuscular injection, and sent on their way, unknowingly, to die. These were not deemed acceptable for repurposing or reclamation because they were not the healthiest of citizens, and the nation's cup already runneth over due to the overabundance of Faux and a backlog of flash-frozen subjects awaiting processing. These individuals were incinerated.

Because AMRS and microchips changed how people felt in real time, everything was universally acceptable to everyone. People accepted the unexpected demise of their friends and loved ones as they were plucked from society for curtailment. Their microchips made them believe that this was normal. Their memories of their loved ones who were thus processed or incinerated were wiped out by their microchips. People were programmed to ignore the fact that they had microchips and to live their lives with a sense of blissful ignorance about such things. That programmed blissfulness was essential in keeping American society productive and stable. These people lived their lives unaware of what they weren't aware.

They didn't know what they didn't know.

CHAPTER 44

One night, a group of double-agent Disciples entered the Americare facility where Kyle and the other three were being held captive. The Disciples disabled the omnipresent security cameras by locking in on a photograph of a stationary view of their surroundings rather than the live view. Two of the Disciples posed as the dinner drones and provided Kyle and the other three with their meals—laced with chloral hydrate. Within minutes of finishing their meals, the four were rendered unconscious. The four drug-induced sleeping bodies of Kyle, Michael, Luke, and Saffron were placed inside of the food trucks by the drone-Disciples, who hurried them to a secure garage facility and into an awaiting van. A clone of each of them was brought out from one of the linen trucks lining the hallway and was placed into their respective rooms. The clones were changed into their night clothes and then situated carefully in their beds by the mock drones. The clones were activated but sedated and asleep, and they were unaware that they were clones. They would continue on as Kyle, Michael, Saffron, and Luke at Americare headquarters as if nothing at all had happened.

The crowing of a rooster split the dawn and awakened Kyle with a start. He only had a vague recollection of what had transpired. One minute, he was sitting in the dining room, finishing his evening meal, and almost instantaneously, he was awakened by the cock crowing. It seemed as if no time had passed, yet he was clearly in an unfamiliar environment. He noticed that he was in a bed and wearing the same clothes that he'd worn the previous day. Likewise, there were three additional beds in the room, presumably one for each of his companions. The three remained asleep; their breathing was audible, and their chests appeared to rise and fall appropriately.

Kyle arose from his bed. With his friends still asleep, he sized up their accommodations. The room smelled of heat, vanilla, and old paper. It was small and had no furniture, aside from the beds. Luke's bed was next to Kyle's, then Michael's bed, then Saffron's. There was a large bathroom attached to the room. Kyle attempted to open the door and leave the room, but he quickly realized that the four were locked inside.

Kyle walked over to Luke and gently shook him. "Wake up, Luke! Wake up!"

Luke awoke, startled by the unfamiliar environment. "Where…where are we, Kyle?"

"Not sure. It smells different."

Luke proceeded to sniff the air.

Within a few minutes they heard a loud noise followed by someone fumbling with the lock on the door.

Michael and Saffron awoke and climbed out of their beds. "Where are we?" they asked, almost in unison.

Kyle raised an index finger to his lips. "Shhhh!"

The door to the room opened, and three people sauntered in. The tallest of the three introduced himself. "Hi, I'm James Christian, the leader of the Disciples. My friends call me Jim. My pronouns are he, him, and his." He reached out his hand first to Kyle and then to the other three. There were no takers on a return handshake. The four were entirely guarded in their responses to this new situation, and they didn't really know what to do, ask or say.

Jim reviewed with Kyle and the other three captives who the Disciples were, how they came to be, what their purpose and goals were, and how they discovered where the four were being held captive. He then entertained questions.

"How large is the Disciples as a group?" Michael asked.

"The Disciples has a huge membership base throughout the United States and even worldwide, with exceptional communication among members." Jim said. "During the past year or so, groups of Disciples have formed throughout the country and within all branches of our local military. We have also secretly organized into the Disciples' military force. We infiltrated the facility at Joint Base Andrews, which is now a Disciples strong hold, and it is where we are right now. No one other than the Disciples is aware that this has even occurred."

The four listened while Jim continued to talk. He touted the availability of double-agents—members of the Disciples who also worked for Americare and other government agencies. "Double agents are able to make changes from within Americare or their respective agencies of employment, as well as provide information from Americare and these other agencies back to me and the rest of the Disciples." Jim said. "The Disciples have been maintained in the strictest of confidence, and no one close to President Dmopvup or Americare is aware of their existence."

"What else has changed since our confinement?" Saffron asked.

Jim related what had transpired since their capture, beginning with the 4th term reelection of President Dmopvup, with Kupevjep Hsacis as vice president. He then reviewed the National Genome Registry, the microchip program, the use of micro-implants, organ and human cloning, the ongoing curtailment of citizens' lives, the human reclamation process, drone conversion, and the development and mass production and mass consumption of Faux. Michael, Luke, and Saffron had no recollection about the specifics of their employment at Americare, with their brains presumably having been wiped clean upon their exit. Unbeknownst to all, Kyle had been receiving daily briefings from the ghost of Sean during his sleep, and he was fully aware of what had been transpiring since their captivity.

"I want to know if you wish to join forces with us to bring about an end to Americare and to bring justice to the perpetrators of these heinous crimes?" Jim asked.

After discussing this with Luke, Michael, and Saffron, it was unanimously decided that they should join the Disciples, provided that Kyle was made their leader. Jim agreed.

The four were then given ample time and supplies

to wash up and get ready for the day. The bathroom was generous and fully stocked with the requisite supplies. Each took turns in the bathroom, and then they headed to a large room across the hallway in which food was available for them to eat. Jim met them there, then he escorted them to the Control Room – an area that looked much as one would suspect The Situation Room at the White House looked. There were people coming and going, and people sitting at various computer workstations. A large digital tactical map of Americare was displayed on the largest wall. Jim took his position at the front of the room, with Kyle by his side. He commanded everyone in the room's attention by his presence there.

"Everyone, I would like to introduce you to Kyle Sanderson." Jim said. "He will be taking my place as the leader of The Disciples. I will serve as his assistant should he require one. I know you are all familiar with Kyle, and his compatriots – Lucas Moses, Saffron Truman, and Michael Jude. Please extend them a warm welcome and assist them in any way you can."

A meet and greet ensued until Kyle and the other three were certain that they had met everyone. Kyle took his place at the lead workstation at the front of the room, facing everyone. The rest of the day was spent with Kyle reviewing the situation in greater detail. Kyle decided that Luke should be working with the double agents, Saffron and Michael with those in intelligence and communication. They continued to work throughout the rest of the afternoon and into the night, taking several hours at the end of their shift to sleep.

CHAPTER 45

The next day Kyle and the Disciples engaged in a full attack on Americare, which had also become the president's office and residence. They attacked it from without and from within, with targeted weapon strikes, infantry, sonic weaponry, kidnapping with information extraction, and electronic surveillance of internet and physical locations. This resulted in the destruction of parts of Americare and AMRS, as well as other sensitive equipment. Yet Americare seemed to continue on, relatively unscathed.

During the Disciples' assault on Americare, Kyle experienced a series of challenges, the end results of which, he hoped, would result in his and the Disciples' success. He fully utilized the Disciples and the resources that they brought to bear. Although their sorties were aggressive and strong, and Kyle gave everything his all, they either weren't targeted enough, or they lacked surgical precision or a specific plan. It was more of a flailing situation, resulting in a series of struggles and failures that caused Kyle and his minions to become fatigued and to lose hope and confidence—overall, to fail. Kyle realized that the harder they fought, and the more weaponry was discharged, the greater were the losses that he and the Disciples incurred. It was as if President Dmopvup had anticipated the Disciples' every move. The more Kyle attacked Americare, the stronger Americare became, at the expense of Kyle and the Disciples fortitude.

What is going on here? Kyle thought. *Why are we failing to overtake this beast? I have been attacking Americare both internally, using our double agents, and externally, using our military resources, but to no avail.*

Kyle received word from a double agent that a microchip with the identical programming and content of President Dmopvup's microchip had been installed within AMRS by Dr. Hsacis. *This is the first time that a microchip has been used to give a computer any human attributes.* Kyle thought. *This has likely given AMRS President Dmopvup's greed, cunning, emotion (or lack thereof), intelligence, and apparent lack of remorse. AMRS has likely become a very rapid-thinking, hyper-emotional, and impulsive version of the president that can anticipate our every move, and at superhuman speed.* It was the addition of a copy of President Dmopvup's microchip to AMRS that was likely responsible for Kyle and the Disciples' failures. It was also likely that AMRS had gained a greater degree of intrusion into Kyle's thoughts via Kyle's microchip. This is likely why the president had been able to anticipate Kyle's and the Disciples' actions.

Learning about AMRS's new microchip was a turning point for Kyle. This changed his overall worldview of the problems at hand, caused him to nullify his previous plans, and necessitated the creation of a new, targeted, and strategic plan. He needed a plan of action that would not mitigate the damage done by the previous flailing efforts. The major focus of the new plan was to obtain control over AMRS, but how? Targeted efforts had begun in that direction but to no avail.

Kyle had lost his confidence; he was unable to see which changes he needed to make within himself to achieve his goals. He was unable to step back and see the big picture and to take the appropriate next steps.

Later that day, Kyle received word that Luke was dead. Luke had gone to the Americare facility with a small group of double agents. He remained in their vehicle while the others went into the building. The vehicle was destroyed in an explosion, without details other than his death was a result of one of their targeted strikes on AMRS. This could have been the result of friendly fire, but that was uncertain.

Kyle had lost his love and his footing and his way, which was almost more than he could bear. The overall situation was worse than it had ever been. Kyle was devastated and entirely spent, and grieving, as were the Disciples. Things were dire.

Grief-stricken, Kyle fell into a very deep sleep. He entered his dreamscape and sojourned there with the ghost of Sean. It was a peaceful and tranquil environment of tropical humidity and warmth, palm trees, and simplicity. They spent what seemed like days reviewing events of the past, as they pertained to what might happen in the future, as if Sean's ghost could see it and have some degree of control over the outcomes.

Sean's ghost revealed to Kyle that he had secretly "viralized" Kyle's broadcasts using Jesús's ham radio equipment back in July 2032. "People who are of good moral and ethical character, and who are not evil, are susceptible to receiving this virus." The ghost of Sean said. "They become infected with it by hearing the broadcast, reading about the broadcast, or even talking about it in the most general of terms. It also causes these people to focus on bringing the Americare scheme to an end, bringing those responsible to justice, and making this a priority. They become happy to help one another." It was this viral infection with Kyle's words that was responsible for the Disciples' formation, influence, and spread. The initial broadcasts, Kyle's words, voice, content, or discussion about it was *the virus*, infecting those susceptible hosts.

"Once a person is thus infected, this '*Kyle virus*' acts in three ways." The ghost of Sean said. "First, it causes those who are infected to seek the company of others who are infected and to organize and act in such a way as to bring an end to the Americare scheme and to bring the president to justice. It also causes the infected person to talk about the broadcast with everyone, thus spreading the virus to other inherently good people. Lastly, it damages the microchips of the infected hosts in such a way that their microchips are no longer able to function, or to generate electromagnetic pulses (EMP). Those people who are evil are not susceptible to this virus, which simply goes in one ear and out the other without any effect. They cannot spread the virus either, and they are not motivated to help anyone except themselves, which has to do with their inherent selfishness and not the virus. Those who are involved with the president in carrying out the Americare scheme are immune to this virus by virtue of the fact that they are inherently evil."

Kyle had been raised to believe that if you were doing that which was morally right, and if you were equally honest, compassionate, and willing to sacrifice your own life in the process of pursuing your own goals, it was highly likely that you would succeed. Likewise, he was raised to believe that crime and evil never paid off, and "what goes around comes around." His recent painful experiences and personal losses because of Americare, and his sojourn with Sean's ghost made him realize a few things. Just because he was morally and ethically proper and was willing to die in trying to bring the Americare scheme to an end and bring about justice, this didn't make his success more likely, or profound losses less apt to occur. He suddenly realized the truth that crime often does pay, and it often pays well. Evil people often profit from being evil and never sustain a loss. It was this realization—that good does not always win, and that crime often pays well—that strengthened Kyle considerably. It also confounded him at times. The harder he had worked, the more he lost, and the more he lost, the harder he had worked. A cycle had established itself that Kyle needed to stop. He ruminated on these thoughts and shared his feelings with Sean's ghost. The loss of Luke had essentially paralyzed him, taking away the meaning in his life, yet giving him a boost of anger that he might need to succeed.

The rest of Kyle's sojourn with the ghost of Sean was spent in prayer and meditation, during which time Kyle's inner strength and resolve increased dramatically, as did his emotional intelligence and his knowledge, as it related to defeating his nemesis. He came to terms with Luke's demise. Sean sat with Kyle, and together, they listened to a recording of Kyle's broadcast from July 2032—Kyle had never listened to it and only recorded it for the broadcast. As a result, Kyle's bond with Sean increased, as did a feeling that he had been selfish. Sean was an innocent victim who was forced to relinquish his life, his world, his family, and his first girlfriend due to a malpractice incident of sorts but a definite crime.

Kyle kissed Sean's ghost gently on the lips, stroked his hair, and said, "Thank you, Sean, for giving up your life for this cause. You were taken as a young man, way too early, without having experienced life. For that, I am terribly sorry." Sean snuggled his cheek close to Kyle's after a glancing kiss and said, "Now you hold me tight, Kyle, and carry me home."

CHAPTER 46

Upon awakening from his sojourn with the ghost of Sean, Kyle had a sense of inner peace that he had never felt before. He was recharged and quick, but calm and at peace. He was still grieving the loss of Luke, but he now had a plan that he would let play out. He relied on his faith in God and Jesús Martinez, with the ghost of Sean as his guide and muse to lead him. He was prepared for a surgically honed battle to win.

Meanwhile, AMRS seemed to have gone rogue. More citizens were being sent for repurposing, reclamation, and incineration, most after being curtailed and flash frozen. It was rumored that Dr. Hsacis had been destroyed by AMRS while trying to deactivate and remove the microchip that had been previously placed within AMRS. Dr. Hsacis was the only one with the training and expertise sufficient enough to deactivate and remove it. Furthermore, it was highly likely that AMRS could read President Dmopvup's mind by virtue of sharing the same chip set, and that AMRS would like nothing more than to eliminate the president from the equation of life. AMRS would then have complete control over the country, and perhaps spread around the world. It was also most likely the President Dmopvup was aware of this and ze was living in fear for hir life.

Kyle's first task was to organize and expand his base of followers. Using media-intrusion techniques developed by the Disciples, he rebroadcasted a recording of his original broadcast, done using Jesús's equipment back in July 2032. He streamed this on all social media sites, radio, network and cable TV, internet, and TV. He encouraged people to meet at least once weekly and to spread the word by talking about the content of the broadcast and what they should do, individually and as a group, to rectify the situation. This infected other susceptible hosts who had managed to avoid prior infection, and it caused significant viral spread among the citizens.

Kyle needed to figure out how to protect his thoughts from being overreached by AMRS, so that the microchip within AMRS would not have access to his mind. He asked Jim to consult with one or more of the Disciples' double-agents to make this so. Kyle decided to leave it up to the double agents how to keep AMRS from accessing his mind. He did not wish to know what they planned to do or how they planned to do it, so he could eliminate this from his thoughts.

Once he received word from Jim that AMRS's access to his thoughts had been quashed, Kyle decided that he needed to have complete control over AMRS. AMRS was major weaponry, the use of which would put one at a significant tactical advantage; without its use, one would be significantly disadvantaged. Kyle planned to infect AMRS with a computer virus that would gradually cause AMRS to stutter and then freeze up, necessitating a reboot. By virtue of the nature of this virus, when AMRS rebooted, the microchip that was installed by Dr. Hsacis would be permanently disabled, and all biometric data used as AMRS login credentials from the president, vice president, attorney general, or the other "bad players" would be blocked, and only Kyle's biometrics would gain AMRS access.

AMRS received this viral inoculation via the AOS (Americare Ordering System) QR code scanners. Millions of QR codes were scanned every day through AOS scanners for patients' medications, drugs, DME, and the like. Sean's ghost appended exceedingly small, seemingly nonsense sequences of data at the beginning and the end of each and every QR code. It was estimated that this would take up to three days to happen, but a reboot would automatically occur, with AMRS no longer in a rogue state and under control of the Disciples. This conversion of AMRS over to the Disciples' control would be seamless and would go entirely unnoticed by anyone, notably President Dmopvup and hir associates, until the very end, when Kyle would assume direct control of AMRS. It would not appear to be undergoing a failure or a reboot, even though that was what would be occurring. President Dmopvup, the vice president, the attorney general, and the FBI director would think that their credentials were being accepted normally and that they were freely using AMRS, when, in fact, they would be logging into and using a sham version. The scanning of the virus began on December 23, 2034, and ended successfully on December 25, 2034. No one was the wiser that anything untoward had occurred.

AMRS had been rendered under the Disciples' control. The microchip implanted within it by Dr. Hsacis had been rendered inactive and destroyed. President Dmopvup and hir cohorts continued to log in to a sham system, unaware that AMRS was now under Kyle's and the Disciples' control.

It wouldn't take long for the president to discover that hir access to AMRS was just a ruse, and that the system had been fully infiltrated by the Disciples, so Kyle had a limited window of time in which to act further.

CHAPTER 47

Kyle had obtained direct access to and control of AMRS using his laptop computer. His biometrics had been entered, and he was now online. It was noon on December 25, 2034, when a video message appeared on all computer screens of the AMRS including the sham AMRS, as well as on all networks, social media websites, CATV outlets, and radio stations. It was Kyle, who explained what had been going on with President Dmopvup and the Americare scheme. The broadcast was brief, and, like his broadcast of July 2032, it utilized the power of the ghost of Sean to immediately access susceptible listeners' hearts, minds, and souls and strengthen the effect of the Kyle virus on them. The broadcast listed all the ways in which President Dmopvup and the regime had harmed and killed the citizens, and what the president had received in return. It revealed that AMRS had likely been in a rogue state, functioning solely of its own accord and lacking control from anyone, even the president.

Next, Kyle outlined what was about to happen. "Those of you who are righteous and good, who are of high moral character, and those of you who are honest are protected from the next step, and you should not worry," Kyle said. "Those of you who are evil and of poor moral character will surely die, and it is too late for you to change that."

Kyle explained what he was doing as he entered several keystrokes on his keyboard. President Dmopvup was witness to this broadcast, and was aghast and panicking, while flailing about on hir keyboard presumably trying to quash hir upcoming and inevitable demise.

"This will cause the microchips of those who are deemed evil to produce a large and powerful electromagnetic pulse that will immediately result in the hosts' death," Kyle said.

To be certain that this occurred, it was programmed to automatically recur three additional times within the span of fifteen minutes. In the corner of the computer screen was a video of President Dmopvup during this entire broadcast, with a progressively more panicked look upon hir face.

"May God have mercy on your souls," Kyle said as he pressed the ENTER key on his laptop.

There came a sudden grimacing, moaning, and drooling from President Dmopvup as ze shook violently, became incontinent of urine and feces, and summarily died. This grimace, moaning, drooling, and shaking occurred a total of four times within a fifteen-minute span. This was visible for all the world to see and to hear, except for those who experienced a similar fate as the president for their involvement in the Americare scheme. Vice President Hsacis (if still alive) and all cabinet members, close associates, and others involved in the Americare scheme met this same fate. They were all too busy dying to watch it live.

By 12:15 p.m. on December 25, 2034, the perpetrators of the Americare scheme had met their demise. AMRS and the Americare, which had become autonomous, was rendered under Kyle's ongoing control, and the citizenry had been released from its powerful grip.

Then Sean appeared to Kyle and everyone who was present. He appeared whole, intact, without any apparent blemish, and wearing a white robe. Standing several feet behind Sean were the unblemished and white-robed Jesús Martinez, Anandakumar "Andy" Canteenwalla, Anne Wilson, Carla Dossier, Lorraine Simons, Scott Smith, Lester Blumenthal, Trinh Nguyen, Karolyn Moses, Doris Chapin, Michael Thomas, and many others whose faces were not discernable. They all had their arms around each other, and their faces appeared angelic, with a sort of a halo around each of them.

Sean then spoke. "Kyle, you have succeeded in bringing the Americare scheme to an abrupt end and in bringing those responsible to justice. Because of this, you will have spared many of our citizens their lives. For this, we are eternally grateful. Like us, you have suffered as a result, and you have put others ahead of your needs. For this, we are incredibly grateful and thankful."

Several "amens" were heard among the crowd of souls who stood before Kyle, those who were victims of the scheme.

"You have asked for nothing in return, other than an end to this genocide and that justice be served. I must admit that I was not entirely honest with you, in that I chose to act without consulting with you first and without your acting in my stead. I apologize for not being forthright. Before Luke was killed, I had the clone of Luke swapped out for the original, allowing the clone of Luke to take the fall and die for our cause. Luke is very much alive and still working within Americare. With your permission, I will bring him to you now, for love is the most precious of gifts, and you both are deserving of this and of each other."

Luke then appeared and was being held in Kyle's outstretched arms, understanding all of what had transpired. Kyle kissed him passionately, saying over and over, "I love you, Luke." Kyle was in tears.

"You found grace in mine eyes," Sean's ghost said. "You had a calling, from me, to lay waste to all that is evil. All other remedies had failed to release the grip of wickedness that had become self-perpetuating, necessitating that it just be ended. You both have our blessings." Sean raised his arms up above the crowd. "You and those who follow you must repopulate this country and perhaps the earth in the name of all that is holy and all that is good. You will be given all the strength and the resources with which to accomplish this. Keep me close and ask for what you need. It will be provided."

With that, Sean approached Kyle and kissed him on the forehead. Then Sean vanished into the ether.